FIERY PASSION

"I want you," Matthew said quietly.

Katherine trembled at his voice. She heard him rise and come toward her, but she didn't dare look at him. He stopped beside her, gently grasped her arms and pulled her to her feet. With one hand he tilted up her face and forced her to look at him.

"Please," she whispered, not knowing what she was asking for.

His head moved down to hers, lips taking hers, softly, tenderly at first, then increasingly more greedily. He tore his mouth from hers and began to kiss her face, her neck, her ears.

"Oh, no," she murmured.

"Oh, yes," he mumbled. "Oh, God, yes."

Also by Candace Camp

Rosewood
Light and Shadow
Analise

Published by
HarperPaperbacks

CANDACE CAMP

BONDS OF LOVE

PREVIOUSLY PUBLISHED UNDER THE
PSEUDONYM LISA GREGORY

HarperPaperbacks
A Division of HarperCollins*Publishers*

HarperPaperbacks   *A Division of* HarperCollins*Publishers*
                    10 East 53rd Street, New York, N.Y. 10022

This book is published by arrangement with the author.

Cover photograph by Herman Estevez
Quilt courtesy of Quilts of America, Inc., N.Y.C.

First HarperPaperbacks printing: March 1992

Printed in the United States of America

HarperPaperbacks and colophon are trademarks of
HarperCollins*Publishers*

10 9 8 7 6 5 4 3 2 1

BOSTON

One

Mrs. James Miller bent her sternest gaze upon her sister, a look calculated to make that timid woman tremble, and said in dire tones, "Amelia, it is all your fault."

"Oh, no, Amanda, truly—you know she never listens to me," Miss Amelia Fritham protested faintly.

"Precisely," Amanda said, nodding her head in emphasis, so that the purple feathers on her hat bobbed perilously. "That is where your fault lies. You have never exercised the least control over that child."

"Hardly a child—twenty-four years old," Amelia murmured.

"From the day you first set foot in this house, she's run all over you. It is bad enough that her father spoils her—after all, he's only a man and doesn't know the first thing about rearing a child—but you give her her head, too!"

"But, Amanda, I tried. The first day I came to live here, I did just as you said and when she disobeyed me, I told her I would send her to her room and she'd get only bread and water; and she said—she said . . ." Amelia paused to gulp back her tears, "she said, 'Auntie, I've been running this household ever since my mother took ill a year ago. 'Tis I who order the servants and 'tis I who carry the household keys. I think it's you who best watch out for the bread and water.' And then she winked at me and laughed."

"You're such a fool, Sister," Amanda said dispassionately. "And no sixteen-year-old chit would have dared to say that to me!"

Leaning forward, Amanda launched into her major campaign. "But that's all water under the bridge. Usually Katherine's common sense has kept her from doing anything disgraceful. But now! The entire city of Boston is talking about her. Going down to the shipyards to work in Mr. Devereaux's office! It simply isn't proper." Mrs. Miller agitatedly began to pace the room. Propriety was, in Mrs. Miller's scheme of things, above cleanliness and perhaps even above godliness. A widow for several years, she had worn black the requisite number of years and then donned her magnificent purple half-mourning, from which she never swerved—not out of respect for the late Mr. Miller (she would be the first to tell you of his many disagreeable attributes) but because it was the proper thing to do.

In amazement, Amelia watched Amanda pace the room; it was most unusual for her stolid sister to so give way to an attack of nerves. Amelia began to twist her handkerchief.

Ever since she came from Amanda's home to this house eight years ago, Amanda had rebuked her constantly for the way she handled Katherine. She just

—*4*—

didn't understand, Amelia would wail to herself. Their sister Alicia had been seriously ill for a year before she died. Gradually her fifteen-year-old daughter Katherine took over the household duties. She ruled the house efficiently and well and was loved and admired by the servants. She was stubborn, unafraid, and independent. And though she had welcomed her Aunt Amelia as a guest, she never thought of looking on her as the new mistress of the house and her substitute mother. Amelia acquiesced quickly. Her meek nature infinitely preferred not being in control. Her life was much more pleasant than it had been at Amanda's, where her older sister had bullied her unmercifully, and where she had had to put up with the vapid giggles and pouts of Amanda's daughters. The only real thorn in her side was Amanda's visits to remonstrate with her over her lax supervision.

Amanda was offended by her niece's independent attitude. Her worst sin was being a spinster. It was not that she disapproved of Katherine's icy demeanor—far from it. In her eyes, Katherine's prim dresses and cool, almost haughty manner were quite proper. What couldn't be tolerated was the fact that despite her many faults she had received some eligible proposals and had refused them. The *most* intolerable thing was that Amanda's own son James Eastland Miller IV had been among the eligible proposals refused.

"Yesterday Matilda Cranshaw told me that she found Katherine's behavior absolutely shocking. Well, I was humiliated," Amanda seethed.

"Are you here bullying Aunt Amelia again, Aunt Amanda?" came a cool voice from the doorway.

"Katherine!" Amanda swung around to face her niece, who stood slim and straight in the doorway.

"Since I am apparently the source of your anger, why not have it out directly with me?" she said, advancing briskly into the room and seating herself. "I'd like some tea, Auntie, if you would please ring for Annie. Would you care for some refreshment, Aunt Amanda?"

"No, I would not. Young lady, you are about to bring ruin on your family!"

"Indeed?" Katherine's brows raised inquiringly.

"Don't look so cool and innocent, missy." It stoked the fire of her righteous anger to see Katherine sitting there in her dove-gray dress with its flawlessly white collar and cuffs and every hair severely in place, her manner calm and collected. "You know very well that I am speaking of your latest escapade."

Katherine's lips twitched slightly, but she said only, "Escapade, Aunt Amanda?"

"Yes, escapade. Working at your father's shipyards! Katherine, it simply isn't done."

"Well, I imagine that dressing up like Indians and dumping tea into the harbor wasn't quite the proper thing, either, Auntie. I'm simply being patriotic. Because of the War with the South, nearly all Papa's clerks have gone to the Army. He has only Teddy Mathias, who's just fourteen years old. Yet the demands on him are greater than ever because the Navy needs ships. I've proved my efficiency and business ability running this house. It would be criminal for me not to help out by keeping Papa's books."

"But for a well-brought-up young lady . . ."

"Really, Aunt Amanda. I'm no longer a girl to sit around being modest and protected and stupid, waiting for someone to marry me. I am twenty-four years old, and I have accepted—even if you have not—the fact that I am going to be an old maid. I need to learn Papa's business; I will have to operate it someday."

"Katherine, there are lawyers and agents and things to do that. Or better yet, a husband. Your chances aren't completely over; why, my Jamie still thinks fondly of you."

"Thinks fondly of my money, you mean," Katherine snapped. "Oh, let's not quarrel about that, too. Believe me, there is little chance of my getting married. I don't intend to entrust my business to strangers, and Papa agrees with me. There's absolutely nothing wrong with what I do. I walk to the yards with Papa and my maid comes down to walk back home with me in the afternoon. The entire day I spend with a young boy and a half-blind old man, and my father is there the whole time! How could that possibly be improper?"

"It's simply not proper to work. If you wanted to help the war effort, why not work with the Ladies' Auxiliary?"

"Oh, pooh—rolling bandages and knitting socks. Why, I'm helping to build ships!"

"Yes, but look at you—ink on your hands. You'll get lines around your eyes from squinting at numbers. Katherine, a lady simply does not work in an office. Not to mention those low people you associate with—that young hoodlum and that crazy old sailor. I despair of you, Katherine!"

"Well, I'm sorry, but if I can't be a lady and still do

something useful with my life, then I guess you'll just have to continue despairing. Because I intend to continue working."

"Well!" In a high dudgeon, Amanda Miller picked up her gloves and parasol and stormed to the door. Amelia fussed along beside her, wringing her hands and pleading with her not to be angry. In the doorway, Amanda halted and delivered her parting shot. "Don't say I didn't warn you."

Katherine sighed and settled down to enjoy her tea. But such was not to be her lot, for Aunt Amelia, summoning her courage, came back into the room to add her mite.

"I do wish you and Amanda wouldn't fight so—but you're just so much alike."

"Alike! Please, Auntie, don't be insulting."

"Katherine, you're stubborn and willful just like her, and that's why you never can see eye to eye."

The girl sighed and looked at her aunt. In the past eight years, she had become fond of her. Heaven knows, she was a silly, fluttery, timid thing, but she was kind and loving. Lacking the beauty of her sister Alicia and the bulldog determination of Amanda, she had never married. The Fritham family was very genteel, but also poor, and so she had become the poor spinster aunt, forced to live off the charity of her relatives. Katherine, knowing that she might well have been forced into the same position had she not had her father's money, felt sorry for Amelia and tried to be patient with her.

"Katherine, I know I may be speaking out of turn, and I hope you won't dislike it, but I feel I must agree with

Amanda. I know how she aggravates you, but this time I think perhaps she's right. It's just not, not—right." Her courage failing, her voice trailed off.

"Well, Aunt Amelia, of course I respect your opinion, but I must do what I think is correct. And I'm just sure I'm doing the right thing. Please, let's not talk about it anymore, shall we?"

Amelia sighed, knowing that, as usual, she had failed in her duty. "Of course, if you don't wish to."

"Good. Then I think I shall check over the household accounts before dinner. Are we having anyone to dinner tonight?"

"Mr. Stephens and his daughter Lillian."

"How dreadful."

"Katherine, please, if you would just make a little effort—"

"I know, I know. I could 'catch' the honorable Mr. Stephens. The only thing is I have no desire to play stepmother to a girl only six years younger than myself. And even less desire to play wife to that avaricious old windbag."

"Katherine!" her aunt gasped.

Katherine swept out of the room and down the hall to the kitchen. There are times, she thought to herself, when I think that if I hear "Katherine!" one more time I shall scream. It seemed the only way she had never heard it said was in love. That thought brought her up short. Never? She cast back in her mind. Her mother, perhaps; not her father—he was always too busy. Old Charlie Kesey, the one-eyed sailor who swept out her father's office—yes, he had shown love for her, whittled toys for her, told her stories of the sea, listened to her problems. But had any young man ever whispered her name against her ear, his voice soft and yearning? Oh, there had been one or two who had cast their eyes upon her and gravely confessed that they wished to marry her. But none had ever loved her; they had only thought "it would be a good match," that she "would make a proper wife." Mentally she shook herself; enough of this nonsense—standing around mooning in the hall. There was work to be done.

Going over the accounts in the housekeeper's fine, spidery writing soon gave her a headache. The accounts were, as always, perfectly in order. Rebecca Woods was an efficient, no-nonsense housekeeper from the top of her tidy iron-gray hair to the bottom of her practical shoes. She was honest and loyal, kept an eagle eye on the maids, knew every item in the pantry down to the last cracker, and, moreover, was an excellent cook. Katherine knew she couldn't have asked for more, but there were times, as now, when she longed for Betsy Carter, the housekeeper of her childhood, who had retired three years before. Had Betsy been here, she would have fussed around like a mother hen, admonishing her for working too hard, and given her a big glass of milk and a batch of sugar cookies. Katherine drew a long sigh, remembering the many hours of her childhood spent in that warm kitchen, listening to Betsy and learning how to cook, to sew, to patch up a cut or a burn. How much more enjoyable it had been than the hours spent on her formal education—learning to draw, to play the piano, to make polite conversation, and to write an elegant hand, to embroider, to cipher, and to read—with every mistake rebuked by a sharp rap across the knuckles. Possessed of a keen mind, she had excelled at Miss Harrington's School for Young Ladies. Although she did not learn Greek as she would have had she been a boy and therefore aiming for Harvard, she was taught Latin and French, progressed to geometry, and delved into the classics and Shakespeare (properly edited, of course, for the eyes of the modest young female). It was an education formidable enough to frighten off more than one timid suitor.

The truth of the matter, though Katherine didn't realize it, was that she herself was simply too formidable for most men. Her looks were quite striking; she was rather tall, with a ripe figure hidden by her high-collared, hoop-skirted dresses. Her face was sculptured, with high, wide cheekbones, a straight nose, strong jaw, and a firm, wide mouth. Her eyes were large and a strange, almost golden color, like rich, dark honey. Her thick curling hair, which she pulled back into a severe knot at the nape of her neck, was tawny, almost the color of her eyes. Her looks were too exotic for Victorian Boston, and she was judged not to be a beauty. Moreover, her demeanor stopped any romantic young man. She seemed icy, indifferent, and overly intelligent. It was no wonder that most young man shied away from her. And as the years passed, she grew more independent, more reserved, and even began to adopt the dull colors of spinsterhood— dark blues, grays, browns. The only men who courted her were dull, unromantic types who thought that she, like they, looked on marriage as a no-nonsense business deal.

Unfortunately for them, Katherine, with an inner warmth that few suspected, had no intention of forming such a marriage. She had almost come to the conclusion that she must be incapable of love, but even so she certainly wasn't going to marry to form an alliance. Which is why, she thought savagely to herself, frowning fiercely, I won't have Mr. Henry Stephens, either!

"Miss Devereaux, is there something amiss with the books?"

"What?" Katherine looked up blankly at her housekeeper. "Oh. No, no. Just fine, as always. I must compliment you, Mrs. Woods."

"Thank you, miss."

Katherine went up the back stairs from the kitchen to her room and rang for her maid, a saucy, redheaded Irish immigrant named Pegeen Shaughnessy. "I must dress for dinner, Pegeen. Mr. Stephens is to be our guest."

"Faugh! That one," Pegeen said, wrinkling her nose in distaste.

"Exactly. And his daughter, too. I have developed a headache, and I think I would like to have my hair brushed out."

"Sure, and we'll fix you right up," the girl said, deftly unpinning the heavy mass of her hair and brushing it out in long, deep strokes.

Under her expert hands, Katherine relaxed and the painful throbbing in her head eased. "Now," Pegeen said, "we'll just bathe your temples in a little rose water and loosen your stays. You lie down and take a little rest while I iron your dress for this evening."

Katherine smiled faintly. "You're an angel, Peggy."

"Which dress is it you'll be planning to wear tonight? The deep blue one?"

"No. Something more—more—"

"Something uglier. You're right. The deep blue is too pretty for the likes of him."

Katherine, snuggling into her pillow, smiled drowsily.

The evening turned out to be everything she had feared it would be. Dressed in a pearl-gray evening gown with a modest white lace bertha—chosen by Pegeen as being the most unbecoming she had—Katherine had greeted her guests stiffly. Mr. Stephens, a portly, graying gentleman, bent gallantly over her hand and murmured that her beauty overwhelmed him. She quickly snatched her fingers from his grasp and turned to his daughter, whose amused look affirmed Pegeen's proud statement, "There, now, Miss Kate, you look as drab as I can make you." Lillian Stephens was the Victorian beauty Katherine was not. Her hair was a mass of soft golden curls, her eyes wide and blue, her mouth a pretty little pout, her complexion the pink and white of a china doll. She was eighteen years old and had just recently made her debut; therefore her wide-skirted dress was a demure white.

"So pleased to see you, Miss Devereaux," she murmured in a soft, maidenly voice, but Katherine could see the pure venom in the girl's blue eyes.

Katherine led the party to the dining room, pondering on the girl's hatred. "She must dislike me because she thinks I'm angling to become her stepmama," she thought, and almost laughed aloud. "If only she knew how little I desire that position."

The dinner conversation, as always these days, centered on the War. Mr. Stephens' pet concern was the inadequacy of the Navy to stop the Southern sea raiders. "Why, look at that rascal Read last summer, sailed all the way up the coast to Portland, wreaking havoc all the way, burning a federal revenue cutter, all with nothing but a little stolen bark that had one six-pounder and a few Quaker guns."

"Whatever are Quaker guns? I get so lost in this military conversation, don't you, Miss Devereaux?"

Katherine, who had taken an interest in the lively chase at the time it happened, said, "They were fakes, Miss Stephens; wooden spars painted and mounted to look like cannon."

"But could the Navy catch them? No! Let him slip through their fingers. Why, it was citizens from Portland finally caught him. And then was he hanged? Hell, no—excuse me, Miss Devereaux. They just locked him up in Fort Warren is all, just like that blockade runner Hampton. A pirate, that's all he is, and he should be hanged for it."

Katherine, nettled as always by Stephens, said, "But it is a war, isn't it, Mr. Stephens?"

"Rebellion, Miss Devereaux." He forced his face into a smile. "Of course, I don't expect a pretty lady like you to understand the difference."

"I understand the difference perfectly, Mr. Stephens, but what to us is treason is to them a war for independence, and I can't help but think that no doubt the British looked upon John Paul Jones as a pirate."

"Katherine Devereaux!" her father said, his voice shocked but his eyes twinkling. "That's the first pro-Rebel statement I think I've ever heard you make."

"It's not at all pro-Rebel, Papa; you know me better than that. But I think this political argument about whether a state can legally secede from the Union is mainly a coverup on both sides of what the real issues are."

"And what are the real issues?" Stephens asked, his voice amusedly tolerant. Mr. Devereaux, who knew his daughter better, hid a smile, knowing that Stephens' attitude—meant to convey that he found Katherine a bright, amusing child—was swiftly killing what little chance he had with her.

"The issues are (1) slavery and (2) which section of the country is to be the dominant one."

"What a cynical remark, Katherine."

"Just realistic, Papa. People don't go to war over legal questions. And though I'm quite an abolitionist, I don't think it's solely over slavery. It seems to me that ever since we started this country, the North and South have been on divergent courses, growing more and more apart every year in economics, modes of life, philosophy, and politics. They have become so opposed that they aren't reconcilable, so one must dominate. The South saw their power slipping when Mr. Lincoln was elected; so they seceded to prove their power. And we must defeat them, in order to show ours.

"And I find it silly to pretend that it's not a full-fledged war but only a treasonous rebellion, just so we can call sailors pirates and hang them for piracy, when they've done no more than what is always done in war."

"Bravo!" Lillian laughed delightedly and clapped her delicate white hands. "Miss Devereaux, you are as smart as a man," she cried and shot her a look of triumph—her father would think twice about marrying such a bluestocking as that.

Mr. Devereaux just sighed a little. He was a hardheaded businessman who had greatly wanted a son and never paid much attention to his daughter. But when his wife died and Katherine had taken over so efficiently, he had begun to admire her. And his admiration grew as the years went by; she was a good companion, able to converse intelligently, and quite interested in what he had to say. She soaked up the information he imparted about his business, and he found himself listening to her opinions. The past few months he had been pleased by her performance in his office, and he found in her the son he'd never had. But while he had come to respect her for her qualities, because he loved her he was distressed at the way these qualities were keeping her from happiness. He wanted to see her happily married, with a home of her own and children. But she intimidated men who were not confident of themselves and pricked the balloons of overconfident ones like Stephens. And she was in fact becoming a spinster. Not that he particularly wanted Stephens for a son-in-law—God knows, Katherine had better taste than that.

But there was a quiet young lieutenant in the Navy that he favored. He had been in the merchant marine before the War and if he survived the War would probably return and steadily rise to a command of his own ship. He wasn't in Katherine's social class, of course, but Josiah Devereaux didn't stand on such formalities; after all, he had not quite been in her mother's social class either. The lieutenant seemed like a good, solid lad to Josiah, one who would care for Katherine and who could—with Katherine's help—take over the shipyard when he died. And it seemed to him that the man was interested in Katherine; after all, he often came by the office on some pretext or other. But no doubt the difference in class seemed insurmountable to him—and just let Katherine unleash that tongue on him one time and he'd be gone forever. Sometimes he wished he could take him aside and tell him that his daughter was not one who chose a husband by the social register and that those things about her which might deter a lover would be highly valued as a wife. But since Mr. Devereaux was a rather reserved man, he did not. Instead he just sighed and wished that Katherine would put a curb on her tongue.

After Katherine's exposition of her ideas, the dinner conversation lagged, as Mr. Stephens was rather miffed. Devereaux was never a conversationalist, and Katherine inwardly seethed at Stephens' condescension, so the brunt of the conversation fell on Lillian Stephens. And she, reared to be pretty and modestly silent, floundered under the burden. Unlike her Southern counterpart, she had not been taught to capture attention with her personality, and she hadn't the spark of one who is naturally entertaining. So the meal limped along through its courses, and the guests did not linger after it was over.

When the Stephenses had gone, Katherine and her father retired to his study to enjoy a companionable glass of sherry before retiring. Josiah (Katherine often wondered how even his very New Englandish parents could have coupled a name like Josiah with one like Devereaux) lit a cigar and sat thoughtfully puffing away for a few moments before he spoke.

"Stephens' mentioning Fort Warren reminded me of something that happened after you left today."

"What?"

"Well, a gentleman from Fort Warren approached me with a proposition concerning some of their Confederate prisoners. They want us to hire them to work on the ships."

"Prisoners?"

"Yes. You know how short of men we are, and the Naval Department wants us to get as many ships built this winter as we can. We're beating them in the West, and with the blockade and now with Gettysburg—well, we hope to make a real push this spring—and to wipe out those raiders of theirs. Our Navy's far superior to theirs, of course—the blockade proves that—but the rebel raiders are a real thorn in our side."

"But is it really wise to use Confederate prisoners? I mean, won't they do shoddy work, perhaps even sabotage it?"

"Well, those are the doubts I had. Here's the argument Major Aherne presented to me: they intend to use the prisoners only on building commercial vessels—we have to get those out, too, after all—and the prisoners would be less likely to do poor work on those than on a ship they knew would actually be firing on their own men. And it would release more workers to build Navy ships. And, of course, we'll be inspecting their work and if they are sabotaging it, we'll stop using them."

"It would speed things up, if they work out. And it would be cheap labor for us," Katherine mused.

"Aherne says they are hoping that the prisoners will be so pleased to spend their days outside the prison that they'll do good work so as not to lose the privilege."

"But aren't they worried about their escaping?"

"They will be in irons and heavily guarded, and it would be so far to go through enemy territory to reach the South that it's unlikely."

"I don't see that it could do much harm to try it."

"Good. I agree. I shall visit Aherne tomorrow and tell him. He will be pleased; they are looking forward to getting the money I'll pay for the prisoners. The only thing is—perhaps it would be better now if you didn't come down to the yards."

"Oh, stuff and nonsense," she said stoutly. "No doubt it will make a few old biddies gasp to think that I'll be only a few hundred feet from prisoners, but I don't care. I don't think my reputation will be forever sullied. I mean, it's hardly as if I'll be associating with them. And now there will be even more work for me to do."

"Yes, but the idea of a young lady being exposed to that element—it's not right, Katherine. Something might happen."

"Oh, Papa, I'm not the sort who would incite men to riot. Please, let's not talk anymore about it. I'm sure it will be all right." She walked over to him and leaned down to place a light kiss on his cheek. "Goodnight, Papa."

"Goodnight, my dear," he sighed. He knew it was not proper for her to continue at the office, but he knew he would let her stay because Lieutenant Perkins would continue to come around to the yards to see her, though he would not have the courage to come calling at the house.

Two

"Oh, miss, I can hardly think straight, I'm that excited," Pegeen chattered cheerfully as she deftly pinned up her mistress's hair.

Katherine smiled. "Whatever for, Peggy?"

"Why, the prisoners, miss, didn't you say that they'd be coming today? Don't you think it's exciting? Why, you'll be that close to them Rebel devils. Why, who knows what they might do!"

"Oh, Pegeen," she laughed, "I'll probably never come close to the prisoners. They'll be working on the ships and I'll be safe inside the office. Why, I won't even pay them; we pay the prison officials. Maybe, just maybe, I shall be able to see them if I look out the window."

"Well, Miss Kate, if you won't be scared, then I'll be scared for you. 'Tis dangerous they are, and there's no telling what they might try. Why, I have a cousin from Kilkenny, coming across from Ireland on an immigrant ship he was—hundreds of people on it, mum. And that Read fellow stopped 'em and made the captain sign a bond for $150,000 not to burn the ship. Proper scared they was, for fear of what he might do. Right in front of their very eyes he stopped another boat and burned it, just to let 'em feel the fear. No, miss, it ain't safe being that close to them."

"Surely they aren't absolutely inhuman, Pegeen."

"Well, Miss Kate, I'm sure I don't know about that. But 'twas you who told me all those horrid things they do to them poor black people down there."

"They do seem to be a particularly violent group of people," Katherine agreed. "And yet think of the great men who have come from the South—Washington, Jefferson, Marshall, Madison. They can't *all* be monsters."

"Well, my brother, who's in the Army of the Potomac, he says they're like the English landlords back home. Very aristocratic, you know, and full of fine words, but cruel tyrants underneath."

"Perhaps so. But these particular tyrants will be guarded and in irons. So I don't think they'll be able to do me any harm." Her hair done, she stood up for Pegeen to lace her stays.

"Suck in, miss," Pegeen said and when Katherine obeyed her, yanked at the strings until the stays were tight enough. Then she quickly tied the laces and proceeded to help her mistress into her hoop and multitude of petticoats.

After breakfast, Katherine, swathed in a heavy cloak, a prim brown bonnet on her head, and her gloved hands encased in a fur muff, set off with her father for the shipyards. Though it was their hardy custom to walk, because of the cold this morning they took the carriage.

When their carriage pulled up at the office, the prison wagons were already unloading. Katherine felt a stir of excitement. Though she had denied it to her maid, she did feel a certain apprehension. She had never in her life seen a Southerner and she had heard tales of their wild drinking and fighting and riding. And in suitably vague and hushed words, she had been told many times that "no woman was safe around them." (Exactly what they did to women, she was not sure, any more than she was sure what happened to a woman to make her "fallen.") Moreover, the abolitionist literature she had read and the tales of their terrors on the seas had implanted a definite impression in her mind that they were merciless, whip-wielding tyrants. So she felt the spice of danger at being this close to them, and a certain thrill of curiosity to see what such ogres looked like up close.

Her father stepped out of the carriage and reached back to help her down the steps. As she stepped out, she looked curiously over at the descending prisoners. They were ragged and generally unkempt, and the heavy iron manacles on their wrists and ankles enhanced their dangerous appearance. But strangely enough, her initial reaction was a thrill of pity at the sight of human beings so chained and at the thought that they were not warmly enough dressed.

One of the prisoners turned after he jumped down from the wagon and, seeing her, insolently returned her stare. He was a tall man, slender but broad-shouldered; his movements were silkily muscular, like the graceful motion of a jungle cat. He obviously had spent his life in the sun, for his skin was brown, his brown hair was sun-streaked with blond, and there were squint lines at the edges of his clear gray eyes. His eyes held her gaze magnetically; though she wanted to look away, she somehow couldn't.

An icy wind from the harbor tore at her, pushing the prim bonnet back from her head and whipping her cloak apart. The man suddenly smiled, his strong white teeth startling against the brown skin, and his heavy black eyebrows rose, conveying a masculine appreciation of her face and figure as strongly as if he had whistled. Flushing hotly, she jerked her hat back on her head, clapped her cloak about her, and, taking her father's hand, descended from the carriage and stalked into the office.

"Miss Katherine, did you see the prisoners?" Teddy Mathias called cheerfully from his station at the window. "Just look at them Johnny Rebs."

"Yes, I saw them," Katherine said, furiously tugging at the bow of her bonnet.

"Katherine, is something wrong?" Her father paused in the doorway of his office to look at her.

"No, Papa; it just unnerves me to see men in chains."

"Katherine, perhaps you shouldn't—"

"Papa, we've already discussed that. I'm staying right here."

He shrugged a little and went on into his office. Katherine unfastened her cloak and hung it beside her bonnet, then began to slam things into place on her desk.

How dare he! she fumed inwardly. He had looked at her so coolly and insolently, not at all like a man in chains should look. And that impudent grin on his face when her cloak had blown open. No one had ever looked at her like that before! It was like the way low, common workers at the yard looked at Pegeen and whistled or called brash comments to her. Not that it seemed to bother Pegeen; she just smiled and tossed back a sharp retort. Katherine didn't see how. That man's grin had made her feel tongue-tied and knotted her stomach.

Teddy Mathias, in his fourteen-year-old boy's excitement, was completely impervious to her mood. He clung to the window, staring at the prisoners and chattering away. "Do you think any of them are Read's men? Or maybe Hampton's? Or Dawson's? They look like a fierce lot, don't they? Why, I wouldn't put it past 'em to try to escape, chains and all. Wouldn't that be exciting, Miss Katherine? What would you do? We'd have to barricade the door, pull a desk across it, maybe. And then I'd shoot 'em out of this window." He shrugged. "Only I haven't got a gun."

"Teddy, don't you think you had best get to work now? I'm sure all those guards can handle the prisoners if they try to escape."

"Yes'm, I guess you're right." Teddy looked at her, his green eyes sparkling and the very freckles on his nose seeming to stand out in excitement. "But it sure would be fun, wouldn't it?"

She had to smile at him. "Your idea of fun and mine differ somewhat, I'm afraid."

It was difficult to concentrate that morning. She found that, like Teddy, her eyes often strayed to the window. It was a relief when Pegeen came in at twelve o'clock carrying a tray with her lunch on it. Teddy took his sack lunch and went out to eat it with the workers. Since Mr. Devereaux went to his club to lunch, Katherine ate by herself, but Pegeen kept up a flow of chatter to keep her amused.

"Law, miss, where are those Rebels?"

"I'll show you." Katherine took her to the window and pointed. "Down there; they're working on that fishing vessel for Wheatley and Sons."

"Well, you can't see much from here," Pegeen said in disappointment. "Maybe we ought to take a stroll down there, miss."

"Pegeen!"

"Well, don't you ever look over the ships and see how they're coming along?"

"Sometimes I do. But not when there are Confederate prisoners all over the place."

"Oh, but Miss Kate, I'd so like to see 'em up close and I'm scared to go by myself! What harm would it do?"

"Why, it would be foolhardy, Peg, you must see that."

"Oh, pooh, mum, they'd probably welcome the sight of a girl, being stuck away in a prison like that."

"They would probably welcome it too much."

"Oh, how exciting."

"Pegeen!"

"Well, they aren't likely to attack me right there in front of the guards!"

"Really, Pegeen, the way you talk sometimes just isn't proper."

"I know, mum." Her pert little face looked downcast for a moment. "But I would so like to get a look at them."

"When you come to get me this afternoon, perhaps you can see them getting back in the wagons. They unloaded this morning right there in front of the office."

"Oh, that'd be grand, that would. Oh, Miss Kate, life's been ever so much more exciting since you started working."

"Has it?"

"Oh, yes, getting to bring you lunch and coming down to walk back with you in the afternoon. Why, Jimmy O'Toole—he's the milkman you know . . ." Pegeen paused and blushed. "At lunch he's taken to walking a couple of blocks with me and sometimes in the afternoon, if he's through, he'll take me up on his wagon and drive me nearly all the way here. Oh, he's a fine lad, with a bold eye and he dances that fine, and the blarney he gives a girl!"

Katherine smiled at the girl. "It sounds as if his 'blarney' must work."

" 'Deed it does," Pegeen said and smiled, thinking to herself that what Miss Kate needed was a James O'Toole who would wheedle and sweet-talk her out of those stiff ways of hers.

Teddy bounded into the room, his skinny little chest swollen with importance. "I been talking to the guards. I went down to the Wheatley ship, and they had them Rebs all lined up getting their lunch, see, from the prison—horrid-looking beans, miss. And one of the Rebs spoke to me, said as how he'd lay a little bet with me if I'd put up my sandwiches, and then they all laughed, and another one said I'd better keep my sandwiches to myself 'cause Jenkins was a riverboat man."

"One of those gamblers?" Katherine asked.

"Yes'm. And one of 'em asked me who the redheaded

lass was, and then . . ." Suddenly he flushed to the roots of his hair and began to stammer.

Pegeen laughed out loud and said, "Go on; you can leave out what they said about me."

"Well, one man, real quiet-like, not loud and laughing like the others, said to me, 'Boy, who's the lady with the gold eyes?' "

Unaccountably Katherine's heart jerked and she said sharply, "Which one, Teddy?"

"Tall one, Miss Kate, strong-looking; brown hair, I guess. Anyway," he went on, impatient at having his tale interrupted, "I said, 'What d'you mean, gold eyes?' and he smiled and said, 'Perhaps you wouldn't notice. I mean the lady who arrived in the carriage this morning. Dressed in brown, with a little fur muff and a silly hat.' "

"Well!" Katherine gasped, indignant at his description of her hat, and Pegeen smothered a laugh.

"So I said, 'Oh, you must mean Miss Devereaux.' And he said 'Devereaux?' and pointed to the name above the office door, and I said, 'Yes, sir, she's Mr. Devereaux's daughter.' And he thanked me and went off to eat."

"Is that all he said?" Katherine pressed him, a little disappointed.

"Yes'm. But they sure do talk funny, all kinda slow and soft. Then I talked to their guards—their names are Jackson and Gunther. And they say that these are a tough lot and they don't know why they let them out."

"They were probably just trying to impress you. But are there only two guards?"

"Oh, no, there's four. Besides the ones that drive the wagons."

"How many prisoners are there?"

"Twenty-five or thirty, I guess."

"Oh, mum," Pegeen broke in, "isn't it exciting that one of them was asking about you? Why do you suppose he was?"

"I'm sure I haven't the vaguest idea, Peg. But I think it's time you took the tray back to the house and regaled everyone with your account of the prisoners. But, Pegeen, don't tell them about one of them inquiring about me. It would only worry Aunt Amelia."

Pegeen, her eyes wide, held a forefinger up to her lips. "I'll be as quiet as a churchmouse about it."

Katherine returned to her work, but found that soon the numbers would recede and in her mind she'd see that man. She was sure it was the same one who had grinned at her so insolently this morning. Why had he asked Teddy about her? Why on earth was he interested in her name? Aunt Amelia would be sure it meant he wanted to "have his way with her," but since Aunt Amelia firmly believed that about every male who called on them, Katherine doubted that she was right. She simply was not the sort that bounders tried to force themselves upon, though if she had ever seen anyone likely to force himself on a woman, it was that man. She wished she knew what his name was and felt that he had some sort of advantage over her because he knew hers.

She was diverted from her reverie by the entrance of Charlie Kesey. He was an old sailor, blind in one eye, and with a lamentable preference for the bottle. He had been blinded, he told her, in a fistfight in Portugal when a drunken French sailor smashed a bottle into his face.

A jagged scar still showed above and below his black patch. His equilibrium had also been impaired, and that, coupled with his loss of vision, had destroyed his usefulness as a sailor. Her father had hired him to sweep the office and do odd jobs about it and sometimes about the house. He had a scraggy, almost piratical look about him, but Katherine had loved him at first sight and had slipped away from her overseers at home every chance she could to come down to the docks and talk to Charlie. She was his adored "Missy," and if Betsy had given her her domestic education, Charlie had given her her naval education. He had taught her how to steer by the stars, how to sail through a gale, how to tell one ship from another, and what every part of a ship was named. He gave wonder and excitement to her childhood, whittling intricate little wooden animals for her and telling highly imaginative tales of his own exploits and those of pirates.

Charlie never seemed to change. As seedy-looking as ever, as inclined to reek of rum, he was also possessed of the same salty humor and admiration for his "Missy." "You've got spunk right enough," he had told her, "spitting in those old biddies' eyes like this."

"Well," he said today, pausing inside the doorway with his broom, "scruffy lot of workers you got out there. Think you'll be taking a shine to one of them, Missy?"

This struck Teddy as so amusing he almost fell off his high stool laughing. Katherine just said tartly, "I hardly think so, Charlie."

"Well, I thought they might be in your line. I've never seen yet any other type of man you fancied."

"The whole lot are worthless." Katherine smiled.

"Don't laugh so, boy; you'll split a gut. I'll tell you truly, I never seen finer dressers than some of them Reb gentlemen. Why, I remember once I sailed under a captain from Charleston—" and Charlie was off on one of his reminiscences.

Katherine, only half-listening, wondered if *he* had been a splendid dresser. How different he would look in a snowy white shirt and well-cut coat and trousers instead of the faded, dirty remnants of the gray uniform he now wore. And, somehow, not so very different—the animal strength, the gathered and waiting power would still be there. Angrily she shook off her thoughts. What nonsense she was indulging in! Determinedly she bent over the books.

So absorbed did she become that she hardly noticed when Pegeen came in. Pegeen, not wanting to leave until she had seen the prisoners closer, took up a quiet post by the window. For a long time the girl was unrewarded but at last she cried, "Oh, they're leaving now!"

Teddy tripped all over himself in his frantic haste to get to the window. Charlie abandoned his efforts at oiling the door hinges to join him. Katherine, with a deliberate air of unconcern, cleaned off her desk and locked it up before she strolled over to stand beside Pegeen. She found him instantly, waiting near the end of the line to get on the wagons. As if feeling her gaze upon him, he suddenly raised his head and looked at their window. He smiled and boldly winked at her. She retreated from the window.

"Did you see that, Miss Kate!" Pegeen exclaimed.

"That pirate winked at us! Bold as brass, he was. Is that the one that was asking after you?"

"I think so. Is that he, Teddy, third one from the end?"

"Yes'm, that's the one."

"You mean one of them scum was asking you about the Missy here?" Charlie demanded.

"Sure was, Charlie."

The old man looked concerned. "I don't like that, miss."

"Oh, stuff and nonsense, you're all making a great to-do about nothing," Katherine said stoutly, but she found to her surprise that her fingers trembled slightly as she tied on her bonnet.

"Well," said Pegeen as they briskly walked home, "I must say, that rascal had a way with him."

"Whatever can you mean?" Katherine said dryly.

Not in the least deterred by her tone, the girl went on, "I mean he was a handsome brute, that one. And it fair sent shivers up my spine when he winked at us like that."

Katherine almost retorted that he had winked at *her*, not the two of them, but bit back the words, realizing what a foolish thing it was to say. Whatever was the matter with her today?

When they reached home, she found a worthy Boston matron and her daughter there, obviously lingering on with their afternoon call in the hopes of her coming in. Sighing, she resigned herself to a tedious time satisfying their curiosity about the excitingly dangerous Rebel prisoners. As if that weren't bad enough, she then had to endure a dinner at her Aunt Amanda's home, where she was plagued by her aunt's alternate scolding and eager questions as well as by her cousin's cloying attentions.

By the time she reached home, she was so tired she could have screamed. She found, however, that she couldn't sleep. At first she fumed about the way the ladies lectured her on her impropriety and then gobbled up the information about the prisoners she could give them. Then her mind turned to the unwelcome attentions of her cousin Jamie—when would he give up? She had refused him twice and still he kept after her, plying her with syrupy compliments. Of course, he was urged on by her aunt, who would have liked to see Katherine's wealth flowing into her own coffers. "As if," Katherine sniffed to herself, "I'd ever marry someone who was too much of a coward to fight, who buys replacements for himself in the draft!"

Then, unbidden, the prisoner came into her mind and, no matter how she struggled, wouldn't leave it. She couldn't understand why he plagued her so—his impudence was unforgivable, and she disliked him heartily. Why should that mean she couldn't stop thinking about him?

She arose the next morning tired but filled with a quiet determination that today she would remain unruffled. And so she did, never once looking out the window at the prisoners as they worked. Nor did she watch them unload, and she left before they returned to the wagons that afternoon. She even managed to repress Teddy's and Pegeen's chatter about them. That night she went to bed feeling triumphant and fell asleep instantly.

* * *

One afternoon a few days later, the door opened and a dark, quiet young man dressed in the blue of the Navy stepped into the office. Katherine looked up and smiled pleasantly.

"Lieutenant Perkins," she said, "how nice to see you again."

"Miss Devereaux. Teddy. Charlie."

"Please sit down. How is the Navy?" Katherine asked.

"Oh, fine. My ship should be sailing soon."

"Where are you going?"

"To join the blockade. I'm not at liberty to say where exactly."

"Of course." Katherine smiled at him. She liked the lieutenant and enjoyed his irregular visits. He had first come to her father's office over a year ago when she had happened to be there, measuring the windows for the curtains she had decided to put in. She had been impressed by Perkins' quiet assurance and steady personality. Rather grave and earnest, he rarely smiled; when he did, his brown eyes lit up and his face was touched with warmth. He was not a particularly handsome man, but there was a certain strength of character in his rough-hewn face that Katherine liked. He had escorted her back to her house that day, and then she had not seen him again until she had begun working a few months ago. Since then, he had taken to dropping in every once in a while, and Katherine always enjoyed his visits, though she was a little puzzled as to why he came so often.

There were times when she felt that he was interested

in her, but she knew she must have imagined that, since he never visited her at home. She had to admit to herself that she would not be entirely averse to his suit. Although she doubted she would ever love him, and the very stolidity of his character made him dull at times, she thought him better than most men who had courted her—more honest, innately warmer, easier to converse with about things that interested her. Because she thought him admirable, it never occurred to her, as it had to her father, that Perkins was afraid she would rebuff his suit because of his background.

"Have you heard about our prisoners, Lieutenant?" Teddy asked eagerly.

"Indeed I have. In fact, I came over just to see them."

Katherine's heart began to pound violently inside her, but she forced herself to speak calmly. "Oh? I'm sure that if you want to walk over to the ship to look at their work, you can. I'll be happy to take you over there if you like."

He smiled. "Why, thank you. I'd like that very much."

Katherine hastened to put on her cloak and bonnet and slip her hands into her muff. She told herself that she was being silly, that there was no reason to be excited, that there was, in fact, no reason to go with him in the first place. Ignoring her inner voice, she swept out the front door. Perkins, pleased because her invitation seemed to him to indicate a liking for his company, followed her out the door and solicitously put his hand under her elbow to assist her down the stairs.

His elation grew as they crossed the yards, for she chattered in a light, excited way that he had never seen her adopt before. It occurred to him that perhaps she was a little buoyant over being alone with him, for they had never been together without at least the juvenile chaperonage of Teddy.

"How thrilling it must be to be going to join the blockade soon," she said, her voice vibrant.

His chuckle was more a release of his turbulent feelings than an expression of amusement. "Oh, I'm afraid not. Blockading is rather dull most of the time—just sitting and waiting and watching. I would rather be out pursuing the Rebel raiders."

She smiled. "I imagine you're right. The raiders are almost like pirate stories, aren't they? Charlie Kesey used to make my hair stand on end with his pirate adventures—and I loved it."

"Did you used to spend a lot of time with old Charlie?"

She looked up at him, her eyes mischievous. "Indeed, yes, whenever I could escape from my governess or my housekeeper or my mother; it was my favorite occupation."

He stared down into her amber eyes, glinting with gold lights, and felt as if he might drown in them. "Katherine, I—I—"

"Here's the hull," she announced gaily. "Now if we can just get past the guards."

"All it takes is assurance—and your name and my uniform," he whispered, firmly taking hold of her arm and feeling a sudden rush of light-headedness at touching her.

"Corporal." He and the guard exchanged salutes.

"Lieutenant Perkins. This is Miss Devereaux. We've come to inspect the prisoners' work."

"Yessir."

They went into the half-finished hull. All around them activity went on, seemingly uncoordinated, with scaffoldings and catwalks at various heights. The guards stayed at the edge, their eyes endlessly watching the prisoners, who worked, not lazily, as Katherine had expected, but in silent concentration. The crew foreman, George MacPherson, came hurrying toward them, smiling and whisking off his cap to properly meet a lady.

"Miss Devereaux." He made a funny little bob, his version of a bow.

"George, this is Lieutenant Perkins. He is interested in seeing how the prisoners are getting along."

"Why, I'll be happy to show you around. You know," he confided, beginning his tour, "I never would have believed it, but this crew has been working right smartly. Just sailors, by and large, but they've at least done repair work and they can handle the simpler tasks, which cuts down the number of skilled workers we need. Why, I think I could practically do it with just them. And they're not shirkers, either, which, I can tell you, surprised me."

"I imagine they're willing to work quite well if it means being outside the prison," the lieutenant said. "I can think of nothing more grim than a prison to a man who's spent his life with the limitless ocean around him."

Katherine walked along with them, barely hearing their words. Now that she was here, her burst of enthusiasm had vanished, leaving her feeling foolish and mad at herself. Why had she come? What did she think she was doing here? Why hadn't she sent Lieutenant Perkins over here by himself? For once in her life, she felt as if she had no control, no understanding of herself. Did she want to see that man again? But how preposterous!

"Now," MacPherson was saying, "if you'll just come up here with me—" He started to climb a ladder, with the lieutenant on his heels, but the young man caught himself and turned.

"But wait, Miss Devereaux can't climb like this."

Katherine looked at the ladder and smiled. Climbing a ladder was almost impossible in a hoop and petticoats, not to speak of the unmentionable view it would present to the men below. "I'm afraid I can't," she said, "but you go on. I'll wait right here for you. I'll be perfectly safe."

"Well—"

"Go on. I know how interested you are."

The lieutenant smiled his thanks and darted up the ladder after the chunky foreman. Katherine, the smile lingering on her lips, turned and found herself staring into cold gray eyes under satanically slanted black eyebrows. Her heart began to pound and she thought frantically of running up the ladder after Perkins.

Then the man smiled, jauntily pulled off his battered cap, and swept her a mockingly elegant bow. "Captain Matthew Hampton, ma'am, at your service."

In her best imitation of Aunt Amanda, she chillingly delivered a snub, looking through him as if he didn't exist and then away.

"Bravo, Miss Devereaux," his voice was softly jeering. "I've never seen even an old Charleston matron administer a better cut. Of course, it's harder to get such an icicle of a look in ninety-degree weather."

Pointedly she turned her back on him. She could hear his chuckle behind her.

"Oh, I am a pariah, aren't I?" he said. "My Grandmama Soames always did tell me I wasn't fit for polite society. 'Course, I'll admit," he continued conversationally, "that I'm not attired in my finest evening wear. My shirt is a little frayed around the cuffs. And my boots—" he sighed dramatically, "well, they no longer have that mirror polish to them." He paused for a moment. "Lord, girl, couldn't you even give a little smile? Just a little look at your face to warm my lonely evenings?"

She whirled on him, longing to shout that he was a rude, insufferable man, but bit back the words. I won't even deign to speak, she thought to herself, haughtily lifting her chin.

"That's a good girl," he said. Slowly, brazenly, his eyes traveled over her face and down her body. She felt suddenly as if he could see through her layers of clothes, as if his burning eyes were roaming her bare flesh. She felt a blush rise in her cheeks, and he grinned wickedly, as if he knew what she thought, and had intended for her to think so.

She bit her lip, trying to think of something sufficiently scathing to say. What had happened to Lieutenant Perkins? Why didn't he return to rescue her?

"Please do not force me to call a guard," she said coldly.

A bitter smile twisted his face. "Oh, yes, we mustn't forget that I am a prisoner, must we? Did you and your friend come down here today to look at the animals? Was the zoo closed? Or is it just more titillating to see men in shackles?"

"You Rebels seem to sing a different tune when it's you who are in chains. Why, I thought chains and whips and such were almost holy to you. I should think you would be proud to wear shackles, a sort of symbol of your homeland, so to speak."

He stiffened in anger, and she recoiled a little at the blaze in his eyes. Then, visibly, he forced himself to relax and his eyes returned to their steely gray. "Miss Devereaux," his former drawl became abrupt and clipped, "I suggest that you take a look at home before you start trying to reform me. Take a look at the women and children dying day by day in your mills. Take a look at your prisons, your insane asylums, your hospitals. Have you seen the food we receive to fortify us for hard manual labor? Have you seen the filth of our cells, the brutality of our guards? Why don't you go home tonight and get out the Bible you stiff-necked Puritans revere so much and read the story about Mary Magdalene. 'Let he who is without sin cast the first stone.' Or is that story considered too risqué for a proper young Boston lady?"

Quivering with fury, she longed to slap him with all her strength or to roar, "Damn your impudence!" as her father would. Then suddenly one of the guards was by her side.

"This man bothering you, miss?"

Shakily she managed to say, "No!"

But Hampton, grinning that vile grin, said, "Just discussing with the little lady whether it's true that if you bed a Boston girl, you'll be frozen stiff before dawn."

Katherine gasped at his vulgar insolence, then shrieked as the guard swung his rifle, clubbing Hampton with the butt end. The prisoner spun and went down at the force of the blow, but sprang back up like a cat. Half-crouching, he warily circled the guard, taut and tense, preparing to spring. Katherine stood frozen at the terrible animal beauty of his predatory movements, at the cold gray death in his eyes, at the fresh red blood trickling from his nose and mouth. The guard slowly raised his rifle and squinted down the barrel at the man.

"No!" Katherine cried, breaking out of her trance. "Don't! Stop it, both of you!" She flung herself between Hampton and the guard. Though the guard held the gun, she faced Hampton, recognizing him as the more dangerous, even though unarmed. "Please, you mustn't do this. He has the advantage over you. You'll be killed. He has a gun."

As though deaf, he sidestepped; behind her the gun tracked him; and Katherine moved again to block them. There was no reasoning with him; she could see the hatred in his eyes. Inspiration seized her and, though she could not imagine later how she had either thought of it or had the ability to do it, she suddenly smiled, forcing a dimple into her cheeks. "Now, really, Captain Hampton," she said in mock severity, with a pretty, flirtatious toss of her head. Lightly she continued, "Didn't your Grandmama Soames ever tell you it's bad manners to kill someone in front of a lady?"

He stopped, nonplussed, and reason returned to his

face. He dropped his clenched fists and then suddenly burst into laughter. "Lord, ma'am, you must have a Southerner lurking somewhere in your family tree. I apologize for my poor taste."

"Now, Corporal, it was really quite innocuous. Why don't you go back to your post and the captain here will return to work, and everything will go quite smoothly."

"Miss Devereaux? What's going on down there? Is something wrong?"

"Why, no, Lieutenant Perkins." She tilted her head to look up at him. "However, I am a little tired."

"Of course," he said solicitously, and descended the ladder. "I'm sorry to have left you down here alone; it must have been quite boring."

A faint smile touched her face. "No, not really, Lieutenant."

Hampton gave her a mocking salute and retreated, as Katherine took the lieutenant's arm and left the ship. Her heart was still racing from the excitement and she felt as if she had enough energy to dance for hours. Mentally, she was in a turmoil, totally confused by Hampton and her own reactions to him. He was really a most abominable man, quite violent and rude and bold; she realized that she disliked him more than any man she had ever met and would have loved to do physical harm to him. The way he had looked at her had been infuriating and insolent, but it had sent the strangest feeling spreading through her. And his lazy, husky voice literally prickled the fine hairs on her neck. His voice, she mused, reminded her of brandy, sleek and smooth but bursting like fire within her.

Lieutenant Perkins, seeing her flushed face and the sparkle that fear had brought to her eyes, was shaken with his love. "Miss Devereaux, would you—that is, might I have the liberty of calling on you?"

She looked up at him, only half-listening. "Why, yes, if you'd like, Lieutenant Perkins."

Stunned by his own good fortune, he almost stopped, but managed to recover. Too happy to speak, he contented himself with gently squeezing the delicate gloved hand resting in the crook of his arm.

Three

The sight of the large, rough-edged Lieutenant Perkins perched on one of the delicate drawing room chairs, holding a dainty Havilland teacup in one sea-hardened hand, was so ludicrous that Katherine had to bite her lip to keep from smiling.

Knowing what her aunt's reaction would be to the casual way in which they had met, Katherine had told her only that a young lieutenant to whom her father had introduced her might be expected to pay a call on them soon. Aunt Amelia, knowing no Perkins in Boston, assumed he was from another city, perhaps even—heaven forbid—another state. She could only hope that he wasn't from some horrid state like New York or Pennsylvania. There was, she thought, a rather prominent Perkins family in Providence, Rhode Island, which would not be too unacceptable, considering the fact that her niece was running out of chances.

He paid a call on them the first Sunday afternoon after he had asked her, as she suspected he would. When the butler showed him into their drawing room, he had bowed awkwardly, looking ridiculously out of place among the fragile furnishings. That didn't surprise Katherine; it had been her experience that many seamen became suddenly gauche and clumsy when removed from their natural habitat. Aunt Amelia, expecting an ordinary civilian parading in a navy uniform, was rather taken aback, but set up a brave chatter about the weather, preparations for the upcoming holidays, and the enormous decisions to be made concerning Christmas presents. The lieutenant listened attentively, a look of grim determination on his face. Katherine, amused, had intervened with an offer of tea, which he gratefully accepted—though no doubt he wished he hadn't, once he was faced with the awkwardness of holding the fragile little cup and saucer.

"What part of the Navy are you in, Lieutenant Perkins?" Aunt Amelia asked him.

Katherine, realizing that the inquisition had begun, perked up so that she might be in readiness to come to his aid.

"I sail under Captain LeGrau, Miss Fritham, on the *U.S.S. Pentucket.*"

"He has been out chasing those Rebel pirates, Auntie. Doesn't that sound exciting?"

But Aunt Amelia, timid though she might be, was, after all, a Fritham and not easily diverted when she was on the trail of someone's background. "Yes, dear, it certainly is. But, of course, the lieutenant is much more used to sea adventures than I, I'm sure. Did you sail before the war?"

"Yes, I was in the merchant marine."

"Why, how nice. Are you intending to return after the war?"

"The sea is the only thing I know. I grew up with it and I guess that I will stay with it until I die."

"I have always thought that if I had been a man, I should have been a sailor," Katherine said conversationally. "I have always felt quite drawn to the sea."

"Katherine," her aunt admonished, "you say the most outlandish things. Tell me, Lieutenant, where is your home?"

"Nantucket."

Katherine could see the wheels spinning in her aunt's mind as she tried to remember any Perkins in Nantucket.

The man gulped and, casting his fate to the winds, said, "My father is a ship's captain, Miss Fritham."

"How nice," Aunt Amelia said automatically.

"Is he?" Katherine said interestedly. "What line?"

"The Stephens Line," he said, wishing he could have said "his own."

"The Stephens Line?" Amelia brightened at the name. "Katherine, are those Henry Stephens's ships?"

"Yes, Aunt Amelia, but in spite of that, it's a very good line."

"Katherine!" Amelia exclaimed as Perkins choked back a laugh.

Lieutenant Perkins, miserably sure that all hope for his suit was lost, soon rose to take his leave. Politely he bowed over Miss Fritham's hand and then Katherine's, a slight squeeze of her hand and a warm look from his eyes telling her that he recognized and appreciated her efforts to draw the fire. Katherine smiled reassuringly at him, glad that, since frail Amelia so intimidated him, he had not had to face the heavy guns of Aunt Amanda.

"Katherine," Amelia said after he had gone, "I really don't think he's quite the thing. A sailor from Nantucket?" From her tone she might have been saying "a convict from Devil's Island."

"Well, I wouldn't worry about it, Aunt Amelia," Katherine snapped. "I think you managed to frighten him off. I doubt he'll return."

"Dear, surely you haven't developed an affection for that young man?"

"Don't be nonsensical. I just think he's a very fine man, and it makes me angry that you can see nothing but his name and where he's from and whether his ancestors came over on the *Mayflower*."

Quick tears started in Amelia's eyes, but her aunt's easy sensitivity simply irritated Katherine further and she flounced off upstairs to her room where she occupied herself by staring out the window and drumming her fingers on the arm of her chair. She had to admit that her aunt was not the source of her nerves; she had been on edge ever since that fight at the yards five days before.

She kept seeing again the rifle smashing into his face, the blood streaming from his mouth. Despicable and insulting as he was, it went against her grain to see a shackled man so brutally hit. No doubt one as insolent as he had to be punished, but surely a crude remark didn't warrant that! To make it worse, she had not seen him among the prisoners the rest of the week. Had he been hospitalized? Or was he being punished by not being allowed to go on the work detail? Remembering what Perkins had said about the effect of prison on a seafaring man, she felt a stab of pain for the Southerner. And somehow she felt that it was her fault. She told herself that he had brought it on himself, that he had delivered a deliberate insult to her. But she couldn't help but feel that she had been wrong to go down to the ship in the first place. It had been a foolish, impulsive thing to do, and she suspected it had been motivated by a wicked desire to see that impudent man brought low, chained and forced to work for his enemy.

Nor could she erase the memory of his bitter words about the treatment of the prisoners. She could see that they were not warmly enough dressed, and that the shackles chafed their skin. Finally, she had been compelled to inspect their lunch herself and was repelled by the watery bean soup that was their fare.

"Man's inhumanity to man," she sighed. Suddenly an idea flashed into her head and she ran out of her room and pelted down the stairs and into her father's study.

"Papa?" she said, a little breathless from running with the iron clamp of her stays pinching her lungs. "Papa, I have an idea!"

Her father looked up inquiringly.

"About the prisoners. I want to feed them lunch."

"What?"

"Well, supplement it, actually. I thought I would add meat and bread and perhaps a vegetable. And vinegar or limes to combat the scurvy."

"My dear, how did you come by this madcap scheme?"

"Oh, Papa, I saw the lunch that is dished out to them;

it's so little, you can't imagine. It—it nearly breaks my heart to see them in irons and see how their clothes are too thin and see the food they receive. And I thought, well, I can help them. Get them some warm clothes and give them decent food at least once a day. Why, it's like charity work and that's something I'm quite experienced at."

Mr. Devereaux looked at her and sighed. "No, my girl, I'm afraid this is one time I must forbid you to do as you wish."

"Oh, but it won't cost much. There can't be more than thirty men. And it will take a minimum of time and effort. Good staple food, nothing difficult, of course. It wouldn't be much more work for Mrs. Woods—I can help her. You know how good I am at organizing."

"Katherine, I know that with you in charge it would be performed quite efficiently. Nor do I begrudge the expense. But if I let you, the military would be offended. These are prisoners of war, not charity cases! Why, your efforts would be seen as a rebuke to the Army. In fact, I doubt that they would allow you to do it."

"Not allow me! Why, that's just so unfair. You're *paying* the prison for the work these men do for you, and the prison won't spend a cent on them. And won't let anyone else!"

"Now, don't get that look in your eye. This is not time for one of your fits of stubbornness. Really, Katherine, they are prisoners of war. A few months ago these very men were no doubt pillaging our ships. And just recently their comrades were tramping through Pennsylvania to

Gettysburg. These are the men you have been reviling for years as monsters, bloodthirsty slaveowners."

"I still decry their abominable slavery. But their wickedness doesn't justify our treating them with the same wickedness. We gain nothing by it, and we release the same evil in ourselves! Can't you see how wrong it is?"

"Katherine, I'm afraid this is one time I'm going to have to refuse you."

Katherine was not used to being refused anything, especially by her father. She had always been so determined, so capable, so forceful that she usually overwhelmed him. She took a direct counterattack.

"Father, if I were to approach the commandant at Fort Warren and get his permission, then might I be allowed to feed these men?"

"Dear God in Heaven, Katherine, you are a stubborn girl! I don't want you pestering the Army about this."

"I certainly shan't pester him."

Her father raised his eyebrows quizzically at that remark, but he replied gravely, "Katherine, I think it would be best if you stopped coming to the yard. It's not the place for you, especially with all those prisoners. It was foolish to allow you in the first place. Of course, these men are a disturbing, pitiable sight to a gently reared young lady; it's quite natural that you have become upset. I think the best thing is for you to stay home."

Katherine was quite happy to be diverted from the original conversation as her father, by sidestepping the issue, had not actually refused her permission to approach the commandant. She started to hotly protest her father's wishes, but stopped. "Let him try without me," she thought, "and see how well he gets along." She had declared war.

Calmly, icily, she said, "Very well, Father. I shan't trouble you with my presence any longer." Regally she rose and exited. Josiah Devereaux sighed and dropped his head to his hands. He found it so difficult to handle his daughter and for the millionth time wished that his wife had not died.

Pegeen Shaughnessy was crestfallen the next morning when she learned that her mistress would not be going to the office. "Oh, Miss Kate," she cried, thinking of the lost walks with Jimmy O'Toole. "How dreadful! Can't you talk your father out of it?"

"Perhaps I could, but I don't intend to try," said Katherine, the light of battle in her eyes. "At least not at the moment. I have other things to do. And perhaps Papa will find out that it's not so easy to manage without me. Don't worry, Peggy, I'll return before too long."

Devereaux, at first smugly sure that he had won on all fronts, soon began to feel a change in positions. It didn't take him long to regret barring his daughter from the office. Orders, receipts, letters, the books—everything began to pile up. Moreover, Teddy did not possess Katherine's spidery copperplate handwriting (and grammar, punctuation, and spelling skills), so that there was no one to write Devereaux's letters at his dictation. Clerks and secretaries were almost impossible to find—certainly none with the brains, quickness, and ready knowledge of Katherine. Devereaux, before a week had passed, was searching for a way to ask her back without losing face.

Katherine's first action was to give a party. She held a small, rather boring recital featuring a string quartet, to which she invited several Boston notables and Colonel Wellman, the commandant of the prison. The latter was quite overcome at rubbing shoulders with Back Bay Society and profusely thanked his hostess. However, not being partial to string quartets, he was not averse to being drawn away from the recital by Katherine.

Propelling him to the edge of the room (to have left the room alone in the company of a man would have been quite improper), she said, "Colonel Wellman, I have been thinking about a project regarding which I would like your advice."

"Oh, Miss Devereaux, you know that I will be more than pleased to help you," he said, flattered.

"I am very interested in good works, as you probably know. I have often been involved in charitable work with Mrs. Castlemaigne—the wife of General Castlemaigne. No doubt you have met her and heard of her interest in charity."

He swelled visibly at her presumption that he communed with generals and their ladies and lied, "Why, of course; she is justly famous for her charity. An admirable woman."

"Yes, I greatly miss her company since they moved to Washington. Needless to say, however, I would like to continue with our work and have been cudgeling my brain to think of some way I could indulge myself and help the war effort at the same time."

"Quite admirable," he murmured, wishing that he

were not a married man, for he found Miss Devereaux's fortune quite appealing and it was obvious that she was enthralled with him.

Katherine, thinking that the dapper little man greatly resembled a sparrow, continued, "Finally, I realized that the perfect solution was the military prison. My father, as you know, employs several of your prisoners, and I thought that I would begin with them—sort of a test case. Don't you think that's a marvelous idea?"

"But of course. Only—what exactly is it that you propose to do?"

"Well, I hoped to save the Army some of the expense of their upkeep—buy their winter clothing, say. And since they are down at the shipyards during the day, how much simpler it would be for us to provide their lunch. And it would save you the expense and trouble of having to bring the food down to them at noon."

"Splendid. Splendid," he said vaguely, thinking that society ladies came up with the most peculiar ideas. "Just take it up with the man in charge of them."

"I think perhaps I should show him your signature. Here, let me get a piece of paper and a pen. Now, if you would just write out your permission for me to give them clothing and feed them their noon meal—"

The colonel, beginning to feel slightly harassed, hurriedly wrote out his permission.

Katherine next enlisted the aid of Pegeen. "Peggy, have you ever been inside a pawnshop?"

"Me, miss? Not likely."

"Well, do you know of any?"

"No. Why?"

"Perhaps a jeweler would be better."

"For what?"

"Well, Peg, Father and I have had a rift, as you know."

"Indeed, I do, Miss Kate, and proper miserable he looks, too. I know if you'd just speak to him sweet-like, he'd be glad to have you come back to the office."

"But it's more than that. He wouldn't allow me my prisoner plan. Well, I've obtained the Army's permission, but now I need to finance it."

"Well, perhaps he'll give in on that."

"He might," Katherine said judiciously. "But I prefer to present him with a *fait accompli.*"

"A what?"

"A—a finished thing—you know, like going ahead and buying a dress instead of asking permission to."

"I see. So you want to pay for it yourself."

"Exactly. But my pin money will hardly cover it. So I shall have to pawn my jewelry my mother left me."

"Oh, miss, not that!"

"Well, not all of it, of course. Just what I need. It's the only thing I have which is truly my own and not given me by my father."

"But you once told me those necklaces and eardrops and things had been in your mother's family for years."

"So they have, and I should hate to lose them. But I'm hoping that Papa will be so convinced of my determination and so scandalized at my pawning the family jewels that he will reclaim them and finance my project."

"Oh, miss, wouldn't it be easier just to ask him? I know my pop has got a dreadful temper, particularly when the drink's in him, but he's always sorry after he yells at me, and if I smile at him real sweet and tease him and call him 'Poppy' like when I was little, he'll always give in and do what I want."

"Well, I don't intend to engage in that sort of subterfuge. I am right, you see, and I intend to defeat him, fair and square."

The maid sighed. "I'm sure I don't know how to— wait, I've got it! My Jimmy will know. He's a smart one, that boy. And he's no doubt been in a pawnshop, for he's a bit prone to gamble a little, you see, and I know he says he's pawned and recovered his gran's gold watch a hundred times."

"Good. He sounds like our man."

He was indeed. A handsome, sharp-featured little man, with bright, knowing eyes and a cocky air, Jimmy O'Toole assured Miss Devereaux that he was just the man for the job. Taking her diamond earbobs, he soon returned with cash, getting a tip from Katherine and a kiss from Pegeen for his pains.

Katherine promptly sallied forth to buy serviceable, cheap, warm, ready-made clothes for the men. She galvanized Mrs. Woods to action by explaining her food needs and then sadly sighing that she was afraid it would be too much for the housekeeper to handle.

So it was that, two weeks after her father's refusal, Katherine and Pegeen, with a bundle of clothing, boxes of bread, and buckets of stew, arrived at the shipyards at noon in the Devereaux carriage. Rather like a warship at full sail, Katherine strode up to the prison wagon where lunch was being dispensed, immediately drawing the attention of all the men. Something was going on, they could see, and they strained their ears to hear what she said to Sergeant Gunther.

"Sergeant, I presume that you are in charge of these prisoners?"

"Yes, miss. Do you have a complaint about one of them?"

"Indeed not." She looked haughtily down her nose at him, firmly believing it best to throw the enemy off-guard with a surprise attack. "I must tell you that I was appalled at the condition of these prisoners."

The sergeant stared at her blankly.

"I can see that you have no excuse for it."

"But—but, miss, I don't—"

"Colonel Wellman quite agreed with me when we dined together last week."

The sergeant, bullied and not knowing how to escape—a friend of the prison commandant!—stammered helplessly.

"Please, Sergeant." Katherine held up one hand imperiously. "I quite realize the difficulties of the Army. I intend to remedy the situation myself—with the Colonel's full accord, of course."

With a flourish she presented Wellman's written permission. The sergeant read it and handed it back to her. "As you wish, miss."

"Good. I'm glad that we see eye to eye." She rewarded him with a frosty smile. "Pegeen!"

The prisoners, who had been listening to the exchange with avid curiosity, were now presented with a new spectacle: a pretty young redheaded girl approached carrying a bundle of clothing. Immediately all eyes focused on her. Pegeen flushed prettily, quite excited at all the admiration. One prisoner, a boy of about nineteen or twenty, sprang to his feet and went to Pegeen. He was a lively lad, thin, awkward in his shackles, but with a wide, generous mouth and merry black eyes.

With a jaunty air, quite oblivious to his chains, he doffed his cap. "Allow me, ma'am. A pretty little girl like you shouldn't be carrying so much."

At the jeers and catcalls of his fellows, he just grinned and called back, "Well, some of us are gentlemen, you know."

"Bring the clothes here, Mr.—" Katherine said and paused inquiringly.

"Fortner, ma'am," he said agreeably. "Ensign Edward Fortner, C.S.N. Where shall I put these?"

"If you would just stand there and hold them, Pegeen and I will dispense them. Gentlemen, if you will please line up, Miss Shaughnessy and I propose to give you each a warmer suit of clothes. It has come to my attention that you are not quite suitably dressed for the rigors of a Boston winter. Feeling that time was more of the essence than fit, I bought these ready-made and primarily in a medium size. I do have a few, however, in a larger or a smaller size. If you will please form two lines, one in front of Miss Shaughnessy and one in front of me. Sergeant, if you and your men would fetch the food from the carriage, I would greatly appreciate it."

After the clothes were doled out, Katherine dispensed the stew and bread, while Pegeen poured out the coffee. The men, feeling slightly giddy at the delicious aroma of stew and coffee and at the unaccustomed pleasure of being so near soft, smiling, fragrant women, laughed and talked excitedly. Katherine and Pegeen caught the festive mood, feeling quite warm with doing a good deed and with the obvious appreciation of the men.

"Ma'am, this is the best coffee I've had since 1861, and that's the truth," the irrepressible Fortner called out. "The only thing good about getting captured is getting away from that chicory stuff. Though I'll tell you truthfully, ma'am, that prison coffee ain't much better."

"But what in the world is chicory coffee?" Pegeen asked.

Fortner explained, "Chicory coffee is made with chicory nuts instead of coffee beans."

"But what does the war have to do with coffee?" Pegeen persisted.

There was an outburst of laughter, slightly tinged with bitterness. "The blockade, ma'am, the blockade. Do you know that coffee beans are grown in South America? Well, they are, and they have to be shipped in. And when the ships can't get in—*voilà*, no coffee beans and therefore no coffee. Actually, we weren't so bad off in the Navy 'cause we could stop in foreign ports and get coffee there. But I pity the soldiers and women stuck on the land."

"Pegeen, I think it's time we left now," Katherine intervened, seeing the girl puzzling out another question. "If one of you men will be so good as to carry these pots back to the carriage? Sergeant, I think that it would be much easier to serve off a trestle table than the end of a wagon. Tomorrow if you would just set up a table— nothing elaborate, of course, just a couple of sawhorses with planks in between—thank you. Good afternoon, gentlemen. Come along, Pegeen."

Before they reached the carriage, Teddy Mathias intercepted them, wide-eyed with suppressed curiosity. "Miss Katherine, your father would like to speak to you in his office."

Katherine squared her shoulders for the final confrontation and followed him. Pegeen went on to the carriage to wait for her, feeling sympathetic pangs of nervousness for her mistress—more than was felt by Katherine, who rather looked forward to settling the matter. Knowing that she had already won, Katherine sat calmly through her father's tirade, simply waiting for his anger to burn itself out. He thundered about her disobedience, her insolence, her extravagance, her stubbornness, her willfulness, and her absolute gall until finally, exhausted, he dropped into his chair.

"Papa, I did not harass the Army," Katherine said mildly. "I simply talked to Colonel Wellman, and he was quite pleased to give me his permission. You see, here is his written authorization. It was *not* obtained under duress. Having his permission, I fail to see that I have done anything wrong."

"Katherine, I expressly forbade you to—"

"Oh, no, Papa, you left the subject open. You didn't say that I could not approach the colonel, nor did you say that I could not feed the prisoners with Colonel Wellman's approval."

"Katherine, you are merely quibbling with words—if you were a man, you would have made an excellent attorney. The import of our conversation was that I did not wish for you to do this."

"Yes, I know you disapprove and that is why I am paying for it myself."

"Paying for it yourself? But how?"

"Well, of course, my allowance would not cover it, and I didn't wish to use your money, opposed as you are to the idea. So I pawned the diamond earbobs Mama left me."

"You what?" he gasped. "Do you mean to tell me that you walked into a pawnshop and pawned your mother's earrings?"

"Well, of course, I didn't enter a place like that myself. I entrusted the job to a friend of Pegeen's."

"Who the devil is Pegeen?"

"Papa, please, your language. Pegeen is my maid. At any rate, I did pawn Mama's earrings—at least they aren't centuries-old heirlooms, like the pearls or the garnets or the ruby drop."

"Katherine, I cannot allow you to dispose of your mother's family jewelry in this manner." He raised his hands in a gesture of capitulation. "You win. I shall retrieve your earbobs and from now on, your project bills are to be sent to me."

"Thank you, Papa." She rose to lean forward and kiss his cheek. "Am I forgiven enough that I can return to work? I should very much like to."

Her father smiled. "You are certainly forgiven that much. Frankly, it's been dreadfully difficult here without you."

Katherine smiled and returned to her carriage. All the

way home, she had to answer Pegeen's anxious inquiries and then attempt to explain the rationale of a blockade to her. She felt rather deflated, oddly enough. She had won, and of course there was the principle of it, and she would be helping those men, but somehow the whole thing seemed so petty and unimportant. While all of life thundered with such mighty battles, the horrendous clash of ideals, the simple, important struggles to survive, she seemed doomed to waste her life on trivialities. She had an awful picture of herself in later years, an aged spinster engaging in petty social battles. Surely there must be more for her than that. She wanted to wrestle, to fight, to build. To challenge the wilderness like a pioneer woman, taking care of husband, home, and children in primitive conditions, struggling to keep alive and bring civilization to a wild land. To have a career, to build a business, to combat the sea and wrest a living from it. To seek adventure—tea in China, gold in California. Anything—anything but moldering quietly away in Boston!

"Miss Kate," Pegeen's voice intruded on her thoughts, "are you all right? You got so quiet all of a sudden."

"Yes, yes, I'm fine, Pegeen. My mind was just wandering."

"Yes'm. You know what I noticed, mum? That bold man wasn't there, the one that winked that day. Why do you suppose he wasn't there?"

"I don't know, Pegeen. I hadn't noticed he wasn't there," Katherine lied coolly.

"I don't know how you could keep from it, miss,"

Pegeen said, shaking her head over Katherine's strange ways. "He's a terribly handsome man, that one."

"Is he?" was all Katherine said.

Two days later, Katherine was dishing meat and potatoes onto plates when she looked up to see Captain Hampton standing in line three men back. Her stomach gave a peculiar lurch as her eyes met his gray ones. He looked thinner, paler—as if he had been ill; but his smile was as self-assured as ever. As she fed the men before him, her pulse began to mount and her muscles tense, as if she were preparing to race.

"I see you have turned to good works, ma'am," he said when he reached her, extending his tin plate. "Surely you didn't take to your heart anything I said."

She raised her eyebrows and said, "I'm sure I don't know; I can't remember what you said to me." She gave him an extra slice of meat, feeling an unwanted stab of pity at the sight of his thin wrists. "Have you—been ill?"

He laughed an odd, hoarse laugh. "No, ma'am, I've been in solitary. Being punished, you see—I have this remarkable ability to get under other people's skins." He winked slyly. "But I'm so indispensable here, your foreman talked them into sending me back." He moved on to where Pegeen was dispensing coffee and bread, leaving Katherine choking back the words of sympathy that had sprung to her lips.

When she returned to the office after lunch, she began to question Teddy. "Once you said something about a Rebel raider named Hampton. Was he captured?"

The boy's eyes lit up. "Was he ever! That was some

battle, Miss Katherine. He sailed out of Wilmington—the one in Carolina—right under the noses of the blockaders, floated out on a foggy night—Lord knows how he got out without running smack dab into one of our ships. But he didn't. Well, we spotted him just as he edged past and we started firing, but then he started his engines and steamed away. Well, it made the skipper of the *San Francisco* so mad that he started out after him. But that Hampton, he headed for Cape Hatteras."

"The 'Graveyard of the Atlantic'?" Katherine said in awe.

Teddy beamed at her knowledge. "That's right. Well, Hampton knew that channel like the back of his hand, but the captain of the *San Fancisco* didn't, and she grounded. Hampton picked up the survivors and put 'em in irons and sailed to Nassau, where he unloaded the prisoners and a cargo of tobacco and stored up on provisions and coal. And then he headed north and proceeded to burn three of our merchant ships. Well, it was July, right after Read, and the Navy was hopping mad and they sent three ships after him.

"One of them found him and engaged battle. What a fight! The Union captain was a canny one, too, and they dodged each other and swooped in and fired a shot and then they'd sweep around right quick to miss a broadside. Well, finally Hampton got the better of him and the Union ship retreated. But Hampton's ship was badly damaged and he was running low on ammunition, so he starts back to a friendly port. Only on his way there, he runs into the second ship we got looking for him!"

"Oh, no!"

"Oh, yes. Now the Reb knows that this ain't the time and place for a fight, so he tries to sneak past them—runs up a British flag and just sails on. But the second ship sees that one of the masts has been snapped and he looks at her real close and can see that she's been in a fight. So he flashes to her to identify herself and explain her condition. Well, Hampton signals back that he had been mistaken for a Yankee ship by a Confederate raider. 'Which one?' signals our ship. 'The *Artemis*,' he signals back—well, that's the name of his own ship, and of course the Union skipper is hot to go after it and goes sailing off in the direction Hampton tells him. Hampton would have gotten clean away if he hadn't had bad luck. One of his engines conked out on him, so he was just limping to port. And meanwhile, our second ship crosses paths with the first and realizes that it was the *Artemis* he'd been talking to. So he goes tearing out after him and manages to catch him because Hampton was so slowed. Well, Hampton was the better skipper and he did some fancy maneuvering, but his ship was crippled and he ran out of shot. And so we got him."

"Bravo!" said a deep voice behind them, and Katherine and Teddy spun around. Matthew Hampton stood in the doorway. "You tell it as if you'd been there, lad."

"I'd like to have been."

"Well, I've brought you an errand to run, boy. Mr. MacPherson has grievous need of a certain sort of nail, and it seems there are none to be found in the yard."

"A broadhead, no doubt," Katherine said and sighed. "We've had terrible trouble getting them since the war started."

"You're absolutely right. And since Mr. MacPherson thinks they might not sell any to one of us," he lifted his hands to show his chains and grinned bitterly, "he wants you to run down some for him."

"All right." Teddy jumped off his stool and bundled himself into his coat and woolen cap, eager to spend some time outside instead of cooped up in the office. He ran out the front door. Hampton closed it behind him, then turned to face Katherine.

She felt a sudden twinge of fear. His hard, masculine presence seemed to fill the room, and she was all alone with him. She forgot that only an hour before, he had seemed thinner and almost ill to her; now she noticed only that his rolled-up sleeves revealed well-muscled arms, that he was poised like an animal about to spring, that his hands were large and strong.

To hide her apprehension, she said calmly, "Are you the same Hampton that Teddy was talking about?"

"I am, and his tale is mostly true." His face was expressionless, but there was an odd glitter in his gray eyes.

"Hadn't you better return now? The guards will think you have escaped."

"I'm not unused to being in disfavor with the guards."

"I'm sure you're not!" she snapped.

He laughed, but there was no amusement in his eyes. Slowly he started toward her, the litheness of his walk marred by the clinking chains. Katherine gulped and retreated a little.

"Captain Hampton, my father is in his office; I think it would be very unwise of you to try to—to—"

"To what? Touch you? Kiss you? Caress that sanctified

—65—

Boston skin?" His voice was low and harsh, and Katherine stepped back before the force of it. "I know you're lying, Miss Devereaux. I've watched, you see, and I know your father never returns from his lunch until two-thirty and it's only one-thirty."

"Well, Charlie will be in shortly, and he'd kill you if you touched me," Katherine said, edging toward the door of her father's office. He stood between her and the outside door; she knew she could not reach that. But if she could just get inside her father's office and lock the door . . .

Deliberately, menacingly, he came toward her, his eyes never leaving her face. "That old drunk? Peljo told me he's been on a binge for two weeks and hasn't come to work. And your Yankee lieutenant has vanished also. Tell me, did you freeze him out?"

Katherine backed away, cautiously feeling for the doorknob behind her. "I'll scream if you touch me."

"The yard's a fair distance—and very noisy. I doubt they'll hear you. And, believe me, I can muzzle you rather quickly."

Suddenly she jerked open the door and darted inside and swung the door behind her. But despite his encumbering chains, the captain was quick, and before she could lock the door, he had turned the knob and pushed the door open so violently that she stumbled back against her father's desk, painfully striking one hip against the sharp corner. She looked at him, frightened almost past thought now, as he coolly closed the door and turned the lock. Desperately, she backed away from him, her eyes fixed in terror on his face. She couldn't seem to tear her eyes away from him; she remembered reading somewhere that there was a snake that fixed its victim with its magnetic gaze, holding the frightened creature transfixed until the snake lashed out and killed it. Finally, her back touched the wall, and suddenly he was on her.

His muscled hands held her arms against the wall above her head, and he pinned her to the wall with his own hard body. No man had ever touched her before, at least no more than a hand under her elbow or a fervent handclasp. Certainly no man had ever pressed his hard, lean body into hers. She gasped with the indignity, and he chuckled, his breath ruffling her hair, and moved his body against her.

"Are you trying to crush the breath out of me?" she said tartly, determined not to admit her fright. "I shall have 'C.S.N.' imprinted on my stomach from your belt buckle!"

He leaned back his head and roared with laughter. "What an absolutely indelicate thing to say, Miss Devereaux."

"I'm too angry to be delicate," she snapped.

He looked down at her, his eyes roaming her face. His gaze rested on her lips and he said huskily, "Have you ever been kissed, Miss Devereaux?"

"I certainly don't intend to tell you!"

He squeezed her wrists. "Answer me."

"Yes!"

He eased the pressure on her wrists. "Good and thoroughly kissed?"

She blushed and said primly, "I haven't the slightest idea what you mean."

"I'm sure you don't," he said, and his lips descended on hers.

It seemed to her as if he wanted to devour her mouth, for his lips crushed hers, forcing them apart. She struggled indignantly against him; never had she received more than a chaste peck on the lips. He was bruising her with the violence of his kiss. Suddenly his tongue darted into her mouth, and she gasped in surprise. What was he doing to her! Her mind reeled; it was barbaric: the kiss seemed to go on forever, his tongue probing, caressing. Then his tongue retreated and the pressure of his lips lightened, and she thought he was through, but he did not end his kiss, only buried his lips in hers once again. It was a shock again, though less this time, but she felt dizzy and faint with his kisses. Would he never stop? His hot breath seared her cheek; his mouth seemed to suck all of the breath out of her. Then suddenly his mouth left her.

"Please," she said shakily. "Let me go; I can't breathe."

He buried his face in her hair, his lips against her ear. "That's the idea, my dear," he said huskily, and his breath on her ear sent the most startling shivers through her abdomen. "Then we take off your stays so you can breathe."

"How dare you—" she gasped, and he chuckled.

"All proper to the end, aren't you, Miss Devereaux?" He nuzzled her neck. "I can feel the fire inside you. Someone should have taken you long ago, ridden you good and hard and with a firm hand, like a temperamental mare. Softened you, made you burn with passion, and you'd have turned into a fiery, loving creature. Instead of the cold bitch you are today!"

"Why you—" she fumed, unable to think of anything horrible enough to call him.

His hands slid down her arms and they fell numbly to her sides. Then boldly he moved his hands down her, his face staring mockingly down at hers. Roughly he touched her breasts, slid his hands along her stomach and abdomen, then back up. Suddenly he groaned and pulled her to him, encircling her with his chained arms, and again he kissed her roughly. He crushed her against him; she could feel the violent pounding of his heart against her chest, feel the hard masculine strength of his body pressed against her. Abruptly he stopped and she sagged against him, feeling dizzy, weak.

"I could take you right now. Do you realize that?"

She nodded weakly.

"I don't intend to—at least at the present." He lifted his arms from around her, but grasped her by the shoulders, his fingers digging in painfully. "I only want you to know that I can defeat you. Even though I am in chains, I am a man; I can conquer you. You may be able to have my back lashed, to have me thrown into a dark hole for two weeks on a diet of moldy bread and water—"

Her eyes widened and she started to speak, but he dug his fingers into her more harshly and said, "Shut up; just listen. You may be able to have me punished for 'insulting' your ladylike ears. But I can still possess you, bend you, force you to submit. Your wealth, your position, your frozen attitude can't protect you from me." His words came out in short hard bursts; he was panting as if he had been running. "Remember that. If I decide I want you, you're mine."

He released her and turned, strode across the room, unlocked the door, and left. She sagged to the floor; her knees had turned to water. "My God," she said, pressing her hands to her face. "Oh, my God."

She ran into the other room, threw on her cloak and bonnet, and flew from the office.

Four

"Miss Kate? Are you all right? Miss Kate?" Pegeen called through the bedroom door.

Katherine had entered the house and rushed upstairs to her room as if pursued by all the demons of hell. Once inside the safety of her room, with the door securely locked, she had collapsed into her rocker. Alarmed, Pegeen had come to see about her, only to find the door locked. Katherine sat numbly in the chair, not even noticing that she hadn't removed her cloak and hat.

"Yes, Pegeen," she roused herself to answer. "Please—just leave me alone. I'll be all right."

Leaning back, Katherine slowly began to rock. Her mind was a jumble of discordant, disconnected thoughts. His breath against her ear. The clean male scent of him. The slightly salty taste of his lips. She clapped her hand to her mouth. Did men really kiss women that way? Would a *gentleman* kiss a lady that way? No, surely not. It was awful, degrading. No doubt that was why a Southerner was considered not to be trusted around a woman. They grabbed you and pawed you and kissed you and—and what? Then they raped you. It was what Boston matrons whispered about when they thought you couldn't hear them. But they wouldn't tell you because you were an unmarried girl. It was what *he* had threatened. But she didn't really know quite what it was.

It must involve kisses like that, consuming, devouring kisses—and it must involve that hot, peculiar feeling in her stomach. Rape was related to what a man did to you on your wedding night, she knew, but being a proper Victorian girl, she had never been told enough to ask what *that* was either—and certainly no one had told her. One went to bed with a husband; husbands could kiss one—but did they kiss like that? She couldn't imagine it. So that sort of kiss must be how rape was different. If he raped her, her life was ruined—that much she knew. She wouldn't be received in polite society; she would be shut up here forever with Aunt Amelia, ashamed to show her face! And she would have a baby; that was always the awful consequence.

Tears began to stream down her face. Why did he want to hurt her? Why should he hate her so much as to want to ruin her life? They had hurt him—whipped him and put him in a horrid cell by himself. And apparently he thought she was the one who had persuaded them to. But why did he think she would do such a thing? And why—why did the thought of his eyes, his husky voice, his strong, brown hands, create this trembling warmth in her? Bewildered, upset, she collapsed into tears, the sobs racking her body.

For two days she didn't go to work, claiming that she

was ill. She spent the two days in turmoil. What was she to do? She would quit work, she decided. Papa would be upset, of course, and her life would be sheer boredom, but anything would be better than having to face him again, having to live in dread that he might attack her. At other times she would burn with anger that he should think her capable of such vindictiveness as to have him beaten just because he had been rude and insulting to her, and she would decide to go right down to the yards and inform him that he was wrong about her. But what did it matter what he thought of her? His opinion was not of the least importance to her. It would be so cowardly not to go back; she had never backed down from a fight before. She had to return—she couldn't let him think that he had won.

Then, unbidden, images would creep into her mind—she would picture him being lashed and almost cry out at the horror of it; she would feel once again his lips on hers, and she would become restless and begin to pace her room. If only she could talk to someone about it! But there was no one. Aunt Amelia would probably faint; any friend of hers would be as unknowledgeable as she; Pegeen would be afraid for her and only urge her to tell her father. And Papa—well, she couldn't tell him, for her would straightway have Hampton punished. And no matter what he had done, she could not bear the thought of his being whipped again. "At least *I*," she thought fiercely, "am not one to beat someone because I have them in my power."

During the afternoon of the second day, there was a knock at her door. "Miss Kate?"

"Come in, Pegeen."

Pegeen opened the door and popped her head in; her eyes shone with excitement. "Oh, miss, Lieutenant Perkins is here to see you." Pegeen was not one to be fooled by Katherine's story of being sick. Love troubles—that was her diagnosis; and she believed it all to be due to the unfortunate lieutenant who had called over three weeks ago and not returned. She knew for a fact that Henry Stephens or the Miller boy wouldn't send Miss Kate into such a high snit. So it was bound to be the lieutenant, and though he wasn't what Pegeen would have chosen for her—too somber by half—she wanted Katherine to have whomever she wanted. Therefore, Pegeen had almost cried out with joy when she saw the lieutenant standing at the door.

"Oh, really?" Katherine brightened. "I'll be right down."

"He's in the drawing room, miss. And," she added conspiratorially, "Miss Amelia is upstairs taking a little nap. It's a good thing I opened the door. That stuffy old Simmons would have sent word up to her." Pegeen, with a large, strict Catholic family, knew how difficult it was to get a little time alone away from nosy relatives.

"Thank you, Pegeen." Katherine patted her hair into place and straightened her collar, then went down to greet her caller.

He was standing by the fireplace when she entered, and she walked over to him, extending a friendly hand. His eyes lit up—she seemed lovelier to him than ever—and he grasped her hand tightly.

"Well, Lieutenant Perkins, I never expected to see you here again," she said teasingly.

"What? Did you think me that cowardly?" He smiled down at her. The nearness of her, the faint rose scent, made him suddenly aware of how much he wanted her in his bed, and he flushed slightly at the thought.

"There are brave men who will run at a spinster aunt's inquisition."

"Well, I am not one of them. Unless, of course, you wish me to discontinue."

"No, not at all."

"I am sorry that I have been absent so long, but just after I was here, I received word that my father had died."

"Oh, I'm so sorry." She laid a sympathetic hand on his arm.

"Thank you. I went to Nantucket on leave, of course, and have just now returned. Unfortunately, my ship sailed last week, and so I have been temporarily assigned to headquarters again."

"How terrible for you. I'm sure the time at sea would have been of great comfort to you."

"You are very perceptive, Miss Devereaux."

"Shall we sit down? Would you like some tea, Lieutenant Perkins?"

"No, thank you." He paused. "I—I hope you won't think it presumptuous of me, Miss Devereaux, but I worried about you a great deal while I was gone."

"Worried about me? But whatever for?" Here was just the sort of calm, sensible person to tell her problem to, she thought. Only he was a man, and of course she could never speak to him on a matter so delicate.

"I thought of you down there at the yards, particularly with those Rebel prisoners. It's just not a safe place for you. Now, don't mistake me—I think you're a very brave and courageous lady. I know how you feel, and I am not criticizing you at all. But still it is dangerous. So I got you a little present."

"Oh, Lieutenant, I couldn't accept a gift—"

He smiled. "Now don't be hasty. Wait until you see it." He reached into his pocket and then held his hand toward her. A little snub-nosed silver handgun lay nestled in his palm. "It's not candy or flowers, but it is more useful, don't you think?"

"Why, what a funny little gun!" Katherine cried.

"Yes, it's made to be carried tucked away in some little place where it won't be noticed. There are gamblers who carry them up their sleeves where they can drop them quickly into their hands in case the game gets unfriendly—excuse me, I know I shouldn't tell a lady about such things."

"Oh, no, please, it's quite all right. And you think I should carry one. But where would I keep it?"

"Make a little pocket for it in your muff. Then if you are accosted, you can just pull your hand out of the muff—with this gun in it."

"As long as I'm outside."

"Well, yes, but your father and Charlie and Teddy are there in the office to protect you."

"But I haven't the slightest idea how to use a gun."

"Well, this is a gun that's used in close situations. It

would be hard for you to miss—and he'll know it. Now let me show you how to load and fire it."

As he instructed her, Katherine was thinking that unwittingly he had solved her problem. Though she was still scared, this gun would give her the courage she needed to return. Just let Hampton try to frighten her again. She would show him that she was smart enough to defend herself. She looked at Perkins's intent face, close to hers as he explained the gun, and suddenly she wondered if he would kiss her as the Southerner had done.

"Thank you very much, Lieutenant Perkins. You are a very thoughtful man."

"I'm glad you accepted it. Some ladies would faint at the sight of a gun."

"Well, I'm not so poor-hearted."

"Why, Lieutenant Perkins!" came Aunt Amelia's voice from the doorway.

Katherine grimaced at him and turned. "Hello, Auntie." She slipped the gun quietly into her skirt pocket.

"You must think it very amiss of me not to greet you when you arrived," Amelia said, shooting her niece a disapproving look. "But the servants didn't tell me you were here."

"I'm sorry, Miss Fritham. I came to apologize to you and your niece for having been so remiss in not calling on you. There was a death in my family, and I was called away to Nantucket."

"Why, how dreadful for you, Lieutenant!" Amelia's ready sympathy rose to the surface, submerging her disapproval. She was also afforded one of her favorite topics of conversation—death and funerals—and she plunged into questions and condolences.

Katherine finally stopped her aunt's morbid flow of words by saying, "Auntie, I fear we have delayed Lieutenant Perkins much too long. I know he must need to return to naval headquarters."

The lieutenant shot her a grateful glance and took his cue. "Yes, I'm afraid I must go. I hope that I might have the privilege of calling on you again soon."

"Whenever you like—you're always welcome here," Katherine said, then added, "Lieutenant Perkins, I realize that of course you are in mourning, but perhaps you might join us for dinner some evening. Not a party, of course, just the family."

"Thank you. I should very much like to."

"Good. Then Wednesday, say? We dine at seven."

"I shall be here."

Aunt Amelia's expression turned to one of alarm, and after the man took his leave, she turned to Katherine, highly flustered. "Oh, Katherine, you shouldn't have done that!"

"Why?"

"Well—because he's in mourning."

"Good heavens, one doesn't become a pariah just because he's in mourning. I should think it would make him feel better to be able to spend an evening with friends instead of alone with his grief."

"Yes, but it makes it seem like he is more than—"

"Than what? He *is* more than a casual acquaintance. I count Lieutenant Perkins as one of my friends."

"Oh, dear, whatever will Amanda say?" Amelia fretted.

"Why should she say anything? What does it have to do with her?"

"Why, she's your aunt."

"That's right. But she's not my mother. There's no need for her to know everything I do. Nor is there any need for her to voice an opinion about it."

"What will your father say?"

"Probably 'Splendid!' He likes Lieutenant Perkins."

Katherine turned and swept out of the room. The weight of the gun in her pocket gave her a pleasantly secure feeling and a brief smile curved her lips. No doubt that loathsome man Hampton thought he'd won; how pleasant it would be to see the look of surprise on his face.

"Let me fix your hair up different this morning, mum," Peg said eagerly as she brushed Katherine's hair the next morning. Pegeen had noticed with satisfaction the change in Katherine's mood; she was sure now that her mistress was in love with the grave lieutenant. And Pegeen intended to do everything she could to help Katherine get him. If only she could get her to take care with her looks.

"Why, Peggy?"

"Just to be different. A little more fullness around the face, Miss Kate, maybe a couple of side curls—"

"Pegeen, I am not a young girl. I am twenty-four years old, and I can't go around with foolish curls all over my head."

"Oh, miss, you never would fix your hair different. It looks like an old maid!"

"Well?" Katherine smiled briefly. "That's what I am, Pegeen."

"Not if you'd take a little trouble to look pretty."

Pegeen made a face, but pulled Katherine's hair back into a severe bun.

"Pegeen, I'd like for you to do something."

"What, miss?"

"Take the muffs I carry and on the inside of each make a little pocket—about this big." She measured with her hands.

"Yes, miss." Pegeen's eyes sparkled. No doubt it was a little pocket for secret love notes.

As she and her father set forth for the office, Katherine found that her heart was beating in trepidation and excitement. Despite her little handgun, she was still frightened of the captain, but she had regained her bravery and looked forward to a confrontation with him—scared she might be, but she'd not back down.

"Captain, your lady's returned," Ensign Fortner whispered, plopping a box of nails down beside Hampton.

Hampton raised his eyebrows and smiled. "Indeed? I guess she has recovered from her illness."

"If you want my opinion, sir—"

"Which I don't."

Fortner grinned and continued unabashed, "The little redhead's worth two of Miss Devereaux."

"Fortner, it's easy to see that you are from Savannah—you have no breeding," the captain said mockingly.

"Well, I'll admit that she's more a Charleston girl than a Savannah one—only time I've seen a haughtier face than a Charleston lady's is on that Boston girl," the young man retorted.

Hampton chuckled. "My boy, I will tell you something. I've about ten years of experience on you, and I have found that true beauty lies in the bones. Look at the Devereaux girl—her face is as beautifully sculpted as a statue."

"And as cold."

"Well, that is where your lack of foresight comes in; you should always imagine how a particular woman would look in bed. Your little Irish maid would be just as she is—pretty and giggly. But my choice, well, picture her hair down, clothes off, face passionate. And all it takes, you see, is to bring that image to life." He grinned diabolically. "Which only takes the right man."

"You, I presume?"

"But of course."

"You two!" a voice cracked out. "Cut the gab and get to work."

"Duty calls," Fortner said. "I wish you luck with your lady."

Hampton returned to hammering, feeling slightly cheered. So she had returned. She had spunk, you had to give her that. He was glad; the past couple of days he was afraid that he had frightened her too badly. She had pulled a typically female trick, having him punished like that. Once they had enthralled your heart, they tormented you, teasing, flirting, firing you with desire, and then retreating. And if they had you physically in their power, then capriciously they had you whipped. He was not the sort to let a woman get away with either trick. But he hadn't intended to completely frighten her away—he wanted her. It had taken all his willpower that day not to go ahead and take her there in the office, despite the danger.

Though no woman had ever managed to capture his heart, and though he thought women vain, foolish creatures, he found them amusing, delectable, and pleasure-giving. He enjoyed their company and their bodies, and he had found the last few months difficult. He was used to periods of celibacy, for such was the lot of a seafaring man, and one compensated with orgies of lovemaking ashore. But months at sea followed by months in prison had made him deeply hungry for a woman.

When she first stepped out of her carriage that day and he had seen those strange gold eyes, he had felt a stab of desire so strong he had almost groaned aloud. Since then she had haunted his thoughts. She was lovely—even her stark hairdo and dark, restraining clothes could not hide that—and the very sight of her sent a delightfully painful tingle through him. When they had thrown him in that hole, his back sore and bleeding, and had starved him for two weeks, the thought of her had helped to keep him sane. Alternately he cursed her for placing him there and mentally un-dressed her and made love to her. He pictured her eyes, dark gold with desire, her wide mouth soft and yielding, her body naked and glistening under his hands, her honey-colored hair like a waterfall across the pillow. He felt her eager body against his and heard her soft moans of desire. The events of three days before had only made him want her more—how full and soft her breasts beneath his hands, how intoxicating the scent of her, how sweet her virgin mouth. He ached to possess her, to awaken her inexperienced body, thaw her freezing hauteur, tutor her in the arts of love. But he would have to wait until there was time and a private place. Wait until they escaped.

Matthew Hampton was not one to sit out a war in an enemy prison, waiting for a prisoner exchange. From the moment he had been captured he thought of escape. His assignment to this duty had presented him with the perfect opportunity. Although only the dark monkeylike Peljo was one of his original crew, he was beginning to form the men into a unit. He had cautiously felt them out, judging them, making sure none would turn informer. Ensign Fortner—hot-blooded, fiercely patriotic, daring—was an easy ally. Peljo was loyalty itself to the captain. The others—well, he had seen better crews, but every one of these men had expressed the desire to escape, and daily they became more and more a united crew that accepted him as their natural leader. There were gaps in their skills, and he had no idea how they would perform in action, but then the prison had not selected them to be his new raider crew, and he must do the best he could with what he had.

He had not yet told any of them what his plan of escape was—even he did not know exactly when it would take place. His scheme was of the sort of daring simplicity that often succeeded through its sheer audacity. Once the ship they were working on was caulked and painted and moved into the water, with only last-minute touch-ups needed, they would overpower their guards, don their uniforms, and simply set sail, as if making a little trial run. It might not cause comment, used as everyone would be to seeing them on the ship, and with the phony guards standing watch. Of course, there were a thousand things that might go wrong. The timing must be absolutely perfect—the ship must be ready to sail, but not so complete that they were taken off it, and it must be done when the civilian workers were not on the ship. They would need food, weapons, navigational instruments—in fact, a whole new ship as soon as possible. It was an enormous risk, but one that he must take; he could not live without the freedom of his own ship under him. And he knew he could succeed; it was possible. The daring wildness that was so often the despair of his family made him a superb raider captain. As his Grandmother Soames had severely told him, "You have the soul of a pirate." And a pirate was what was needed in this situation.

Fiercely he hammered in a nail. He would pull it off, he told himself. It required only patience and the ability to move quickly and without second thoughts when the time was right. It would come off; he would see to that. And when it did, he would take *her* with him.

The days quickly fell into a pattern for Katherine, interrupted only by the activities of the Christmas season. Every day but Sunday she went to the office to work, and each day at twelve she and Pegeen handed out lunch to the prisoners. Gradually she came to learn their names. The cheerful young man was Edward Fortner; the earringed man was called only Peljo; the dark man with the heavy accent was Jenkins, Teddy's riverboat gambler from Louisiana; the flaxen-haired silent man was Mason. There were twenty-two of them and eventually she knew them all; some she found herself grudgingly liking. She was almost disappointed to find that the captain stirred up no more trouble. He kept her aware of his presence, nearly always fixing his gaze upon her, sometimes coldly, sometimes with an odd glint in his eye. Every now and then he spoke to her, usually saying something lightly teasing or sarcastic, always with that exasperating grin. When she handed him back his plate, he often slightly caressed her hand, not noticeably, but enough to send a chill up her spine. Once, helping her put the empty boxes back into her carriage, they were shielded from the sight of the others by the carriage, and he took her hand and raised it to his lips. The moment was over quickly, but her hand seemed to burn where his lips had touched it.

Such moments were few in the months that followed, however. Usually he was rather aloof. Curiously, she felt almost piqued—certainly none of the men kept their admiration for Pegeen a secret, always hanging about her, laughing and joking, and following her movements with their eyes. Katherine did not know it, but Hampton was keeping a tight rein on himself; he could not afford to let passion sweep him into anything that might destroy his escape plan. He found it difficult to keep his head when near her, and so he kept his distance. Katherine, however, had the vague feeling that he was merely trying to irritate her, as always. It was irrational, she told herself, to feel that way; certainly she didn't want him bothering her again. It was just that she had primed herself for a showdown, and it seemed rather deflating that it never materialized.

The personal pattern of her life came to be centered on Lieutenant Perkins. As the cold winter days straggled by, he became a more and more frequent visitor to their house. Often he ate dinner with them, now and then arriving with a box of candy or a precious nosegay of hothouse flowers. He and Katherine talked contentedly, usually about the ships or the War or foreign policy or naval history, leaving Aunt Amelia quite stultified with boredom. Determinedly she fought off dozing to sleep and never left the room; after all, she was the guardian of her niece's reputation. Sometimes she was relieved of this duty by Mr. Devereaux, who rather enjoyed the conversations and skillfully steered them toward his business concerns. He was delighted with the way things were proceeding.

Amanda constantly reprimanded both Amelia and Katherine. It was a personal insult to her that Katherine so encouraged that nonentity of a lieutenant. In vain she implored Katherine to remember her family, her breeding, her ancestors. "After all, who *is* this man?" she stormed.

"He is a very nice, very capable lieutenant in the United States Navy and a good friend of mine."

"He's a nobody; that's who he is. And he's only after your name!"

"Really, Aunt Amanda, I believe that a wife takes her husband's name, not vice versa."

"A wife! Has he spoken to you of marriage?"

Katherine colored slightly. "No, of course not. We are only good friends. It is you that implied Lieutenant Perkins wanted to marry me."

"Only friends—hah! You can't fool me. He calls here far too often to be only friends. He wants to marry you, and—mark my words—he wants your money."

"Is there anything so unusual about that? Mr. Stephens wants my money; your precious son Jamie wants my money. In fact, I think Lieutenant Perkins is about the only man who ever showed an interest in me who isn't after my money!"

"Katherine!" her aunts chorused.

Though she denied that he intended marriage, Katherine secretly suspected that marriage was the lieutenant's goal. His handclasp was always warm; often she caught him off-guard, looking at her intently; twice he had, on taking leave of her, raised her hand to his lips in a kiss much more personal than the usual polite grazing of the lips against the hand. Someday, she thought, he would propose. And what would she say?

She wasn't sure. There were times when she thought she might agree. He was so much preferable to men like Jamie Miller and Henry Stephens. She enjoyed his company, liked talking to him and listening to his ideas and plans. He respected her, sought her opinion, obviously thought her very competent. He would not be the sort of husband who would object to her being involved in the operation of her business. She knew they would work together, perhaps build a new ship line or expand the yards. It would be a very satisfactory marriage— except that she didn't love him! There were times when she wondered if he would kiss her when they were married, kiss her with his lips and tongue and whole mouth as Matthew Hampton had done. Would he touch her intimately as the Rebel had, press his body into hers? She blushed hotly at the thought. She didn't *want* him to, of course, being a respectable girl. And yet—somehow it made marriage seem more exciting. Of course, Lieutenant Perkins would be much more respectful, not frightening, and it wouldn't be so dreadful to feel that limpness in her legs when her husband made free with her body. But did wondering about her wedding night with him mean that she loved him? She seriously doubted it.

Sternly she told herself that she was being nonsensical about it. That roseate glow of love in the novels did not exist in real life—at least not for her. Better to be practical about it. She knew the horrors of spinsterhood. She also knew that she wanted a home of her own, children, a focal point to her life. And Lieutenant Perkins would be the perfect husband. Then, unbidden, would come an inward wail—"But I don't love him!"

The weeks quickly passed. Katherine worried and weighed the alternatives and went through her daily life. Lieutenant Perkins tried to judge her feelings for him and pondered when would be the correct time to ask for her hand—would he be too soon? Too late? Would she turn him down or tilt up her lovely face for his kiss? The thought of her lifting her delectable mouth to receive his kisses made him almost ache with pleasure. He day-dreamed about kissing her—should he seize her and devour her mouth with the raging passion he felt? No, better to be slow, gentle, not frighten her; at first only a chaste kiss. Later he would deepen his kisses, softly break down her reserve, until on their wedding night he would gently introduce her to love. The thought made him tremble. But all that would come, he reminded himself, *only* if she accepted him—whenever he got up the nerve to ask her.

The matter was finally forced to a reckoning by the United States Navy: he was given his orders to sail on the blockader *Henry Kemper* in a week. He felt he had to ask her now; he could not bear to sail with their relationship still in limbo. The evening he received his orders, he called on Mr. Devereaux. Josiah, somewhat surprised, greeted him affably. Perkins sat down, his hands clenched nervously. Twice he started to speak, then stopped.

Finally, he said, "Sir, I've come to ask your permission to ask your daughter to marry me."

Devereaux looked at him thoughtfully, and the lieu-tenant rushed on. "I know I am only a lieutenant, sir, and my prospects are not outstanding. I plan to rejoin the merchant marine after the War is over, and someday I hope to own my own ship. It would not be a life of luxury, but I can provide for her, and if Miss Devereaux would be content to be a sea captain's wife, I know we could make a go of it. Sir, I sincerely love and respect your daughter; I would cherish her always."

"I'm sure you would, Lieutenant Perkins. And I have no doubt that Katherine would be a splendid sea captain's wife. However, Katherine doesn't come by herself. She is my only child, and she carries along with her my shipyards, my fortune."

The young man colored hotly. "Sir, I have no desire for your daughter's wealth. I—"

"Tut, tut, young man, what would you have me do with it? Bestow it on some distant cousin? I am sure you are no fortune hunter. But you must be realistic. Katherine will inherit from me, and I fear that, capable as she is, she will be unable to run it entirely by herself as well as raise a family. Are you prepared to help her with that burden?"

The lieutenant looked at him steadily for a moment. "I think that I would be capable of operating it, sir, with Miss Devereaux's help, and I believe that I will be able, when the time comes, to stop sailing in order to run the yards."

"Well, Lieutenant Perkins, I will tell you frankly that I favor your suit. However, I will also tell you that the final decision rests with my daughter. Katherine is, as you know," he smiled briefly, "an independent young woman. She will marry as she chooses. Therefore, I suggest you take your suit up with her, with my blessing."

"Thank you, sir." He rose and gratefully shook the older man's hand. "Is she at home?"

"No, she is at a concert with her aunt and the Stephenses. May I suggest that you wait in the library. She should be here within the hour. I shall send her to the library—and her aunt up to bed." His eyes twinkled.

Katherine, caught between Henry Stephens's warm glances on her left and his daughter's murderous gaze on her right, was at the moment wishing she were home. Why had Aunt Amelia ever accepted the Stephenses' invitation to the concert? Their private box was too small, Lillian too spiteful, and Stephens too phonily lovesick. He sat beside her and had twice that evening secretively taken her hand in his clammy grasp. Both times she had jerked it away in irritation.

"Auntie," she said suddenly, "I hate to spoil your pleasure, but I have developed the most awful headache. Do you think we could return home?"

Immediately everyone was all concern, Mr. Stephens solicitously insisting on their all leaving and taking her home in his carriage. When finally he left them at their door, Katherine sagged in relief. The butler's information that her father had left word for her to see him in the library made her sigh. All she wanted was to tumble into bed.

When she stepped into the library, Lieutenant Perkins sprang up from an easy chair. "Miss Devereaux, you are home early."

"Why, Lieutenant Perkins, what a pleasant surprise. But where's Father?"

He smiled ruefully. "I'm afraid that was a ruse on his part to separate you from your aunt. You see, I—I have his permission to speak to you."

Katherine sank onto a couch. It was coming—his proposal. And what was she to say? The lieutenant nervously strode to the bookshelves and seemed intent on the book titles. Finally he took a deep breath and turned to face her.

"Miss Devereaux, you must know of my regard for you. I think you are a lovely, gracious, intelligent lady. I have respected and admired you for many months. I—I would like to ask you to—become my wife." His voice ended almost in a whisper.

"Lieutenant Perkins, I hardly know what to say. I, too, have a great deal of feeling for you," she paused, "but marriage is such a great undertaking. I—I must have time to think. Could I think about it for a few days and tell you later?"

"Of course," he said formally. "However, I would like to know before next Tuesday. I sail then on the *Henry Kemper.*"

"To the blockade?" Why did he speak so coolly, so formally, if he loved her? Why didn't he pour out his passion for her, cover her face with tender kisses? He hadn't even spoken of love. She told herself not to be silly. He was not a man overcome with passion, but one who approached life and marriage sensibly, rationally. He wanted to marry her because they would get along well together, be able to form a firm, solid marriage. He was not looking for love but companionship and a peaceful, industrious life together. And wasn't that exactly what she should be looking for also?

"Yes, to the blockade," he answered, keeping his voice level. His hands trembled and he wanted to throw himself at her feet, to beg her to marry him, to hold her close and kiss her passionately, but he refrained. He knew he must not frighten her, must not make her bolt. Go slow, keep calm, he told himself, give her time to think. "I'd like to know that you were here, waiting, promised to me. Somehow I'd feel easier about leaving you. Please let me know before then."

"I will. Just let me have tonight to think it over. Come tomorrow afternoon at four; I'll get Aunt Amelia out of the way."

"I'll be here." He didn't trust himself even to kiss her hand, but turned and left quickly.

Katherine went up to bed and tossed and turned all night, trying to solve her problem. It seemed so right, and yet—and yet, he didn't love her or she him. Quietly she wept into her pillow and fell asleep finally as dawn was breaking.

She awoke feeling and looking terrible. Staring at her tired, wan face in the mirror, she said, "Pegeen, I think I'll wear that pale blue dress today. And I'll let you dress my hair differently." Somehow she felt she must look her best today.

Pegeen clapped her hands excitedly. "Oh, miss, is it the lieutenant? Do you think he's going to ask you today?"

"He already has and I must give him my answer this afternoon. Come to get me early, about two. And when he comes, we must keep Auntie from coming in."

"Oh, no, miss, I'll let him in myself and keep everyone out, even if I have to bar the door. Oh, Miss Kate, a wedding! I'm so excited."

"Wait, hold on a minute. I said I was going to give him my answer; I didn't say it was going to be yes."

Pegeen's face fell. "Oh, but, miss, I know you love him. Why, think of the way you moped around when he was gone those three weeks. And he loves you."

"Does he?"

"Of course; anybody can tell that by the way he looks at you. Sure now, it's 'yes' you'll be saying this afternoon."

Katherine sighed. "I wish I were as sure as you."

When Pegeen finished with her mistress's hair, she stepped back to admire her handiwork. "Oh, Miss Kate, you look beautiful."

Her dress was a pale ice blue, its frosty look softened by a tiny frill of white lace at collar and cuffs. Her hair was pulled back into a chignon, but was looser, fuller about the face with two carefully astray tendrils escaping from the temples. She looked softer than usual, beautifully aloof. Even Katherine had to admit that the effect was good. She smiled at her reflection, and behind her Pegeen smiled, too.

The morning at the office seemed to drag; she couldn't keep her thoughts on her work. Like a mouse in a cage, her thoughts ran around and around in the same path. She was relieved when a diversion arrived in the form of two naval officers. They seemed somewhat surprised to see a girl in the office, but greeted her politely and went into her father's inner office. After a few moments, Mr. Devereaux stepped out of his door.

"Teddy, run down to MacPherson and tell him I'd like to see a prisoner of his crew. A man named Hampton."

Katherine looked up in interest. What did the officers want with Hampton? Had he done something wrong again? Was he to be removed from the yards forever?

Her father turned toward her. "While he's getting the prisoner, I'm going to show the major and the lieutenant over the new blockader we're building."

"All right, Father," Katherine said absently, her mind on the possible reasons for the Navy's visit. She gave the men a perfunctory smile as they trooped out.

Hampton was as mystified as she when MacPherson called him from his work to tell him his presence was requested in the office. Walking toward the brown brick building, he pumped Teddy for information, but the boy knew no more than that two Navy officers had arrived and now Mr. Devereaux wanted to see him. He felt a touch of uneasiness. Surely it wasn't the girl. She had had the perfect opportunity to report him a couple of months ago when he attacked her, and yet she had not. Nor did her generosity toward his men betoken vindictiveness. In fact, he sometimes wondered if she had really had anything to do with his punishment; it was as likely that it had been solely because he had almost attacked a guard.

More likely, his escape plan had somehow been discovered. In his mind he reviewed his men; was one of them a traitor? He could hardly believe it. Perhaps a guard had overheard a comment.

His thoughts suddenly stopped when he crossed the threshold of the office door and saw Katherine seated at her desk. How lovely she looked—delicate, expensive, aloof. Desire for her washed over him and his eyes moved over her hungrily. She colored slightly at his gaze and dropped her eyes to her desk. He drew a shaky breath, fighting to control himself, and took a seat with an air of nonchalance. He stretched his legs out in front of him and crossed his arms behind his head, regarding her with his cool, lazy stare.

Katherine was glad to have her desk between them. Even across the room she was as aware of him as if he had been standing beside her. An invisible current seemed to leap from him to her, tensing her muscles, making her nerves stand on end. She felt as if she were being drawn toward him against her will, pulled by the very intensity of his gaze. He didn't speak, but his eyes caressed her, disrobed her. Thoughtfully he ran his fingers slowly across his lips, and she, watching him, was reminded of the feel of his smooth, warm lips on hers. Unconsciously, she moistened her lips with her tongue, and he smiled, his eyes glinting. She flushed hotly and tried to turn her attention to the work on her desk.

"I'm afraid you'll have to wait, Mr. Hampton. Father has taken the major and the lieutenant on a tour of a new ship."

"I don't mind waiting," he said in his soft drawl. "In fact, I enjoy it. You've done your hair a new way, haven't you?"

"Yes, I—I'm surprised you noticed."

"I notice everything about you, Miss Devereaux." His voice caressed her name, making it sound more intimate than if he had called her by her Christian name. Katherine, feeling strangely warm and uncomfortable, avoided meeting his eyes and instead stared fixedly out the window. She was not the only one to feel uncomfortable—Teddy could feel tension in the air, though he was mystified as to why. He shifted uneasily on his feet.

"Why don't I go get Mr. Devereaux and tell him you're here?" he volunteered, struck by inspiration. He was out the door almost before Katherine could open her mouth to tell him to stay, and Katherine was left staring at the closed door. She froze—what was she to do?

"Have you any idea how lovely you are?" he asked, and his husky voice sent prickles down the back of her neck.

She shook her head a little, afraid to answer, afraid to listen to him, afraid not to hear what he said. He continued in his quiet, smooth voice, "I want you. I want to kiss you, to feel your sweet tongue in my mouth. I want to undress you, to touch you, to fondle you."

Uncontrollably, she trembled at his voice. She heard him rise and come rapidly toward her, but she didn't dare look at him. He stopped beside her, gently grasped her arms, and pulled her to her feet. With one hand he tilted up her face, and she was forced to look at him. Mesmerized, she stared into his gray eyes, now strangely alight with something she did not recognize or understand.

"Please," she whispered, not knowing what she was asking for.

His head moved down to hers, his lips taking hers, softly, tenderly at first, then increasingly more greedily. He tore his mouth from hers and began to kiss her face, her neck, her ears. His tongue probed her ear and she stiffened, strange darting flashes of warmth assaulting her.

"Oh, no," she murmured.

"Oh, yes," he mumbled, nibbling at her earlobe. "Oh, God, yes."

Fiercely his lips swooped down on hers again and he wrapped his arms around her, pressing her against him as if he wanted her to melt into him. His tongue ravaged her mouth until instinctively she responded and her tongue crept timidly into his mouth. A violent shudder shook his frame and a half laugh–half groan sounded deep in his throat. He crushed her to him harder and kissed her hungrily, his tongue teasing hers, first retreating, then thrusting deep, lightly caressing. She felt dizzy and faint from his kisses and wrapped her arms around his neck, clinging to him as to a rock in an unsteady world.

His lips left her, and she gasped at the loss, but he kissed her face, her ears, nuzzling and nibbling at her neck until he evoked little involuntary whimpers from her throat. "My little girl, my sweet little girl," he murmured against her ear. "It's been so long, so long. Please." His breath was hot and swift. "Please." His fingers fumbled at her hair, jerking out pins until the heavy mass came tumbling down into his hands. He groaned and buried his face in her hair. Again he kissed her lips; then his mouth began to travel down her throat. Limply she let her head fall back, leaning securely against the steel band of his arm. He unbuttoned the tiny buttons of her dress, his burning lips following the trail of his hands. Her bodice undone, he slipped one hand inside her chemise, cupping and caressing her breasts. He pulled her to him and turned her sideways, supporting her yielding body against his chest and arm while he pulled her chemise down and explored her breasts, his fingers teasing her rosy nipples into hardness. "Beautiful," he whispered and bent his head to kiss her, his mouth retracing where his hands had roamed, until she smothered a moan against his chest.

"Oh, Katherine," he said shakily, "I take back what I said about Boston women. There's fire in you." His hand strayed downward, delving through layers of dress and petticoats and hoop, until his hand rested against her bare stomach, and she gasped at his touch. He quieted her gasp with his mouth, kissing her until she felt that she would swoon. She clung to his shirt, awash in a haze of desire, assaulted by wild, strange feelings she had never suspected existed. He lost himself in her, her lips and her succulent body under his hands setting him aflame.

They were shaken back into reality by the sound of men's voices coming across the yard. Her father and the officers! He tore his mouth from hers and stood staring down into her face, breathing heavily, his face flushed with desire. She stared back, numb with fright. He drew a deep breath and closed his eyes for a moment, then slowly released his breath.

"Get into that office and put yourself back together. I'll hold them off out here," he said tersely.

She whirled and raced into her father's office, closing and locking the door behind her. Hampton threw himself into a chair and assumed a casual air, holding his hat in his lap to hide the telltale bulge in his trousers. Katherine leaned against the door and with trembling fingers pulled up her chemise and buttoned her multitude of tiny pearl buttons.

The outside door opened, and she pressed her ear to the door to hear. There was a great deal of noise of feet entering, then her father's voice saying, "Where is my daughter?"

Hampton's lazy drawl answered him. "Locked herself in that office. Doesn't seem to fancy my company."

Katherine pressed her hands to her burning cheeks. How could he sound so casual and offhand after what he had done to her! She knew that guilt was written all over her face. Clumsily she tried to twist her thick hair back into a knot. But all of her pins lay scattered on the floor in the next room. Hot, scalding tears slid down her cheeks. Whatever had possessed her? All those horrid, shameful things he had done to her; she would never be able to hold her head up again. And she hadn't fought him, hadn't threatened him with her gun, hadn't even protested! She had just stood there and let him do what he wanted—had even responded. She thought of the way she had kissed him and clasped her hand against her mouth. She had actually enjoyed his kisses and caresses, enjoyed them in a wild way she had never before enjoyed anything. Good Lord, was she a wanton? One of those loose women proper ladies whispered about?

In the room beyond the murmur of voices was broken by Hampton's clear, amused laugh. "Surely, gentlemen," he said coolly, "you can't really believe that I will tell you about the waterways around Charleston. Have I ever given you any reason to think that I am a traitor?"

Katherine wished she could hurl a heavy object at him. How could he dare to be so calm and collected when she was all in disarray and trembling? She couldn't marry Lieutenant Perkins now—he would be so revolted to discover this vulgar tendency in her. Only—only perhaps that was what married people did; perhaps Perkins would be pleased with her as the captain had been. Maybe this sinful streak in her would be satisfied in marriage. If she did not marry, might not her nature betray her into doing something awful, perhaps become a "fallen" woman? Perhaps marriage was the only honorable recourse open to her. And yet, wouldn't that be deceiving poor Lieutenant Perkins?

"Katherine?" Her father tapped lightly on the door. "You can come out now. The ogre is gone."

Katherine gulped. How was she to face her father? Sternly she willed herself to be calm—he must not suspect. "Oh, Papa, I wasn't hiding from him," she said, amazed to find that her voice didn't tremble. She opened the door. "I had such a horrid headache, I had to undo my hair and rest a minute on the sofa."

"Are you all right?" Katherine could detect no hint of suspicion, only concern, in his voice.

She managed a slight smile. "I think that it is really only nerves, Papa. Lieutenant Perkins has asked me to marry him."

Her father followed her red herring. "And what was your answer?"

"I haven't given it yet. I told him I would tell him this afternoon. And I can't decide what to say."

"I approve of Perkins, Katherine. I hope you accept him."

"I just don't—I don't love him," she said in a small voice.

"Love is not the only thing in marriage, my dear. Respect, similarity, companionship—all those are important, too."

She looked up at him, her eyes shining with tears. "Perhaps I'm not worthy of him."

"Come now, Katherine, don't be foolish. You'd make the lieutenant an excellent wife."

"If you don't mind, Papa, I think I shall go home now. I must have a little time to think before the lieutenant calls."

"Of course, my dear."

Katherine, her tumbled-down hair hidden by her bonnet and cloak, started for home, but partway there suddenly turned and headed for a poorer, though carefully kept, section of Boston. Coming to a small, clean red brick house, she knocked on the big brass knocker. Moments later, the door opened to reveal a tiny, white-haired woman with bright black eyes.

"Katherine!" she cried, holding out her hands.

"Oh, Betsy." Katherine rushed into her old housekeeper's arms. "Betsy, I have the most dreadful problem."

"Why, my dear, you've been crying. Whatever is the matter?"

Betsy guided her into a neat little yellow and white

kitchen and seated her at the table, with a cup of hot chocolate and a plate of cookies before her, just as she had always done.

"Now tell me all about it," she said, comfortably settling herself into a chair across the table.

Her tale of woe tumbled out—the lieutenant, his proposal, her feelings for him, the Rebel raider captain (the latter a carefully expurgated account, since she could not reveal, even to Betsy, that more had happened than that he had kissed her).

"Now, now," Betsy soothed. "It doesn't sound so terrible."

"Oh, Betsy, you don't understand!" Katherine wailed. "I hate him. He's everything that I despise—cruel, hard, rude, insolent, no respect for me or any woman. And yet I enjoyed his kiss! What kind of person does that make me? I can't marry Lieutenant Perkins and let him discover this wanton streak in me. Yet he is the perfect husband for me—only I don't love him. But I don't want to be an old maid, with nothing in my life but teas and charities and gossip. I want—oh, I don't know what I want. I can't think straight." Her jumbled thoughts poured out.

Betsy patted Katherine's hand consolingly. "Katherine, I have never seen you so confused and disorganized. I think it can indicate only one thing: you are in love."

"Nonsense."

"Not at all. You're all confused and upset because for the first time your emotions are engaged. You aren't used to having your feelings try to control you, and so it makes you upset, and you try to fight it—and wind up feeling worse than ever."

"But surely I would *know* if I were in love."

"Sometimes people just don't realize it. Or they won't admit it. But if you aren't in love with Lieutenant Perkins, why should you feel all this turmoil? It seems to me that you would be able to make your usual clear, rational decision."

Katherine stared at her, considering.

"You have always had a great deal of love in you, Katherine, but you have been forced to restrain it. Now, when I was a girl, things weren't as strict as they are now, even in Boston. People didn't go around pretending they didn't enjoy kisses. Of course, one must not give in to one's impulses and be sinful and allow a man liberties before one is married, but it's a normal and fine part of marriage. My guess is that you really want to kiss your young lieutenant." She paused.

"Well, I have wondered what it would be like," Katherine admitted.

Betsy bobbed her white head in emphasis. "Perfectly natural. You must restrain yourself until marriage, of course. But this silly notion that a young girl shouldn't even want to be kissed is sheer nonsense. You love the young man and want him to kiss you, only you won't admit it."

"But what about Captain Hampton?"

"Oh, him!" Betsy sniffed. "You see, Lieutenant Perkins is a fine young man who respects you and wants to marry you. He wouldn't dream of compromising you. So though he no doubt wants you, he will wait until after you are married. Whereas that Hampton fellow is one of those wild Southerners who has no respect for anything. He wants to kiss you and so he does, with no thought to your reputation. And you enjoyed it—there's nothing wrong in that. It would be sinful, of course, to give way to your passion, but it's only natural to feel it. Particularly when you are desirous of being kissed—even though by a different man."

Katherine traced a tiny crack in the table with her finger, mulling over what the old woman had said. It made sense in a strange way. If Betsy said it was all right, then it must be. Perhaps she did love the lieutenant; perhaps that was the reason for her turbulent feelings; perhaps she had enjoyed the captain's advances because she wanted Perkins to do those things to her.

"But what should I do?" she said finally.

"Why, accept your lieutenant. You must channel these instincts of yours into their proper outlet. I think you love him, but even if you don't, you still have the basis of a good marriage. I came to love my husband more and more every year of our marriage. And it will be the same for you, my dear. Marry Lieutenant Perkins. And steel yourself against Hampton. Don't allow him to make any more advances to you. He has no love for you, no respect, and you no love for him. It would be wrong to let him have his way with you."

Katherine drew a deep breath. "You're right, of course, Betsy. I shall be quite chilly and remote with Captain Hampton, and should he try again, he will find there is quite a bit of fight in me. And I think that I shall accept Lieutenant Perkins."

Betsy, seeing Katherine's chin lift in her usual determined way, beamed. "I am sure you are doing the right thing."

Her mind made up, Katherine cheerfully settled down to enjoy her chocolate, sugar cookies, and a good gossip. She left an hour later and returned home where Pegeen, somewhat puzzled at her mistress's erratic behavior, was nevertheless pleased to hear that she had decided to accept Lieutenant Perkins's proposal. The maid skillfully redid Katherine's hair, and then Katherine retired to the library to read while she awaited Lieutenant Perkins. Pegeen could only shake her head in wonder at the other girl's calm. If it had been she, Pegeen knew, she would have been all in a dither.

Lieutenant Perkins fortunately called during Aunt Amelia's afternoon nap, and Pegeen, who opened the door to him, quickly ushered him into the library before any of the other servants could see him. Then she took up her post at the foot of the stairs, where she could distract Miss Fritham if she came down from her room.

When Pegeen quietly closed the library door behind him, Perkins paused uncertainly. Katherine arose from her large leather chair, greeting him with a smile and an outstretched hand.

"Why, Lieutenant," she cried when he took her hand, "your hand is as cold as ice."

He managed a weak grin. "Frankly, Miss Devereaux, I am scared to death."

"Of what?"

"Your refusal."

Katherine smiled. "Well, you needn't be, Lieutenant, for I accept your proposal of marriage."

He looked stunned. "Miss Devereaux—I mean, Katherine. Oh, Katherine." Fervently he raised her hand to his lips and kissed it. "I never thought you would. I was at the point of despair."

He seated himself on the sofa and drew Katherine down beside him, still retaining her slender hand in his grasp. For several minutes he simply gazed at her, seemingly incapable of speech. He felt dizzy at the closeness of her, at the sweetness of saying her Christian name, at the wonder of her acceptance. Achingly he yearned to trace the outlines of her face with his fingers and to kiss her invitingly wide mouth. Suddenly he realized how soon he would have to leave her and how desperately unsatisfying it would be to be only engaged to her.

Katherine waited, a little disappointed. His eyes certainly glowed in a loverlike manner, but she had hoped that he would take her in his arms and kiss her as Hampton had. A tiny sigh escaped her.

"Katherine, is something wrong?" he asked anxiously.

"No, it is only that last night, when you gave me all the reasons for wanting to marry me, you never said— does love enter into it at all?"

"Katherine, how can you doubt it?" he exclaimed in a shocked voice. "My God, yes, I love you. I worship you. You must know that."

A little hesitantly he reached out to cup her face in his hands, then bent to kiss her lips. His lips were firm and warm; his kiss, close-mouthed and brief. Katherine felt a stir of disappointment. Was this a husband's kiss? Was this what Betsy had meant when she spoke of her husband's kisses replacing Hampton's? But this wasn't the sort of kiss she had meant at all!

"Do you think that we could marry before I leave?" he asked.

"But, Lieutenant—I mean, William, that's only four days away. We couldn't possibly—"

"I know; I know," he sighed. "I was just hoping. Look, I brought your ring." He pulled a gold ring from his pocket. "Your engagement ring, not your wedding ring, of course. It was my grandmother's. I hope you like it. If not, I can—"

"Nonsense. Of course I like it; it's quite lovely." Katherine slipped it onto her ring finger. It was a plain, narrow gold band with a square onyx stone set in it, very simple and yet beautiful against her slender fingers. Suddenly she felt like crying.

Five

Aunt Amelia was predictably appalled. She received the couple's news with a fixed smile and, as soon as the intended groom left, collapsed on the drawing room couch in a fit of hysterics.

"Katherine, whatever am I to do?" she wailed.

Katherine, grimly pacing, said, "Oh, hush, Auntie, you're giving me a headache. What do you mean, what are you to do? Just think, now this house will be yours to run."

"Amanda will die! She'll say I've never had any control over you—and I haven't. She'll say none of her daughters would ever do a thing like this."

"Well, I am not one of her daughters. And if I were, I certainly wouldn't let her browbeat me, like those ninnies do—and like you do."

"Katherine, please. Fetch my smelling salts; I think I'm going to faint."

"Oh, stuff and nonsense! *I'm* the one who's just become engaged. If anyone has a right to the vapors, it's *me!*"

"You never had an attack of the vapors in your life, and you know it."

"I certainly haven't."

"Well, it just isn't ladylike."

"For Heaven's sake, Auntie, sometimes you make me want to curse like Mr. MacPherson does at his crew!"

Her timid aunt burst into full-fledged tears. "Oh, Katherine. I never meant to anger you. It's just that it's so wrong—he isn't of your class."

Katherine stared out the window, absently twisting her ring. There was a cold, awful feeling in the pit of her stomach—what if she had done the wrong thing? She was committed to him now forever, and the vastness of it made her tremble. How much more familiar and pleasant to spend the rest of her days here, with her family and the things she knew and loved. Why, he was a stranger, really, and she had just pledged herself to spend the rest of her life with him.

"His family is a bunch of nobodies from Nantucket! And you could have had Mr. Stephens."

"I didn't want Mr. Stephens."

"Why did you have to rush into this? Why couldn't you have waited to become engaged until after he returns from this trip of his?"

"He wanted to know we were engaged before he left."

"Well, we can at least wait until he returns to have the engagement party. It won't be official until then, and you can still retract your acceptance."

Her poor aunt, in her usual bumbling way, had said the wrong things. The light of battle sprang into her niece's eyes. "Indeed?" she snapped. "Well, we shall have an engagement party before he leaves."

Amelia began to fan herself with her handkerchief. "But, my dear, think. He leaves in four days. We couldn't possibly get together a ball on four days' notice!"

"Not a ball. Just a small dinner party, for family and friends. After all, he's still in mourning."

Her aunt seized upon this. "But you can't possibly get engaged while he's in mourning."

"Oh, Aunt Amelia, there is a war going on. If everyone waited until mourning was over, there would be a total halt to all parties and balls and weddings. I intend to marry him as soon as he returns, so we must have the party now."

"But, Katherine," her aunt's voice was deeply shocked, "you can't mean you are not going to be engaged for a full year. It just isn't done."

"I am sick to death of hearing those words." Katherine was rapidly working herself into a heat. "Open your eyes, Aunt Amelia. Men are dying by the thousands. No one stands on ceremony any longer. What does waiting the proper period of time mean when your fiancé may be dead by then! I plan to marry William when he returns, whether that is a year or six months or three weeks. And that is absolutely final! I refuse to even discuss it any longer."

"Oh, Katherine," her aunt moaned.

Katherine did not return to work that week. For one thing, her fiancé called on her every afternoon. For another, she had too much to do preparing for the engagement party. She had to write and send invitations, all without the help of her aunt, who had taken to her bed, prostrate with shock and grief. Her dressmaker was making a dress for the occasion—a special rushed order for which she must be constantly available for fittings. Pegeen kept trying new hairdos on her until she managed to come up with one pretty enough for a bride and subdued enough for Katherine. Most of all, there was the party itself to plan for. Katherine decided on a large, elegant dinner, with fifty of her family and friends attending. The ballroom had to be decorated, tables and chairs brought in, flowers ordered, the meal planned— all with wartime shortages and delays. And through it all, she had to withstand a constant barrage of disapproving visits from Amanda Miller.

Aunt Amelia had notified her sister immediately, of course, and Amanda had come over the day after the engagement, every aspect of her (even her clothes) bristling. She stormed to no avail and finally left, but she did not give up. Time and again she returned to try a new tactic or repeat an old one. Katherine either listened in white-lipped fury or stormed back at her. Her final visit on the afternoon of the dinner turned into a battle royal. Katherine was already nervous and exhausted from the rushed preparations, and it didn't take long for her composure to crack.

"After all the things Amelia and I have done for you, to turn against your family like this!" Aunt Amanda wailed after delivering her usual lecture on the inadequacy of Perkins's family and finances.

"I would hardly say I am turning against my family, Aunt Amanda. Father is in favor of the match."

Amanda airily waved away her father as insignificant. "As for what you and Aunt Amelia have done for me—I really fail to see what you have done. Saddled me with a fluttery, silly, crying woman who is worse than useless. Given me constant, unwanted advice and criticism. Tried to foist your son on me. Believe me, I would have been much happier without your aid!"

"Katherine, how dare you speak to your own mother's sister like that! I have never been so offended in my life. You have always been a stubborn, heartless child, with absolutely no respect for your elders. Not a bit of consideration for our feelings. How am I to ever hold my head up in society again, with you married to that common, penniless Perkins person?"

Enraged, Katherine picked up the closest thing at hand, a delicate crystal vase, and hurled it against the wall, where it crashed with a satisfying sound. Her aunt stared at her, dumbfounded.

"I'll not have it!" Katherine roared. "Lieutenant Perkins is to be my husband, and I will not hear another word against him. I am used to the criticism you heap on me, but I refuse to listen to you revile Lieutenant Perkins. If you cannot refrain from it, then I must ask you not to come here."

For once in her life, Amanda was speechless. Haughtily she stalked to the door. In the doorway she turned and said, "To think that I would ever live to see the day when my sister's child would turn me out of her house.

Poor Alicia." Theatrically, she dabbed at one eye with a handkerchief. "I'm glad she is not alive to see this."

The look in Katherine's eyes at that remark made her leave hastily. Katherine sat down and indulged in a small fit of tears. There were times when she even felt amazed and appalled at what she had done.

She could receive no lover's reassurances from William, since Aunt Amelia chaperoned them as closely as ever—she was not about to relax her vigilance just because they were engaged. So their talk was confined to speculations on when he would return, tentative wedding plans, what sort of house they would have, and general talk of the War. After the South's defeat at Gettysburg, with the North's blockade stranglehold, and with the Mississippi River in the Bluecoats' hands since the fall of Vicksburg, surely the war could not last much longer. The spring offensive would certainly bring an end to it. So might not this be William's last tour of duty? Happily they conjectured that within a few months he might return forever. Always, however, there lay between them the unspoken thought that he might not return at all, that he might be killed in the last gasp of the Southern rebellion.

The couple were unable to shake their guard until the night of the party. The party was successful despite the hurried preparations. There was no gap where the Miller family should have been, since Amelia's tearful apologies and pleadings and Katherine's own more formal apology (combined with Amanda's consuming curiosity) persuaded Amanda to attend with her son in tow. The guests were pleasantly amazed at how lovely Katherine suddenly seemed. Dressed in a rich peacock-blue satin and with her hair swept softly upward and back in a mass of gleaming curls, she looked elegant. Her sailor, as Amanda called Perkins, felt his pulse race at the mere sight of her, and he spent the rest of the evening trying to maneuver the two of them away from all the other guests. After the announcement of their engagement, however, they were besieged with congratulations and, being the center of attention, it was extremely difficult for them to disappear.

When the guests finally departed and Perkins thought that he, too, would have to take his leave without having had a chance to be alone with Katherine, he was surprised and pleased to see Mr. Devereaux take Aunt Amelia by the arm and firmly lead her off toward the stairs, quelling her protestations with a stern look. Katherine smothered a giggle at the outraged expression on her aunt's face. William seized her hands and held them tightly between his own. He discovered, now that his opportunity had finally come, that he had nothing to say—or maybe too much to even begin to express it. So he stood gazing down at her, drinking in her loveliness, as if he wanted to memorize every line of her face.

"Katherine," he said finally, "I love you."

"I love you, too," she responded, wondering inwardly if she were telling the truth.

"I had a farewell all thought out to say, but now I can't remember it. Oh, Katherine, I only know that I shall miss you unbearably. For the first time I am very reluctant to put out to sea. I want to stay here, to marry you, to live the life we plan."

"It's what I want, too, William. I shall pray that the war will be over soon and always, always that you will be safe." She realized suddenly that whether she loved him or not, she cared for him very much and that he might be killed. "Oh, William, keep safe. Come back to me. I'm so very frightened for you."

"I will," he said, gratified at her concern. "Very soon, I promise."

He bent to kiss her, and she flung her arms around his neck. He pulled her to him and kissed her hard, their mouths opening against each other. Finally he pulled away from her shakily.

"I must go. I can't bear this," he said.

He raised her hand and kissed it fiercely, then turned abruptly and left. Katherine stared after him for a few moments, then covered her face with her hands. Why didn't his kiss affect her as that man's had? Whatever was the matter with her?

Hampton was afraid that he had frightened her off again, so it was a great relief to look up and see her dishing out food at the head of the line. It was disturbing to realize, however, how intense his desire for her was. The risk he took had been foolish, with her father and two Yankee officers lurking about the yards. But he guessed, considering everything, the questioning about Charleston Harbor that he had been put to was worth the chance it had given him to see her, to kiss and caress her. Perhaps that opportunity had even been worth the tremendous risk he had taken. Had he been discovered with her locked in his arms, it would have meant solitary confinement for the duration—and the complete destruction of his plans for escape. He would be more careful in the future to avoid her, but when the escape was made, he was damned sure going to reward himself by taking her with him.

Dreamily he contemplated her. What a lovely, changeable creature she was. Out here in the sun, her hair blazed golden; indoors it seemed a rich red-brown; and her eyes, changing from a clear gold to a hard, dark amber. Those spinsterish clothes and beneath them those full breasts. Her tart, brisk manner and that passionate yielding the other morning. He smiled, remembering her little whimpers of desire and her eager, questing tongue. Given a little time with her, he knew he could turn her into a passionate creature who wanted to give and receive pleasure. And he would dress her more fittingly—deep, vibrant colors with low necklines to show off her flawless ivory shoulders and breasts. Diaphanous nightgowns that would be for his eyes alone.

Bitterly he shook himself back into reality. Once he could have showered her with such clothes, with jewelry and trinkets, with anything she desired. But the Hampton fortune had vanished in the War, lost in their merchant ships moldering in the harbor and their rice and indigo crops lying ruined in the fields. The blockade had crushed them, as it had so many, crippling the Jackton Shipping Line and leaving no outlet for the export of the Soames plantation's crops. Thinking about it, his hatred flared. Damn them all, including this lovely golden girl, smugly sitting out the War, well-fed and far away from battle. While his country starved and bled, while his mother and sister were forced to make do with mended dresses and too little food, while even his mistress had been reduced to waxing ecstatic over occasional black net stockings or French lace petticoats that he brought with him from Nassau when he managed to slip through the blockade.

It was in this frame of mind that he stepped up to receive his plateful of food and, glancing down at her left hand, saw the ring on her third finger. Quickly he looked up at her face and saw it confirmed in her face.

"May I congratulate you, Miss Devereaux?" he murmured.

"Thank you, Captain Hampton," she replied stiffly.

Irrationally he was furious. What a two-faced bitch she was! To respond as she had to him when she was on the point of becoming engaged. He did not stop to consider that if anyone had a right to feel betrayed, it was her fiancé rather than he. Angrily, he found a place to sit by himself and began to devour his food without really seeing it. He had no feeling for her except physical desire, he told himself, for she was a cool Yankee bitch. It was just that he felt somehow used; she had merely been trying out her powers on him, teasing him, indulging in a little virginal curiosity, knowing that he was chained, powerless, at her mercy, knowing that with the officers nearby he could not satisfy the desire she aroused. He had seen the same sort of thing done by a Southern belle to a slave—leaning forward to innocently expose a view of her breasts, showing more leg than necessary when entering a carriage, laying a soft little hand on the arm while giving instructions—all in an attempt to provoke a frustrated desire in him which he knew would be death to fulfill. It also showed itself in the way a young lady teased her devoted beau. In more objective moments, he was prone to think that it was women's way of revenging themselves against men for having all the power over them, using the one weapon at their disposal. Now, however, he was simply enraged to think that she had been taunting him. No doubt she felt smugly sure that he would burn without fulfillment; no doubt she felt quite pleased with herself for putting a Rebel through a little agony. Damn her; he'd show her soon enough that she was unable to pull her tricks on him. It would not be long now until he was able to satisfy his craving for her.

Fortner squatted down beside him and said, "I see the woman of your dreams has become engaged." Cheerfully he shoved a forkful of potatoes into his mouth.

Hampton answered him with only a noncommittal grunt.

"Guess you'll never get to taste her charms," the young man teased.

"I wouldn't count on that, Ned. I'm taking her with me when we leave."

"What! Sir, you can't be serious."

"I am," he replied coolly.

"But to kidnap her! To—to—you can't really mean to take her by force."

The captain shot him an amused glance. "I can—and shall, if force is needed."

"But, Matt—I mean, Captain—even though she's a

Yankee, still she's a lady—gently reared, no doubt a virgin."

"More trouble, I'll admit, but I think she's worth it."

"Really, sir—" Fortner spluttered, unable to express his outraged chivalry.

"Come now, Fortner, don't be childish. I am not your vision of a Southern gentleman. Normally this is not the sort of activity I engage in, but the circumstances are extraordinary." He looked at the young man, his eyes hard and implacable. "Don't cross me, Ensign. When I want something, I get it, and time and circumstances don't permit me to play leisurely chivalrous games with Miss Devereaux. I plan to take the lady with me, and I fail to see how it concerns you."

The young man gulped at the steel of the other's gray eyes. "Of course, sir, there is nothing I can do since you're my superior officer. But I must protest; I think it's very unwise. She'll impede us, sir. This is a very dangerous and uncertain enterprise to drag a girl along on!"

"Ensign, I am the captain of this crew, and I think that I have proved that I am quite capable of planning and directing this venture. I am quite aware of the hazards involved." Suddenly he grinned to soften the rebuff. "I prefer a few dangers in war—and love."

Fortner had to return the smile. "I'm sorry, sir. I know I'm out of place trying to tell you what to do. It was just that, well, she's been rather kind to us, you know."

"I know, Fortner. Believe me, I don't plan to harm the girl. She may even enjoy it." He winked and laughed.

* * *

The time passed slowly for Katherine after Lieutenant Perkins sailed. She found herself something of a minor scandal for becoming engaged to a nobody. Lillian Stephens said maliciously that, considering her age and unmarried state, Katherine had had to accept the only thing that came along. Others came to call on Katherine to quiz her on her reasons for marrying him. Aside from these annoyances, her days were monotonously uneventful. Amanda maintained a huffy silence, and Captain Hampton kept his distance. Pegeen talked of nothing but the wedding and her Jimmy O'Toole. The wedding was too indefinite for Katherine to begin any preparations, and it was too early for any bridal parties. The only thing she found to do was choose and be fitted for a wedding dress. Even the daily routine of the office grew dull, particularly after the new ship was moved from dry dock into the water for testing and final touches, and she could no longer see the workers. The days and weeks crept by, as February drifted into March; and slowly the weather showed signs of warming.

One day in early March, as the prison wagons pulled into the yards, Hampton knew that the time had come. The ship was seaworthy now, though lacking final graces; soon the prisoners would be taken off it. What decided him in favor of this particular day was that four barrels of fresh water stood nearby on the docks, waiting to be used in cleaning the decks of another ship. He and his men had to have water on board ship to make good their escape.

Casually he turned to Fortner and said, "Tell the men

to overpower the guard as soon as we reach the ship. We have only an hour before the civilian workers arrive."

Fortner gaped at him in astonishment, then gulped and said, "Yes, sir."

"You and I will take Gunther. Peljo and Emerson will get Jackson; Mason and Carter take Bannion, and Jenkins and Puryear take Sanderson. Remember, no noise, and all of them at the same instant. I'll give the signal."

Fortner quietly passed the word as the men jumped from the wagons and walked toward the ship. Hampton could feel the familiar tightening in his stomach, the sudden lightness of head and rush of adrenaline that he always felt before battle.

"Tippins," he leaned toward one of his men as they walked up the gangplank. "Start a fight aft—enough to bring the guards."

"Yes, sir."

As Tippins purposefully headed toward the rear of the ship, Hampton and Fortner hung back by their guard.

"Say, Sergeant Gunther, when we gonna move to another ship, you think?" Fortner said conversationally.

"Dunno. You boys just get to work."

Hampton kept one eye on the brewing quarrel, and just as Tippins swung, he said lightly, "Sure would like to get back up to where I can keep my eye on that Devereaux girl."

"Why, you—" The Yankee turned on him wrathfully, as the other guard ran toward the fight. His back was now to Fortner, who quickly dropped his chains around Gunther's neck and jerked back, choking off his breath.

Hampton swept one arm up in a signal and with the

other grabbed the guard's rifle. Quickly he took the guard's pistol from his holster and the keys to the irons. He glanced toward the knot of struggling men and hurried toward them, but by the time he reached them the three guards had been knocked unconscious and disarmed.

"Strip 'em," he said. "And four of you men put on their uniforms and pretend to stand guard. Mason, here are the keys. Unlock everyone's chains and put irons on these guards and take them below. Peljo, come here."

He drew the dark little man off to one side. "Peljo, you know Miss Devereaux?"

The earringed man grinned and nodded.

"Good; go up to the office, very excited. Tell her there's been a fight here and one of the men has been hurt badly."

"You, sir?"

"No, not me," he grinned ironically. "She might not come. Say Fortner. Tell her we need her assistance immediately. Don't let anyone else come. Bring her down to the captain's quarters. Got that?"

"Yes, sir." He took off at a run.

Turning back to his men, he assigned stations and had them draw up the anchor. Mason undid his chains, and Hampton rubbed his chafed wrists. God, it felt good to be able once again to spread his arms wide.

"Are the guards taken care of?" he asked Mason.

"Yessir. In the hold. Shall I dump these chains below decks?"

"Yes. We may need them later."

"Sir—" came a worried hiss. "MacPherson's coming."

"Damn. I had hoped we wouldn't have to take him. Any of the other workers coming yet?"

"No, sir."

"Well, let him on board. Have the guards hit him on the head as soon as he steps on. No noise—and try not to kill him."

MacPherson came up the plank and was rendered unconscious before he had taken two steps across the deck. Hampton stationed men at the moorings and gangplank, ready to untie the ship and pull up the plank as soon as Miss Devereaux was aboard. Anxiously the captain kept glancing toward the yards. Where the hell were they? What if she was late to work today? Or perhaps had decided not to come in at all? He sincerely hoped Peljo wouldn't be fool enough to wait for her if she wasn't there.

Then suddenly they came into sight. Though both were hurrying, they were slowed by her skirts and Peljo's chains to an awkward gait. Hampton sighed in relief and turned away.

"Get ready. As soon as she's aboard, we sail."

Katherine had leaped up in alarm when Peljo burst into the office. "What in the world!"

"Ma'am, he's hurt; the ensign's hurt. Down at the ship. Mr. MacPherson said to fetch you and your medical kit. Right now."

"Of course. Teddy, get the first-aid kit. It's in the third cabinet, bottom shelf." She quickly wrapped her cloak around her, tied on her bonnet, and grabbed her muff.

"What happened?" Teddy asked excitedly, pulling out the metal box which housed their bandages and ointments.

"Fight," Peljo said succinctly. "I'll take that, lad. The foreman says no one but the miss here is to come."

"But I wouldn't get in the way—" Teddy protested.

"You certainly would," Katherine said briskly, already heading for the door. "You stay right here. Come along, Peljo."

"Is he seriously hurt?" she asked as they hurried toward the ship.

"Lots of blood. I don't know how bad."

She concentrated on trying to run, tightly corseted as she was and with her hoop swaying wildly. She felt scared and, strangely enough, excited.

"He's below deck, ma'am, in the captain's quarters," the little man panted as they neared the gangplank.

She swept up the plank, hardly glancing at the guards, and hastened across the deck and down the steps to the captain's quarters. Flinging open the door, she rushed inside. Just as her mind registered that there was no one there and then that everyone on deck had looked somehow wrong—no chains—an arm encircled her from behind and a hard hand was clamped across her mouth. Wildly she began to struggle, but the arm was like a steel band pressing into her, and, already short of breath from her run, she slumped into a faint. The room went suddenly black and spinning, and when it finally righted itself, she found that her hands were bound and tied to a small post in the center of the room. The dark figure of Captain Hampton loomed above her. Taking a deep breath, she opened her mouth to scream, only to have Hampton stuff a piece of cloth in her mouth and quickly anchor it with a handkerchief bound around her head.

"I was afraid you might try that," he said genially. "I can't stay to talk to you now, but I promise to explain all this later. Soon we'll be out to sea where you can scream to your heart's content, and I'll remove that gag. But for now, you must be patient. Good-bye, my dear."

He placed a light kiss on her forehead and left the room. She rested her head against the post, trying to recover her breath and her scattered wits. What on earth was happening? The men without chains . . . the captain had spoken of the open sea. . . . She could feel the ship begin to move. . . . They were setting sail, and the only explanation could be that they were escaping! Escaping—and for some reason taking her along with them.

THE SEA

Six

Quietly, easily, the fishing vessel slipped out of the harbor. The few who noticed the ship presumed that it was being tested. As Hampton anticipated, the familiarity of seeing prisoners aboard made their sailing the ship appear natural. Moreover, the sight of blue-uniformed guards quelled any suspicions that might have been aroused. Until out of sight of the harbor, Hampton gave every indication of going south, but once concealed from view, the ship made a wide sweep and sailed north. No one would expect them to go north, and so that gave them a slight advantage.

The captain's main worry was time. The fishing vessel was slow, and he needed to put distance between him and his pursuers. The civilian workers should not arrive for another half-hour. Then there would be the time it took to speculate and then ask questions. Time to work through natural channels back up to Devereaux. He would notify the Navy of the disappearance of his ship and daughter, and then the Naval Department would take a while to determine its course of action, and then they would sail, hopefully southward. Surely an hour to two hours' head start. And if he had thrown them off with his directional trick, longer than that. How long would it take them to realize that he must have changed course? With luck, he would find a faster ship before they found him. And then he would sail for England. He needed a real warship, swift, with both steam and sail, and, most of all, armed. When his ship was captured, he had been on his way to England to take command of a new battleship. Perhaps it was still waiting for him. If not, he would at least be able to contact his government and receive instructions on obtaining another ship.

He looked around at his crew with deep satisfaction. For a crew unused to each other and a long time not at sea, they were performing very well. No ship in sight on the horizon. It appeared that he could leave them for a while to release Katherine from her bonds. Whistling softly, he strode toward his cabin.

Katherine, meanwhile, had managed to recover her wits; she was not the sort to allow herself to remain dazed. Forcing herself to examine her situation calmly, she came to the conclusion that the prisoners had at last executed a long-prepared escape plan and that she had been taken hostage. It sounded like just the sort of thing that awful Hampton would do. No doubt he hoped that with the young, genteel daughter of a rich and influential man on board, the Navy would be reluctant to fire when they caught up with them. Perhaps he even planned to bargain with them, to release her if they allowed him to escape. Her mind shied away from the idea of what he could do to her in the meantime, having her completely in his power as he did.

Sternly she commanded herself not to dwell on such nonsense, but to think and plan what she should do. She must be calm and clear-headed and do everything she could to impede Hampton and aid the Navy in capturing him. "Logical," she told herself, "be logical and fair." She must not let her dislike of him spoil her judgment. He was a very good sailor and quite adept at chases; undoubtedly he had used some evasive maneuvers that would delay the pursuers. And he would have the advantage of time; probably no one would even notice anything was wrong until the regular workers arrived. So Hampton probably had a good hour's head start. But even so, he could not escape them long. This was not a raider, not even a swift-sailing clipper. It simply could not outrun the Navy's sleek, fast vessels. Surely it was only a matter of hours until they were caught.

And when the Navy reached them, there could be no battle; the Rebel ship had no cannon. Their only hope would be in using her as a bargaining factor. Well, there they would be in for a little surprise: her father was not the sort to use his influence to urge the military to treat the captain more easily because his daughter was the enemy's hostage. No, he was a fighter; it was from him that much of her stubborn attitude came. He would more likely urge them to fight. But still the Navy would probably be reluctant to refuse to bargain for the life and honor of a young lady. It seemed to her, therefore, that she must do two things: attempt to delay and slow this ship and also try to escape or somehow negate her usefulness as a hostage. But how? Particularly bound and gagged as she was.

He had said he would return and release her. If she were to fight him, to scream and struggle, it would keep him occupied, and without him on deck, surely, the crew would be more inefficient, wouldn't react to any emergency as well as he. That could possibly slow them down, but not for very long. And she would quickly be retied and gagged and once again totally ineffectual when she might be really needed. No, the thing to do was to talk to him, argue, plead, anything to take up as much of his time as possible. Get him to let her move about, where she could try some sabotage if the possibility were presented, get herself in a position where she could be useful if the occasion arose.

She heard heavy footsteps outside the door, and her heart began to race. He was coming! Everything in her tightened for battle with him. He walked in and paused to look at her, taking in at once the fact that there was no fear in her. She simply sat on the floor, looking up at him mutinously. Smiling, he shook his head in admiration; you had to give her credit for bravery. Although he didn't know it, she had felt a sharp, quickly stifled stab of fear at the sight of his long, lean body in the doorway. With the sun behind him, he had seemed dark, featureless, evil. Then he had stepped inside and she could see his clear, handsome features, including his lazy, infuriating grin, and anger flared in her.

He squatted beside her and untied her gag, taking the cloth out of her mouth. Her mouth was so dry that she couldn't speak and so she glared at him impotently. He chuckled quietly.

"I am sorry, my pet, but I simply did not have the time

to reason with you, so I had to take more drastic measures. You may scream if you want, of course, but we are at open sea and there is no one to hear you but my crew—all enemies, I'm afraid. I will also untie you and let you have the freedom of the ship since, as you no doubt realize, there is no way you can escape."

"You are insane!" she managed to croak. He just smiled and set to work on the rope binding her wrists. "You cannot possibly hope to escape in this tub."

"But of course not."

"Then why are you doing this! They're bound to capture you, and you know it will go much harder for you and your men this time."

"There is that risk," he agreed thoughtfully, and she realized that he was teasing her.

"You're insufferable!" she snapped. "I try to speak to you reasonably and you refuse, as if I were a child."

"Don't worry about my plans, my dear. Believe me, I have thought of the consequences, and I will take the course that seems best."

She curled her lip contemptuously. "Well, if you plan to use me as a hostage, I can guarantee you that it won't work. My father is not such a pudding-heart as to urge the Navy to let you escape in order to save me. Nor is the Navy likely to. They will blow you out of the water even though I am on board."

"Is the U.S. Navy that unchivalrous? To try to kill a young maiden, abandon her to a cruel fate, just to capture a minor villain?" He shook his head in mock despair, his gray eyes dancing with mirth. "Grandmama Soames will feel quite vindicated; she always said that the only person more ungentlemanly than I was a Yankee."

"You and your Grandmama Soames!" Katherine said furiously. "Don't you realize how much harsher you will be treated for trying to use me as a hostage?"

"Don't worry about that, dear," he said, a wicked smile lighting his face. "I have no intention of making you a hostage."

"Then why on earth have you brought me along?"

His smile widened and he softly traced the delicate lines of her face. "Why, to comfort me during the empty hours at sea."

Her eyes widened in shocked disbelief. "You can't be serious. You brought me along to—to—"

"Umm. To make love to you. To rape you. However you want to express it. You see? You are my cherished possession, not something to hide behind." He leaned forward to kiss her, but she scrambled away.

"I am not your possession, nor anyone's!" she hissed furiously. "You vile, wretched, abominable—"

"Please, you'll turn my head with all your compliments."

"How really low you are—to take a woman from her home, her family, her fiancé, and force her to submit to your filthy—"

"Come now, it's not so bad; you might even find you like it."

"Like it! Your touch makes my skin crawl."

"There have been times when you have not seemed so averse to it."

"How dare you throw that up to me! I despise you, and I despise myself for letting you touch me that day. I only did it because—because I was angry with William and wanted to get even with him. I hated every moment of it."

"Did you now?" His voice was soft, but with a hint of steel beneath it. Suddenly his hand whipped out and grasped the back of her neck like a vise, holding her face immobile. "I am sorry, for your sake, that you have such a revulsion for me. For I intend to have you, anyway. It's been far too long since I have had a woman; you shan't deny me my pleasure. I plan to keep you with me, and I plan to take you, wherever and whenever I desire you. Don't waste your breath appealing to my better nature; I don't have one."

He pulled her to him and kissed her roughly. She tried to pull away, but his iron grip held her head motionless. His kiss was long and thorough, as if he were putting his stamp, his seal upon her, demonstrating his possession of her.

"Shall I begin now?" he said. Then, glancing around the bare room, "I'm afraid we could not wait until my cabin was furnished. Of course the floor would serve our purpose well enough." He smiled into her stormy eyes. "But I'm afraid you'll have to wait, my pet. As close as your friends are, I am needed on deck almost constantly. Don't despair, though; it won't be too long."

Almost casually he rose and swept her an elegant bow, then walked out the door. She longed to storm after him and scream her hatred of him, but she controlled herself. More than ever, she needed to keep a cool head. It was imperative now that the Navy catch them as quickly as possible. If she could just fend him off until then, she would be safe. She needed to delay them so the Navy could rescue her, and that could be done by keeping him below decks. But by keeping him off the deck, she would be risking the very thing she wished to avoid. Perhaps she could lock herself in; she flew to the door, then slumped in disappointment—the locks had not been installed yet. And there was no furniture with which to bar the door. She could hide, but there were very few places to hide on board ship, and she would be found quickly. But at least that would give her a little more time for the Navy to arrive; it was certainly a possibility as a last resort. The thing for her to do, she decided, was to go up on deck and scout. He would be unlikely to attack her in plain view of everyone. She could see how swiftly they were traveling, how well the men worked. There she could look for a place to hide and note whatever she could use to advantage later. Feeling full of purpose, she retrieved her muff. As she slipped her hands into it, she suddenly remembered the squat little pistol inside it; in her excitement, she had forgotten all about it.

"Thank God for you, William," she whispered, drawing the little gun out of its pocket. Suddenly she felt braver, more secure. Here was her real last resort. When he attacked her, she would face him with a weapon in her hand. No doubt he thought he was dealing with a silly, faint-hearted female. Well, he would discover differently. She could not kill him, of course; she could never kill anyone. But she could threaten him with it, and if he persisted, well—she smiled grimly—she thought she could manage to wound him. Right now, more than anything, she would like to choke him or hit him with her fists. In fact, the idea of doing him bodily harm filled her with morbid delight.

How she hated that man! He had insulted her, threatened her, abused her—but this was the crowning blow! To abduct her and rape her! She would be ruined forever, unable to face society again. William, indeed no man, would marry her with her honor so tarnished. She slipped the gun back into its hiding place and determinedly left the room.

Maintaining what she hoped was an air of calm, she strolled around the deck. There wasn't a ship on the horizon in any direction. She looked around at the men; they appeared to be good sailors, each busy at his tasks and instantly obedient to commands. The captain was getting every ounce of speed out of the ship that she was capable of. Katherine sighed. She wasn't dealing with amateurs; in fact, the only amateur on board was herself. How could she ever hope to outwit them, to singlehandedly delay them?

"Miss Devereaux," said a cultured voice behind her. "May I take a turn around the deck with you?"

She turned to see Ensign Fortner. "Why, Mr. Fortner, that's very nice of you. But aren't you needed?"

"An ensign, ma'am, is probably the least useful man aboard ship," he smiled. "Most of the time I just relay orders. And I keep an eye on the men, which I can do just as easily with you on my arm."

"That doesn't say much for my ability to distract one, does it?" she smiled.

"Oh, ma'am, I didn't mean that," the young man spluttered, his face turning a deep red.

"Never mind. I long ago faced the fact that I was not the sort to turn heads," she said, amused at his embarrassment, and took his arm.

"Well, you have certainly turned my captain's head."

"That beast," Katherine sniffed.

"Oh no, ma'am, Captain Hampton's really a very fine gentleman."

"He may be a very fine captain, but a gentleman he is not," she said with asperity. "Unless, of course, it is the Southern idea of good breeding to kidnap a lady and rape her!"

Fortner blinked, somewhat taken aback at her bluntness. "No, no, I'm sure that is not his intention," he murmured vaguely.

"He told me so himself."

"He's not an unkind man; I know that he has a great deal of feeling for you. He often speaks of your beauty. It is just that he is so entranced by you, and couldn't bear to leave you."

"Poppycock," she said sharply. "He is not in the slightest entranced by me. I just happened to be the only female around."

"Oh no, that's not true. The captain would never run such a risk to his crew unless his affections were very much engaged."

"That man thinks of no one but himself."

"You're wrong there, ma'am. A good captain always thinks of his crew, and he is a good captain."

"So everyone tells me. But he must be insane to try this escape. The Navy couldn't be more than an hour behind you, you must know that, and with sailing vessels far swifter than this crate."

"More than an hour, I should think. Look at the sun; what direction are we going?"

"North."

"Which way would you presume we would go?"

"South; maybe due east."

"Exactly. And south is the way we sailed until we were out of sight of the harbor. How long will it be before they realize that we couldn't have gone in that direction? And then won't they go east, not north? Or maybe waste time searching inlets and coves, to see if we're hiding there? Rather more than an hour behind us, don't you think?"

"So it is several hours before they find us. But eventually they will; this tub can't possibly outrun them," she said scornfully, but inside her heart plummeted. That small difference in hours was all-important to her.

"With luck, we won't be on this 'tub' much longer."

"What do you mean?"

"Well, madame, we plan to practice our profession— piracy, I imagine you'd call it."

"You're going to steal a ship?" she asked incredulously.

"Stole this one, didn't we?" he said and grinned boyishly.

"You're all insane," Katherine decided, and he laughed.

"Yes, ma'am, a little."

"Miss Devereaux." Katherine whirled around at the sound of the captain's voice. "Must you bewitch my crew, too?"

"Sorry, sir," Fortner replied. "I'll take my leave now. Ma'am. Captain."

Katherine swept the captain with a haughty glance and maintained an icy silence. He pulled his mouth down in a lopsided grin.

"Come now, Miss Devereaux, is this fair? Here you have captured my heart, but won't comfort me with even one word or a smile."

"Play your games elsewhere, Captain. I'm not a silly child to be taken in by your flirtatious manner and phony compliments. You have already revealed your true nature to me."

He heaved a mock sigh and leaned back against the railing, watching her. "I know. Abominable, am I not? So absolutely horrid as to find you desirable. So utterly lost to the finer things in life that I find your skin delightfully soft to touch and your lips very kissable. Indeed, so low that I can't sleep at night for thinking of your honey-colored hair and how much I long to let it run through my fingers, to bury my face in it."

She colored and looked away, too embarrassed to speak.

"What?" he said, his voice lightly mocking. "Have you nothing to say? Surely I cannot have rendered you speechless."

"Please," she said, a trifle shakily.

"Please what?" He reached out to smooth a wind-whipped curl back into place.

"Please don't say such things."

"Why not? They're true." He laughed softly. "You know, you are the oddest creature. When I storm at you, say vile things to you, you don't even flinch, just stare me straight in the eye and storm right back at me. But when I compliment you and tell you how lovely you are, you blush and look away and ask me not to say such things."

Gently he pulled her to him and slid one hand beneath her cloak. He let his hand roam freely, stroking her back and stomach, caressing her breasts. Involuntarily, she responded to his touch.

"Take your hands off me!" she snapped.

He clucked his tongue in reproof. "Now, is that any way to talk? I'm only trying to gentle you to my touch."

"I am not a mare for you to tame, sir. I am a woman."

"I am well aware of that."

"A human being, Captain Hampton, with feelings and pride and—"

"And weaknesses and desires, also, Miss Devereaux. Why deny them?"

"What do you mean?"

Softly his lips brushed her temple, her cheek, her ear. "I mean, relax; let me give you the same pleasure you'll give me. Give your passions free rein. You'll find that it's far more enjoyable."

"If you think that I would ever enjoy having you touch me—why, it makes me ill."

He sighed. "What a cold Boston bitch you are," he said conversationally. "Permit me to leave you alone with yourself, since that is the only company proper enough for you."

She glared at him as he strode away. "I hate you! I hate you!" she muttered through clenched teeth.

She resumed her inspection of the ship, more determined than ever to find a hiding place. She found a small, high ledge near the brig where MacPherson and the guards sat in chains. She held a short, whispered conversation with the prisoners, but they could not help her, chained as they were. Nor was the ledge a good place to hide since it had no covering. At the top of the stairs leading to the sailors' quarters, there was a tiny closet. She was able to squeeze inside it, and could even look out at the deck through the hole where the lock would have gone. But what use was it? That would probably be the first place they would look. What more obvious place to hide than a closet?

Sighing, she walked to the railing and looked out at the ocean. A heroine of any novel, she thought, faced with such a situation, would have dramatic hysterics (indeed, would have been having them for the past three hours) and hurl herself over the side. Suddenly she straightened—but what a perfect idea! She began to pace, deep in thought. It just might work, close as the closet was to the railing. If it did, it would at least slow them down for a few minutes, and perhaps even enable her to hide without being noticed at all.

She looked around her; there was no one near or looking in her direction. Calmly she untied the ribbons of her hat. With a last quick glance around, she tossed it into the ocean and hurried to the closet. Opening the door, she uttered a high, piercing shriek and darted inside, closing the door after her. Quickly she heard the thud of running feet and, from high above up in the sails, a voice calling, "Man overboard."

"Good God, it's her!" boomed a voice so close it made her jump. "That's her hat in the water."

Katherine quietly sank to her knees and peered through the keyhole. A knot of men were clumped at the railing; Fortner was tossing out a life preserver. She could feel the ship slowing and heard the sails being taken in. She smiled to herself—they believed it; they thought she was in the ocean with her bonnet. Hopefully they would waste a good deal of time looking for her and then, believing her dead, never bother to search the ship for her. She would be safe until the Navy arrived.

There was the thunder of a man running, and Hampton came into view.

"She's overboard, sir," Fortner said.

The captain paled. "Jesus Christ! That little fool!" Swiftly he pulled off his boots.

"Sir, you aren't going in after her, are you?"

"Of course."

"But, Captain, that water's cold as ice. We don't even know where she is; she hasn't come up that we can see."

"That heavy cloak and all those damned petticoats would pull her down."

In one fluid motion he jumped up onto the railing, stood poised for a moment, then dove cleanly into the water.

"Put down a lifeboat, Mason," Fortner ordered.

"Aren't any, sir—they haven't been put on board yet."

"Damnation!"

Katherine watched the quiet, tense group of men until her neck and back ached from the strain of her position.

Why was he persisting in swimming around in that freezing water? He'd catch pneumonia—if he didn't drown.

"Sir!" Jenkins called. "You'd best come in now. It's been over fifteen minutes. You couldn't save her now. Grab the preserver and we'll haul you in."

They began to haul on the rope, and finally Hampton appeared and crawled over the railing to drop onto the deck, exhausted from battling the heavy northern seas. Unsteadily he rose to his feet, dripping wet and gasping for breath.

"Sir, you'll die if you stay out here in this cold with those wet clothes on. Why don't you go to your cabin and get those off?"

The man swung his face toward Fortner, and Katherine caught a glimpse of his weary face. The strange bleakness in his eyes almost made her gasp. Quickly she covered her mouth; this was no time to be discovered.

"Mason, check the ship; see if you can find any blankets or cloths so the captain can dry off. Try that closet there."

"Yessir."

With horror, Katherine watched him approach her closet. She scrambled to her feet and pressed herself back against the wall, but the door swung open, revealing her to the group of men. Mason's hand dropped from the door handle and he stepped back as if he had seen a ghost. She looked at Hampton. He stood straight and still, his face cold, his eyes glittering like ice. Then he sprang forward and seized her wrist in his iron grasp.

"Damn you! What in the hell kind of game do you think you're playing!"

Katherine felt numb with fear; desperately she wished that she had never come up with this idea.

"Do you realize that we thought you were dead? That I nearly drowned trying to save you?"

She gulped and willed herself to speak. Through frozen lips she said, "And do you realize how much time you have lost?"

His nostrils flared in anger and for a moment she thought he was about to strike her. Instead, he snapped, "Full sail, Fortner!" Then he turned on his heel and strode off to his cabin, dragging her with him. Wryly she thought that it was a good thing she was not a delicate woman or her wrist would be crushed by now.

Once inside his quarters he slammed the door and with one quick motion of his arm flung her across the room. She thudded against the far wall, knocking the wind out of her, and sank to the floor.

"Damn it, woman, I'd like to throttle you with my bare hands!" he roared.

The pain in her shoulder where she had smashed into the wall turned her fear to anger, and, struggling for breath, she managed to gasp, "Well, I am very sorry that it so displeases you that I am alive."

Water dripped from him, puddling on the floor, and involuntarily he shivered. "You scared the living hell out of me."

"I can't imagine why it should have mattered to you."

"It is a little disconcerting to think that a woman has drowned herself rather than endure your attentions."

"You needn't worry," Katherine said scornfully. "Believe me, I would not kill myself because of you!"

He simply stared at her, visibly struggling to suppress his rage.

"You ought to change clothes. You'll catch your death of cold if you stand about in those wet garments."

His eyes were splinters of ice. "I shouldn't be surprised if I murder you myself before this is over."

She tossed her head, feeling more confident; the worst of his anger had passed, and she could breathe again. "I wouldn't be so sure of that. It might be the other way around."

He said nothing, but purposefully began to unbutton his shirt. Katherine stiffened and her eyes widened in fright. She had provoked him too much and now he was going to do that awful thing to her. Seeing her reaction, he grinned.

"No, my pet, I am not about to punish you by inflicting my horrible demonstrations of affection on you. I am simply trying to avoid pneumonia, as you suggested." He wrung out his shirt, his eyes fixed tauntingly on her. "I'm afraid that little dip in the ocean has somewhat cooled my ardor."

She couldn't think of a suitable retort and so swung around to face the wall. What a crude man he was to undress right in front of her. Behind her she heard the wet slap as each of his soaked garments hit the floor, and fought the urge to sneak a look at him. It was an awful urge, she knew, but she had never seen the naked male body, and she was more than a little curious about it.

His footsteps approached, and then his voice sounded close behind her. "If you would be so kind as to lend me your cloak, madame, I would be far more comfortable, and you wouldn't have to stare at the wall."

She shrugged and unfastened her cloak. Standing up, still without looking at him, she pulled it off and held it out behind her. He took it from her hand and retreated.

"All right," he said, "it is safe for you to turn around now."

Katherine turned and looked at him, then bit her lip in an unsuccessful attempt to keep from smiling. Though her cloak was quite plain, it was still obviously a lady's cloak, and looked ridiculous on him, especially ending as it did just below his knees.

"I fail to see what is so amusing," he said stiffly.

Katherine tried to choke back her laughter, but it tumbled out anyway. He stalked to the opposite end of the room and sat down, carefully wrapping the cloak around him.

"I'm dreadfully sorry," Katherine said, though her grin would not be stifled. "It's just that you look so—so silly in that." She dissolved into laughter, made hysterical by the fear and tension bottled up within her for the past few hours.

He shot her a murderous glance and then pointedly closed his eyes against her. Eventually her laughter subsided, and she settled down on the floor against her wall. A battle of silence raged between them, finally broken by the entry of Peljo.

"Captain, brought you your boots and one of them Yank's uniforms to put on." He grinned at Katherine, obviously delighted at her escapade. "Glad to see you still among us, ma'am."

"I wouldn't be so damned amused if I were you, Peljo," Hampton growled. "Since this little lady has managed nicely to cut our lead. Or do you want to return to a Yankee prison?"

"More likely a yardarm," Peljo said cheerfully.

At a dark glance from the captain he forced his face into a more somber line, but winked at Katherine. As the captain stood to dress, Katherine once again turned to the wall. She didn't turn back around until the slam of the door told her that they had left. Then she hurriedly donned her wrap again. If only there were a stove in the room—suddenly she felt cold and deserted and miserable. Before long the steady motion of the ship rocked her to sleep.

It was the cessation of motion that woke her. She blinked drowsily, trying to collect her wits. It was a moment before she realized what had awakened her. They were stopped, the only movement caused by the surge of the waves. Quickly she scrambled to her feet. Had her rescuers found them? She headed for the door, pausing only to grab her muff. Just as she stepped out the door, she met Ensign Fortner scurrying down the steps.

"Oh, Miss Devereaux, I was just coming to fetch you," he said woodenly.

So, she thought with a flash of amusement, he, too, is highly offended by my ruse. These stiffnecked Southern men, angered not so much because she had delayed them as because she had tricked them, pulled the wool over their eyes.

"Indeed? Why?" she said coolly, raising her eyebrows.

"The captain wants to see you."

"Oh, well, in that case, we must not delay, must we?" she said sarcastically.

Stiffly he stood aside to allow her to precede him up the narrow steps. She swept past him and at the top of the stairs did not pause to take his arm, but sailed right on to where Captain Hampton stood at the railing. Suddenly she gasped and went rigid—a ship on the horizon! Katherine ran to the railing and peered out anxiously over the sea.

"Who is it?" she asked eagerly. "Is she approaching us?"

"Hopefully," Hampton said calmly.

She looked at him in amazement, then frowned in thought. Of course, he must have some trick up his sleeve. But what?

"What's going on?" she asked. "Why are you so cheerful at the idea of meeting a Union ship? And why aren't you running instead of waiting for her like a sitting duck?"

"I can't hide anything from you, can I?" he said lightly.

She bridled at the amusement in his voice, but before the hot words spilled out of her mouth, he went on, "Well, I shall explain it to you. Look up there."

She raised her eyes to see the ship's American flag flying upside down. "The distress signal," she breathed.

"Very good. I have decided to take a leaf from Captain Read's book. I think we need a faster, better-equipped ship, don't you agree? But since we are unarmed and easily beaten in speed by almost anything on the water, open battle does not seem the best way to get one. What this vessel *can* do, however, is look very much like an innocent fisherman in trouble. If we're lucky, we will be able to fool that ship and their master will board us, only to find himself a hostage. His loyal crew, not wishing to see his brains blown out, will then surrender. And *voilà!* You will have more luxurious sleeping quarters tonight."

"Sounds rather chancy to me," she said.

"But of course. That's the fun of it." He grinned down at her.

It occurred to her that his grin was demonic; the man must be insane. "But why did you want me on deck?" she asked.

"Don't you think this Yankee uniform resembles that of a ship's captain? I, you see, will play the part of the master of this fishing boat. And you, my dear, will play the part of my wife."

"What!"

"Just think how the presence of a woman will add verisimilitude to our little drama—especially a woman so obviously a true blue New Englander. You'll make us ruffians look downright respectable."

"You must be crazy!" she blazed at him. "I will not participate in this trickery of yours! As soon as she's close enough, I'll scream and wave her off."

"I suspected that might be your reaction. But you see, your frantic gestures will only convince him that we are in need of help. He will think that you have merely succumbed to feminine hysteria and are trying to get his attention. And when he gets close enough to hear you and see that your gestures are warnings, why, I will simply put a husbandly arm around you—so." He wrapped one arm around her, effectively pinning her arms to her sides. "And if you scream, I will tighten my grip and—with the aid of your corsets, of course—cut off your air. You will be unable to make a sound, and, moreover, will provide a most touching fainting scene."

"Why, you—"

"Please, I've heard it from you before."

She coldly turned her shoulder to him and stared out across the water at the other ship. She was under no illusion that he would fail to carry out his threat. No doubt he would quite happily crack a few of her ribs, to boot. She could return to her cabin and refuse to come up. But what would it accomplish? He would probably be able to trick the other ship without her assistance anyway, and she would have thrown away any chance to warn them. If she succeeded in warning them, they would probably just sail away, leaving her in the same predicament without consuming the time that would be taken up in boarding and overpowering the other ship. She was on the verge of giving in to him when it struck her that if she could warn them away, it would save their lives; whereas, if she didn't, lives could be lost in taking over the clipper ship. And if he lived up to his reputation, it was quite possible that Hampton might slaughter them all once he gained control of their vessel. She couldn't just callously leave them to their fate. She had to try to warn them off.

Hampton, looking at her, saw her eyes darken with thought. His mind was split between thinking what a lovely color they turned and wondering what plan she was cooking up. Angry as he was at her tricks and insults and mockery, he had grudging admiration for her. He could think of no other girl who would have the gumption and nerve to battle with him and try such an effective tactic to delay him. It would be quite a challenge to tame her, to defeat her, and yet win her over mentally and bodily. He touched her cheek, and she looked up at him, the sun turning her eyes the pale gold of some fine white wine.

At his quick intake of breath, she said, "What's the matter?"

"I want you," he said simply.

She blushed and looked away. "Please let me go," she said in a small voice.

Gently he pulled her into his arms, and she found herself resting her head against his chest. His strong arms wrapped protectively around her and he leaned his head down to whisper in her ear, "Don't be so afraid, little one. I shan't hurt you. Trust me."

"Trust you!" She jerked away from him. "Trust a man who steals ships, who abducts girls and does physical violence to them? No, thank you. I'd rather trust a snake."

He smiled and shrugged. "I never have understood a Yankee's preference in companions."

"Oh, shut up!" she snapped.

Seven

$\mathcal{I}$mpatiently Katherine waited for the other ship to draw nearer; as it did so, she felt excitement build in her. She did not know that at the opposite end of the ship, Captain Hampton, despite his casual, almost languid expression, felt the same surge of anticipation. She gripped the railing and watched the other ship and savored the new feeling. She had longed for something more exciting, more strenuous—well, here it was. She had to grasp the chance now, while it was offered; surely there would never be another one. In a way, it almost seemed a dream come true: the ship beneath her feet, the wild band of sailors, the approaching fight. Even the Rebel captain fit in; after all, how could one struggle without an opponent and where would the excitement be if there were no danger?

So intent was she on her own emotions that she scarcely noticed when Hampton came to stand beside her. Lazily he leaned against the railing and joined her in gazing at the approaching ship.

"I think, my dear," he said, "that it is time we strolled

down toward the middle of the ship; we must station ourselves where we are most clearly seen."

She sent him a withering look, but obediently took his arm to walk back. When they came to a halt, she remained quietly at his side, her hand still in the crook of his elbow. He tensed when she withdrew a dainty handkerchief from a pocket of her dress, but she used it only to wave circumspectly at the other ship. He almost roared with laughter; she looked just like a proper lady waving very correctly to the boats in a race. What a cool one she was; that was the perfect touch for a New England sea captain's wife.

The clipper signaled them, inquiring as to their trouble. Hampton, having no equipment, was unable to signal back. The other ship seemed at a loss, but soon lowered a longboat, carrying the captain, a civilian, and sailors to row the boat.

"What now?" Katherine said, turning sideways to look up at him; he would not be able to put his arm around her so quickly from this position.

He looked down at her, a faint alarm going off in his mind. She was pulling something—but what? "Why, when they come aboard, we cover them with our guns and explain our urgent need for their ship."

Suddenly she flung her arms up and wide and screamed a high, piercing scream. Immediately he threw both arms around her and crushed her against his chest. The men in the boat looked disconcerted, but when Hampton patted her back and stroked her hair and bent his head solicitously toward hers, to all appearances comforting her, they only wondered curiously what had caused her to give way to hysterics and kept rowing. Helplessly Katherine struggled, but he had her arms pinioned to her sides and her body tight against his; painfully her face was pushed into his chest to muffle her.

"Damn you, I ought to break your neck," he whispered into her ear. "Fortunately, they did not heed you. But, believe me, I'll take care of you later."

She gave up her struggles as futile. How did he always manage to get the best of her?

"Good girl," he said, but he didn't relax his hold.

Although she could not see, she could hear the steady slap of the oars, then a man calling, "Ahoy there! Identify yourself!"

"We have no name yet," Hampton called, giving a fair imitation of a nasal New Englander's twang. "We were taking her out for a trial run."

Now she could hear them climbing up the rope ladder over the side of the ship. Those fools!

"Captain Sloane, the *Susan Harper,*" a man said, coming toward them across the wooden deck. There was the sound of more men coming over the side.

"Captain Hampton," she heard him say above her head, his voice reverting to his Southern drawl. "C.S.N."

There was a shocked silence and Hampton released her. She staggered back from him, red with anger, and whirled on the luckless clipper captain.

"You idiot!" she said furiously. "Why did you think I screamed? Just for the fun of it?"

The men from the clipper blinked at her, still stunned. Hampton chuckled. "Please, dearest, they are not used to your way of expressing yourself, as I am," he said, amused.

"Oh, shut up."

"What—what is going on here?" Sloane managed to ask.

"Oh, nothing," Katherine said bitingly. "You have just been captured by a Rebel pirate, that's all. A Rebel pirate who, by the way, happens to be sailing a fisherman that you could sail circles around, and who has no cannon, only a few handguns, and who—"

"Katherine, for heaven's sake, calm down. Don't berate the man so. After all," he winked meaningfully, "he is not the only person I've tricked into coming aboard."

"Oh, you—" she fumed helplessly.

"Now, Captain Sloane, I'm afraid you and these men are my prisoners. Moreover, we are about to get back in your boat and return to your ship, which your men will turn over to me."

"Don't count on it," Sloane said stoutly.

"Well, for your sake, I hope they do." He turned to the civilian. "And who, sir, are you?"

"Dr. Edward Rackingham. We thought perhaps your crew was ill."

"Well, I am happy to have a doctor aboard. I certainly hope I don't have to shoot you. Now, gentlemen, if we may proceed to your ship?"

Hampton climbed over the side and down to the longboat and held a pistol on the clipper crew as they got in. Then Peljo and two other men with guns and manacles climbed in also. Katherine watched them row across to the other ship. She had no doubt that he would succeed.

Her only hope now was that the delay would be costly. She watched Hampton standing in the boat, his pistol at Sloane's head, calling up his demand to the first mate. Apparently he won, for Peljo went scrambling up the side of the ship, then Mason, and they began putting the irons on the crew. Then Hampton and his hostages went on board, and Mason and the other Southerner rowed back for more men to search the other ship for hiding crew members and weapons.

Katherine and the prison guards were transported last, after Hampton was sure the clipper was completely subdued. Fighting for delay, she made a great fuss climbing down to the longboat, pointing out how extremely difficult it was in her wide skirts and how frightened she was of trying it. Fortner, who had been assigned to bring her over, seemed nonplussed and plunged into begging and cajolery. Peljo, however, simply tossed her medicine kit down to the men below, then picked her up and unceremoniously threw her across his shoulder like a bag of meal.

"You wretch!" Katherine hissed at him. "How dare you manhandle me this way! You're as bad as your wicked captain. When the Navy catches up with you, I hope they flay you alive."

Peljo just laughed and scrambled down the ladder into the boat. She kept up a steady stream of vilification all the way across the water until Fortner began to look quite pale and weary, but Peljo merely grinned through her abuse and when they reached the clipper swung her over his shoulder once again to carry her up on board.

On deck she scrambled out of his grasp and slid to the

deck. "Captain Hampton, did you see what he did to me? Are you going to allow your men to treat me like that? I have never been so humiliated in my life!"

"Ma'am, he did precisely what I would have done had I been there."

"I don't doubt that, for you are the lowest creature imaginable."

"Please, what will our guests think if you talk that way?" he mocked.

Furiously she stamped her foot. "Damn you! You selfish, maniacal, murderous, traitorous pirate!"

"She sure has a tongue on her, don't she, Captain?" Peljo said admiringly.

"Yes, she does. But I am greatly shocked to hear a lady curse so. What would your Great-Uncle Ebenezer say?"

"Who?"

"I thought all Bostonians had a Great-Uncle Ebenezer—you know, the one who wrote the book of edifying essays for Christian boys."

"Don't be so frivolous," she said severely.

"Come, come, now, my girl, don't be a poor loser. If it's any comfort to you, had it been I approaching, your scream would have warned me off."

"Had it been you, you wouldn't have been stupid enough to have rowed over in the first place!"

"Why, thank you. I didn't realize I was so highly esteemed."

"Don't make me laugh." Suddenly her attention was caught by the longboat returning to the fisherman. "Why are they going back?"

"We no longer need it, so they are setting it afire."

"You're going to burn it?" she asked incredulously.

"Certainly. Why not?"

"But you built that ship!"

"We built it to escape in, and now it has served its purpose. I don't intend to leave it around for the Yankees to use in any way. Even a fishing vessel destroyed is some loss. Nor do I wish to leave such an obvious indication of what we have done lying about."

She watched the figures scurrying about lighting fires and then clambering down the ropes to the longboat. Something clutched at her throat as the flames began to climb. She felt some sort of an attachment to that craft. She hated to see it destroyed, although it was no more than one of her father's ships. Yet he, who had actually built the thing, could burn it without a qualm.

"What a heartless man you are."

"So I have been told. Now, if I may escort you to your cabin?"

"I would rather stay on deck," she said quickly.

"Now, now. We have too much to do and you will only get in the way. Besides, I don't want you pulling another one of your tricks on us."

He grasped her arm firmly. For a moment she hung stubbornly back, but he jerked her forward roughly. He led her to the captain's cabin and ushered her inside. "As you can see, the accommodations here are somewhat nicer. *And* the doors lock. Sorry to lock you in, but I haven't the time to play hide-and-seek with you again. I am sure you will be quite comfortable," he said and then left quickly.

Immediately she ran over to the door. There was no

inside latch; it locked only with a key, inside and out, and he had the key. Sighing, she turned back to face the room. The cabin was small, but pleasant. It contained a comfortable-looking bed, a desk, a small table and chairs, a wardrobe, and a short chest of drawers with a mirror above it. At the foot of the bed was a large trunk. All the furniture was fastened to the floor. A small stove by the desk warmed the room. Grateful for the heat, she removed her cloak and muff and tossed them on the bed, then began to explore the room.

The wardrobe contained a few shirts and suits, a uniform, and a pair of boots. The captain's desk held the usual paraphernalia of instruments, charts, maps, and logbook, as well as pens, ink, paper, a bottle of whiskey, and a bachelor's sewing kit. A shelf above the writing area held several well-thumbed books and a traveler's chess set. Katherine ran her index finger along the spines of the books: the Bible, Shakespeare, a set of Sir Walter Scott novels, an English naval history, *Tom Jones*, and *Vanity Fair*. Then she moved away and sat down on the bed. There was nothing left to explore; she could not bring herself to look in the trunk—that was too personal.

Her mind whirled. What was she to do? A poor loser, he had called her. Well, she had a lot to lose. She was in a worse position than before. Any delay she had caused and the time spent trapping this ship would soon be made up by the clipper. It might be only sail, but it was built for speed, light and sleek. With good winds, they might be able to escape the Navy entirely; certainly, it would give Hampton several more hours. There was no hope that he might relent; he had already shown himself a ruthless, selfish man. And her trick about jumping overboard had enraged him. Now he was more determined than ever to make her submit, to hurt her. She longed to throw herself on the bed and indulge in a fit of tears.

Sternly she reminded herself that she could not be so weak. All she could do now was wait for the Navy and hope. Perhaps it would be calming to read; perhaps it would even bolster her courage. She went back to the desk and paused for a moment. Suddenly a half-grin flickered across her lips. No doubt she ought to reread *Ivanhoe*, just to refresh herself on the noble example set for her by the virtuous Deborah. Determinedly, she sat down in a chair and opened the book.

Above her the deck swarmed with activity. While the fishing vessel burned steadily, some of the *Susan Harper*'s new crew scrambled up the masts to set full sail. Others secured the prisoners in the hold and stacked the arms they had discovered so that they would be ready for immediate use. When the sails were set, the men were put to making Quaker guns after the fashion of Captain Read's. Spars were cut off and painted to resemble small cannon, then lined up at portholes below deck. The ship was already equipped with two real six-pounders on deck. Finally the men were able to eat and then go to their quarters to sleep in shifts, with only a skeleton crew on deck.

Hampton, after issuing orders and supervising the work, had to check the work on completion. He had a new crew, and he could not take chances until they established their reliability. So as the sun gradually inched down over the horizon and night came, he continued to work, checking, supervising, charting an immediate course. He paused only to eat and to have some food sent down to Katherine. When finally he was through, with the ship on course, watch set, and everything seemingly secured, he went down to his cabin to join the girl.

She was sitting at the table, every hair in place, calmly reading a book. He grinned; she could be cool, certainly enough.

"Good evening, my dear," he said, locking the door and tossing the key onto the desk. "Have you had a pleasant evening?"

"Quite, thank you," Katherine said coolly and turned a page, not even glancing up. Inside her stomach knotted. She had been waiting in fear for several hours, not really reading, just staring at the pages while her mind raced. Every minute had seemed an eternity, waiting, hoping, dreading, until she was almost anxious to get it over with.

Nettled by her indifference, he searched for something to say to spark her temper. It occurred to him that that was silly: he wanted to bed her, not fight with her. So he stopped the taunts that sprang to his mouth and instead searched the room for liquor. He found the bottle of Irish whiskey in the desk and poured himself a stiff drink. Katherine watched him out of the corner of her eye, keeping her head resolutely bent over her book. She did not look up when he sat down across the table from her and placed his glass and bottle on the table. He downed his drink, then poured himself another, never taking his eyes off her. The whiskey spread warmth along his veins. Slowly his taut nerves and muscles began to relax; for the first time that day, he had a moment in which to luxuriate in his new freedom. No chains, no guards, no ever-present enemy. He was back at sea, once more in command; free, and in the company of a desirable woman. His eyes roamed over her face and body; it was exquisite pleasure to have the time to slowly appreciate her, to know that his desire could run its full course without the fear of someone's interference.

"Look at me," he said quietly.

She raised her head and stared defiantly into his face. His eyes were bright and his face flushed. He had removed his coat and partially unbuttoned his shirt against the warmth of the liquor, revealing a V-shaped patch of his chest, hard and brown and covered with crisp, curling brown hair. Her stomach dropped peculiarly, and she primly averted her gaze from the sight of his bare chest.

"I want you," he said baldly. "And I will have you. There's little point in your struggling; I can overpower you. And I think you'll find it much easier and more pleasant if you don't fight."

"I am sure *you* would much prefer it," Katherine replied scornfully, the color rushing into her cheeks. "But I am not the sort to acquiesce in my own shame and dishonor. I promise you I shall fight you to the utmost."

"Somehow I suspected that would be your answer," he said wryly. "You're a damned difficult woman."

"Because I have the temerity to oppose your base plans for me?" she sniffed.

He reached out to touch her face and she jerked away. He rose and came toward her; she dropped her book on the table and backed away from him. Suddenly she darted toward the door, but Hampton was too quick for her, and he grabbed her wrist and pulled her back against his chest. His arms imprisoned her like bands of steel; she struggled wildly, but to no avail. Holding her with one hand, he tore out the pins from her hair with the other, so that her hair tumbled down wildly over her shoulders. Shoving his hand into the luxuriant mass of her hair, he held her head immobile. Fiercely his mouth descended onto hers, forcing her lips apart. His tongue took possession of her mouth and his lips crushed hers against her teeth.

Katherine brought her foot down hard on his instep, and he gasped in pain, loosening his hold on her. She tore away and darted toward the door, but he was on her before she reached it. With one hand he tore down the front of her dress, ripping the bodice apart. She gasped and tried to cover herself, but he pulled her hands firmly away and to her sides.

"Lovely," he murmured, staring hungrily at the swell of her creamy breasts above her chemise. Then he bent to kiss the top of each ripe breast. Slowly his lips roamed over her neck and chest, his breath softly tickling her skin. Backing her against the door, he kissed her again, a burning, consuming kiss, grinding his body into hers. His hands released her arms to slide up and cup her breasts. She kicked and screamed and struck out at him, but it had no effect.

Suddenly Katherine simply went limp; her shift in weight caught him off balance and she managed to slide away from him. He grabbed for her and the rest of her dress came away in his hand. She dived for the bed, reached into her muff, and turned to face him, a tiny silver gun in her hand. He stopped in mid-step, stunned.

"Don't come one step closer. I promise you I won't hesitate to shoot, and at this range, I can hardly miss."

"Exactly what do you think you will accomplish?" he said, keeping an eye on the gun. Guns in the hands of women made him very nervous; in some ways a novice was more dangerous than an expert. "Are we to remain like this all night? Who do you think will relax his guard first, me or you? You can't watch me every second; you will get tired, sleepy; you'll blink. And I shall take it away from you. Or suppose you manage to kill me. What then? You would be fair game for all the men. Do you enjoy the prospect of being passed around from man to man, of being raped over and over, until you scream for death?"

Suddenly he dived at her; a bullet whistled past his ear. His shoulder slammed into her at the waist, sending them both to the floor and knocking the breath out of her. He grabbed her wrist with both hands and slammed it against the floor, sending the pistol flying from her grasp. Unceremoniously he hauled her to her feet and shook her until she felt her head would separate from her spine.

"Never," he hissed fiercely, "never try anything like that again."

He flung her away and she fell onto the bed, gasping for air. Savagely he ripped away her multitude of petticoats and her hoop. They were damn nuisances at any time, he thought, but with her squirming and struggling, they were almost impossible. The last straw was her stays; corsets were as effective as armor. Exasperated, he pulled his knife. At the sight of it, she paled and scrambled across the bed away from him and flattened herself against the wall.

He grinned wickedly and said, "Ah, a little more compliant now, aren't you?"

With one swift stroke, he sliced her laces neatly. Her eyes narrowed. What a brute he was to scare her so, knowing he only meant to cut her laces. Furiously she sprang at him, scratching, biting, and kicking; it was all he could do to subdue her. It was like trying to hold a twisting wildcat in his arms. Finally he managed to pull her back against him and wrap his arms around her, pinning her arms to her sides and holding her still. She was able to do no more than kick backward at him and turn in his grasp. He held her thus until finally she exhausted herself with struggling and stopped, limp and trembling like a horse after a hard race.

Quietly he nuzzled her hair and neck, while one hand roamed freely over her body, caressing her breasts and traveling down her stomach and abdomen to come to rest at the joining of her legs. She gasped and flinched at the intimacy of his touch.

"Hush, little one," he murmured. "Soon you'll come to know the feel of my hand."

She felt tired, numbed, drained of all emotion, even fear or anger. She felt only a deep, still hatred for him like a cold lump in her stomach. Her eyes closed and she steeled herself to endure her humiliation, choking back her tears—she refused to give him the satisfaction of seeing her reduced to tears. His arms relaxed around her, then released her altogether. Quickly his obviously experienced hands unfastened and removed her thin chemise, pantalets, and stockings, until she stood before him completely naked. Desperately she tried to cover herself, but he gently pulled her hands away.

"No, I want to look at you," he said, his voice husky with desire.

Good God, what a magnificent creature she was! Her skin was velvet smooth, creamy; her breasts ripe and firm, deliciously rosy-peaked. Her slender waist flowed into a flat, satiny abdomen, down to the soft triangular tuft of hair, and into her long, shapely legs. And what a delightfully rounded, squeezable little derrière!

He could feel desire rising in him, pounding along his veins. Hastily he began to disrobe. Katherine crept into bed and pulled the covers up to her shoulders to hide her nakedness. She huddled up against the far wall and buried her face in her arms. Soon she felt the bed sink and then felt Hampton's warm presence beside her.

"Here, little one, come here." His voice was soft. Gently he pulled her to him and turned her on her back. He began to kiss her, his lips traveling over her face and neck and returning to her mouth, until she was breathless. All the while his hand cupped and caressed her soft breasts, his fingers circling her pink nipples until they hardened. Then his hand drifted down over her stomach and in between her legs. She stiffened, and he gave an odd little laugh.

"No, darling, do not close against me." Teasingly his fingers opened her legs, stroking her soft inner thighs, then crept up, finding and entering her, while his mouth lazily kissed her breasts and stomach, his tongue making little circles on her skin. A treacherous warmth spread through Katherine as his lips and hands explored her, and gradually she relaxed under his expert caresses. Hampton rolled over on top of her, his weight pressing into her. Suddenly he entered her, and she felt a searing pain. She cried out and tried to scramble away from him, but he held her firm. He murmured unintelligibly against her cheek and then took her mouth in a fierce kiss as he began to move within her. The pain was intense, and she stiffened against it, struggling ineffectually. At last he jerked spasmodically, then collapsed on her. Softly he kissed her face and caressed her gently. Katherine bit her lip, trying to hold back her tears, but when he rolled away from her, she could no longer restrain herself and burst into loud sobs.

"There now, hush, little one," he whispered, taking her into his arms. He held her tightly against him and smoothed her hair and stroked her back comfortingly, murmuring quiet endearments into her ear. Illogically she clung to him and cried her heart out against his chest.

* * *

Matthew awakened the next morning with his arms still around Katherine. Looking down at her tousled head, he smiled. Last night she had fought him to the limit—cursed him, struggled against him, even tried to bring his life to a premature close—and now she lay snuggled against him, soft and innocent as a kitten. Lightly he touched her hair, then drew back their covers to look at her. Lovelier, if anything, in the daylight. He felt desire stirring in him and reluctantly turned away. He needed to be up and about his work.

Katherine woke at the sudden absence of his body heat. For a moment she could not remember where she was, but her scattered wits came back together in a rush that almost made her cry out. Oh, yes, she remembered all too well. She was in the bed of a Rebel sea captain, shamed, humiliated, and ruined. I wish I were dead, she thought miserably. Was wedded bliss as gruesome as that? Surely it wasn't always so painful.

And yet she remembered how soft and gentle he had been when she cried, how he had whispered to her and comforted her. Yes—after he had what he wanted! She blazed with anger, remembering his exploring lips and hands. Never had she imagined that anyone would do such things to her. How low his opinion of her must be!

Surreptitiously she glanced across the room at him. Immediately she closed her eyes at the sight of his nudity, but they soon crept open again in curiosity. She had never seen a man undressed before; even last night, it had been dark and he too close and she too scared. He was lean and well-muscled, emanating lithe power. And well she knew that power, she thought wryly.

She had never realized before that there was a sort of animal beauty to a man's body. Covered with clothes, they did not reveal that sleek, supple grace reminiscent of a wild cat. She remembered the hardness of his body against hers, and then she blushed, remembering that extra hardness.

Feeling her gaze, he looked over at her and grinned, totally without embarrassment. Katherine felt embarrassment enough for both, however, at being caught looking at him, and she turned her face away.

"No," he laughed, "go ahead and look. I don't mind, and it will advance your education."

"Thank you," she replied tartly, "but I had just as soon receive no further education at your hands!"

He smiled. This girl was certainly no milk-and-water miss. She had the tongue of a termagant; he felt sure that she had frightened away many an eager lad. But he found her tartness refreshing and rather piquant, coupled as it was with a succulent body. He had felt guilty this morning that his anger and desire had led him to rape a gently reared virgin. Had she been tearful and passive now, his guilt would have increased, but his ardor would soon have been quenched. But that bravado of hers piqued his interest and made him feel, somehow, that she deserved better than what she had gotten.

"Katherine," he spoke her name, liking the sound of it in his mouth.

She raised her eyebrows haughtily. "I was not aware that I had given you permission to use my Christian name."

Matthew burst into laughter. "You mean we haven't

been formally introduced?" How enchanting she looked, all prim and Boston-proper in her tone, with her hair tumbled about her shoulders, clutching a bedsheet to her bare breasts. He felt desire rising in him, and he started toward her.

Katherine immediately regretted the quickness of her tongue. She recognized that look in his eyes. In terror she scrambled to the far side of the bed. He stopped, pulled up short by the real fear in her eyes as she cringed against the wall. He felt a pang of remorse and pity.

"Here now, child," his voice soft and gentle. "Surely it isn't as bad as all that." He extended his hand to her. "Come now; come here. I won't hurt you."

She snorted. "No more than you did last night, no doubt."

He smiled. "I think you'll find it different this time. I shan't hurt you again."

She looked at him disbelievingly. He sat down on the bed and patted the space beside him. "Come sit here. I want to explain something to you." Cautiously she moved to sit beside him, still clutching the sheet to cover her nakedness.

"Now then," he said, putting an arm around her in an almost paternal way. "Has no one ever told you about sex? Marriage? The ways of men?"

Blushing, she shook her head and stared fixedly at her hands.

"Not at all?"

"No." Her voice was barely discernible.

"Well, then, I suppose it's up to me. Here, let me under the sheet; it's chilly out here." He slipped under the sheet and lay down, gently pulling her down beside him, her head on his shoulder.

Funny, she thought, how perfectly her head fitted into his shoulder; for a brief moment, she wanted to snuggle into him, like a child. Curiously, she listened.

"You know that people have children."

"Yes."

"Well, this child that grows in a woman's belly gets his start through sex; and, fortunately, we are so made that the process is highly pleasurable. Now, there is in a woman, in you, an opening. All your life, until now, you have had a thin piece of tissue here; that's the mark of a virgin. The first man you have breaks it. That's where the pain comes from, and you have it only once."

His gentle, exploring fingers made her feel strangely limp and warm. Her voice trembled slightly as she said, "Then it was not something you did to hurt me?"

"Heavens, no! I have no desire to hurt you. In fact, my intention is quite the opposite. Before too long, I think you will find it quite enjoyable."

"Yes, but what about a man—about—you know," she said, her voice small and embarrassed.

"Ah, now, a man has the seeds of the child inside him, which he must put into the woman when he enters her."

"But how can you help but hurt me with such a huge thing?" she blurted out, then flushed to the roots of her hair.

His chuckle was rich and deep. "You must have rocked the foundations of Boston society with questions like that."

She bit her lip in anger and self-hatred.

"Here now, don't go all huffy again. There's nothing wrong with what you said. Believe me, it doesn't hurt a man's self-esteem one bit." He kissed the top of her head and then laid her hand on his chest. "Here. Touch me. Satisfy your curiosity."

"No!" She jerked her hand away, but inexorably he drew it back and guided it across his chest.

His skin was smooth and warm, the hair on his chest prickly. She buried her face in his shoulder; she was avidly curious, but ashamed for him to see it. Now he moved her hand down, off the plateau of his ribs, onto the softer flesh of his stomach. She could feel the ripple of his abdominal muscles beneath his skin. And then as he drew her hand lower, she pulled away in fear and shame.

"There now, it won't hurt you. Come back." His voice was low and raspy, and when he replaced her hand a smothered groan arose from his throat. "I think I must halt our lesson for a little practical application."

He pulled her head up and kissed her, not the consuming kiss she had come to expect from him, but a light, gentle kiss. Then his lips moved to her ear, gently nibbling at her lobe, sending a tremor across her abdomen. Softly, his hands caressed her, stroking her silky skin until she felt lost in an enclosing haze of peculiar sensations. All her nerves seemed to scream within her; she wanted crazily to push out of herself into him, to arch against his weight, to *do* something. Achingly, she wanted something, but didn't know what. His mouth returned to hers, and, as if breaking out of her frustration, her tongue plunged into his mouth. A tremor shook him and he wrapped his arms around her, encircling her like steel. But somehow now it didn't hurt; now she wanted him to crush her into him. He rolled over onto his back, pulling her on top of him, his legs wrapping and unwrapping around her as he kissed her, an interminable kiss, delightful, tormenting. Wildly they rolled on the bed, locked in embrace, until finally he moved her legs apart and slid into her. Slowly he moved inside her, thrusting and retreating, circling his body against hers until she moved in rhythm with him, swept along in swirling pleasure until he burst within her.

When he left her, she felt bereft. Tenderly he kissed and caressed her, sheltering her in his arms.

"That is the way it is, Katherine—and better," he whispered in her ear. "I'll teach you things you can't imagine; I'll make you wild with wanting."

Soon he left the bed to dress. Katherine lay there, stunned by her passion. After he had dressed he returned to her bed. Casually he stroked her hip.

"You make me lazy, Kate. I must get to work." He paused, then smiled. "My instincts were right. I think you will be a wild and passionate mistress." He bent and lightly kissed her lips, then left.

His words jerked Katherine from the haze created by her passion. Dear God, what had she done! In shame, she covered her face with her hands. She had yielded to him, yes, enjoyed herself with that devil, abandoned her genteel upbringing. No doubt he felt confirmed in his belief that she was a slut. Of course he did; hadn't he just said that he planned to make her his mistress? Weakness, wickedness—never again would she allow herself to act so. She would never willingly be his mistress, no matter what his opinion of her morals.

After dwelling for some time on his evilness, lack of morals, and generally degenerate character and on her own shocking lapse into sin, she arose purposefully and set about to correct her error. She went to the wash basin and scrubbed her body until it was almost raw, trying to rid herself of the taint of his lips and hands. Dressing presented something of a problem. While her petticoats were largely intact and her pantalets and chemise at least repairable, her dress was absolutely ruined. Well, he would just have to find her something, as it was he who ruined the dress. Calmly she wrapped her cloak around her and searched the cabin for needle and thread. Taking out the small bachelor's sewing kit, she began to repair her undergarments.

Once she had finished her needlework Katherine dressed as far as she could, putting on all her underclothes, including petticoats and hoop, though she had to omit her stays as they were as demolished as her dress. She left off the cloak, as it was really too warm for the cabin. Carefully, she brushed out the tangles in her hair, then thoughtfully studied her reflection. She could not leave her hair like this, for it gave her a much too wanton look. She searched the cabin floor for her hairpins, then attempted to fasten her thick hair into her usual bun. She found, to her amazement, that she couldn't do it; strands kept sliding out of her fingers and sticking out where they should not. How infuriating it was not even to be able to dress her own hair! Pegeen had always done it for her, just as she had always helped her dress, just as servants had always done everything for her, just as her father had always protected her from want and danger and the cruelties of life. Thinking of how insulated from the world she had always been, she was tempted to give way to another outburst of tears. She had thought herself so realistic, so self-sufficient, so capable. Now, thrown into the harsh reality of a dangerous, uncaring world peopled only by enemies, she realized how ill-prepared and sheltered she really was.

Sternly she shook herself. This was not like her at all—hurt and terrified by Hampton's advances one moment and the next positively transported by them; feeling excited and almost glad to face danger yesterday, and today cowering in her cabin, unable to function without her protectors. It was utterly ridiculous. Determinedly she attacked her hair once more. Perhaps she could not fix it as Pegeen did; she would just have to practice. And for the present—well, she had often done her hair as a child. So Katherine carefully braided her hair. Certainly that was a plain enough hairdo, not likely to incite a man to lust.

To keep herself occupied, she turned to cleaning the cabin. She dusted everything, including the books, and organized the contents of the desk. She began to make up the bed, but stopped at the sight of the bloody sheets. That was her blood! It reminded her all over again of what a loathsome creature he was. Angrily she ripped the sheets off the bed, searched the drawers until she found clean ones, and remade the bed. Since the room was small and not too disorderly to begin with, it did not take her long to finish cleaning it. She sat down and tried to resume reading *Ivanhoe,* but could not for the hunger gnawing at her stomach. She had had nothing to eat since the day before at breakfast, having been too nervous to eat anything of the unappetizing plate of beans Peljo had brought her the evening before. What was he trying to do, starve her to death? He could at least have been thoughtful enough to have breakfast sent down to her. Unable to sit still, she got up and went to the porthole to look out. The sea stretched out endlessly before her, gray and cold under a similarly gray sky. It was bleak, yet somehow, as always, soothing to her.

Footsteps sounded outside the door and she whirled to face it just as Captain Hampton entered. He stopped, a trifle stunned at her appearance. What a changeable creature she was. One day a prim old maid, the next a yielding, voluptuous woman, now a little girl with braided hair, surprised in her petticoats. He smiled—life was certainly more interesting around her.

Hurriedly Katherine grabbed her cloak and wrapped it around her, then turned to face him with some of her old hauteur. "Captain Hampton, is it your custom to starve your prisoners?"

His lips twitched, but he replied gravely, "No, madame. In fact, lunch should be here shortly. I'm sorry that I sent you no breakfast. I must admit that it slipped my mind. It won't happen again, I assure you. Though I have to admit that our food supply will soon become a problem."

"Why?"

"Because the *Susan Harper* was just completing a transatlantic passage, and therefore her food supply is rather low. It will never last us to England, especially considering all the prisoners we have."

"Is that where we are going? England?"

"That's our first port of call, yes. Have you ever been there?"

"No."

"Odd sort of place. Very stuffy, in some ways worse than Boston. Now don't get your dander up. Very full of what is proper and decent and correct. Yet certain parts of London are so teeming with bordellos and taverns and thieves that it makes San Francisco seem tame."

"Really, Captain Hampton, what a shocking thing to be telling a lady."

"Oh, yes, dreadful, isn't it? You, of course, have absolutely no curiosity about it, just as this morning you had no curiosity about a man's anatomy."

Katherine flushed clear up to her hairline and started to speak, then clamped her mouth shut. He smiled and continued, "Then in other ways, England is very similar to the South, very concerned with being aristocratic and riding and shooting and partying. I think you'll find it interesting."

"Not if you're with me," Katherine snapped.

Hampton grinned. "You didn't seem to mind my company this morning."

"Please don't throw that up to me. I was very distraught and disturbed; I didn't really know what I was doing. The past day has been rather unsettling."

He choked back a laugh. "My dear Katherine, only you would describe being kidnapped by enemy prisoners of war and capturing a ship and pretending to jump into the ocean and fighting with me and being rather forcibly deprived of your virginity as 'rather unsettling.' "

She glared at him. "Well, you can be amused if you like, but *I* do not find it so. I think you are a low, vile, inhuman beast!"

"I fear you're not alone in that analysis of me. Oh, Katherine, come here." He reached out and pulled her into his arms and cradled her there, resting his cheek against her hair. "Sweet girl, I have no desire to hurt you. I'm sorry I hurt you last night; believe me, it would have been the same pain had it been your wedding night and the sour Lieutenant Perkins instead of me. No doubt you are right—I am not much of a gentleman, I'm afraid. Charleston society has been informing me of that for years. Generally, when I want something, I go after it, and damn the consequences. I wanted you, and I am not noble enough to stand by and see you wasted on that cold, grim Yankee."

"How dare you speak of Lieutenant Perkins that way! You are not worth one-tenth of him."

"Please, don't extol your fiancé. I'm sure he is a splendid citizen, but I have no desire to talk about him. Look, Katherine, I am sorry; I have wronged you. But you cannot deny that you are attracted to me—"

"Oh," Katherine cried, "what a conceited man you are!"

"My dear," he nuzzled her ear. "I heard you moan with pleasure, felt you move against me, saw your eyes hot and bright with desire."

"Oh, please, don't; I am so ashamed," she whispered.

"For God's sake, don't be; it's perfectly natural and good and right. Katherine, stop fighting me. Let me draw you out of your Puritan shell, let me teach you, let me remove all your prim barriers to happiness. Why not call a truce, forget our past differences, begin from right now? Let us just be Katherine and Matthew and enjoy each other. Talk to each other, give pleasure to each other, discover a thousand delights you never dreamed of."

"No!" She twisted out of his arms. "I gave in to weakness this morning, but never again! I despise you; I hate you; you are everything I have always held in disfavor. You are a cruel, unthinking brute, and now, having abused me, hurt me, ruined my life with never a thought for me, you say, 'Let's forgive and forget. All you have to do is submit willingly to your degradation.' Well, I won't! I'm not some weak, girlish thing to be swept off my feet by your soft words. I am made of sterner stuff than that. You won't find me a willing bed companion. I shall fight you every inch of the way."

"So I have to rape you every time I want you, is that it?"

"Yes."

He looked at her for a moment and then shrugged. "So be it. You are only making it harder on yourself. It won't deter me; I shall take you whenever I want. Though I can't guarantee you will receive the same consideration that I give to a pleasant bed partner."

"Don't threaten me, Captain Hampton. You don't scare me; you have already done your worst to me."

His thick eyebrows rose mockingly. "You think so? It's obvious that you are a very naïve girl."

Katherine felt a rush of fear; she was suddenly very much aware of his power, of the way his sheer male presence dominated the room. It came back to her how ruthless he was; his gentleness this morning had made her forget temporarily his true nature. He would not be lenient if thwarted.

To cover her fear, she said acidly, "You are right, of course; I have very little knowledge of torture. Unlike you, I did not have slaves around to experiment on."

He went white around the lips, as if she had struck him. Tightly he said, "As usual, madame, you have no idea what you are talking about."

She was about to retort hotly, but they were interrupted by a tap on the door, followed by Peljo's entrance with a tray of food. The monkeyish little man was completely unperturbed by the tension in the room. He grinned merrily, his teeth flashing white against his swarthy skin, and went about putting their meal on the table. As he went out the door, he turned to wink at them.

"What a peculiar man," Katherine said, uncomfortable because her remark had had a greater effect than she had expected.

"Yes," Hampton said stiffly. "A little odd, but extremely loyal when he has attached his affections to one, as he seems to have done to you."

"I am sure it will come as a shock to you, Captain, but there are people who like me."

"It doesn't shock me at all. I rather like you; that is, when I'm not wanting to strangle you."

Katherine could not repress an amused smile. She dug

eagerly into her food, as did Hampton, and both found their mood lightening as their empty stomachs filled. By the time they finished eating, the silence was no longer oppressive, only practical. Matthew smiled at her ability to put away her food. She could be amusing in her innocent, natural moments, when she was not striving to be correct or fighting with him. He had to admire her courage. Few women would have had the nerve to pull a gun on him, as she had last night, and still fewer would have been cool enough to actually fire it when he dived at her that way. His sister, he knew, would have screamed and dropped the gun—not that she would ever have had the wit to carry or draw it. Nor could he think of another woman who would have dared to try to warn the clipper after his threats, as she had done yesterday. Or have coolly regrouped her forces and taken up the battle anew after having met defeat, as she had today. His admiration, however, tended to be obscured by the blinding anger she so often provoked in him. He had never met a woman who could make him fire up so easily. She was a stubborn woman, and it would be difficult to vanquish her and destroy her repression. But when he did—he smiled at the prospect. He had tasted the passion that lay buried deep within her. She would be worth the effort, he was sure of that.

Katherine pushed away her plate with a satisfied air and said, "Captain Hampton, I have a favor to ask."

He smiled. "What? You must know I would grant any wish of yours."

She snorted indelicately at that and said, "My dress is ruined beyond repair, and I need something to wear."

"And you think I might have one hidden up my sleeve?"

She glared at him. "It seems to me that it is up to you to remedy the situation, since it is your fault my dress is ripped apart."

"Perhaps I don't wish to remedy the situation," he said and reached across the table to run a casual finger between the edges of her cloak and lightly down the valley between her breasts.

She jerked away and said angrily, "All right. I shall just go around like this then." She flung off her cloak and sat facing him defiantly in her thin chemise. "Shall I wander about the deck like this, too?"

"That might be a trifle cool, don't you think?" he said lightly, but his eyes devoured her hungrily. He swallowed hard. "Perhaps we had better find you something to wear. Otherwise I would be too tempted to spend all my time here in my cabin. Let's look in the good captain's trunk; perhaps he was taking home some French creation to his wife."

The trunk was locked, but he found a key in the desk and opened it. On top lay a frothy white lace scarf to lay delicately around a woman's shoulders. Katherine pounced on it with a pleased cry and had to try it on, standing on tiptoe to see how it looked in the little mirror above the dresser.

"It looks lovely on you," he said, and she blushed at being seen doing such a vain, feminine thing.

Next he pulled out a crimson satin evening gown with a plunging V-neckline and held it up, laughing, "I think I have more respect for our friend."

Katherine gasped. "That couldn't be for his wife!"

"Not unless he has a highly unusual wife. No, I think he must have a mistress hidden somewhere. Here, put it on."

"No, I cannot wear that!"

"I'm not asking you to parade around deck in it. Just try it on for me; I want to see how you look in it."

"Absolutely not!" Katherine said stoutly, though her fingers itched to snatch the dress from his grasp. She longed to see what such a wicked dress looked like on her.

"You are the most exasperating wench," he said and tossed the gown onto the bed and continued digging in the trunk.

"Ah, here is the wife's dress," he said triumphantly, holding up a sensible brown wool dress.

"Why, how awful!" Katherine exclaimed, and Hampton roared with laughter. "Well, it *is* awful: to bring some wicked woman a beautiful satin dress—even if it is outrageous—and bring your wife only a plain, ordinary day dress. I'll wager this lovely scarf isn't for his wife, either."

Hampton sat back on his heels and looked at her. "No doubt his wife is fortyish and quite plain and very monotonous; whereas his mistress probably has wild tawny hair and golden eyes like a lioness and a very sensual mouth."

Katherine blushed and looked away in confusion when she realized that he was speaking of her. He rose and came to stand very close to her. He adjusted the lacy scarf about her shoulders and then cupped her face between his hands and turned it up so that he was staring down into her eyes. She looked up at his face, hovering hawklike above hers, at his wide gray eyes, his high, fierce cheekbones, his wide, full lips. Suddenly she realized that she wanted very much to feel those lips on hers. He smiled at her as if he could read her thoughts, and lightly ran his thumb across her lips.

"You would like to be kissed, wouldn't you?" he said in his low, husky voice. "My dear, all you have to do is just stretch up a little and put your lips on mine."

She frowned at him, looking like an obstinate child, and he smiled and released her. "Have fun with your new possessions, Katherine. Until this evening." He bowed slightly and left.

Katherine grimaced at the closed door and stuck out her tongue. "Monster."

Eight

After Hampton left, Katherine tried on the red dress. Without her stays it was a little tight, and it was too short, ending at her ankles, but even in the inadequate little mirror, she could see that it looked very good on her. It was shockingly indecent, of course; she could not wear any underclothing under the bodice, it was cut so low—but her unusual coloring could take the strong red as many could not, and it set off her figure admirably. The neckline revealed a great deal of her breasts, as well as the flawless ivory skin of her chest; it was the sort of dress that kept a man trembling in hope that some sudden move would expose even more. All it needed, she decided, was her ruby drop nestling in the hollow of her throat. She smiled to think of what Matthew's expression would be if he were to see her in this.

Which is why, she told herself firmly, taking it off, he will not see me in it. She folded the dress and put it back into the trunk. Then she tried on the dark brown dress. It also was too short, and hung loosely on her, even uncorseted as she was. Sighing, she rummaged through the trunk some more and found a girlish print with a scoop neckline, which was much too tight as well as too short. She decided that this must have been meant for his daughter.

Once again, Katherine dug out the sewing kit and whiled away her afternoon altering the brown dress. When she finished, she put it on and looked at herself in the mirror. Serviceable and dull, she decided, and heaved a profound sigh. Donning her cloak and muff, she went to the door, determined to scream until someone let her out, if necessary. To her surprise, the door was unlocked. She shrugged. He was right; no point in locking the door now, since what she had been trying to escape had already happened.

The brisk sea air immediately lightened her spirits. She leaned against the railing and looked out to sea, remembering how desperately she had searched the horizon yesterday for sign of a ship. Now she hoped the Navy would not catch them. It would only mean bloodshed. As for her, Hampton would doubtless have tired of her by the time they reached London and would gladly release her. It did not really matter that she would have spent weeks with him instead of only days; she was ruined either way. Of course, they should be punished for stealing the ship and stopped before they could do any harm to Union shipping, but she did not want to see any of the men hurt. After all, she had fed them, given them clothes, knew their names. Compared with their lives, military considerations didn't seem so important.

Her gloomy thoughts were interrupted by the arrival

of a thin, distinguished-looking older man. "Pardon me, Miss—"

"Devereaux," she said automatically and then stared at him. Who on earth was he?

"Dr. Rackingham," he said helpfully.

"Of course, the doctor who was with Captain Sloane. But I thought all of you were in irons."

"Well, I was only a passenger on the *Susan Harper*, returning home to Portland. Captain Hampton apparently regards me as a civilian and has allowed me to remain in my cabin. He counts me, I think, as rather harmless. Moreover, he is quite pleased at having a doctor aboard, and I believe he wants to keep on friendly terms with me."

"I didn't know he ever tried to be on friendly terms with anyone," Katherine said sarcastically.

"He has been most amiable to me. I hope that you will be also."

"Of course, Dr. Rackingham. We are, after all, the only 'Yankees' on this ship not in chains."

"I thought your accent was that of a New Englander. Tell me, how did you come to be with all these Johnny Rebs?"

Katherine spilled the story of her abduction into the doctor's receptive ear. The doctor seemed quite taken aback at the story.

"But, my dear," he said, "this is dreadful. Kidnapping a genteel young lady! He must be a madman."

"Just a Southerner and used to having his own way, I think."

"But he seems to be a gentleman."

"That depends on your definition of gentleman. If it means only a certain suavity of manners, he is capable of being a gentleman. But if it means true nobility of mind and spirit, he will never reach it."

"Dreadful affair," the doctor said, shaking his head. "He—he hasn't harmed you, has he?"

"He has raped me, if that's what you mean, but he has not beaten me or tortured me."

The older man looked shocked. "My dear girl, I hardly know what to say."

"There isn't much to say. I hope this won't make you take back your offer of friendship to me."

"No, of course not. How could you think such a thing?"

She gave a crooked smile. "Oh, I think there will be quite a few who will think it quite shameful of me not to have killed myself."

"I doubt that happens very often. It is my belief that that idea is one that is more 'honored in the breach.' Don't allow what some old biddies will say to bother you. Some fine young man will love you and it won't matter to him except to make him angry that someone has hurt you."

"Oh, really?" Katherine said in a tone of disbelief.

"Really." He patted her hand. "Believe me. A man who really loves you wouldn't hold it against you. Perhaps even Hampton can be awakened to his duty as a gentleman and marry you."

"Him?" Her voice was scornful. "I wouldn't marry that snake for anything. Please, let us talk of something more pleasant."

"All right. Do you, by any chance, play chess? Captain Sloane was my chess partner, but now he is clapped away in irons."

"Why, yes, I do."

"Good. Then you and I can while away a good deal of our time playing chess."

"I should love to, Dr. Rackingham."

"Good. Well, I must go now. This cold wind bites into these old bones, and I must retreat to my cabin."

"Shall I see you tomorrow?"

"But of course. We can have our first game."

"I shall look forward to it. Good afternoon, Doctor."

"Good afternoon, Miss Devereaux—and be of good cheer."

"I feel much better now, thanks to you," she replied.

She did feel better, somehow; the doctor and the sea air had revived her spirits. She took a turn around the deck, feeling the gaze of interested eyes with every step. Her face burned and her good spirits evaporated. All the sailors knew, she thought. They all knew and were watching her, leering at her, thinking of what she had done. She wanted to sink through the floor with shame. Worst of all was that Hampton waited in front of her, lounging casually against the railing. Everyone would observe their meeting, wanting to see how they spoke and acted toward each other, wanting, no doubt, to see him inflict some further humiliation on her.

Katherine started to sweep past him without a word, but he forestalled her by springing to her side and offering her his arm.

"Taking a stroll around deck, Miss Devereaux?" he asked politely, grinning that insufferable grin.

She could not refuse without causing a scene, so she rather ungraciously took his arm. He covered her hand with his other hand and patted it, smiling down into her face. She realized suddenly that he possessed great charm when he wanted to, that his smile was reassuring and his eyes warm.

"Are you being charming for the benefit of your men?" she said caustically.

"For the benefit of *you*, dear lady. You see, I'm trying to entice you into my bed."

She attempted to pull her hand away, but he held it firmly where it was. "You are insufferable. As if you had to entice me."

"Ah, you mean that you are quite willing?"

"You know very well that I mean that you *force* me."

"Only if enticing doesn't work," he laughed.

"You are a pig."

"Are you always so kind to your suitors?"

"I would hardly consider you my suitor."

"No, you are right, as always. I am your lover."

"Really, Captain, must you—"

"I enjoy seeing you blush in confusion. Most of the time, you are far too much in control."

"Please take me back to my cabin."

"What? Won't you take another turn around the deck with me?"

"I wish I'd never come up here," she said in a muffled voice.

"Whatever is the matter, Katherine?"

"I'm so embarrassed. All the men watch me. They *know,* don't you see?"

"Has any of them said anything to you?" he said, his voice hard.

"No. It's just that they look. They know what you did to me; they think I'm—that I'm—"

"That you're what, Katherine?"

"You know."

"No, I don't know. I never know what you are thinking."

"That I'm cheap, loose, fair game."

"Don't talk nonsense. They think nothing of the kind."

"Oh, you just don't notice it."

"I will tell you what they think. They think you look like a pretty little girl with your hair in braids, like an innocent waiting to be taught. And they want you and no doubt speculate on how you look without any clothes. I know that because that is what I think, too, when I see you. And they envy me because you are mine and they wish they could be me tonight. Then they think about how they must restrain themselves because they know I would keelhaul any man who approached you."

"And you think that shouldn't embarrass me?"

He shrugged. "It's the lot of a beautiful woman."

"Oh, really!"

He looked at her quizzically and she said, "I am hardly beautiful."

He chuckled softly. "Don't be foolish. You may try very hard to appear not beautiful, but you cannot hide it from me. Nor from very many other men. Your problem is you have spent all your life around Bostonians, who wouldn't know a lovely woman if they saw one. Now, don't fire up; it's the truth. New Englanders have cash registers for hearts. I see your hair, your eyes, your skin, your breasts, your luscious lips. But a Bostonian goes: 'Click, click, father's business; click, click, jewelry and expensive clothes; click, click, how big is her house; click, click, ping.' Now isn't that the truth?"

Katherine burst into laughter. "Stop it. You're dreadful."

"I know," he said with sham repentance. "But isn't it more fun to be with me than sitting in a drawing room in Boston, sipping tea and saying, 'Yes, Aunt Prudence, isn't it shocking that Sally Throckmorton actually smiled yesterday at a man she has met only six times!"

"My aunts are named Amelia and Amanda, not Prudence," she said lightly.

"Good God."

"Yes, quite so. And my mother's name was Alicia."

Hampton chuckled. "How did you come by such a nice name, with all that precedent?"

"Well, my father's name is just as bad as Mama's—Josiah. Mamma said my name could not begin or end in an *a* and Papa said it must not sound like a Puritan or something out of the Old Testament. So they chose Katherine, which is, you must know, a terribly wicked name. I cannot imagine how they came to choose it."

"Why is it so wicked?"

Her eyes dancing with mirth, Katherine said, "Why, it's the name of that licentious Russian queen. And *three* of Henry VIII's wives were named Katherine—two of them most sinful and the other a Catholic! And worst of all, it was the name of John of Gaunt's paramour, the ancestor of the Tudors."

"That is quite a list of evildoers," he smiled. "You seem to know a great deal of history."

"I do," she said simply. "I find it interesting."

"Tell me, then, whom you admire."

"Queen Elizabeth of England," she said promptly.

"I should have known. You two are a pair."

"And whom do you admire?"

"Oh, Lord Nelson, I guess; Sir Francis Drake."

"They were great sailors," Katherine admitted. "But what about rulers?"

"Well, I think Edward IV and Charles II have both been slighted."

"Womanizers," she sniffed.

"What's wrong with that? I happen to like women myself. But, you see, that's all people remember about them; they ignore all the constructive things they did. But I guess, all in all, the king I admire most was Henry II."

"Another libertine."

He grinned. "Perhaps it's a factor of greatness."

"Certainly it's a factor of your admiration. However, I have to admit that he made a great many improvements, particularly in the judicial system."

"And in pruning church influence."

"And in pruning the nobles' influence."

"There," the captain said triumphantly, "we have made a second circuit of the deck and you didn't even notice the stares."

"That's true. Thank you."

"Thank you; it has been a most agreeable conversation. I have never before met a woman who even knew who Edward IV or Henry II were."

"Perhaps, Captain Hampton, you, like Bostonians, look for the wrong things in a woman."

"I stand rebuked," he said and bowed over her hand. His lips faintly brushed her fingers, sending a strange thrill through her. "I am sorry, but I must return to my duties. Until this evening."

She nodded her head formally, and went back to the cabin. It was amazing to think that they had had such a normal, enjoyable conversation. And he had been so pleasant and really rather considerate to get her through that first stroll around the deck by distracting her. It would not be so difficult again; she would no longer be such a novelty. Then she grimaced to herself. What a fool she was to feel grateful to that man! After all, if it weren't for him, she would not have had to face the situation in the first place. Angrily she picked up the cotton print dress and flounced into a chair to begin altering it. She had better not forget that, she told herself. He was only trying to charm her into forgetting her resolutions.

Before long, Hampton returned to his quarters, and dinner followed soon after. It was an odd mixture of normal seafare—beans and salt pork—together with expensive luxuries—fine French wine and oranges from Spain. Matthew explained that they were supplementing the ship's sparse food supply for the crew with some of the delicacies which the *Susan Harper* was importing from Europe.

"We may starve to death," he joked, "but at least we'll die with the best wine in our stomachs."

He received only a sour look for his attempt at jollity. Inwardly he sighed: there was no understanding her. Their brief camaraderie of this afternoon had vanished. All through the meal she was gloomily silent. Well, if that was the way she wanted to be, he was not about to spend all his time trying to improve her mood. As soon as Peljo removed the dishes, Hampton seated himself at his desk and began charting a course to England. He chose a common route, hoping to waylay some merchantman to restock his provisions.

Katherine, weary of sewing, passed the time reading *Ivanhoe*. She was unable to remember a word she had read the evening before and so started the novel all over again. However, she had little more luck now, as she could not keep her mind off the coming night. Would he try to rape her again? What course should she follow? It seemed so pointless to struggle, yet she could not just meekly give in. When at last he put away his charts and instruments, rose, and stretched, she tensed and slowly stood up to face him.

"Why, my dear," he said mockingly, "you are trembling. In anticipation, I hope."

"In dread," she snapped.

He sighed. "And I thought this afternoon we were getting along so well."

"I should be quite happy to converse with you, if that is what you wish."

"No, it is not what I wish." His voice was teasing. "What I wish is your not-quite-virginal body."

"How dare you, you—animal, you brute, you—"

"Please, Katherine, I'm beginning to get tired of your epithets."

"And I am tired of your unwelcome attentions!"

"Katherine, I am weary and would like to go to bed. Now, tell me," he said, coming toward her, "do you propose to fight me? I'd be careful if I were you; your supply of dresses is somewhat limited, you know. Or do you want to remove your dress before we tussle? You may begin in any amount of clothes you wish."

"Damn you," Katherine said evenly.

"We're wasting time, my love. Just tell me your rules for our battle. I wouldn't want to do anything that isn't proper or damage your property in any way. Perhaps you would prefer to just flip your skirts up over your head like a two-bit whore."

"Oh!" Katherine gasped and slapped him hard.

His eyes darkened with anger, and he just looked at her for a moment, his jaw set, the mark of her hand plain on his face, first white, then swiftly turning to red. Her slap made him furious. He had always disliked women who, secure in the knowledge that a gentleman would not return their blow, slapped one whenever they were in a tiff. It galled him not to be able to return a blow, especially this one—Katherine delivered a real hay-maker, not a little ladylike slap.

Suddenly he reached out and threw her onto the bed. Before she could scramble off, he was on top of her, kneeling across her, holding her so that she could not move. She lashed out at him with her fists, raining blows on his face and chest, but he quickly grabbed her wrists and firmly shoved her arms down against the bed above her head. She writhed helplessly beneath him.

"Well, what will it be, madame? Shall I make love to you? Or shall I toss up your skirts and take you? It's up to you. You enjoyed it this morning, but that's awful, isn't it? You cannot let yourself realize that you enjoyed my caresses! You have to make me force you. If I rape you, it's not your fault, is it? Perhaps you would prefer it if I tied you down—that would really satisfy you, wouldn't it? You would be so completely at my mercy, so completely innocent. Now, Miss Devereaux, what is it to be? Are you going to face up to your passions or are you going to continue to lie to yourself?"

"You bastard!" she hissed through clenched teeth.

"Ah, I see you have come up with a new word. It warms the cockles of my heart to see you sliding further and further into the sinful depths of profanity."

It was difficult to breathe with his heavy weight on top of her, but she continued to struggle and to gasp out a tirade of abuse against him, using every word she had ever heard around the docks, though she didn't know the meaning of half of them. He ignored her, casually unbuttoning his trousers and shifting his weight momentarily in order to pull up her skirts and roughly pull down her pantalets. Brutally he entered her, climaxed quickly, and then abruptly withdrew, and she felt his weight leave her entirely. She gave a soft moan of humiliation, and rolled to the far side of the bed, making feeble efforts to right her clothing.

Behind her, she could hear him moving about the room getting undressed. She pressed a fist against her mouth to stifle a sob, her mind a jumble of hot, vengeful thoughts. Someday, somehow, she would pay him back for this. She would hurt him, make him suffer. The bed creaked beneath his weight, and he put one hand up her skirt on her bare leg and squeezed it.

"That is more what rape is, little one," he said.

"I wish you were dead!" she rasped. "I would love to see you killed! I would love to see you sliced up into little pieces. I wish I had a gun and I'd blow your head off."

"Bloodthirsty wench, aren't you?" he said dryly and rolled away from her.

Soon his heavy, even breathing told her he was asleep, and she slipped off the foot of the bed. She pulled up her pantalets and smoothed down her skirts. Her legs were trembling so that she had to sit down in a chair. Her thoughts were incoherent, but one thing was clear in her mind: she would not spend the night at that brute's side. Soon, however, she grew quite sleepy, and her back began to hurt from sitting in the hard, straight chair. There was no sofa to sleep on, or even a comfortable chair. But she refused to go back to his bed. Finally she took a blanket from the foot of the bed and reached across his sleeping form for the other pillow. Then she moved as far from the bed as possible, threw down the pillow, wrapped the blanket around herself, and curled up on the floor to sleep. She found the floor a highly uncomfortable bed, but, after much twisting and turning, finally fell into a shallow sleep.

When Hampton awoke the next morning, the first

sight that greeted his eyes was Katherine lying asleep on the floor near the door. It took a moment for his fogged brain to sort out the reason for her peculiar behavior, and then he grimaced. The little fool. She was the most stubborn chit he had ever met. Cursing softly, he got out of bed and went to her; the floor was cold as ice beneath his feet; no doubt she would catch her death of pneumonia. Kneeling, he picked up her limp body, blanket and all, and carried her back to bed. She gave a little sigh and laid her cheek against his shoulder. After removing her shoes, he put her in bed and pulled the covers up to her chin. Her hands and feet were freezing, and he crawled back into bed to hold her body close to his own warmth and rub her hands and feet. When he was satisfied that she was warmer, he got out of bed, dressed, and left.

Katherine slept most of the morning, and when she awoke, she was stiff and sore from sleeping on the hard floor. She felt miserable, irritable, and ashamed. As she dully sewed away on her frock, her mind teetered between the scalding things she would like to say to Hampton and a horrible feeling that she could never again look him in the eye for the shame of knowing he had seen her in such a debased position. It had been terrible enough that he had raped her, but to so deliberately degrade her as he had last night! It was as if he was trying to show her how low his opinion of her was.

Don't give in, she told herself sternly; don't let him lower your self-esteem. That is what he wants—to make you feel so low and humiliated and worthless that you just give up. You have to oppose him. The only problem is how to fight him.

Hampton did not come back to lunch. Peljo explained that he was busy on deck giving chase to a ship. Katherine looked at him in amazement: she had been so immersed in her own troubles, she had forgotten that the outside world existed. Good heavens, there was still hope of the Navy finding him or of some victim defeating him and releasing her from his clutches. Hurriedly she bolted down the food Peljo had brought, grabbed her cloak, and dashed out to the deck.

Dr. Rackingham was standing at the rail and she joined him. "Oh, Miss Devereaux, what a pleasure," he said, turning to her. "I believe the captain is giving chase to that vessel out there."

Katherine strained her eyes to see the ship he pointed at. "What is it, do you know?"

"I have no idea. Even if I could see her closely, I would not be able to say what kind of ship she is. I am the sort who often calls a ship a boat."

Katherine smiled. Gracefully the *Susan Harper* swooped down upon the other ship. One had to admit that Hampton was an excellent sailor—and a seasoned predator. Soon Katherine was able to make out that it was a stolid merchantman wallowing heavily through the waves. Her heart sank.

"It's only a merchantman," she said in disappointment. "We'll catch her easily. She's far slower than we and well-loaded to boot. I doubt she will put up any kind of fight."

Katherine was right. They raced down upon the hapless ship and made a lovely *en point* turn to bring themselves broadside. Hampton was showing off, she thought, no doubt trying to throw more fear into the merchant captain with his little display of skill. The *Susan Harper*'s real guns fired a shot across the bow and called on the other ship to surrender. The other captain refused, putting a brave face on it, but Hampton flung wide his portholes and displayed his neat row of false cannon. The merchant ship quickly surrendered. Katherine sighed. It had been a good show, but she was still imprisoned.

Listlessly she watched the transfer of food and medical supplies from the captured ship. Then Hampton's crew began heaving the other's cargo over the side. Finally, near the end of the short winter afternoon, the captain's prisoners were rowed across to board the other ship. As Katherine and the doctor watched, Hampton approached them.

"Good afternoon, Doctor, ma'am."

"Good afternoon, Captain," the doctor replied, but Katherine studiously ignored him.

"Dr. Rackingham, I have too little space and food to accommodate more prisoners. Therefore, I am putting them aboard that ship. No dobut they will be back in the States in a couple of days. You, of course, are free to go with them, although I am afraid I must keep your medical kit."

"My medicine! But what if an emergency should arise? I would have no supplies."

"I'm sorry. I hope that won't happen. However, as you must realize, perhaps the one thing my country is most sorely in need of is medicine. I am afraid that I must seize every opportunity to get medical supplies. You are certainly most welcome to stay, if a trip to London appeals to you. I can always use a doctor."

"What about Miss Devereaux here? Is she free to go also?"

"Miss Devereaux?" His eyes flicked over her coldly, as if she were a horse or piece of furniture he was judging. "No, Miss Devereaux remains here."

"But, Captain, consider; you can't go about forcing well-bred ladies to—"

"Well-bred?" Hampton repeated, his face amused. "I would hardly apply that term to her."

"Really, Captain!" Rackingham gasped.

Katherine merely shot him a venomous look.

"Please, Doctor, this girl is staying right here. She is, shall we say, a prize of war, my possession, and I intend to keep her as long as she amuses me. Let's hear no more about it."

The doctor simply stared at him aghast. Katherine glared, longing to slash her fingernails down his insolent grinning face.

"Then I must remain here, too," the doctor said finally. "I cannot abandon Miss Devereaux in her distress."

"A very noble sentiment," the Rebel murmured.

"I am quite capable of taking care of myself, Doctor!" Katherine flared.

Hampton chuckled at the other man's dismay. "I am sure you are, my pet." Lazily he encircled her arm with his thumb and middle finger and lightly ran the circle down her arm to her wrist, then slowly back up. A shock seemed to run up her arm and she jerked it away, glared at both men, and stormed back to her cabin. Hampton's eyes followed her retreating figure. Then he straightened and looked at the older man. "Well, then, have you decided to stay?"

"If you insist on imprisoning that girl, yes."

"Excellent! You are most welcome. However, a word of advice: she is right, you know. She doesn't need a champion; she fights quite well for herself. I don't think she will particularly welcome any interference from you on her behalf. And I can guarantee that I will not welcome it at all. Now, if you will excuse me." He nodded and turned on his heel, leaving the doctor staring after him dumbfounded.

After the *Susan Harper* had pulled away from the other ship and Hampton had satisfied himself that everything was in proper order, he retired to his cabin to freshen up before dinner. Katherine, from his entrance through to the end of the meal, maintained a deathly silence. Hampton, after a few attempts at speech, gave up the effort and said nothing more until he had finished his meal and made his log entry for the day.

Then he turned to her and said, "Well, my dear, are we to have another battle royal tonight?"

"No," Katherine said coldly. "My revulsion for you obviously matters not at all to you. You are much stronger than I, and I have no hope of anything but being vanquished every time. No one is hurt but me. Therefore, I no longer plan to resist you."

"Good girl," he said, buoyed by his victory. "You are beginning to show some sense." He paused. "Katherine, forgive me for mistreating you last night. I have a damnable temper. But it's easily pacified; if you had but turned your charm on me a little, you could have easily cooled my wrath."

"Oh, Cap'n Hampton, you are such a mahvelous, big, strong man—please don't hurt little ole me," Katherine mocked, simpering. "I am not the sort to wheedle and cajole and debase myself to such as you in order to make you act like a human being."

"You learned your history, ma'am, but I think you must have failed your lessons in femininity," he said smoothly.

"Oh, is it unfeminine to try to preserve my honor from a madman?" she asked innocently.

"Damn it, woman, you are mine, and you will obey me. I am a man, and a man rules a woman. I rule you."

"No man rules me, unless I give him permission."

"Indeed? Did you give me permission to use you as I did last night?"

"You filthy monster!"

"Apparently the men of your acquaintance have been mice who never stood up to you. But I am a different sort. You will do as I tell you."

"Yes," Katherine hissed furiously, her eyes narrow with anger. She reminded him of a jungle cat, and some primitive instinct surged in him, a desire to tame her, conquer her so completely that she would ask to submit to him. "Yes, I will do as you tell me. Whatever you say, I will do, because you can force me to do it. Physically, I am your slave, as you well know. But mentally I shall never give in to you. I won't fight you, but I will not respond to you. I will never be yielding, never soft, never passionate. You'll find me a cold and passive bed partner."

"That I can well believe," he snapped, "for you are a veritable snow queen now. God, woman, do you think I would bother with you if there were a real woman around? I had as soon make love to an iceberg! But since you are the only female available, I must make do with you."

"I despise you. Remember every time you touch me that I loathe you, that your touch makes my flesh creep," she rasped at him. "In my mind I will be defying you, resisting you, hating you. Though I obey your every order, we will both know it is only because your brute strength is greater than mine."

He smashed his hand down on the table. "You are a selfish, spoiled little bitch. All your life everyone has jumped at your command, from your spineless father down to the lowest servant. You are imbued with your own superiority—cold, haughty, and self-righteous. No doubt you would have led your poor Yankee lieutenant a merry dance. But you'll not do the same with me. For I intend to master you, dear girl. I am going to gentle you to my hand. I shall treat you as you should have been treated long ago. Do you understand me!"

"Pig!"

He stepped back, panting with anger. He stood for a moment, regaining cold, hard control. Then he sat down in a chair and lounged back against his desk, as Katherine continued to stand, glaring at him. His voice was calm when he spoke. "Undress."

"What?"

"You heard me."

"I won't."

"I thought you vowed to obey my every command."
She stared at him unmoving. "You can't be serious."

"I am perfectly serious and growing impatient. Must
I remind you that you are completely in my power, that
if you disobey me, I am capable of taking my whip to
you?"

Her face paled and he smiled evilly. "Yes, my dear,
don't forget that I am a wicked slaveowner and well
versed in such things. Or perhaps you would like for me
to call in a few of my men to help you undress."

With trembling fingers, she began to unbutton her
dress, but she said through stiff lips, "You son of a
bitch."

"What do my mother's morals have to do with anything?"

"Bastard." She slipped out of her dress, then paused.

"Continue. Would you like for me to teach you new
curse words, my dear? I may grow weary of having the
same ones hurled at me all the time." His voice was soft
and dangerous.

Katherine stepped out of her shoes, then removed her
hoop and her petticoats one by one, until she stood clad
only in her chemise. She stopped and glanced at him
uncertainly, but he said nothing, just kept his obsidian
gaze on her. She swallowed hard, trying to force back the
acrid fear that rose in her throat. Never had he seemed
so hard, so cold, so cruel. Summoning up her courage,
she tugged off her pantalets and then stockings, under
cover of the thin petticoat. Then in one swift movement,

she tore off her chemise and stood before him. Desperately she tried to conceal herself with her hands, blushing furiously, and averted her head to avoid meeting his eyes.

"Take your hands away," his voice cracked out. "Why be so ashamed of your body? I see no deformity."

She forced herself to drop her hands to her sides and with a great effort of will raised her head to stare back at him defiantly. He inspected her from head to toe, his insolent eyes taking in every detail. He lit a cigar to hide the trembling of his hands. Desire flooded through him but he forced his voice to be casual.

"Now come here."

Seething, she obeyed him. When she stood by his chair, he tilted his face up to look at her and said, "Now, undress me."

She looked as though someone had thrown freezing water in her face. "You can't—I, I don't know how!"

"Discover."

Katherine looked at him helplessly, gulped, then knelt and removed his boots. She stood up again, but he did not speak or move to help her. Gingerly she leaned down and unbuttoned his shirt. He felt dizzy with the scent of her and the closeness of her bare breasts, swaying with her movements. Carefully she slid his shirt off one shoulder and arm and then the other, then flung it furiously on the table.

He watched her without moving and finally she said, "You will have to stand up."

"I beg your pardon?"

"Dammit, I'll not beg you. If you want those trousers off, you'll have to stand."

Laughing, he rose. Tentatively she reached out, then snatched her hands back, then forced them back to his waistband. Accidentally she brushed his stomach and the lean stomach muscles jumped involuntarily. Her hand recoiled as if bitten by a snake, but he grabbed her hand and replaced it. His stomach was warm, the skin strangely soft to her touch, fuzzy with hair.

"Go ahead," he said huskily.

Her hands shook violently as she unbuttoned his trousers, very conscious of the male bulge beneath her fingers and what it meant. She pulled them to the floor and off his feet, then stood, eyes downcast, hands clasped tightly behind her back.

"You haven't finished."

"I can't."

"You will."

Desperately she glanced at the drawstring of his underwear, then reached out and quickly untied it. But his close-fitting long knit underwear did not fall to his ankles, and she had to pull them down, which forced her to look at his naked legs and hips close up, even touch them. Nor could she avoid the sight of his swollen manhood.

"Get into bed," he told her, and she scurried toward it as if to a refuge.

He followed and crawled in beside her. Almost carelessly he began to stroke her body, running his hands all over her breasts and stomach and legs. Turning her over onto her stomach, he caressed her back and lingered over her buttocks, then stroked the backs of her legs, even reaching down to run a finger up the soles of her feet. Again he returned to her buttocks, squeezing, soothing, brushing with his fingertips. As he continued to caress her with his hands, she felt his lips begin to roam her back. His body slid lower along her, and she jumped with shock when he nipped gently at her buttocks.

"What are you doing to me?"

He laughed a low, soft laugh. "Oh, wicked things, my love; things quite frowned upon in Boston." He kissed her hips, her thighs.

"Please—no!"

"I plan to kiss you many places, my love," he said thickly. "Look, I even kiss your dainty feet."

"Matt—Captain Hampton!"

"Go ahead. Say my name. Say Matthew." He hovered over her, his face buried in her hair. "I want to hear you say it," he breathed into her ear. "Say it softly, caressingly, bitterly, loudly, reprovingly. I don't care. I just want to hear it in your mouth. I want your teeth and tongue and lips to form it. 'Matthew.' 'Matt.' " He shoved her hair aside to nibble at her ear and his body moved against hers. "To please me. Say it just once."

"Captain Hampton," she flared.

"Damn you, Katherine. See how I will say your name. Katherine. Kate. Kathy." His lips roamed her cheek, twisting her around to kiss her deeply. "Katherine. I won't stop until you answer me. Katherine. Lovely, infuriating. Beautiful. My Kathy." He let her return to her back, all the while kissing her, murmuring her name.

She steeled herself against his hands and mouth and words. Once she had felt sorry for herself that she had never heard her name spoken ardently; now she felt close to melting at the sound. How could he be so changeable, so humiliating, so enflaming? It was torture to hold herself still, to keep from saying his name. As he entered her, she realized with horror that even though he purposefully humiliated her, she delighted in his possession of her. She wanted to move with him, against him, anything but remain cold, immobile, and silent. As soon as he withdrew, she rolled away from him to huddle against the wall.

"Get back here," he said roughly, pulling her into his arms. "I'm not through with you." Tenderly, softly he kissed her hair and face and mouth, then settled his head on her breast and immediately fell asleep.

Cautiously she touched his face, lightly running her fingers along his cheekbone and jaw. "Matthew," she whispered into the dark silence.

Nine

$\mathcal{A}$ loud knocking at the door awakened them both. "Captain! Yank ship south-southwest. Looks like Navy."

Hampton was immediately alert. He left the bed and quickly threw on his clothes. Katherine sat up sleepily, fighting the fog in her mind.

"What's going on?" she asked, yawning.

"It may be that your saviors have arrived," he said shortly, pulling on his boots.

"The Navy?"

"Perhaps."

"But what will you do?"

"Hope they have not crossed the path of the ship I let go yesterday. If they haven't, we may be able to bluff our way through as the *Susan Harper.* But if they have encountered the crew of the *Susan Harper* on that merchant ship, they'll know we aren't and we'll have to run or fight. If it's a sailing ship, we can probably outrun them. If steam, we probably cannot. And they are bound to be better armed than we. Our only hope in a battle is that their captain is incompetent." He paused and looked at her shrewdly. "Do you know much about the Navy? Names of ships, their captains, that sort of thing?"

She shrugged. "A fair amount about the ones we built. And of course Teddy told me about the Navy constantly."

"Good. Then get dressed and come up on deck. Perhaps you can identify our friend."

"What makes you think I would tell you anything if I recognize it?"

"Because you know I'd break every bone in your body if you deceived me," he said pleasantly and turned toward the door.

She picked up the closest thing at hand, which happened to be a pillow, and threw it after him. It bounced harmlessly off the door as it swung to behind him. She slipped out of bed and dressed hurriedly, her curiosity about the ship overcoming her desire to defy his commands.

When she came on deck, she found Hampton gazing through his telescope at what was little more than a speck on the horizon. He turned to her and smiled.

"It seems that we cannot use your expertise yet."

"How could they tell it was a military ship?" she asked.

He shrugged. "I think Peljo smells them out. I certainly can't see her well enough. But Peljo's seldom wrong, so I must presume it is Navy. I have ordered full sail; perhaps we'll outdistance her before she suspects us. Or keep in front of her until nightfall when maybe we could lose her."

Katherine stayed on deck for a while, but soon hunger lured her down to the cabin to eat. Afterward she read for a while, though her thoughts constantly intruded. She ran over and over how he had humiliated her, degraded her for the past two nights. And just because she had dared to stand up to him. No doubt he expected her to throw herself at his feet, as countless other women probably had. Piqued because she did not, he had decided to abuse her. He used her as if she were a thing, an inanimate object, almost as if she didn't exist. She pressed her fist against her trembling lips to hold back her tears. Wasn't it enough that he impose himself on her physically? Why did he have to hurt her mentally and emotionally, too?

Her gloomy thoughts were interrupted by a polite rapping at the door. Katherine swallowed her tears and went to answer it. Dr. Rackingham stood outside; he had come to begin the chess games they had promised each other. He was a good player and, though she played rather distractedly at first, she soon settled down to her usual form, and they passed the morning quite enjoyably. She asked him to join her for lunch and he accepted. The meal was pleasant and they found themselves talking and laughing companionably. When Hampton arrived to eat his lunch, he found them at the end of their meal, chuckling over some story of the doctor's. The captain bowed politely.

"Excuse me, my dear. I did not know you were entertaining."

"Dr. Rackingham kindly stopped by to relieve my boredom," she said airily. "He and I have been playing chess all morning."

"Ah, then you have spent a more pleasant morning than I."

"Do you play, Captain Hampton?" Rackingham inquired.

"Sometimes."

"Perhaps we could have a game ourselves some evening."

"I would enjoy that, Doctor."

"Though Miss Devereaux plays so well, you will probably find me a poor substitute."

"Yes, Miss Devereaux is indeed a worthy opponent," he said, shooting her a mischievous glance.

Mason entered with Hampton's food, and the doctor excused himself to return to his quarters for his daily nap.

After he left, Hampton said, "You seem to have made a new conquest. Be careful or you'll make me jealous."

She looked at him, startled, and saw that his eyes were twinkling. "Must you always be making fun of me?" she said coldly.

He smiled. "If Dr. Rackingham were not at least sixty years old, I would probably be deadly serious."

"I can't imagine what you mean."

"Only that I am very possessive, and I want no other man sharing your favors."

"Well, since I was obviously happy and enjoying myself, you can be assured that he did not do the sort of things you do to me."

He winced exaggeratedly. "A direct hit, Miss Devereaux." He ate in silence for a moment. "She's gotten

—215—

close enough for me to make her out. Peljo's right—she's military."

"What kind of ship?"

"Sail. Very sleek, built for speed. Faster than we are and sailing full speed ahead. Several years old, I think." He went on to describe in detail the sails, masts, body design, and equipment.

Katherine listened interestedly, building a picture of it in her mind. "If it's out of Boston, I know of only three like that, the *Pandora*, the *Susquetack*, and the *Dorsey*."

"Do you know their captains?"

She shook her head slowly. "I don't know who commands the *Dorsey*. The *Pandora*'s captain is a New Yorker, I forget his name—something Dutch. I don't know anything about him. But that's the best ship; we built her ten years ago—she's solid and fast."

"What about the *Susquetack?*"

"I know her captain—Harold Camberton. He's professional Navy. Lieutenant Perkins thinks highly of him."

His gray eyes turned icy. "And am I to trust Lieutenant Perkins's judgment?"

"It matters not at all to me whether you do or not. Whatever you may think of him personally, no matter how stupid you may think he is to want to marry me, he is a very good sailor and he knows ships. I think he's a fairly good judge of men also."

"Then what does Lieutenant Perkins say about him?"

"That he's strong, solid, steady, tenacious, respected by his men. He's not flamboyant. He's conservative in battle, but not prone to making mistakes. Slow, but persistent. He doesn't dazzle, but he's tough."

Hampton looked at her, weighing her comments. Finally he said, "Then I guess perhaps I should hope it's not the *Susquetack.*" He rose. "I have to get back on deck. Thank you for your information; you never cease to amaze me. Come here." He put his hands on her shoulders and she tensed at his touch. "Don't be so stiff, girl. I only want to kiss you."

He bent and kissed her full on the lips; his mouth felt warm and soft against hers. His kiss was neither passionate nor gentle, but a sort of firm, warm reassurance. She wasn't sure whether the reassurance was for her or for him.

"I must go," he said, paused as if to say something, then shrugged and said, "Come up if you like."

Katherine picked up her cloak and followed him out the door. He allowed her to look at the ship through the telescope.

"There is one bad thing about the sea," he said. "There's no place to hide." He clenched his fist. "If only I knew whether they intercepted that ship."

"It's not a heavily armed ship," Katherine said. "It's too light and speedy."

"Yes. It won't be so bad if I have to do open battle with it. But I prefer to avoid that. Too chancy, as poorly armed as we are. And I can't afford to lose any men; my crew's too small. Worst, these men have very little experience together—tricky maneuvers might be difficult."

"How do you feel when you go into battle?"

"Tense, excited, scared to death. How do you feel?"

"I've never battled with anyone but you."

"I know." He smiled down into her face, his eyes shooting into hers. "That's what I mean."

Her stomach began to dance. "The same, I guess." Her voice was small; she could hardly get it out.

"Foolish girl. I won't hurt you. Don't you know that you have only to surrender to conquer me?"

"I don't understand."

Lightly his fingertips grazed her cheek. "Someday you will."

Nervously she turned away and returned to the subject of battles. He followed the change without comment, and they passed some time discussing ships, wars, and maneuvers. Katherine was so interested in the subject that she forgot her animosity and questioned and listened to him eagerly. He found that he enjoyed explaining things to her, for her questions were bright and knowledgeable, her understanding excellent, and her interest flattering. It helped to ease the tension of waiting as the other ship crept closer.

As the afternoon wore on, the naval vessel gained steadily. When it came within signaling distance, Hampton decided to go on the offensive. He signaled to them, stating the name of his ship and requesting them to identify themselves. The answer came back U.S.S. *Susquetack*. Hampton raised his eyebrows and made a faint bow toward Katherine.

"It seems your fiancé's captain is upon us."

"Do you think he knows?"

"If we presume that he is one of the ships sent after us, doesn't it seem strange that he wouldn't question us about whether we had seen the stolen ship? That would seem to indicate he knows we are what he is looking for. On the other hand, perhaps he is not one of those ships, knows nothing about us, and then it isn't odd at all."

"Why else would he have chased us all day?"

"I'm afraid you're right." Decisively he turned and began snapping orders to his men. They raced to do his bidding. The ship turned gracefully and swooped back toward the *Susquetack*.

"What are you doing?" she asked, her heart leaping into her throat.

"Attacking," he replied calmly. "We shall see how well a good conservative sailor can fight against unusual tactics. And you, my dear, are going below."

"I most certainly will not," she answered heatedly. "I am staying right here, where I can see everything."

His brow contracted thunderously. "You'll do as I say. I won't have you hurt. And I can't afford to have my mind wandering to how you're faring. Besides, you'll get in the way."

"I won't," she pleaded. "Please let me stay. I promise I'll stay out of the way and I will not get hurt."

"How can you promise that you won't get hit by a shell?"

"Please."

"Absolutely not. Now get below."

She glared at him, not moving.

"Katherine, I haven't time to fool with you. If I have to pick you up and carry you down there and lock you in, I shall do so," he threatened.

She turned and flounced away. Hampton turned his

attention to other things and didn't notice that she got no further than the stairs, then hid herself behind a pile of ropes and boxes to watch the battle.

The *Susan Harper* ran down her U.S. flag and replaced it with a makeshift Confederate flag, then fired a neat shot with the six-pounder, which hit the other ship broadside. Hampton fired on the run, made a graceful sweep, and got off a second round before the enemy gunners were ready to fire. The *Susquetack*'s first shot went wide, giving the *Susan Harper* a few spare minutes in which to circle and attack from the other side. Katherine sucked in her breath in admiration of Hampton's skill.

Suddenly Hampton swung, presenting a narrow target to the other's next broadside, and scurried away. Within two volleys they were out of range, with little damage incurred. The *Susquetack* gave pursuit, but as it came within range, the *Susan Harper* again turned and engaged battle. This time, however, a broadside smashed into it, shaking the ship and sending wood flying. Again Katherine's ship twisted out of range, and the deadly dance continued.

Katherine realized what Hampton was doing. He was slapping at them, darting in and out, keeping control of the battle in his hands, and eating up valuable time. No doubt he was hoping to elude them when dark came. Also, he was attempting to inflict enough damage to keep them from following or at least to slow them down. Hence he was using his limited firing power on the masts. While the *Susquetack*'s captain was good, his nature nullified the advantages of his ship. His craft was smaller and speedier, but his methodical slowness lengthened the ship's reaction time too much; he could not counter Hampton's quick, wasplike darts and retreats. He was caught off-guard by the other's unorthodox approach; he was puzzled, uncertain. He shot to cripple, not to slow, but the *Susan Harper* was larger and could withstand more punishment. What Camberton didn't realize was that Hampton did not intend to settle down to a full-scale fight, that he was just trying to escape.

One of the *Susan Harper*'s balls hit a mast directly and it toppled. Katherine wanted to cheer, then realized she was supporting her enemy. She heard her name called and turned reluctantly, fearing the captain's wrath. But it was Dr. Rackingham signaling to her. She quickly made her way to him.

"Have you ever done any nursing? I need help with the wounded," he shouted above the roar of the wind and guns.

"No, I haven't, but I have a strong stomach and won't faint."

"You'll do. Come with me."

Katherine followed the doctor around, carrying his supplies, holding broken limbs as he set them, handing his instruments to him, swabbing gently at wounds. At first she thought she had been too confident in her estimation of her abilities, but she forced down her nausea and steeled herself to the awful cries of pain, knowing that a display of her sensibilities would not help. Time crept by. She kneeled, pulled, crouched, shoved, carried until her muscles and joints ached. Her head pounded from the vibration of the guns. Her face had frozen into a mask of concerned reassurance. She soon felt infinitely weary, but there was no rest. Beneath her the deck shuddered as they were hit; the guns pounded; the ships swerved and turned and raced; the air reeked of gunpowder. But she was oblivious to the battle, oblivious to everything but the wound of the man in front of her, oblivious even to the blood splattering her dress or the gash in her arm where a flying splinter had hit her. Hampton, catching sight of her, felt the anger flare in him—didn't she realize the danger she was putting herself in?—and almost went to snatch her away. But he stopped and gave a rueful shrug. She was needed and making herself useful, and it just would not be Katherine not to be in the midst of things. He might as well tell the wind not to blow.

It was not until she turned to the next patient, only to see there was not another one waiting, that she realized it was over. Somewhere along the way it had grown dark; the guns had stopped booming. She looked dazedly up at Dr. Rackingham. He smiled wearily.

"Is it over?" she said. "What happened?"

"We are giving them the slip," said Matthew behind her.

She whirled to face him. "We've escaped them?"

"It's night and difficult to see us; cloudy, no moon or stars. And we are sailing south instead of in our original direction. We will lose them by morning. We cut their speed in half, and by the time they repair mast and sails—if they can—we will be very far away."

Peculiarly she almost felt relieved. "And what of us? Are we damaged?"

"A few holes in the hull; we'll make it. As for the men, well, that is what I came to see the doctor about."

"You're lucky. No dead. Only one critically wounded—a gut wound. I'm afraid he will be gone before long. A couple of fractures. Several cuts from flying wood or pieces of shell. Probably three of them will be out of commission for a while. The others will be able to do at least some work."

"You mean we tended no more than that?" Katherine asked, astounded. "It seemed like hundreds."

"No, Miss Devereaux, there were only about five or six serious cases. But here, you are cut yourself. Let me see that."

Numbly she extended her arm to him. She saw him clean the wound and swab it with antiseptic as if she were very far away from him and quite unconnected with the injury. He bandaged it carefully with clean white gauze. Peculiarly he and Hampton seemed to move away and grow smaller. They were talking but she couldn't hear their voices, only a faint roaring in her ears like the sound in a seashell. Suddenly they and the ship began to tilt crazily, and then darkness rushed in on her.

"My God!" Matthew cried, catching her limp body before it hit the deck. "She's fainted."

"She's had a rough day," Rackingham said. "I suggest you put her to bed. Here are some smelling salts."

Hampton swung her into his arms and carried her like a child back to his quarters, where he carefully laid her on the bed. He waved the bottle of salts beneath her nose, and her eyes fluttered open. She wrinkled her nose and coughed, pushing the vial away.

"Get that away from me. What are you trying to do?"

"Bring you back to life. You fainted on me, my love."

"I never fainted in my life," she protested weakly.

"There's a first time for everything. Now if you'll just stand up, we'll get you undressed and into bed, and then you're going to take a nice sleep."

"It's silly to be so weak," she said, clinging to his arm to help her stand.

"Even you are allowed to be weak sometimes," he replied, supporting her with one arm and unbuttoning her dress with the other hand. "You have had a rough time today."

"You didn't faint," she said and yawned.

"It was not my first battle, either. Besides, I just stood around shouting orders. You were doing actual work."

She tilted back her head to look at him. She felt strange, light-headed, with little control of herself. "Why are you being so nice?"

Hampton looked down into her wide, luminous eyes and breathed in sharply. How lovely she was, even with a sweat- and dirt-streaked face. "Relief that we're not dead or captured, I guess. Anyway, you're not up to it tonight," he grinned. "Tomorrow I plan to be very severe, however, about the fact that you disobeyed me. You could have been killed, you know."

"I know," she sighed, and rested her head wearily against his shoulder.

"All right, now." He pulled off her dress, then unfastened her hoop and petticoats so that they dropped to the floor. "Into bed with you."

She crawled in obediently and he tucked the covers in

around her shoulders, then bent down to kiss her cheek.

"Sleep well. I'll join you as soon as we're out of danger."

"Goodnight." She was asleep almost before he reached the door.

She slept fitfully, dreaming harried, confused dreams, still hearing the boom of cannon fire. A few hours later, she woke up as Hampton crawled into bed beside her. He was large and warm and smelled still of gunpowder. She snuggled up against his back and fell sound asleep.

The sound of his chuckle awakened her the next morning. She opened her eyes sleepily and looked at him.

"Good morning, Katherine," he said and kissed her lightly.

"What is so funny?" she asked sourly.

"You. You look like a chimney sweep."

"What are you talking about?"

"Your face, dear. And mine, too, no doubt."

He was indeed covered with soot. She crawled over him and went to the dresser to look in the mirror.

"Good heavens!" She gasped at her reflection; her face was smudged and streaked with gunpowder.

Immediately she poured water into the wash basin and began to scrub her face and neck and arms with soap and water. When she finished he took her place, washing off the grime, stripping off his dirty shirt to scrub his chest. Katherine began to dress, pulling the light flowered dress from the trunk. The other was dirty and splashed with blood and needed a good cleaning before she could wear it again.

"Very attractive," he said and she turned.

Katherine glanced away uneasily at the sight of his bare chest, firm and well-muscled, little droplets of water still glistening on the crisp brown hair.

"A little girlish for me."

"A little, for your personality," he agreed. "But still very pretty. The neckline shows off your lovely bosom."

She blushed, then shivered. "I'm afraid it leaves too much uncovered. I am freezing."

"Well, it won't be high fashion, but you could wear one of my shirts over it."

"Could I?"

"But of course. My generosity is boundless. Anyway, they belong to Captain Sloane."

"That's true," Katherine said, as though the idea made her feel better.

As she put it on, he said, "Katherine, what I said last night is true. You should not have disobeyed me. I realize you were a great help to Dr. Rackingham. But I want you in the safest place, not the most exposed. I did not bring you along to get you killed or even to put you to work as a nurse. You know that a captain's word is law on his ship."

"I know," she said petulantly, feeling herself to have been in the wrong. "But I just couldn't stand to miss it."

"I am sure you couldn't, and your bravery is commendable. But during a battle, during any crisis, it is imperative that everyone obey quickly and exactly. You could endanger everyone by disobeying. Surely you un-

derstand that. No matter how you react to me personally, you have to obey my commands as captain."

"Oh, all right. I won't do it again."

"Good girl. Now how about some breakfast?"

She wanted very much to pout, but instead assumed
a dignified air. "As you wish."

He winked at her. "No sulking. You know I'm right."

She stuck her tongue out at him and felt better. He
grinned.

After breakfast, he went out to set the ship back on
its course and attempt to repair some of the damage that
had been inflicted. Katherine tried to read, but found it
dull, still feeling the overflow of tension and excitement
from the day before. Soon she gave it up, put on her
cloak, and went up on deck to survey the situation.

Hampton was too busy to notice her and she observed
him undetected. She had to admit that, no matter how
low he was as a human being, as a captain, a sailor, a
warrior, he was superb. Calm, quick, daring, respected
and obeyed; she had seen him in a different light when
she watched him coolly outwitting and escaping a faster,
better-armed ship. Before she had thought of him only
as her hated enemy, a swaggering, conceited brute. Now
she saw him as his men did, a trusted leader, competent,
bright, responsible. And she felt a pang of hopelessness.
What chance did she have against such an opponent?
Implacable, a master of strategy, quick-witted, strong—
he was sure to defeat her.

Her gloomy thoughts were interrupted by Dr. Rackingham, who took her down to visit the men she had

helped nurse the day before. It improved her spirits to see their gratitude and to cheer them and make them feel better. She promised a man with a broken arm to write a letter at his dictation and was immediately swamped by requests from many of the men who were illiterate. She agreed, feeling useful and needed. Then she proceeded further to improve her attitude by soundly defeating the doctor at a game of chess.

Soon after the doctor left, Hampton came in for lunch. Katherine greeted him coolly. She might feel moments of despair, but that did not mean she was about to give in easily. He responded to her icy demeanor with a sardonic smile. So the companionship of the day before was gone. Well—he shrugged mentally—the excitement of yesterday had caught her off-guard, causing her to reveal herself more as she really was. Today, she had recovered her image. He didn't expect to win her over that easily. Still, it was a little disappointing.

"I see you are as ingratiating as ever," he said. She merely raised an eyebrow.

She was too cool by half, he thought. He came up to her and lightly traced the neckline of her dress, running one finger down the valley between her breasts. Katherine looked at him, startled out of her composure for a moment. He bent to kiss her neck, his lips lingering over her smooth flesh. She simply stood stiffly.

"I would like to eat lunch," she said crisply. "I am rather hungry."

"I have a hunger of a different sort," he murmured.

"You're mad. It's the middle of the day!"

He chuckled. "Have I offended your sensibilities?

Can't it be done by light of day? I think I will enjoy looking at your body in full light."

She flushed and bit her lip. "Please, Captain Hampton. This is really most—"

"Most what?" His lips traveled down the quivering flesh of her breasts. She stood still as a mannikin, her face averted, while he removed her clothes. He led her to the bed and she got in and lay perfectly straight and unyielding, her face blank and her eyes closed. He took off his clothes and joined her in bed. He explored her with his hands and mouth, delighting in the sight and feel of her rounded, silken body. He teased her by naming the parts of her body that he touched; he kissed and caressed her until he himself was at a fever pitch of passion, but she remained cold, never softening or returning a kiss or caress. And when he had finished, his passion spent, she still said nothing, but slipped out from under him, washed and dressed, then sat down at the table.

"When will supper come?" she asked coolly.

Anger spurted in him. Damn her for a frozen Yankee bitch! His lovemaking had not touched her at all; she seemed perfectly indifferent to him. He wanted to storm at her, to shake her, to slap her, anything to wipe that cool indifference from her face. He leaped from the bed and strode across the room to her. Her face filled with fright at the sight of his enraged countenance.

"You goddamn little—" he broke off and kissed her savagely, violating her mouth with his tongue.

Hampton bent her back onto the table, pinning her down with one arm, and jerked down her undergarments. He stroked and caressed her, concentrating on bringing her to pleasure, lightly brushing her skin with his fingertips and mouth, touching all the hidden secret places of a woman that brought her pleasure. Again his manhood enlarged with intense desire and, standing before her, he parted her legs and entered her, moving within her until finally, in spite of herself, she groaned with desire.

"What, my pet?" he breathed. "Was that a sound of pleasure I heard?"

She nodded in shame.

"Then you enjoy this?"

She stubbornly remained silent and he began to withdraw. "Yes," she forced out.

"What do you want?" he whispered. He pulled down the bodice of her dress and began to lazily nuzzle her breasts, as though he had quite given up what he was doing. She trembled violently beneath him.

"Please," her voice was an urgent whisper.

"I have a name," he said, tracing intricate designs on her hips with his fingers.

She swallowed hard and said, "Please, Matthew."

He grinned wickedly. "Please what?"

"You're awful!" she choked.

"I know. What is it you want?"

"You. Please make love to me. I want you."

"Do you now?" he said and suddenly pulled out of her. "May I suggest exercise and a cold bath?"

He began to dress. She struggled to sit up, gasping, "Matthew!"

"I leave you to your own cold company, ma'am, since

that is what you prefer. I hope you find comfort for the fire in your loins—and reflect upon your actions." Jauntily he went out the door, saying over his shoulder, "I'm sure your lunch will be here soon to satisfy your hunger."

"Damn you!" she screamed after him.

Never had she hated him so much. He took every opportunity to debase her. Her legs felt weak and inside she burned, aching to feel him inside her again. She almost cried in frustration. It was weak and wicked to so long for him to do those dreadful things to her. He was cruel and inhuman to treat her so. He had done it purposely, calculatingly working on her treacherous body. (And how many women he must have had, to know so well how to excite her!) She had begged him! Oh, God, she could never live that down. And worst was that if he returned now, she would probably throw herself at him, she wanted him so. Even yet she longed to run after him and beg him to return. It was only with great power of will that she held herself back from making more of a fool of herself. Instead she threw herself on the bed and dissolved into hot, angry tears. Finally, when she could cry no more, she lay quietly staring at the far wall, feeding her hatred of him and conjuring up wonderful scenes in which she managed to hurt him. Somehow, someday, she would get back at him.

Almost immediately, Matthew regretted what he had done. Had he gone on, made love to her, he would have made a large breach in her defenses, as well as bringing himself great pleasure. But because of his damnable temper, he had humiliated her once again. Perhaps it had been a step in proving to her his dominance over her.

However, he knew her well enough to know that it would harden her stubborn determination to oppose him, to refuse to give in to her desires. If he hadn't lost his temper, he might have been able to win her over then and there. Now he was in for a harsh, bitter struggle; he would have to steel himself to be hard and prepare himself to take her barbs and silences. He sighed and leaned against the railing; to win her he was going to have to curb his temper.

The wind was with them and the *Susan Harper* slipped swiftly across the waves toward London. Katherine's and Matthew's private lives did not pass so smoothly. She maintained a furious silence, speaking only when it was absolutely necessary. He, nettled by her stony silences and barbed comments, found it very difficult to keep his temper in check. She could make him angrier faster than any woman he had ever known.

If their days were a field of battle, their nights were more so. He made love to her frequently; he was amazed that his desire for her seemed to increase daily, rather than lessening as it usually did. No matter how many times he took her, he never felt completely satisfied. It was because he never completely possessed her, he decided. Always she lay still and stiff beneath him, no matter how he battered at her senses. He varied his approach, hoping that the uncertainty caused by changes would help crack her defenses. Sometimes he was rough with her, at other times as gentle as if she were a sixteen-year-old virgin. Now and then coldly businesslike, almost as if she were a chore. Often he took care with her, assiduously stoking the fires within her, using every trick that experience had taught him sent shock waves of desire through females.

Only once did she break her silence. She had cursed him roundly, using words she had picked up from his men. His rage dissolved. He drew her into his arms and onto the bed. "My little lioness," he said fondly, rubbing his cheek against her hair. "Do you have any idea what half those words mean?" Her huffy silence told him she didn't. "Shall I tell you?" She blushed as he told her, but listened curiously. Soon the topic at hand, and the feel of her soft body curled against him, made him feel desire for her steal through him again. Gently, slowly, he began to kiss her, losing himself in the warm sweetness of her mouth. Although he could not be sure, he thought he heard a whimper of pleasure escape her throat. Except for that one time, however, he elicited no response from her. Daily the tension increased in him.

Neither was Katherine immune to the tension and frustration that pervaded their relationship. Though she managed to keep herself from responding to him, it took all her will and kept her irritable and constantly yearning in a way she could not understand or explain. He was an expert lover, and his hands set her on fire in ways she had never suspected existed. Mentally she recited all the poetry she could remember, mathematical equations, genealogies of royal houses; she walked through the streets of Boston, took inventory of her linen closet and pantry. Anything to keep her mind off what he was doing to her.

Shamefacedly she discovered that her pulse began to race as bedtime neared; that sometimes, looking at him seated at his desk, she longed to go to him; that she day dreamed that he came to her to beg her to forgive him and marry him. Of course, in her dream she coolly refused him (at which he vowed to blow his brains out), but still she wondered what it would be like to be married to him, to be able to give in to the feelings he evoked in her.

It was hard, too, to maintain silence with him. She missed her conversations with her father, with Lieutenant Perkins, with Pegeen, even with Aunt Amelia. It had been very interesting talking to him the day of the battle; she would have enjoyed discussing such things more with him. Perhaps she could even persuade him to explain the intricacies of navigation and charts and graphs. Moreover, she was very curious about him; she would have liked to ask him questions about his home, his family, his former life. Often she thought of things she would like to tell him and visualized how she would make him laugh with stories of her aunts. The long evenings were dull without conversation: he worked at his desk and she read. The time dragged by, and all the while she brimmed with things she wanted to talk about.

The days were not so bad. Though she would have liked a little needlework to do, she passed her time rather pleasantly, tidying up the cabin, reading, and playing chess with Dr. Rackingham. She took several walks around deck every day, either with the doctor or alone. Now and then Ensign Fortner joined her on her strolls and enlivened the time with his cheerful exuberance. She visited the men, at first to see her mending patients, but as time went on, to write letters for them or to bring some comfort to one who was ill. Peljo for some reason had become attached to her and was usually her self-appointed guardian on these visits. He also decided that it was necessary to give her some instruction in the art of using a knife. Although he assured her that he or the captain would always be there to protect her, he thought knowing a little about self-defense a wise precaution. Sailors tended to be a rough lot, he said, and the docks and wharves were wild places. One never knew when something might happen. He showed her where to thrust to go between the ribs and into the heart or lungs, how to go in under the ribs and plunge upward, the way to attack from front, side, or rear, and the art of thrusting a knife downward at the base of the neck, avoiding the collarbone. Daily she practiced on a dummy Peljo fixed up for her, and she progressed so rapidly that he soon increased her instructions to include knife throwing. Katherine found to her surprise that she enjoyed it. She had always been eager to learn new things, to perform well, and this appealed to her especially because it seemed exciting, something her femininity had always blocked her from doing. When they reached London, Peljo promised, he would buy a knife for her, one in a little scabbard that could be strapped to her arm and concealed beneath her sleeve.

Katherine smiled at that. Apparently it never occurred to him that she might use such a knife against his captain. Or that she would not sail with them from London. He must think that she and Hampton loved each other—or at least liked one another and enjoyed their relationship. No doubt he thought that, like other women, she had succumbed to the Southerner's lazy good looks and his expertise in bed. Well, she was made of sterner stuff.

Ten

Katherine awoke in the dead of night. Something was wrong. For a moment, she lay quietly, listening to Matthew's steady breathing. What had awakened her? Then she realized: the rhythm of the ship was altered; the pitch and roll of the ship, to which she had become accustomed, had suddenly grown stronger, more violent. There must be a storm approaching. Just as she decided that, there was a loud knock at the door.

"Cap'n! Wind's up."

Hampton opened his eyes and said quietly, "Damn."

"Cap'n!" The voice sounded again. "There's a storm brewing."

"Yes, I'll be there in a minute," Hampton called, sitting up and sliding from the bed in one fluid motion. He dressed quickly, muttering to himself, "Damn North Atlantic storm is all I need."

"Captain?" Katherine said sleepily, struggling to sit up.

"Go back to sleep, Katherine. It's just a storm."

"Just a storm," she repeated derisively.

He smiled briefly. "All right, so you've heard about North Atlantic storms. But not even you, my dear, could command the waters to be still. So I suggest you try to get some rest—you may need it later."

"All right." She yawned lazily.

He opened the door; an icy blast swirled into the room. Katherine snuggled down deeper into the covers, edging into the warm spot left by Matthew's body. She felt very snug and secure, shut away from cold and wet and wind. Matthew would take care of it, she told herself groggily, then slipped pleasantly back into sleep.

When she woke up the next morning, the roll of the ship had greatly increased. She had difficulty keeping her balance enough to climb out of bed and get dressed. It was even more difficult to choke down her cold and soggy breakfast, the way her stomach was swaying with the ship.

"It's bad outside, miss," Peljo informed her, for once without his usual grin. "Captain says you're to stay in here."

Katherine could not find the heart to protest; she had no desire to go up on the pitching deck. After Peljo left, she spent the day attempting to control her wretched stomach. Sternly she reminded herself that she was not some ordinary frightened landlubber. She had grown up around ships, had sailed many times, and never once had she been seasick. (She ignored the fact that never before had she sailed the mid-Atlantic, her longest trip having been from Boston to Philadelphia.)

Lunch was never brought down, but she did not notice its absence. The only things she did notice besides her stomach were the lashing of the rain, the wind whipping around the vessel, the agonized groans of the ship as it tossed about in the sea. Katherine huddled on her bed in terror. The elements were an awesome enemy. There was so little one could do to save oneself, and nothing one could do to defeat them. Incoherently she mumbled prayers.

"Don't punish him for his wickedness; don't kill us all. Don't let the ship break up. Make it strong enough to withstand the storm. Forgive me. Forgive me. I have sinned; I am in sin. But please don't let it capsize; please let him pull us through."

She lost all track of time. Once Hampton came in, soaked and weary, to gulp down some food. She could barely raise her head to ask how they were doing. He tersely replied that he did not know yet, that the gale still blew strong as ever.

"Please save us," she whispered, and he smiled briefly. "I'll try."

"I have never been so scared."

"I'm sorry." He came to the bed and looked down at her, curled up into a tight ball, her face deathly pale. "I shall do my best to keep anything from harming you."

"God is punishing us."

"Don't be absurd, Katherine. And don't work yourself up into a lather." He bent and brushed his lips against her forehead. "What kind of a God is it that would kill you and a whole crew of men just to punish me? Do you want me to send the doctor to you?"

"No; it's only *mal-de-mer*. I'll try to pull myself together." She forced herself to assume a more normal air. "Shouldn't you rest? You look dreadfully tired."

"No. I can't take the time now. I have to leave. Try to eat something, you'll feel better."

The terrible pounding of the ship continued. The *Susan Harper* lurched sickeningly from side to side, threatening to break up and fall apart under the pressure of the huge waves. Katherine fell into a semisleep, often waking, always aware of the constant noise and tossing of the helpless ship.

Gradually the storm began to abate, so slowly that Katherine did not notice, but was lulled into a deeper sleep. She didn't awaken until Hampton came into the cabin.

"What is it?" she said groggily, trying to collect her wits.

"I think we've made it," he replied, his voice heavy with exhaustion. "The wind has died and the waves have gone down. It's still raining hard as hell and we have been blown off course. But I think we're safe."

She sat up and a joyful smile lit her face. He was right. The awful noise was gone and the rolling much less. He had brought them through safely. Thank God he was so skillful!

He took off his slicker. Even beneath his slicker, his clothes were soaked. Katherine saw that they were also stiff with ice particles.

"Get out of those clothes!" she cried in concern, bounding out of bed. "You'll catch pneumonia for sure."

Quickly she pulled off his clothing. Why, he was practically blue! She wrapped a towel around his wet head and with another vigorously rubbed him dry. Peljo appeared like a godsend with a pot of steaming coffee. Katherine forced cup after cup of the scalding liquid down his throat. Then she propelled him to the bed and piled the covers on top of him, adding all the extra blankets she could find. Climbing in beside him, she wrapped her arms and legs around him and clung to him to warm him with her own body heat.

"Good to me," he mumbled thickly and drifted into sleep.

When Katherine awoke the next morning, she found the whole bed trembling with Matthew's convulsive shivering. She felt his skin with her hand; it was hot as fire. Quickly she dressed and hurried down to the doctor's cabin. He came to the door, sleepy and surprised to see her there.

"Dr. Rackingham, Matthew's caught a fever. Please come look at him. He is burning up and has a lot of cover, but he shivers as if he were freezing!"

"All right. Go back to your room. I shall dress and come right away."

She scurried back to her cabin. He was no longer shivering. Now he was pushing back his covers, mumbling incoherently that it was too hot. She pulled the covers back over him and nervously paced the room. Where was the doctor? Why was he taking so long? Peljo brought in their breakfast but she ignored it. Peljo went to tell the ensign that the captain was ill and he would be in charge of the ship. Katherine frowned. What if Hampton didn't get well? What if he died? Her heart contracted. Dear God, they would be out here on the ocean with only an ensign to lead them. Perhaps he could steer them toward England, but what if an emergency arose? Oh, he had to get well! She went to the bed and looked down at Hampton.

How strange he looked, weak and helpless like that, his mind wandering in delirium. He could not die, she thought staunchly. Not Matthew Hampton. Nothing so slight as a fever could conquer him, surely. He was too strong, too obstinate. She couldn't imagine him dying. But then, she reminded herself, she couldn't have imagined him sick, either.

Dr. Rackingham entered the room, with Peljo on his heels. The little man hung back close to the door, but wouldn't leave. Katherine looked at him with pity: he was so fond of the captain. The doctor examined Matthew, then forced some medicine down his throat. It was a fever and chills, he announced. Matthew must be kept covered heavily to sweat out the fever and given medicine every four hours. He did not know how long the fever would last, but until it broke, there must be someone by his side constantly. He proposed that he and Katherine—and Peljo, if he wished—stand watch over him in shifts.

So the three of them watched over him in turns all through the day. When night came, Katherine insisted that the doctor get some sleep, and she and Peljo continued the vigil. Matthew alternately shivered with chills and fought his blankets as too hot. His temperature remained high and his face flushed; he sweated profusely beneath the heavy covers, but his fever would not break. He moaned and mumbled a great deal, often calling out names, the most frequent and clearest of which was "Charity." Often he thrashed about in the throes of some delirious nightmare, and Katherine or Peljo, sometimes both, had to hold him down to keep him in the bed and with his covers pulled up. They bathed his burning face in cool water, and now and then Peljo held him down while Katherine forced soup or tea down his throat to keep up his strength.

Katherine stayed glued to his side, feeling somehow that she could make him well through sheer strength of will. She struggled with him, bathed him, force-fed him, sat by him until her back felt as if it would break in two. She couldn't eat, though she forced down a few reluctant mouthfuls at the doctor's insistence. It was so important that he get well that she felt she couldn't spare any of her concentration for any other task. Had she stopped to consider, she would have wondered why it was so important that he get well. But she was far too concerned with what she was doing to stop to ask herself questions. Instead she watched him like a hawk and recited a litany of jumbled prayers, some addressed to God and others to Matthew.

His fever rose and with it his agitation. His voice was louder now, more tortured. "I hate the sight of him!" his voice rang out and then dropped to a moan, "Oh, Selina, I'm sick, so sick." Another time, he laughed and said, "The captain'll have our hides for this. Run away." Once he rasped, "Not Shel. Not Shelby. Oh, Davie, why not me?" And constantly he called for Charity, plaintively, like a child.

Trying to soothe him, Katherine would take his hand

and say, "Here I am, Matthew. Charity's here with you."

Who was this Charity? A long-lost love? His mistress? Maybe a dead wife?

"Peljo, who is Charity?" she asked.

"Don't know, miss, never heard him mention the name."

Katherine looked at him shrewdly. "You wouldn't tell me if you knew, would you?"

He grinned and shrugged. "That would depend on who she was."

"Franny, you dunce!" Hampton exclaimed sharply.

Peljo gestured toward the restless figure. "Now that one I know. Miss Fran is his sister."

"He doesn't seem to think much of her," Katherine said dryly. "Well, who's Selina?"

"Dunno."

"Shelby?"

"The captain's brother. So is Davie. Mister David's a blockade runner, but Mister Shelby was in the cavalry. Killed at Antietam."

"How awful." Katherine felt a little flash of pain for Matthew.

"Better him than Mister Davie; he's the captain's favorite. Younger than him, always tagging him around."

Katherine suddenly realized that she could ease her curiosity somewhat through this little man.

"Have you known Captain Hampton long?" she queried politely, hiding her eagerness.

"Aye, since he was thirteen, ma'am. Rascal ran away and joined my ship as cabin boy. Course, I knew he was a planter, even though he used another name—you could tell by the way he talked and didn't take kindly to orders. I sort of looked out for him, pulled him out of scrapes and the like. 'Cause I liked the look of him—game as hell (begging your pardon, miss). He'd take on any and everything." One bright little black eye winked at her. "Kind of like you, ma'am."

"Like me? Whatever do you mean?"

"Why, you're a real scrapper, too, Miss Kate. Never mind the odds—you just start swinging. Got him into trouble, too. But I saw to it that he made it back to Charleston. Course, the old captain took his cane to him, but he was so grateful to me for seeing Mister Matt got home safe that he gave me a job on one of his ships. And once he started sailing in earnest, I been following the lad ever since."

"Who is this captain you talk about?"

"The old captain? That's our captain's grandfather. Old Randall Hampton. He's a tough old coot, and crazier'n hell (begging your pardon) about Matt."

"I see. He—he owns a shipping line?"

"You bet he does. Biggest one in Charleston, with an office in New Orleans, and New York, too, before the war."

"He owns Jackton Shipping?"

"You're a canny one, miss. That's him, all right. His partner was Arthur Jackson. So Jackson and Hampton—Jackton. But he bought old Jackson out."

"And Matthew sailed for Jackton?"

"From the time he was seventeen—when he was chucked out of William and Mary."

"He was expelled from college?"

Peljo beamed with pride. "And he got kicked out of The Citadel, too."

"Whatever for?"

"Pranks. He was always getting drunk, sneaking out at night, playing jokes. That was at The Citadel. At William and Mary, it was something to do with a woman—anyway, he got into a duel with another student."

"Well, that doesn't surprise me," Katherine said with severity.

"Then his family let him sail, which was what he wanted anyway."

"And you've been with him since then?"

"Yes, ma'am."

"Has he always been like this?"

"Like what?"

"Hard, cruel, dangerous—"

"He has his moments," Peljo admitted. "But there's not another I'd rather sail under. Not even Raphael Semmes himself."

Katherine smiled. "You're loyality personified, Peljo."

He looked at her intently. "Well, it's not exactly hatred you've been showing toward him today."

"I would do the same for any ill person," she sniffed.

"Would you now? Well, no doubt you'll snap my head off for saying so, but I think you have a little fondness for the captain."

"I think you are a little touched in the head."

"And I'll tell you the truth, Miss Kate, though he would snap my head off for it, I've never seen his interest so captured by any other girl."

Katherine simply raised her eyebrows in cool disbelief.

* * *

Hampton did not improve; in fact, his fever worsened. They had difficulty keeping the heavy coverings on his thrashing form. His skin was like fire. Peljo held him still and Katherine forced a spoonful of medicine into his mouth. That set him off cursing violently. Peljo retired to curl up on the floor and sleep. Katherine sat down on the edge of the bed and began her struggle to keep him quiet and covered.

He looked straight at her and said fiercely, "You're a heartless bitch, Susan. Why Shelby, of all people?"

"Be quiet now," Katherine said soothingly. "Be still and get some rest."

Hampton flung back his covers and started to rise. Firmly she pushed him back down and pulled up the blankets. Leaning down, she hissed in his face, "You listen here, Matthew Hampton. You are going to get better. Do you hear me? Damn it, I won't let you die. I won't let you. I am going to get even with you, and I will not let you thwart me by dying. So shut up and be still."

He glared at her and fell to cursing again. He began to toss and turn so much that she knelt on the bed and held him down by pushing against his chest with both hands, leaning all her weight into him. Finally, however, he roughly flung her aside, sending her hurtling off the bed and onto the floor. Frantically she awakened Peljo and the two of them managed to restrain him.

It seemed hours to Katherine that she had held this position, firmly holding down his ankles while Peljo pinned his torso and arms to the mattress. Her back ached dreadfully and her fingers and arms were beginning to cramp. Suddenly she realized that she was no longer straining against resisting muscles. He was limp. She let go of his legs; he didn't move. She looked up at his face; it had gone slack, dead.

"Oh, my God!" she cried and thrust past Peljo to touch a trembling hand to his still face.

His cheek was wet, clammy, and much, much cooler. She simply stared at him, her mind not comprehending, feeling his breath against her wrist. He was not dead, she realized.

"Oh, Peljo," she gasped. "It's broken. His fever has broken!" She burst into tears.

Hampton slipped into a shallow but quiet sleep, and Peljo, cheered by the change in him, left to return to his quarters. Katherine picked up Hampton's watch, which lay on his desk. Four-fifteen in the morning. Sighing, she tried to settle herself comfortably in the chair; it was next to impossible. Everything about her ached, and she wanted desperately to lie down beside him and sleep, but she was afraid of disturbing his rest.

A couple of hours later, a soft knock at the door aroused her. She was surprised to find that she had actually fallen asleep. The visitor was the doctor, who looked at Hampton, took his temperature, and declared himself satisfied with his progress. He administered another dose of medicine, advised Katherine to get some rest, and left. Soon her breakfast arrived and she devoured it, suddenly realizing how little she had eaten the day before.

"Katherine?" It was Hampton's voice, weak almost beyond recognition, and she turned to look at him.

He looked tired, his face strangely gray. There was still a feverish glint to his eyes, and his expression was bewildered.

"Shhh. Don't talk." She walked over to him and felt his forehead; he was still too warm. "You caught a fever and you have been delirious for a while. But Dr. Rackingham's taking care of you, and you'll be all right. You need to eat. Let me feed you something."

She held his head up with her hand and made him sip some tea, then fed him toast softened in tea and an orange which she fed him slowly, section by section. About halfway through the orange, he slid back into sleep. His breath was more even and regular and his sleep seemed deeper this time, so she risked lying down beside him to sleep.

When he awakened several hours later, she was able to feed him a whole bowl of soup, as well as an orange and a cup of coffee. He was still weak and confused, and she had to explain again to him that he had been ill. However, his fever continued to drop, and he fell into a sound sleep. The doctor was cheered and declared Hampton a very strong individual and Katherine a competent nurse.

"Some of the men have taken sick also," he told her. "I'm surprised they aren't all so, being out in that weather, and with their constitutions weakened by prison."

Katherine's heart leaped with happiness remembering that she had given them those meals; surely that had helped keep them from being too weak. She said only,

"He seems deeply asleep. Would you like for me to come help you?"

"No, I can manage. However, I do recommend that you get outside for a little while, take a turn or two around the deck. And then get some more rest. We don't want you coming down sick, too."

She followed his advice. It was refreshing to get outside again, even though it was cold and drizzly. Ensign Fortner joined her to inquire about Hampton and reassure her that they would reach London safely. His breezy manner had not deserted him, but it was strained. Katherine soon left him to rejoin Hampton.

"Hello, Katherine," he said as she stepped in the door.

"Captain," she said, inclining her head. "How do you feel?"

"Hungry," he said, a ghost of his old smile touching his face.

"Good. You must be better. I'll go get you something."

She came back from her raid on the kitchen with a number of small dishes to tempt his appetite. It didn't need much tempting; he gulped the food down rapidly, finally stopping only because he was too weak to chew anymore.

"I feel ridiculous," he said, his voice stronger than before. "Like jelly."

"Fever drains you, weakens you," she said. "You still have some, you know."

"Peljo tells me you hung over my sickbed like a ministering angel," he said.

"Peljo?"

"He came in to see me while you were out strolling. He admires you excessively."

"Well, he was with you quite as much as I."

"Ah, yes, but Peljo doesn't profess to hate me."

"I am not in the habit of allowing someone to die just because I have a great deal of personal dislike for them. You were in a serious way—delirious, coughing. It might have turned into pneumonia. I intend to help Dr. Rackingham with the other men as soon as you are well enough to be left alone for a while."

"Tell me, don't you find sainthood a bit taxing sometimes?"

"How can you be so infuriating even when you're sick? I suggest you shut your mouth and go to sleep."

"I am sorry. You have the damnedest effect on me. I meant to thank you, not get in another argument."

"There is no need to thank me," she said shortly. "I would have done the same for anyone."

He grimaced and turned his face away from her. Soon she could hear his breathing slow and deepen. She sat down wearily in a chair. Suddenly everything seemed so drab and hopeless, and she wanted to cry. The tension of the past days, the euphoria of today when he passed out of danger—all to come down to this anticlimax of their sniping at each other. It wasn't that she had expected anything to change. It was just that during the storm and his illness, she had somehow had a different relationship with him: complete trust during the storm and then a sense of jointly fighting against something while he was sick. It was unsettling to suddenly be thrust back into their usual roles. For a few days they had been allies; now they were enemies again. It jarred, like sitting down too hard. Sighing, she rested her head on the table, pillowing it with her arm. Before she knew it, she had drifted asleep.

Hampton proved to be a poor patient. He disliked being in bed and wanted to be up and working; it frustrated him to be too weak to do so. Moreover, by the next morning, his fever was gone and his mind clear, and he was bored with lying in bed staring at the ceiling. His irritability was increased by the fact that he felt rather guilty that Katherine had repaid him in opposite coin, being kind and devoted even though he was often harsh with her. It indicated, perhaps, that she had more feeling for him than she would admit, but even that did not offset the bitter feeling that he was in the wrong. It did not improve his humor any, either.

Though Katherine tried to resume her old silent attitude, she found that she could not, out of sheer self-defense. It added so greatly to his boredom and irritation that he became much more upset than he should; he was almost impossible to keep down and quiet. Besides, it was difficult to return to precisely the former status. So she unbent some and began to converse with him.

"Who is Charity?" she asked casually, bending her head over the shirt she was mending.

"What?" His voice was bemused.

"You called her often while you were delirious."

His eyes began to twinkle. "My dear Katherine, do I detect a hint of jealousy?"

"Don't be ridiculous!"

"Well, you needn't worry. Charity is my childhood nurse. You know, fed and dressed me, nursed me when I was sick, that sort of thing."

"Oh, I see."

"What else did I say?"

"A great deal, but very little of it was understandable—which is probably just as well. You spoke of someone named Selina and kept talking to her about coffee."

"Caffy—it's a person." His face suddenly looked older and more tired. "Selina's his mother. They're slaves, too."

Katherine snipped off her thread, maintaining a disapproving silence. Finally she relented enough to say, "And you mentioned someone named Susan."

He grimaced. "My brother Shelby's wife. I must have been having nightmares."

She repressed a grin. "Then you talked about the captain, too, and David and Franny."

"My brother and sister. The captain's my grandfather."

"Peljo told me he owned Jackton Shipping. Why didn't you tell me?"

"You didn't seem particularly interested in me or my family."

"Tell me about them now."

He shot her a puzzled glance. "Why all this sudden interest?"

"I should think it would be obvious. I'm trying to pacify you."

He chuckled wearily. "You are incurably blunt, aren't you? Well, I shall tell you. My grandfather is Randall

Hampton; he was wealthy, but only a merchant. Not landed aristocracy. It caused a minor stir in society when my grandmother married him. *She,* you see, was a Rutledge. They had three daughters and one son, my father, Shelby, Sr. He was more Rutledge than Hampton. The ultimate sin, to my father, is to do something that is not genteel."

A laugh escaped her lips. "The same with my aunts. 'But, Katherine, that just isn't proper,'" she mimicked.

"Well, the worst thing in my father's life was that he didn't own a plantation. He practically grew up on the Rutledge plantation, but he wanted one of his own. So he married Mary Anne Soames, who was the sole heir to her father's rice plantation."

"Oh, surely that's not why he married her."

"Oh, she is a very proper wife. Pretty in a fluttery sort of way. Silly and feminine; would never dream of doing anything out of the ordinary. Never questions Father about his gentlemanly pursuits. My sister Frances is just like her—stupid, vain, and vapid."

"No wonder you think I'm so spoiled and strong-willed. Not all women are like feather pillows, you know."

He smiled. "I've learned that. But very few of them are like brick walls, either."

"Don't be rude. What are your brothers like?"

"Shelby is—was—a great deal like Father. He rides well, shoots well, drinks well, wears his clothes well, never does anything that is not exactly what a gentleman does. He's a planter." His face turned hard. "He was shot

—254—

at Antietam, killed in a charge. Typical of Shel—all courage and no sense.

"Now David's more like me. Always had a feeling for the sea. Like Grandpa. Not quite the gentleman that Shel was. Though, you will be happy to know, not as wicked as I. I, you see, was always the bane of my parents' existence. I was forever doing something improper."

"Like getting thrown out of college?"

He looked startled. "How did you know that?"

"Peljo told me."

"That's Peljo—loyally silent to the end."

"He seemed rather proud of your educational exploits."

Hampton shrugged. "Boyish pranks. I wanted to go to sea, but the family wouldn't let me. First I must have the proper Southern gentleman's education and then the proper tour of the Continent. By then, they hoped, I would be over such nonsense. So I went, but I was hardly a prize student."

"And did you abduct young ladies then, too?"

"No. The one I got expelled over was quite willing—but off limits to students. You are the only girl I ever kidnapped, you know."

"What an honor," she said dryly. "I think you should rest some now."

"All right. Why don't you read to me?"

"What would you like to hear?"

"Not that awful *Ivanhoe*. My sympathies were always with his enemy."

"Naturally, since he was a rapist, too."

"Read *Tom Jones*."

"Oh, I couldn't." She blushed. "That's a highly improper book."

"What nonsense. Just read it."

She sighed and fetched the book. Before long, both of them were convulsed with laughter. Katherine felt deprived that she had been kept from reading it all these years. She wondered whether her enjoyment of it stemmed from her general lack of ladylike sensibilities or the fact that now she was a fallen woman and understood what it was about.

The next day, while she sat watching Matthew rest, she turned over in her mind some of the things she would like to ask him. There were so many forbidden things she was curious about, things she would never have dared ask anyone else. She was sure Matthew would answer them. At least he wasn't all nonsensical about sheltering her from evil knowledge. The problem, really, was that she hated so exposing herself to him in all her dreadfully unladylike, improper, wicked curiosity. No doubt it would confirm his estimation of her as a secret wanton.

His eyes opened, and her stomach fluttered a little. His eyes were so handsome, shadowed by lashes so long that it was criminal for a man to possess them. Without thinking she blurted out, "You must have had so many women."

Hampton blinked, trying to orient himself. "What a peculiar thing for you to say."

Katherine blushed, realizing how what she had said must sound. She pulled herself up to full height and said haughtily, "I don't fool myself that you are not an attractive man, Captain Hampton. It's a pity that your soul is not equal to your looks."

"I stand reproved," he said in a chastened tone. "In answer to your rather impertinent question, I suppose I have known a fair number of women. None quite like you, if that's what you want to know."

"I had nothing of the kind in mind," she sniffed.

"I'm not sure what you want to know. Do you want me to tell you about all of them?"

"I do not," she snapped. "I'm sure that would take too much time."

He grinned teasingly and she picked up *Tom Jones* and began to read aloud. However, that night, when she had climbed into bed clad in her chemise and lain down by his side, her head resting against his arm, she began to question him again, feeling sheltered and concealed by the darkness.

"Captain Hampton?" she said softly.

"Don't you find it a bit ridiculous to be lying in a man's arms and addressing him as if he were a total stranger?"

She remained silent and he sighed. "What is it, Katherine?"

"I—I wanted to ask you a question—if you promise not to laugh at me."

"Good grief. What?"

"You've been to—that kind of place, haven't you?"

"What are you talking about?"

"One of those places where bad women are—you know."

"A brothel?"

"Yes."

"For heaven's sake, why don't you just say what you mean? Yes, I've visited brothels."

"What are they like?"

"You show the most shocking lack of propriety," he said, his voice warmly teasing.

She nudged him with her elbow. "Stop being obnoxious and tell me."

He turned toward her more and pulled her closer to his chest, casually running a hand down her side to rest on her hip. It felt warm and good to lie like this with her, talking to him without strain between them, as natural as any couple.

"Well, it depends on how expensive the place is. Some of them are just broken-down houses, but the fancy ones have plush red carpet and red velvet curtains. Couches and chairs and benches covered in velvet. Usually a big marble bar. And the walls are covered with big, gold-framed mirrors and paintings of nude women."

"You're joking. Actually nude?"

He chuckled. "Yes, my dear. Actually nude, or perhaps with a filmy scarf draped across them."

"What happens when you go there?"

"Well, you sit around and have a few drinks. Maybe there's a buffet to eat from, too. Girls wander around in various stages of undress, and you talk to them and look at them. Choose the one you want."

"Are they pretty?"

"Some are; some aren't. Few as pretty as you."

"Really?"

"Really."

"You think that I am pretty, don't you?" she asked, sounding slightly amazed.

"Of course. You are beautiful."

She lay quietly, digesting this thought. No one had ever thought her beautiful. Or desirable. Yet he had stolen her simply because he desired her. Not for her money, like other men; he had just wanted her for herself. Not even for her good stable nature and common sense, like Lieutenant Perkins. It was sort of a heady feeling, being desired and beautiful. Perhaps she *was* pretty. Perhaps Pegeen had been right; maybe it was just her demeanor and clothes and the way she wore her hair that made her unattractive. She felt a sudden desire to test out her desirability on him; she found herself wanting to touch him, to arouse him with teasing kisses, to wantonly drape herself across him.

Sternly she restrained herself and said, "And when you've chosen one?"

"Then you go upstairs to her room. Those differ also with the quality of the house. Some are very fancy, even have mirrors on the ceiling above the bed."

"Mirrors?" Katherine repeated in a shocked tone.

"Yes. It can be rather erotic."

"What do they do to you?"

"Varies. What they *don't* do is lie beneath you, stiff as a board and teeth clenched."

"I didn't say I cared to emulate them," Katherine flared.

"Calm down, now. Mostly they try to please you. They do what you ask them—different positions, or doing certain things that stimulate you."

"Like what?"

"I shall be happy to show you," he said quietly.

"Don't be silly. You're too weak. You have been sick."

"I could never be too weak if you want me to make love to you."

"Well, I don't; so don't trouble yourself. I was curious what they did differently."

"They don't do anything differently from what any woman will do if she is warm and passionate. It's just that most women are too bound by propriety. Maybe they'll do no more than just caress you; a man enjoys being touched and kissed, too." His voice was husky. "Oh, Katherine, it stirs me just to talk of it to you. I want so to feel your hands on me. Your mouth."

He turned her face up and tenderly his mouth covered hers; her lips were soft and yielding and for a moment she responded, pressing her mouth against his. A shudder shook him and he crushed her to him. Her tongue crept into his mouth and a moan escaped him as she softly explored his mouth. Suddenly she tore away and averted her face.

"No, please."

"Damnation, Katherine, don't tease me." His voice sounded tortured.

She looked at him, realizing that she could excite him, even with her inexperienced responses. She could arouse him, heighten his desire. A strange, heady sense of power swept over her—she could exercise some control over him, arouse him against his will if she wanted to. Desperately she longed to try out her power over him, to caress him, let her hands wander over him and see his face light with desire and hear his breath become harder, quicker.

Exerting her willpower, she pulled away from him. "No, I can't. It's wrong."

"Katherine, do you have any idea what you do to me?"

"I'm sorry." Her voice was close to tears. "I didn't mean to. Oh, please, please, I just can't."

"All right. I haven't the energy to fight you tonight. Come back here; I won't do anything. I just want to hold you, talk to you."

His voice went on, quiet and impersonal, but she scarcely heard him, so aware was she of his body against hers and her aching desire to touch him. It was a long time before she was able to sleep that night.

The next morning Hampton insisted on dressing and moving about the cabin some. In the afternoon he took a stroll around the deck, one arm around Katherine for support. He ate heartily and soon began to recover his strength. By the day after, he was spending hours on deck, and in another day or two seemed fully recovered.

The ship steadily approached England, and Katherine anxiously awaited their arrival. He did not try to make love to her again, but she found that she wanted him to. Lying beside him at night became more and more difficult; she was constantly aware of his hard, masculine body and his lean, strong hands. If they didn't reach London soon, she would give in, she knew.

ENGLAND

Eleven

"Well, my dear, we're almost there," Hampton said casually one day as they sat down to lunch.

"What?" Katherine gasped.

"We should reach Liverpool this afternoon."

"Liverpool? I thought we were going to London."

"Yes. I am going there by train when we dock. But I shall sell and buy my goods in Liverpool. You may come with me to London if you wish."

"I—I guess that would be the thing for me to do. Go to the American embassy there," she said uncertainly.

"What makes you think you will be going to the American embassy?"

"Well, surely you intend to release me when we reach England. You can't seriously expect to continue holding me prisoner."

"Why not?"

She stared at him in astonishment. "But—I mean a ship is one thing, but how can you keep me a prisoner in the middle of a crowded country? Believe me, I don't intend not to make a fuss."

"Very simple. If you want to get off the ship, all you have to do is promise me, give me your word that you won't attempt to escape. I'll trust you to keep your word. Otherwise, I shall leave you locked up here in the cabin and leave Peljo outside the door to guard you."

"I shall scream until someone investigates," she threatened.

Calmly he began to peel an orange. "Number one: I think it would be unlikely that anyone would hear you from inside this ship clear across the noisy docks. Number two: I doubt that in Liverpool anyone would pay attention if they heard you. Number three: If it becomes necessary, Peljo will have instructions to bind and gag you."

Katherine went white with rage. "You monster! I wish I'd never lifted a finger to help you get well. God help me, I should have let you die."

"I think it would have been more in character if you had. Care for a slice?"

"I don't want your orange—or anything else of yours. You are the most hard-hearted, cruel, soulless devil I have ever met."

Hampton kept his eyes steadily on the spongy orange peel in his hand. He could not bring himself to look at her blazing face. He knew that he had destroyed what little friendliness had sprung up between them during his illness. She had treated him kindly, and now he was repaying her selflessness with harshness. There was no doubt but that she would think him evil and despicable.

But he could not let her go. This morning he had decided that the right thing for him to do would be to release her. But on the heels of that thought came the searing realization that he couldn't bear the thought of losing her. No matter how irritating and exasperating and spoiled she could be, she was so increasingly desirable, so challenging, so interesting, that he knew he could not rest until he had captured her mind and spirit as well as her body. If he kept her, he was sure he could do that. After all, he had detected definite signs of weakening, hadn't he? All he needed was enough time. It would set him back to retain her as a prisoner, but he would have time to work it out. However, if he let her go, she would pass right out of his life, and he would have lost all hope of ever winning her. He didn't know why it was so important to have this woman more than any other. In the past he had gone quite easily from one woman to another, never regretting giving one up. He did know, however, that this one he would regret bitterly, and that no matter what, he had to have her.

"Katherine, I won't try to explain it now. You are too furious to understand—or even listen. Later I shall try to explain my actions, and I hope you will understand. But for now, please just accept it."

"I will not accept it!"

"You must." His voice was devoid of emotion.

Katherine stood silently glowering at him, too overcome with anger to speak. Finally he bowed slightly to her and left. After the door shut, she stormed around the room in an uncontrollable rage, crying, cursing, hurling everything she could put her hands on against the blank, uncaring door.

All her past dislike of him boiled up in her, thickening

and bubbling like cooking candy. She despised him. He was a totally inhuman, evil man, with no grain of sympathy for the girl he had mistreated, no regret for what he had done, and no gratitude for the fact that she had nursed him so tenderly. Eventually she worked out her fury and was calm enough to sit down and think.

Though it was frustrating to be denied the freedom she was depending on, realistically her situation was at least far better than before. If she could manage to escape now there would be someplace to go, whereas before there had been nothing but boundless ocean all around. For a while she contemplated promising not to run away and going with him to London and then breaking the promise. But he would probably watch her so closely that he would be able to catch her before she reached the embassy, and then there was no telling what he would do. No, it was better to stay here and hope for a chance to escape.

There was a tap at the door and a voice said, "Miss Devereaux?"

Katherine leaped from the bed. Dr. Rackingham! How could she have forgotten about him? He would help her. She raced to the door, but could not open it; Hampton had locked it. "Dr. Rackingham, the door is locked. Can you hear me?"

"Yes. Why is the door locked?"

"Oh, Doctor, you have to help me. He is *not* going to release me when we get to England; he told me so at lunch."

"Well, I shall have a talk with that young man."

"Oh, no, please don't. He won't listen to you, and I'm

afraid he might harm you to keep you from helping me. I think you ought to just leave the ship, and when you get off, get the police and come back. They won't engage in combat with the English, surely."

"All right, Katherine. Don't worry—we will rescue you. I will leave now, before someone sees me here talking to you. Stay calm."

"I will," Katherine said, triumph surging through her. She snapped her fingers at the room as if he stood there—that would show him, all right. She would outwit him, after all. She laughed with delight and threw herself onto the bed, where she lay back and happily contemplated her victory over him.

The doctor was not quite as cheerful. He realized that it would not be as simple as Katherine thought. He did not think the English police would be too eager to board the ship of one nation to recover a citizen of a second nation that was at war with the first. Or would it be a matter for the military? Certainly the Americans would not be allowed to board it in a neutral port. It had all the makings of an international incident, especially with two such hotheads as Hampton and Miss Devereaux involved. He imagined the British would enjoy having it dropped in their lap about as much as if it were a hot potato.

He decided to approach the captain first and feel out the situation. Perhaps it was not as bad as the young lady had painted it. He went to search out Hampton and found him near the bow of the ship.

"Well, Captain," he said cheerfully. "Almost there, eh?"

"Yes. We should dock late this afternoon."

"Good. Good. I shall be more than happy to escort Miss Devereaux to London."

"Oh? That is very kind of you, but it won't be necessary."

"Ah, then you are escorting her yourself?"

"No one is escorting her; she's not going to London."

"Indeed? Why not? You can't be planning to force her to remain here!"

"But of course not," Hampton replied coolly. "She has decided not to leave."

"She has?"

"Women do change their minds, you know, even ones like Katherine. I think she has realized how little she has to return to."

"Oh, I see." Rackingham fell silent. To confront his lie, Rackingham would have to reveal that he knew the truth. Katherine was probably right; if he was capable of kidnapping and ravishing her, the doctor doubted that he would hesitate to incapacitate one old man in order to save himself. And it would do Katherine no good at all if he was out of operation. The best thing to do was to pretend to believe the captain's story and execute Katherine's plan. So he said, "Well, then, I guess that I will leave the vessel by myself. You have been a most considerate host, even though rather forced on me. I shall look forward to meeting you at some future time, when we are no longer at war."

"I, too," Hampton replied politely. "I have enjoyed your company and am most grateful for your medical assistance."

The older man bowed and moved away. Hampton watched him return to his cabin and his gray eyes narrowed in thought. He did not trust the doctor. The old man had accepted the story too quickly, without even a murmur of protest or a demand to hear it from Katherine herself. And he had not even mentioned a desire to bid Katherine farewell. The good doctor was up to something. It would be prudent to have him watched.

"Peljo!" he roared, and when that grinning little man appeared, he said, "I think we may need to impede Rackingham somewhat. Nothing serious. Just a light tap on the head perhaps as he leaves the docks and a few days shut away in a room somewhere."

"Will do, Captain. I have a friend in Liverpool who's just the man for the job."

"I am sure you do," Hampton said dryly. "But, remember, no harm is to come to him."

"Aye, Captain."

Matthew and Katherine spent an uncomfortable evening together in the midst of the fruits of her destruction. Katherine maintained a cold silence, but Hampton thought he detected a hint of smugness in her stance that confirmed his suspicions that something was afoot. He simply kept his face stripped of all expression. They slept the night in the same bed, but coldly and separately.

Dr. Rackingham spent a more unpleasant evening, however. First Hampton delayed him—quite unnecessarily, he thought—on the ship for over an hour. Then he had to wend his way through the crowded, noisome

Liverpool docks at dusk. Suddenly a large, hard, painted old woman stepped into his path and swayed her hips in a pathetic attempt at seductiveness.

" 'Ey, mister, wanta 'ave some fun?" she cawed.

Just as he started to step around her, he felt a sudden crack of pain at the back of his head, and he slumped to the ground.

When he came to, he found himself lying on a lumpy bed in a cramped, dirty room. He groaned and sat up slowly, trying to collect his scattered wits. Cautiously he edged off the bed and tottered to the door. It was locked from the outside. Turning, he went to the small window; it, too, would not budge, and it was so coated with grime that he could not see out. He sighed and returned to the bed where he ingloriously passed out again.

Katherine found that she was much more able to make Peljo suffer than his captain. Heretofore, her relationship with the monkeyish little man had been warm and friendly. He was very fond of her and thought her the first woman he had ever met who was suitable for Matthew. They had joked and laughed; he had taught her to use a knife. He would have sworn himself to die to protect her if need be. But now he was her jailer, commanded by one to whom he had greater loyalty, and Katherine turned against him the wrath she usually reserved for Matthew. Every time he unlocked the door and brought in her tray of food, she greeted him in icy silence, despite his jocular efforts to converse with her. She simply looked at him as if he had turned into a toad or a snake. He cajoled her, made excuses, cut jokes, all to no avail. After three days of this treatment, he revised his estimation of Hampton—he had more courage than Peljo had thought to have been able to stand this sort of treatment for so long.

However, after three days, Katherine was getting so worried, she decided to unbend in order to pump Peljo for information. She was afraid that something had happened to Dr. Rackingham. Otherwise, surely the police would have been here by now to rescue her. It occurred to her that perhaps the doctor had been stupid enough to confront the captain with his knowledge. If that were so, it wouldn't surprise her to find that Hampton had callously done away with the old man. She spent many hours worrying about the condition of his health and regretting that she had involved him in her troubles; she should not have asked anyone else to fight the captain when she had such a difficult time of it herself. After a time, though, she realized that the doctor's absence, whatever the reason, meant that she was once again on her own. If only she knew for certain what had happened to Rackingham—

"Peljo." For the first time since docking in Liverpool she addressed him when he brought her supper. "How long will Captain Hampton be gone?"

"Dunno, Miss Kate," Peljo replied, happy to be back in her good graces. "Depends on how long it takes him to get us a ship."

"Oh, is he going to steal a British ship now?" she couldn't resist asking.

Peljo grinned. "No, ma'am, not unless he has to."

Katherine had to laugh, in spite of herself.

"He has to get some instructions if he can and hopefully the ship they was building for us before we got caught. It's like piloting in a fog, you see—can't get word in or out of the South. The captain's always fighting his own little war."

"I am sure that is the way he prefers it." She paused, frowning. "Peljo, has he done anything to Dr. Rackingham? Has he hurt him?"

Peljo assumed an air of innocence. "Dr. Rackingham?"

"Peljo, please tell me. Did he kill that dear old gentleman?"

"Good God, no, Miss Kate. Don't you know the captain better than that?"

"No, I don't. It seems to me very much like something he would do."

"Oh, Miss Kate, you're too hard on the captain. He wouldn't kill the doctor, after the way he worked to help save our wounded, and knowing what a special friend of yours he is."

"I think he is in danger *because* he's my friend."

"Then you did have a plan cooked up!"

"Peljo," she said sternly, "for heaven's sake, tell me."

"The old doctor's all right, ma'am; he's just where he can't get to the authorities. As soon as he got off the ship, a ruffian just happened to kidnap him, and he's sitting very safe and sound right now in a locked room."

Suddenly her knees felt like rubber and she sat down heavily in a chair. It was true, then, what she had suspected—there would be no help coming. She was all on her own against him. Despair washed over her. She could not hope to escape him; he defeated her at every turn.

Peljo felt a little frightened at the pale, broken look on her face. "Ma'am—" he began tentatively.

"I hate him," she whispered. "I hate him. Why does he torture me so? I can't stand being locked in here; I shall go mad. He despises me; he does nothing but abuse me."

"Miss Kate, that's not so!" Peljo exclaimed, shocked.

"Isn't it? He knows what it's like to be imprisoned; he knows how locking me in here would make me feel. Can you call that anything but cruel?"

"This cabin is hardly like the prison me and the captain was in."

"It's a prison nonetheless!" Katherine flared. "How can you defend him? He treats me as if I were his possession, his property, like a horse or a piece of land or a slave. He stole me! He raped me! And now he refuses to release me, locks me in here like a dog in its kennel."

"Oh, no, ma'am, he didn't *want* to lock you up like this!"

Katherine gave him a withering look. "I suppose someone forced him to?" she said bitingly. Her rush of anger had given her back her strength, cleared her head. After all, it wasn't Hampton she had to overcome; it was Peljo. The captain was far away in London. By the time he learned of her escape, she would be safe with the police, and he would not be able to get to her. All she had to do was overcome Peljo. Her mind raced while outwardly she kept her face set in weary, bitter lines.

"He just couldn't let you go, ma'am. I have never seen him so taken with any other woman."

She got up and began to pace the room distractedly, glancing around her in a seemingly vague and distraught way. In reality, her sharp eyes were searching for some heavy object to use to stun her jailer; her gaze fell upon the heavy crystal decanter on Hampton's desk. She moved toward it slowly, keeping up her act of despair.

"Then why treat me so? Oh, Peljo, I am at my wits' end." She turned to face him and stealthily slipped one hand behind to grasp the heavy bottle.

"Please don't judge him so harshly. He's never met a woman with your spirit before, and he doesn't quite know what to do with you."

She slumped against the desk, her face sullen. "Oh, stop it. I don't want to hear any more of your excuses. Just go away and leave me alone. And take that supper tray with you; I am not hungry."

Peljo sighed. She and the captain were a pair, all right, both as stubborn as mules, and both blind to their true emotions. He walked across to the table and bent down to pick up the tray, his back to her. Swiftly, Katherine raised her arm and swung; with a heavy thud the bottle crashed into his skull. He slumped to the floor amid the wine and broken bits of glass. Katherine bent to feel his pulse, fearful that she had struck him too hard. Reassured that he was only unconscious, she took one of Matthew's handkerchiefs and pressed it against his wound to stop the bleeding. Then she took the keys from his belt, snatched up her cloak, and scurried out of the room. She stopped long enough to lock the door from the outside, then dropped the keys beside it. It would give her a little extra time if he had to yell for someone to release him, but she was afraid to buy more time by tossing the keys in the water. What if they couldn't get him out?

She hurried toward the gangplank, but when she reached it she was stopped by a sailor guarding the exit. Inwardly she cursed herself for her foolishness. She should have realized that there would be a guard at the gangplank. Why hadn't she grabbed Peljo's gun?

"Excuse me, ma'am," the sailor said nervously. "Uh, the captain's orders were for you not to leave the ship."

Katherine fixed her haughty, glacial gaze upon him. "I beg your pardon?"

The young man cleared his throat. Damn. He was roasted either way. If he let her go, the captain would have his hide, but neither was it wise to get the captain's mistress set against him. "Ma'am, I can't let you pass. I'm sorry."

"Your loyalty is commendable, sailor, but Captain Hampton is waiting for me in London. He sent a wire to Peljo, telling him to bring me to London to join him. And I don't think he will be very pleased if you make me miss my train."

"I'm sorry," he said doggedly. "But I would have to hear that from Peljo himself."

Katherine sighed impatiently. "Then why don't you go ask him? He's back in my cabin getting my baggage."

The sailor turned to go, and Katherine made a slight move toward the gangplank. The young man caught the movement and swung back, stepping onto the plank to bar her way. Instinctively Katherine pushed him with all her strength and he, caught off balance, stumbled backward, teetered on the edge for a moment, and then tumbled ingloriously into the water. Katherine picked up her skirts and scampered down the gangplank.

At first her only thought was to evade her pursuers, and she ran at top speed, turning frequently. At last, however, she had to stop to catch her breath and she realized that it was growing dark and she was lost somewhere on the Liverpool waterfront with absolutely no idea of where to go. Sternly she forced down the panic that rose in her. It would gain her nothing to lose her head. Looking about her, she chose a direction and set off briskly.

As night fell rapidly and she remained in the twisting slum streets, she found it hard to suppress her fears. Once a drunk stumbled out of a pub and knocked into her. She began to walk faster, and her heart raced as if it would outstrip her feet. A sailor called out an indecent proposition to her, and she broke into a run. Rounding a corner, she ran full-tilt against two men.

"Hey, little girlie, where you going so fast?" one said jocularly, grasping her arms.

"Let me go!" She tried to twist away from him.

"Now, you're a pretty little thing, ain't you?"

"I would hardly call me 'little,' " she snapped at the man, who wasn't an inch taller than she.

His companion chuckled. "She's right there, Ned. I'd say she's a real handful." He pinched her bottom and she shrieked indignantly.

"How dare you! Why, you—" She tore away from the

short man and began to run, but they were on her instantly. She struggled wildly, clawing, kicking, biting, but she was no match for the two. They dragged her into a dark, dirty alleyway and pushed her down onto the ground amid the dirt and garbage. Desperately she tried to free herself, half-crazed with fear. One pinned her shoulders to the ground; in vain she lashed out with her feet at the other. He grinned down at her, the pale moon glittering on his round, lust-filled face, and began to unbutton his trousers.

"Quite a fighter, ain't you, girlie?" he said and smiled unpleasantly. "Well, we shall see how much fight is left in you after we get through with you. I don't mind a little fight—makes it more fun."

The other laughed and slid his hands down over her breasts, squeezing them painfully. She battered at him with her fists and tried to rise, but he shoved her hard back to the ground. The one standing suddenly bent and gripped her legs and spread them apart, shoving her skirt and petticoats above her waist and tearing away her pantalets.

"Ain't that a sight?" he crooned, his voice thick with lust.

"Don't take too long, Ned," the other joked. "I'm all ready for my turn."

"I won't," Ned said. "Next time around I'll take a little longer, but this one will be quick." He slid his hands up her thighs and she cringed. Dear God, why had she run away?

"Matthew," she whispered, "oh, save me."

Suddenly a peculiar look crossed Ned's face and then

he slumped on top of her, a red stain spreading across his back. She stared at him in disbelief, for one wild moment almost believing that her prayer had been answered, that somehow Matthew had been magically transported from London to Liverpool to save her. Then she looked up and saw a tall, thin man holding a cane, from the end of which protruded a stiletto blade, stained with her assailant's blood. The dead man's friend gulped and took to his heels.

"Dreadfully sorry, madame," the man said, politely extending a hand to help her up.

She struggled to her feet, staring at him in amazed silence. By his manner, he might have just been introduced to her at a tea, rather than saved her from rape.

"Liverpool at night is no place for a lady alone. Here, you seem quite shaken up. Let me escort you to my aunt's house; it's very near here. She will give you a cup of tea and you can rest a bit and freshen up and then I'll take you back home."

Dazed, she took the arm he offered, and they began to walk. Her thoughts were careening around wildly in her head. Who was this man? He talked like an English gentleman, but why did he wander about with a walking stick that concealed a knife? Gradually, she began to regain her senses; her heart stopped pounding quite so madly.

"Thank you," she managed to say.

"Not at all, my dear, not at all," he said airily. "Couldn't just stand by, could I? Lucky for you, though, that I was there."

She nodded. "Yes; very lucky." Very lucky, indeed;

she knew that it would have been much more horrible than anything she had ever suffered at the hands of Matthew Hampton. She felt weak with relief.

"I—I was trying to reach the police—the constable."

"Whatever for?"

"I was a prisoner aboard an American—I mean, a Confederate ship at the docks. I escaped and was looking for the police."

"My, you do lead an exciting life, don't you?"

"Never before," Katherine said, on the brink of tears or laughter, she wasn't sure which.

"Well, then, as soon as we calm you down a bit, I'll take you to the constabulary."

"Yes, yes, please. Right now, please; I don't need to rest, really. I won't feel safe until I've reached the police."

"Nonsense, you are so upset you can hardly stand up. My aunt will fix you up in a second. Now, I won't take any argument."

Too confused and weak to protest, Katherine could only give in and cling to his arm. She felt as if her head would burst from all the wild, discordant thoughts and images and aches. What on earth would his aunt be doing living near here? What was a gentleman like him doing wandering around slum streets, for that matter? And how could anyone be as imperturbable as he? Although his clothes were expensive, they seemed a trifle flashy. Or was it just that she was so used to only sober Bostonians dressed in blacks and grays?

"Here we are," he said, approaching an unprepossessing brown building.

"Here?" Katherine asked doubtfully, glancing at the squalid surroundings.

Without answering, he rapped sharply on the door. It was quickly answered and her savior propelled her inside. They stood in a small hallway that was dimly lit; but Katherine could see that the walls were a deep red and the carpets thick and plush. What a strange place! Through the half-opened door she could glimpse a large room with several people in it, men and—near-naked women. She remembered things Matthew had told her.

"Why—why, this is a broth—" she exclaimed as her companion's hand clamped over her mouth. It held a sickeningly scented handkerchief. Feebly she tried to struggle, but the world began to whirl around her and then go black, and she slumped against him.

Twelve

The memory of their angry parting stayed like a bitter taste in his mouth. Matthew wished she were here in London with him: they would go to plays and eat intimate midnight suppers in sumptuous private rooms; he would take her dancing, to the races, to wicked clubs that she would be eaten up with curiosity to see. He would introduce her to a thousand pleasurable vices that prim Boston had denied her. Instead, she was sitting alone in their cabin, imprisoned, unhappy, no doubt feeling abandoned because the old doctor had not come to her rescue.

To add to his depression, his embassy had been singularly uncooperative. The ambassador referred him to Mr. Redfield, whom he termed a "special representative." Mr. Redfield put off his questions about a ship and instead referred mysteriously to a plan, one that had not been quite worked out yet.

"I think perhaps you just might be exactly who we're looking for. We need a man of your daring, your skills."

"For what, man, for what?" Hampton had exploded,

leaping from the chair to pace the room. "What is this plan you keep hinting at?"

"Calm down, Captain Hampton; there's no need to shout—I'm not a Yankee ship to be taken. I am afraid I can't tell you about the idea until I have all the details. I expect a vessel any day with orders from Charleston."

"And in the meantime am I just supposed to sit around waiting?"

"Exactly."

"Look," Matthew said harshly, "I have a crew in Liverpool. They deserve a rest, a little time to satiate themselves with booze and whores. But if we have to wait too long, they will dissolve, begin to leave, lose their sense of unity, and remember how much they hated that prison and think how much nicer some merchant ship would be. I can't afford to cool my heels here for very long."

"You will have to, Captain. Do you think I can just pull battleships out of my pockets? We have no ship sitting ready for you in the harbor. I have no instructions to order one built for you. Moreover, I have no money to pay for one if I could find it. Captain, the Confederacy is strapped for money. The blockade is strangling us— destroying our economy. What money we do have is hell to get out. And our friends the English are somewhat leery of extending credit to us."

"I realize the South's financial situation; my men have received no pay in two years; I have to give them shares in the merchandise we take to keep them with me."

"That must appeal to your piratical instincts," Redfield said dryly.

Hampton grinned and sat back down in his chair. The special representative rather intrigued him. He was a dry, wispy little man, bespectacled, plainly dressed, his nondescript sandy hair thinning on top. But for all his meek looks, Matthew sensed a hardness in him, a quiet, dogged, steely determination. Every day he fought a losing battle, juggling diplomats, money, supplies, and men, usually without any communication from headquarters. It took a kind of gritty patience Hampton didn't have.

Redfield favored him with a thin smile. "Aside from the problems in obtaining a ship for you, we may need you more in a different capacity."

"The secret plan?" Hampton teased.

"Yes, Captain. You do understand?"

"I suppose."

So for the past three days, Hampton had found himself idling away his time. Taking his share of the bounty, he multiplied it in the gambling halls of London. He knew that skillful operators lured the naïve into gambling halls and let them win the first night so that they would return succeeding nights, when they would be sure to lose heavily. Hampton roamed London, playing the gullible American, allowing himself to be lured into the halls for one night of winning, but not returning for the losing nights.

Matthew's winnings grew, even though he squandered much of his money on whiskey, good food, and ladies of the night. He luxuriated in his freedom, in the good taste of food and liquor denied him in prison, in the pleasures of soft, eager bodies that didn't struggle or stiffen at his touch. His enjoyment was lessened, however, by memories of his fight with Katherine and by the realization that he would have enjoyed London much more if she had been with him. He missed the feel of her soft form cuddled up against his back at night, the sight of her lovely face and amber eyes, her sharp, witty comments, her interest and easy understanding, even—yes, he even missed their battles.

The third day Matthew pulled himself out of bed by noon and went shopping for something for Katherine. He had made up his mind to change the situation between them when he returned. He had treated her too roughly, he realized. To hell with her spoiled ways and stubbornness; maybe he didn't even really want to tame her. From now on he would woo her, win her, seduce her. And he would begin with presents. First he bought her material for dresses: yards of pale gold satin for a ball gown, emerald-green wool and a deep rose cotton for every day, with ribbons and delicate underthings, an ivory fan thrown in for good measure. The crowning glory was a thin, shimmering, almost-transparent nightgown, virginal white, with a deep neckline, the sides slashed from top to bottom and caught here and there with delicate loops of ribbons.

Next he went to the jewelry stores. Once he would have lavished jewels on her, and he chafed at his present lack of funds. After much searching, he managed to find a fragile gold chain to encircle the slender column of her neck, beautiful in its delicate simplicity. He could imagine it lying soft as a breath against her ivory throat, and he felt a sharp stab of longing for her. Perhaps he ought to return to Liverpool to see if she was all right; after all, he was just marking time here until Redfield came through with his orders.

He made his way back to his hotel room, his mind busy with departure plans, only to find Redfield waiting. The little man looked worried and nervous; he was sweating profusely. At the sight of Hampton he jumped to his feet.

"Captain Hampton, this is the outside of enough. Kidnapping some genteel Yankee girl. Really, don't you raiders realize that you are not pirates! I won't have it, sir; I won't have it."

Hampton stared at him stonily. "Whatever are you babbling about?"

"Katherine Devereaux, that's what I'm talking about."

The captain's eyebrows rose lazily. The devil!—had that wretched girl managed to escape?

"Don't play the innocent with me, Hampton. Oh, I fobbed off that Englishman with just the same air of wounded innocence. But it sounds like just the sort of thing you would do."

"Would you please calm down and explain yourself?"

"*You're* the one who needs to do the explaining. Some old fool of a doctor is kicking up a fuss with the police in Liverpool, claiming that you kidnapped a young lady and are holding her captive aboard your ship. Katherine Devereaux yet—whose father happens to be a very wealthy shipbuilder. My God, man, if you must go about abducting females, couldn't you choose an ordinary one? Must you take someone so influential?" He paused, red in the face and panting with anger.

Matthew smiled, his eyes lighting with a cold flame. "Ah, but I didn't want an ordinary girl; I wanted Miss Devereaux."

"Don't you understand?" the little man exploded. "You've created an international incident. I spend every waking hour trying to influence the proper British that we, too, are proper and staid and sound, and then you pull a stunt like this! The English can't ignore Rackingham if they intend to be neutral. Why, they are threatening to search your ship!"

"I'll be damned if I let them search my vessel!"

"Oh? And how do you plan to stop them? Are you going to declare war on Great Britain? Dr. Rackingham is on the train to London right now and he'll be here within the hour; the English insist that he confront you with his charges. And you cannot deny them."

"Why not?"

"Do, and they'll search your ship. You could touch off a spark that could blow up all our friendly relations with England! Damn it, there's only one course open to you."

"And what is that?" Matthew grinned sardonically.

"Let the girl go. We shall turn her over to the British with our profuse apologies and hope for the best."

"I certainly am glad that you aren't in the military: you haul down your flag before a shot's been fired."

"Captain, we are not at war with England."

"Mr. Redfield, you're a diplomat—you should be able to lie. Deny everything, and leave the rest to me. If I ruin it, then you just shrug and say I deceived you."

"But what about Rackingham?"

"I'll telegraph Peljo and tell him to take Miss Devereaux off the ship and hide her in town. When the good doctor gets here I shall simply give in to a search of my ship and lie through my teeth. In fact, we'll go back to Liverpool on the next train."

Redfield looked at him skeptically. "I shall be very surprised if you pull this off. However, as you say, I can disclaim all knowledge."

Hampton grinned. "You won't have to, Mr. Redfield. Remember, just put up a good bluff, and half the battle's won."

"Someday that attitude's going to get you killed, Hampton."

After Redfield left, Matthew cheerfully packed to return to Liverpool, carefully concealing his presents. It wouldn't do to let Rackingham see those. He dashed off a wire to Peljo, informing him of his impending arrival and the necessity of hiding Katherine. Then he sat down to await the doctor's arrival.

When Dr. Rackingham did arrive an hour later, he found Hampton as calm and poised as ever. He quirked one eyebrow at the doctor, the faintest trace of a smile on his lips.

"Dr. Rackingham. Good to see you again."

"Captain Hampton, this is Major Revington."

"Tenth Hussars, sir, detached," the man with Dr. Rackingham said in crisp British tones, and saluted.

Hampton returned his salute. "Pleasure to meet you, sir."

"The pleasure is mine, Captain. I've admired your exploits for some time."

"Whatever Captain Hampton may be militarily, Major, in his personal life he is a low violator of innocent women!" the old man snapped, annoyed at his companion's friendliness.

Hampton smiled and exchanged a glance with the Englishman. He was a dashing young gentleman officer. Beneath his fierce waxed mustachios his lips twitched slightly, and his blue eyes twinkled.

So, Hampton thought, he is on my side already. He thinks that the doctor is an old fool and that we are fellow gentlemen whose indiscretions are to be winked at.

"Come now, Doctor, don't tell me you still believe that rubbish?" Matthew said indulgently.

"Captain Hampton, you know that it is no rubbish, just as I do. You kidnapped and ravished Miss Devereaux."

Hampton laughed. "The chit sold you a bill of goods, my dear doctor. She is a girl of ordinary virtue, which fact she tries to conceal. She was afraid of your disapproval, and so no doubt she made up this silly story of abduction, just to gain your sympathy. Katherine, I am afraid, is afflicted with that dreadful middle-class morality, and since she cannot control her actions, she just denies them. The fact of the matter is, I asked her to come, and she did. And just as I told you, she decided to stay with me. But, alas, I brought her to London and lost her to a young baronet, I'm afraid."

The major's lips threatened to burst into laughter, and he covered his mouth with one hand.

"That, sir, is a damnable lie," the doctor exploded.

"If you were not so old, I would call you out for that insult, sir," Matthew said coldly.

"She is a prisoner on board your ship!"

The Southerner sighed and said, "I see it's useless to argue with you. You are making a fool of yourself, and it's an insult to me. However, I see the awkward position our British friends are placed in; so, to clear the entire thing up, I suggest that we return to my ship and let you discover for yourself that she isn't there."

Rackingham stared at him suspiciously; Major Revington looked relieved.

"What game are you playing, Hampton?" the doctor asked.

"Oh, come now, Dr. Rackingham. The captain's being very obliging," the major expostulated indignantly.

Hampton chuckled. "Don't be hard on the poor man, Major. Had you ever met Miss Devereaux, you would know the kind of spell she can work on a man."

The major grinned back at him. "A high stepper, eh?"

Matthew felt a sudden urge to smash his fist into the Britisher's leering face, but he swallowed his inexplicable anger and smiled. "A beauty, Major, a beauty."

They took the night train to Liverpool; the doctor was suspicious and reluctant but could hardly refuse the search he had been requesting. Hampton could not help but feel some respect for the old man. He was no fool and not so negligible an opponent as Hampton had first thought. If nothing else, he was persistent. And he had escaped from the grasp of Peljo's criminal friend.

"Tell Captain Hampton about your escape from those rascals in Liverpool," Revington prompted the doctor in an attempt to create a convivial atmosphere at their late supper aboard the train.

"Oh, were you set upon by thieves?" Hampton asked blankly. "I should have had one of my men escort you to your hotel."

"Not thieves, sir, kidnappers." Rackingham looked meaningfully at him.

"Another kidnapping?" Hampton's lips twitched with amusement. "I never realized before how much abduction went on in this world."

"Certain types seem to be quite fond of it."

"Well, what did these kidnappers want—money?"

"I believe not; I think they wanted only to silence me."

"Silence you?" Matthew looked puzzled. "What do you mean?"

"I think you know."

Hampton looked at him, his face perplexed, for a moment, then shrugged. "Well, never mind. Go on— how did you escape the scoundrels?"

"They locked me in a room with boarded-up windows. However, I managed to pry one of the boards loose with the fireplace poker. Then I attracted the attention of a young urchin in the alley below and persuaded him to come up and open the door—for a suitable price, of course. He was a resourceful young man and soon succeeded in unlocking my door without a key. For another reward he led me to the nearest constable."

"Remarkable, Doctor, quite remarkable. I can see you're a good man to have on one's side."

Rackingham just looked at him silently. Matthew returned his gaze steadily, and the doctor soon gave up the battle. He retired early, claiming age and fatigue. Revington and Hampton, however, stayed up a good many hours more, growing quite comradely over card games and whiskey. Though he gained the major's confidence, Hampton awoke the next morning with a fierce headache and a jaundiced outlook on the day. It annoyed him almost past endurance to see the doctor's chipper attitude, and he felt a churlish pleasure in anticipating the doctor's defeat.

The trio took a hansom to the docks, then boarded the *Susan Harper*. Peljo came hurrying toward them.

"Cap'n." He gave something close to a salute. "Didn't expect you back so soon."

"Well, I had not expected it either, Peljo. But Dr. Rackingham would like to search the ship; he is under the impression that I have Miss Devereaux secreted somewhere on board." He turned toward his companions. "Well, gentlemen, where would you like to start? My cabin?"

The search was gratifyingly fruitless. Dr. Rackingham was thorough, and they covered every inch of the ship, but Katherine was nowhere to be found.

"Are you satisfied, Doctor?" Hampton asked when they had finished.

Rackingham said nothing, but the major cut the silence. "Well, I certainly am, Captain Hampton. It was terribly good of you to allow us to come on board like this. I promise you—"

"He's hidden her somewhere in town," Rackingham interrupted him.

"Good God, man, this is really too much." Revington, whose head felt no better than Hampton's, swung on the doctor in irritation. "The captain has done more than enough already. What else can you want? You have blackened his name, totally without proof, demanded that we search his ship as if he were a common criminal instead of a gentleman. And then, when he is generous enough to allow us to search his ship and naturally we find nothing, you insist that he has somehow spirited this young woman off his ship and hidden her in town!"

"He could easily have telegraphed his men and had them remove her. No doubt he knew we were coming; his compatriots would have told him as soon as your attaché approached them," Dr. Rackingham said stubbornly.

Major Revington sighed heavily. "Precisely what would you have me do? Have him arrested? You have absolutely no proof; it is only your word against his. The only solid evidence we have is that Miss Devereaux is not aboard his ship as you claimed."

The old man glared at them both for a moment, then turned and stalked off down the gangplank. The Englishman shrugged and said, "Dreadfully sorry about all this, Captain. I hope you realize the position we were in."

"Of course, Major," Matthew said smoothly.

"I can assure you that we won't trouble you again."

"Good. I'm glad it's all settled then."

"Returning to London? We could have another go at the cards."

"No, I'm not really needed there for a while. I think I shall stay here for a few days."

"Well, do call on me when you come to London."

"Of course, Major; I shall be happy to."

When Revington at last followed the doctor down the gangplank, Matthew turned to Peljo. "You did a good job, Peljo. Make sure Rackingham isn't loitering about and then you can bring Katherine back here. I'm going to try to catch some sleep."

"Captain, didn't you get my telegram?"

"No, what telegram?"

"I guess you had already left by the time it got there. I didn't hide Miss Katherine in Liverpool. She—" he hesitated and then forced out his words, "she escaped last night."

"What? Good Lord, Peljo, can't you keep hold of anything?" Matthew thundered. "First Rackingham gets loose and now Katherine!"

"I know, sir. I'm sorry; I haven't any excuse. She just tricked me."

Rage surged through Hampton. "Damn that girl!" Why must she be so obstinate and willful and defiant! Every time he turned around, it seemed she had played another trick on him. The thought of his presents for her even now being carried down to his cabin—their cabin—added fuel to his anger. She hated him to the marrow of her bones, while he, like a fool, had been out eagerly buying things to pacify her. Savagely he growled, "Well, let her go then. Let her go. I've got no more stomach for forcing her."

* * *

Slowly Katherine crept from the fog of sleep. She opened her eyes and blinked; how peculiar the cabin looked. Then she drifted back into sleep. Later she came to semiconsciousness to find a maid tugging her awake to force her to eat a bowl of sticky porridge. Of course, she realized drowsily, she was a little girl and sick and Betsy was making her eat this awful porridge. Slowly her heavy eyelids shut. The next time she awakened, her faculties were clearer, and she stared around her at the dingy, cramped, bare room she was in.

"Matthew?" her voice came out a frightened whisper. She wet her dry lips and swallowed. Hadn't she escaped from Matthew? But of course—she had escaped and there had been those two awful men and then that gentleman had stabbed one with his cane. How ridiculous; how could he stab anybody with a cane? She pressed her hands to her swimming head. It felt as if it would inflate and float up to the ceiling at any moment. Tears started in her eyes and she wanted to whimper. Where was she? Where was the captain? Peljo? The ship?

Suddenly the door opened and a woman entered. She was of medium height and very full-figured; her filmy wrapper was pulled tight against her, revealing every line of her body, and the globes of her breasts pushed up impudently from the low neckline. Her hair was long and loose, jet-black; it tumbled freely down her back. She looked at Katherine contemptuously and tossed back her luxuriant mane.

"I do not think you are so much," she sneered. "Parker said you were a beauty, a 'Venus.' Ha! Let me tell you, missy, you haven't a tenth of the appeal I have."

Katherine stared at her. Who on earth was she? *What* was she? Her face was pretty, though covered with heavy makeup, bright red on her cheeks and lips, globbed black on her eyelashes. But now it was set in petulant lines, and hostility radiated from her. Why? Katherine struggled to sit up, clutching the bedsheet to her in an attempt to maintain some dignity. (Why was she in her shift, and where was her dress?)

"What do you mean?" Her voice came out cracked and small.

The woman laughed. "What do I mean?" she mimicked. "What do I mean? Why, just that you're a pale little nothing, no spark. Why, they'll probably have to pay the men to climb on top of you!"

Suddenly Katherine remembered standing in the red hallway, remembered quite clearly the elegant stranger who had rescued her—but, of course, there had been a thin blade concealed in his cane; he *had* stabbed that man. That room, all velvet and mirrors, filled with men and half-naked women.

"Wait a minute!" she snapped, her old self returning with a rush, and the woman looked slightly taken aback. "Where am I? Why did that man bring me here?"

"Can't you guess? You are in a bordello, dearie. And he brought you here to set you up in business."

"You are mad! I'm not a—a—"

"No?" she jeered. "Well, you soon will be. Ain't you never heard of white slavery?"

"No." Katherine shook her head in bewilderment. "What are you talking about?"

—*297*—

Her guest cackled. "My, but ain't you the innocent! Well, that won't last long, either."

"Hazel!" a strident voice cracked out in the hall. "What are you doing in there? Get out this instant!"

The girl's face changed instantly, became younger, fearful, and she scampered out of the room. The owner of the voice loomed in the doorway. A massive woman, tightly corseted, swathed in purple. Her face was a mask of paint, her hair brassy gold, her skin sagging from age. Heavy rings covered her fingers and jeweled bracelets encased her fleshy arms; a ridiculous lavender feather was stuck in the stiff mass of her hair and curled down against her cheek. Katherine choked back a hysterical giggle. What a comical sight she was and yet, strangely, how frightening. She swung the door to behind her and advanced into the room.

"I'm Pearl," she said in a voice to match her bulk. "This is my house and now you are one of my girls."

"I haven't the faintest notion what you're talking about," Katherine said haughtily.

"Oh, my, high and mighty now, ain't we, girl? Mind you, you be careful now or I'll have to turn you over to Parker. In general, he ain't too fond of girls, preferring little boys, if you catch my meaning." She winked lewdly.

"No, I don't," Katherine said flatly.

"But he don't dislike a little taming job, now and then, when one of the girls gets too uppity. American, ain't you? I could tell by your voice." She sighed and shook her head. "Never got a Yankee girl before, but I hear they're fearful independent. But," she brightened, "we'll soon take that out of you."

"Mrs.—Pearl, I'm afraid you have made a dreadful mistake. My name is Katherine Devereaux, and my father owns a shipyard in Boston. My disappearance will not go unnoticed, and my father is not a good man to cross. I suggest you release me before you get into serious trouble."

The harridan cackled. "Nice try, lovie, but I don't believe a word of it. Parker told me you were running away from prison."

"Not from prison. I was a prisoner, but illegally. I am from Boston, and a Confederate raider kidnapped me. And when we docked here, I escaped. Don't you see? The Union Navy is searching for me and no doubt the English authorities, too. Not to mention Captain Hampton, the man I escaped from."

The woman listened, faintly smiling, as if she were being told a very entertaining story. "My, my, you are an important little girl, aren't you? The Union Navy is looking for you; the Confederates are looking for you; the English are looking for you. Why, half the countries of the world seem to want you! Don't worry; I'm sure you will be just as big a hit here, too."

"You dolt!" Katherine said wrathfully. "I'm telling you the truth. Hampton will be furious at my leaving and will not rest until he finds me. And I can guarantee that when he does and finds you've harmed me, he will be enraged. He'll—he'll kill you. He has a vicious temper and no compassion at all; he won't hesitate to shoot you."

"Then I should think you should be the one in fear of him, seeing as how you ran away from him. Besides,

I think you think a little highly of yourself, if you imagine he's going to be so hot and bothered because you've thrown him over. Much more likely, I should think, to bury his sorrow in a fling with a few waterfront doxies. Besides, even if he did look for you, he could never find you here. Nobody is ever found once they enter the 'Pool docks. Even the police daren't venture here, except to collect their bribes, of course."

Katherine tried to hide the ice-cold stab of fear that went through her, but the old witch caught it and smiled. "That's right, dearie, you just think of it for a while and I think you will begin to see reason. I shall just leave you alone with your thoughts now."

She left, closing the door behind her with an ominous click. Katherine raised her chin mutinously and whispered, "He will come. He will."

Of course he would find her; the old hag was simply trying to frighten her. Yet nagging doubts crept into her mind. She remembered how she had stormed at him the last time he saw her. He was in London, no doubt surrounded by women who fawned on him. Probably he regretted not letting her go. Wasn't it likely that when he saw the beauties of London he would laugh and realize that prison had so starved him for women he had thought her beautiful when she wasn't at all really? And when Peljo told him she had gone, wouldn't he just heave a sigh of relief?

"No," she whispered fiercely. "No!" No matter what he thought of her, no matter how cold and cruel he was to her, his pride would be wounded because she had escaped, outwitted him. He *would* search for her simply because he wouldn't be able to stand to let her best him. He would come; he would. And Pearl underestimated him. *He* could find her. Maybe no one else dared venture here, but Matthew would. Matthew would search for her, comb the docks—and Peljo, and his friend who had trapped Dr. Rackingham, and the crew. He would find her; of course he would. She summoned up a picture of him, hard and lean and brown, his eyes as cold and gray as the Atlantic. Oh, no, Pearl just didn't know Matthew, or she could not be so confident.

Katherine closed her eyes. "Matthew, please, please, you must come." Oh, why had she ever left? She pressed her fist against her lips to choke back a sob. "I'll be good," she whispered. "I will do anything you want. Only, please, please come."

She lay paralyzed by fear and doubt. Time crept by, and she was left alone. Hunger began to gnaw at her, and still no one came. She left her bed and crept to the door; it was firmly locked; so were the shutters on the window. She searched the room thoroughly and could find her dress and shoes nowhere in it. Why didn't they bring her any food? Or water? She was dying of thirst. Did they intend to murder her slowly like this? Oh, God, what was to become of her? Matthew was far away in London; when he learned that she was missing, what if he were with a girl, what if he casually tossed aside the message and continued making love to the girl? Oh, how bitterly she regretted not giving in to him. If only she had not been so stubborn—she would be with him right now, safely snuggled up in his arms in some bed in London, miles and miles away.

The pale light that seeped in around the shutters gradually faded away and she was left alone in utter darkness. She curled up on the bed. Sternly she told herself that she must not give way to her fear. She pretended she was back on the ship, lying against Matthew's chest. She felt his even breath ruffle her hair, felt his smooth skin against her cheek, heard the gentle rumble of his breathing. Softly she slid into sleep.

Katherine was awakened by the tepid light creeping in through the shutters. She sat up and looked around the room. Her head felt much clearer and her hunger seemed to sharpen her senses. The terror of the night before was gone. They had been trying to frighten her, of course. Weaken her so that she would accept her fate without a fuss. She grimaced; they would discover that Katherine Devereaux was not so weak.

Assessing the situation calmly, she felt that Hampton would look for her; his pride would not let him permit a mere girl to defeat him. And knowing him, he might very well be able to find her. The thing to do was to hold fast until he showed up, and in the meantime wait for an opportunity to escape, just in case she had calculated wrong and he did not bother to look for her or could not find her or found her too late.

The major problem was time. If she could just stave them off long enough—she smiled faintly. Her thoughts were so similar to those right after Hampton abducted her; only then he had been the villain and now he was the rescuer. Mentally she shook herself—this was no time to dwell on the oddities of fate. How long had she been here? It had been evening when Parker knocked her out with that foul-smelling stuff—chloroform? Light when she awoke—must have been the next day. Then another night. And now it was day again. A full day and two nights. How long would it take Hampton to find her? No doubt Peljo would look for her before he notified the captain; he would want to find her and not have to report to Hampton that he had lost her. A few hours, perhaps, and then he would telegraph Hampton. There probably would not be a train until morning. That meant that Hampton arrived the afternoon or evening before. No doubt Peljo would have checked out the logical places for her to go—the train, the police, and so on—and they would have decided that something had happened to her in this area. They would begin searching, asking questions, tavern by tavern. She felt a flash of despair; it would take forever! She must escape. If only Peljo had given her that promised knife—or if she had thought to take the little gun that she had used against Hampton.

First she took a pin from her hair and worked assiduously at the lock. At last it clicked and she felt a brief moment of triumph, but the door still would not budge. There must be a bolt on the other side, and there was nothing she could do about that. Disheartened, she moved on to the shutters. The lock would not open. Then she remembered her hoop which had been tossed carelessly on the floor when they undressed her. Quickly she ripped out the hem and pulled out the thin whalebone band and managed to break off a piece which she used to pry open the shutters. Three of the whalebone pieces snapped before the shutters gave way. The window they revealed was small and so grimy with soot and dirt that she could barely see out. She did manage to see that the window looked out upon the blank wall of another building less than three feet away and that between was a sheer drop of at least three stories. She sat down and almost burst into tears. No way out, unless she could manage to slip out sometime when they entered or left the room. Heaven knows how she would manage to get out of the house undetected. Well, she would worry about that impossibility when it came up. Right now, she must face the impossibility of getting out the door.

First, she needed a weapon. She roamed the room. No washbowl or pitcher. No mirror to smash for its sharp pieces. Not even a small chair to hurl. Obviously they knew their business. Katherine sighed in exasperation. Then suddenly she rushed to the bed, knelt, and crawled under it, emerging a moment later with a sturdy bed slat. That would stun one or two people, she thought triumphantly. But she mustn't use it until the last possible moment. She slid it back out of sight under the bed.

A few minutes later the door opened to admit Pearl, who was today dressed in shrieking orange. "Well, dearie," she said cheerfully, "are you in a more cooperative mood this morning?"

Katherine lifted her chin in a manner that Matthew would have easily recognized. "Don't think you can starve me into submission. I am not that easy."

"No, I dare swear you're not. You seem like a sensible girl, not one of these weak, silly fools. So let me put this to you sensibly. You are a very pretty girl, but has it ever gotten you anywhere? Of course not. Nothing but a lot of heartache. But here, dearie, with my aid, you could make a fortune from that body of yours. I give you good, decent food, a place to live, pretty clothes, and a nice bit of spending money. A smart girl like you, before long you'll have grabbed some wealthy old joker and be sailing off as his mistress. Now ain't that better than spending your time with men like your captain?"

"Your proposal does have merit," Katherine conceded coolly. "But I dislike being pawed by all those different men."

"Pshaw, chit, it won't be any worse than what you normally go through for free. Some of 'em can even be real gentlemanly sometimes."

"Give me some time to think it over."

"All right. I'll give you an hour to decide. But if you decide wrong, I shall have to turn you over to Parker, and, believe me, you'll wish I hadn't."

Thirteen

Hampton turned and stalked off toward his cabin. He felt sick with anger and disappointment. His head throbbed violently and his stomach churned. Damn her. He decided to get good and thoroughly drunk. Lock himself in his cabin with its painful memories of her and get blind drunk, wallow in his hurt. And then he would proceed to forget her, the cold, spiteful wench. What a fool he had been to let her get so close to him, to let her sink her nails into him like this.

Peljo stood for a moment in indecision, his worry about Katherine warring with the fear his captain's enraged face arose in him. He gulped, crossed his fingers, and hurried after Hampton.

"Sir! Cap'n! Just a minute, sir."

Hampton paused and turned toward the little man, his face and stance exuding irritation and impatience. "Good God, man, what now?"

"The thing is, Cap'n, I'm worried about Miss Katherine."

"Worried about her?" Matthew laughed shortly. "I

think there's one who is quite capable of taking care of herself."

"Please, sir, just listen to me. I have been looking for her ever since she escaped last night and she hasn't turned up anywhere."

"Surely you don't think she would let herself be found so easily."

"But wouldn't you figure she would go straight to the police, sir? We have checked all the police stations and not a word of her."

"Well, after the British didn't come storming to her rescue, no doubt she mistrusts them. She probably went straight to the embassy."

"No; I checked there, too. And I've got two men at the train depot, and she's not there, either. And I personally went to every hotel where the likes of Miss Katherine might go, and she has taken a room in none of them. And she's one who would be remembered, sir. This morning, I thought, 'Of course, she just went straight down the dock to a Union ship.' So I checked, and there's not a Yankee ship in the harbor."

Matthew frowned, his anger turning to apprehension. "Perhaps she knows someone who lives in Liverpool, some shipping acquaintance of her father's."

Peljo looked at him skeptically. "Then why didn't she tell the old doctor to go to them? They would have swung more weight with the Limeys than him."

"So you think something's happened to her."

"Well, sir, it was evening when she escaped. Going through the docks of Liverpool at night like that—why, she didn't even take that little popgun of hers with her.

There's no telling what could happen to her—she could be raped or kidnapped into white slavery or—" He stopped abruptly.

"Or murdered," Matthew finished grimly. He stood for a moment, staring off into space, his eyes as cold and hard as glass. "Gather up the crew, and enlist the aid of that friend of yours, incompetent though he is. Keep the watch at the depot and put some of the men to checking the pawnshops for that engagement ring of hers. She will need money if she's all right, and if she's not, they would take her jewelry and sell it. Everyone else is to comb this area looking for her. Every street, every alley, every bar. And this time I will not brook failure."

"Yes, sir." Peljo scurried off.

Hampton closed his eyes and leaned against the railing for support. There was a cold, hard knot of fear in his stomach. At this moment she might be dead or hurt or locked in some dingy little room, half-crazy with terror. And if she was, it would be his fault. He had brought her here, driven her to make a desperate attempt at escape. If anything happened to her, he was to blame.

Suddenly, he realized—how obvious it was—he loved her. He, who had remained undisturbed by the wiles of flirtatious Southern girls and fragile Asian women and seductive European beauties, had been ensnared by that stubborn, willful, icy Yankee. His mouth twisted in pain. That beautiful, sharp, brave girl. Now he understood the inexplicable rage and desire and black depression she could plunge him into. He loved her, and she could hurt him and please him as no other woman had ever been able to. Determination boiled up in him. She could not be dead. He must get her back; he had to find her. He had to make it up to her.

Katherine's hour of decision ran in fits and starts, now leaping forward, now crawling, as she paced her room, her mind skittering over her problem. She must get control, she told herself, must calm down and think clearly, but the next moment, she found herself wringing her hands helplessly, her mind a jumble of disconnected thoughts. What was Matthew doing? When would he find her? Would he even find her at all? And how was she to answer Pearl when her hour was up?

She pictured Hampton, cool, unruffled, even when facing death or capture, his eyes clear, his face faintly contemptuous, his hard body misleadingly graceful and relaxed. Somehow that calmed her. Nothing scared him; at least, he never showed it. She sat down on the edge of her bed, her brow furrowed in thought. Despicable as he was, he was also a fighter. What would he do in this predicament? She smiled—aside from the obvious impossibility of his being in this predicament, that is. Well, of course, he had a brute strength she lacked, but when he had fought that battle with the *Susquetack*, he had been fighting from a very weak position. Yet he had won because he had been daring and quick; because he had taken them by surprise; because he had outbluffed them. And that was exactly what she must do. Bluff them; make them relax their guard; buy time until Matthew could rescue her; and if the chance came, strike quickly, take them by surprise, and run like hell.

The door opened and Pearl unceremoniously entered.

Her eyes flicked over Katherine shrewdly, and Katherine tried to keep her own gaze steady. Pearl sat down heavily on the bed.

"Well, dearie? Made up your mind yet?"

"Your proposal has its merits," Katherine said, amazed at how calmly her words came out. "It is true that I would be making them pay for what they would only take by force otherwise. And I like the thought of making my own money, not having to depend on them." Would the woman buy this about-face? She certainly looked suspicious. Perhaps she ought to put up more protest. "But the thing is, I'm not very good at it. I don't like men and I don't enjoy their pawing me."

Pearl laughed harshly. "Nobody says you have to enjoy it, luv. In fact, you're better if you don't. Girls who get too concerned with their own pleasure forget to concentrate on giving *him* pleasure, and that is what you get paid for. Best whores I've known have been cold as ice or found their fun with other women."

Katherine stared, and again Pearl cackled. "Shock you? But no matter; you won't be innocent long. We'll fix you up. Dress you right. Show you a few tricks of the trade. I think gold would be best for you. Set off those wild eyes of yours."

Katherine's heart leaped. She had believed her bluff. Now they would let her go down into the red room and from there it would be easy to escape, surely.

As if she could read her thoughts, Pearl snapped, "Don't think for a minute that I trust you. I've got my eye on you, and if you try anything, you'll regret it." She opened the door and called, "Paul! Come in here. It's

time for a little demonstration. Bring Sally with you."
She closed the door and turned back to Katherine. "The
first thing to remember is to do whatever a customer
asks. If he wants you to stand on your head, then do it.
That's what he pays for. And always pretend you enjoy
what he does to you. Pretend he brings out passion in
you. Build him up; admire him; praise him."

She broke off as the door opened and a large, muscular man entered followed by a woman with red-tinted
hair and aging skin. Katherine felt sick—what were they
going to do?

"This is Paul, dearie, he throws out the customers
when they start breaking up the place—and helps keep
my girls in line." She grinned evilly and Katherine felt
more than a touch of fear. He could break her in half.
"Now, Paul, this girlie don't know much about men; so
we are going to show her. Take off your clothes."

Paul grinned and began to disrobe, obviously proud
of his physique, but Katherine blushed furiously. Yet to
her shame, she found herself comparing him to Matthew
and thinking with longing of Matthew's lean, sinewy
frame.

"Now, unless he tells you different, you don't attack
a man; tease him at first. Touch him very lightly, like a
feather. Sally, show her what to do."

Katherine watched, shocked, as Sally began to caress
him. She reeled inwardly, watching the two obey without
question any direction given them by Pearl.

Good heavens, she thought, what was she doing; she
ought to be thinking about escape. The door was unlocked and the guard naked and hardly paying attention.

But Pearl stood between her and the door. If only she could maneuver to get closer to the door, get Pearl on the other side of her. She slowly moved away from the bed, as if to get a better view of the demonstration. She stood a little behind Pearl and to one side. Pearl didn't seem to notice; she was intent on the couple on the bed.

So that's it, thought Katherine: she enjoys watching. No wonder she wanted to hold a demonstration for me. Suddenly Katherine shoved Pearl hard and she went tumbling onto the bed on top of Paul and Sally. Katherine whirled and darted through the door and closed it behind her, shoving the heavy bolt to. Let *them* be the prisoners, she thought in satisfaction. Then she scampered down the narrow, winding staircase. The stairs ended abruptly after one flight, and she found herself in a sumptuous red-carpeted hallway. Above, Pearl and her employees were shouting and beating on the door, and all along the hallway doors opened and curious girls peered out. Katherine ran blindly down the hall and at last came to the main staircase. None of the girls tried to stop her; she caught a glimpse of her voluptuous visitor of yesterday, laughing.

Down the stairs she darted and across the salon to the heavy double doors leading into the hallway. Futilely she tugged at the doors; they were locked tight. For a moment she froze. What on earth was she to do? Over her head the clamor continued, and now she heard heavy, running footsteps. There must be another guard. Frantically she looked around her. A window! She ran to it and tried to push it up, but it wouldn't budge. Then she saw a small hassock, lifted it—Lord, how heavy it was!—and hurled it through the window. The glass broke with a gratifying crash, but before she could throw herself through it, someone grabbed her from behind, squeezing the breath from her. Ineffectually she flailed about with her arms and legs. Painfully he twisted one arm behind her, and she cried out. But one frantic hand grabbed a heavy ashtray and she blindly struck back at him with it. Luckily she managed to hit his head and he released her, crumpling to the floor.

Katherine retained her wits enough to kneel beside him and relieve him of his knife and pistol. Then she ran for the window and crawled out, not even noticing that she cut her arm in doing so. She looked back to see Paul and Pearl at the top of the stairs, he ludicrously naked and wielding a gun. She fired at him to slow him down, but didn't come close to hitting him. She whirled and ran out into the street—and stopped short at the sight of her phony rescuer casually strolling down the street. He at once took in the situation and begun to run toward her. She raised the gun and fired again, but it clicked uselessly. Damn! It wasn't a revolver, just an old single-loader. She hurled it from her in disgust. Then she remembered the knife still gripped in her other hand, took it, aimed, and tossed it at him. He went down heavily, clutching his shoulder. Thank God for Peljo's lessons. She dashed across the street and began to run in earnest, hoping she was running in the direction of Matthew's ship.

Behind her she heard running footsteps, but forced herself not to look back; it would only slow her down. The sound gained on her; it was right behind her—soft, slapping steps. Barefoot? Paul! Had she had the breath or time, she would have laughed. A woman clad only in her chemise and a stark naked man racing through the city streets. Suddenly he thudded into her and she went tumbling to the pavement, striking her head sharply. Everything went black.

When she came to, she was back in the room in the bordello. Softly she began to cry. They had caught her; she was back—worse than when she started. Her head ached terribly; her throat and mouth were dry, her stomach nauseous. And she couldn't move. Was she paralyzed? She turned her head and the world swam sickeningly. She closed her eyes and waited for the world to right itself, then cautiously opened her eyes again. She was tied! Her arms were outspread and a rope tied around her wrists and around the bedposts. Gingerly she lifted her head and looked at her legs; they were tied the same way. And she was naked, with no cover.

The door opened and Pearl entered. She walked to the bed and leaned over Katherine, her face filled with anger. Suddenly her hand lashed out and slapped Katherine twice. Katherine's head buzzed and she almost passed out again. Those pudgy hands, covered as they were with rings, packed a wallop.

"That was stupid, girlie," Pearl spat out. "I gave you a chance to cooperate. Now I'll have to be less pleasant. You have wounded Parker so badly, I'm afraid he is not up to dealing with you. But we have a customer who enjoys a little taming; I have sent a special invitation to His Lordship. Just think—you'll be entertaining a baron tonight!" She grinned wickedly. "But for right now, we have Paul to help prepare you for the honor this evening. Poor boy, he's somewhat out of sorts. You see, his feet—and his pride—are somewhat sore. Paul!"

His bulking shape loomed above her; his look was far from pleasant. He unbuttoned his trousers and began to stroke himself until his manhood stiffened. She tried to restrain her fear as he lowered his body onto hers and roughly entered her. She refused to cry out, biting her lower lip until it bled, digging her fingernails into her palms. Finally he stopped and removed the crushing weight of his body from her. Gratefully, she relaxed her tense body, but then she realized that he was not leaving. He unfastened the ropes from the bedposts and roughly turned her over on her stomach. Then he began to retie the ropes. What in the world was he doing to her? She began to struggle, suddenly struck with terror. Her arms and legs were stiff from being tied and he was far stronger than she, but Katherine managed to land a few blows before he got her retied.

For a moment he did nothing, just looked down at her, then said, "You put me to a little trouble, girl. And I intend for you to remember me."

The bed creaked under his weight as he straddled her. She choked back her cries as he entered her, held in her tears of pain and humiliation; she wouldn't give him the satisfaction. At last his body shuddered and he withdrew. He patted her bottom and strolled out of the room. Only then did Katherine burst into tears, burying her face in the bed to stifle her sobs.

"Oh, Matthew," she moaned. When would he come for her? He had to come.

Hours crept by. Her arms and legs ached from their spread-eagled position. She was hungry and thirsty. Her face was sticky and itching from crying. Stubbornly she refused to call out, to ask for anything to eat or drink. That was what they wanted; they wanted to break her, to bring her so low that she would submit to anything. Well, she wouldn't; she would show them they could not break her. She would hold out until Matthew arrived.

At last someone came and untied her and turned her over. She was too stiff and cramped to move, let alone put up a struggle as they retied her. Tears of rage sprang into her eyes and she began to curse them, screaming every insult she had ever heard Matthew or his men use. Pearl just chuckled gleefully.

"Go ahead, dear; His Lordship will like that. Gets him all excited."

Her tormentors left the room and Katherine subsided. A few moments later the door again opened and a well-dressed, graying man entered.

"Hello, my dear," he said pleasantly and strolled over to look at her. "Very nice. Very nice indeed. My compliments to Pearl."

He squeezed the inside of her thigh painfully, then slid his gloved hands up over her body. His hands roamed her, squeezing and pinching, till she yearned to cry out. Why on earth did he keep on his gloves? It was so ludicrous that, but for the pain and humiliation, it would have been almost funny. His eyes took on a new glitter as he withdrew a small stick from his pocket, a stick to which were attached tiny leather thongs. Katherine flinched involuntarily and he smiled. He applied the tiny whip to her in sharp little slaps. The little strings of leather hardly cut her flesh but were extremely painful, like hundreds of stinging little nettles hitting her skin. Finally she began to cry from the pain of it, and then he unbuttoned his trousers, shoved himself into her, and came quickly. He withdrew, rebuttoned his trousers, replaced the tiny whip in his pocket, and withdrew a small brown bottle.

"A parting gift," he said and smiled agreeably.

He took a little dab of ointment from the bottle and rubbed it into her wounds. It felt nice and warm; how peculiar he was. Then he replaced the bottle, removed his gloves, and said, "Good-bye."

Katherine stared after him in stunned silence. Her mind and body felt so bruised and battered she couldn't even come up with any coherent thought. Gradually the warmth of the ointment changed into a burning, itching torment and she writhed with the pain of it, choking and gasping on her own sobs. They left her for hours in her debased position, racked with the burning. At last they came and untied her, threw a blanket over her, and left her to huddle into a little ball and cry herself to sleep.

The next morning the terrible burning was gone, though her legs and arms still ached. She also felt as if she were dying of hunger and thirst. So when a maid brought in a bowl of the vile porridge, she gulped it down eagerly and was even grateful for the weak tea that accompanied it. After that she was left alone all day, free to torment her mind with the impossibility of her situation and the awful things that were no doubt planned for her this evening. She received no more food until another bowl of porridge late that afternoon.

About an hour later, she began to feel very peculiar— listless, sleepy, yet she could not sleep. Her room began to slant oddly and for the first time she realized that the floor sloped downward to the door. How very odd. And how odd that the ceiling was rising, moving away from her. It made her feel dizzy. Soon Pearl and a maid came in; their faces were strangely distorted.

"How do we feel?" Pearl asked brightly and patted her cheek.

"You're all hazy," Katherine said.

Pearl smiled and she and the maid pulled Katherine to her feet. She swayed slightly and stared at Pearl; she seemed so far away, but when Pearl reached out, she could touch her—her arms were fantastically long.

"I'm glad to see you becoming agreeable," Pearl said pleasantly. "Now we'll just get you all prettied up here."

The maid pinned a brief piece of gold material around Katherine's hips, then a longer diaphanous gold scarf. Another scarf was wrapped around her torso, barely covering the tops of her breasts and leaving her shoulders bare. Then a final veil was draped over her hair and down across her shoulders.

Pearl clapped her hands in delight. "Now, ain't that just beautiful? You're going to be a great success. Oh, the toe ring, Bessie, that will be just the right touch."

The maid knelt and slipped a ring with a great amber jewel onto her left large toe. Katherine looked down at herself in bewilderment. Pearl reached out and took her hand. Docilely Katherine followed her out the door and down the stairs. She was led into the red room, now full of noise and smoke and people. Katherine shrank back from it, but Pearl firmly led her in.

Pearl's booming voice rang out across the noise. "I have a special treat for you tonight, boys! Straight from a sultan's harem."

Immediately all heads were craning to see her. Pearl said something to Paul and he picked Katherine up and stood her on the black marble bar. Every eye in the room was riveted on her. Across the room, Katherine could see her reflection in the mirrors; surely that couldn't be she. Not that voluptuous creature wrapped in golden gauze, her breasts boldly thrusting out, her tawny hair tumbling wildly to her shoulders, her eyes huge and velvet-soft. She did look like something from a harem. That wasn't Katherine; no, Katherine was above her, floating up to the ceiling. She smiled to herself; how she had tricked them. They were all looking at the girl on the bar and here was Katherine on the ceiling, escaping them.

"Yes, gentlemen, this beauty was purchased at great expense from the harem of the great sultan Ibn Saud. Now, I was quite puzzled about who should get her her first night here, seeing as how you'd all be wanting her. And then I thought: Why not give her to the highest bidder? Huh, gentlemen?"

There was a murmur of approval. Slowly Pearl drew off the veil covering her head, then the gauzy material that covered her breasts. The room grew hushed in lustful anticipation. Pearl paused at the next scarf.

"No offers, gentlemen?"

Immediately men all over the room began to call out amounts, the numbers rising rapidly. Pearl laughed merrily and detached the next filmy veil. The voices rose in volume and number.

Katherine looked out numbly at the sea of faces, flushed with desire, eyes glittering. Dear God, why couldn't she move? Why did she feel so detached and filled with lassitude? Why couldn't she lift her feet to run from this new humiliation? Why couldn't she call out or even cry?

Keeping up a running chatter, Pearl pulled off each seductive veil. The clamor rose as they all leaned forward in anticipation, their faces lust-crazed. The figures they shouted rose staggeringly until finally the last veil fell away and her whole lovely ivory body was revealed. At the sight of her firm, smooth flesh, bewitchingly golden in the soft light, their voices reached a fever pitch.

"Calm down! Calm down," Pearl cackled. "Since you are all so fired up to have her, we'll have to do a little compromising here. Now this little beauty says she's willing to give you all a chance. Ain't that right, dearie? Highest bidder first and then on down. How does that sound? She *claims* she can handle the whole sultan's army. Let's just see what she can do, huh?"

Matthew slumped at his desk, his head cradled on his arms. It had been so long since he had slept. With one shaky hand, he reached out and poured himself another whiskey and downed it. Wearily he dragged a hand across his face. Three days—they had been frantically looking for her for three days, with no luck. She seemed to have vanished into thin air. Dear God, what had happened to her? Had she been seized and thrown into a ship headed for the brothels of Europe or the West Indies? Or was she still in Liverpool, locked away in the dark bowels of some filthy building? Either way, she would not have gone tamely. She wouldn't submit, he knew, and he also knew they would feel no compunction about hurting her. Or maybe—maybe she was dead.

All through his own selfishness. Hurt or dead, it was because of him. All his waking hours, while he searched the vice dens of Liverpool, his thoughts haunted him; he was plagued with guilt and remorse. He remembered the unkind things he had done to her, the way he had teased her, had forced her to submit to him, had tried to bend her will to his. And for no reason except that he wanted her and was angry because she didn't want him. Her spirit and independence—the very things that had made him love her because she was so different from all the others—he had tried to break, to conquer, even while realizing that no mastery over her was worth having unless she accepted it willingly, lovingly. He had been an impatient fool.

She hated him for the way he had treated her and now, rightfully, she would blame him for whatever horrible thing happened to her after she escaped him. He realized that if he found her, he would still not win her. But if only he could find her, that wouldn't matter. He would gladly give her up, return her to the American embassy, if only he could find her safe and sound. He could accept the awful, bleak pain of living without her, if only he could save her.

But after three days of searching, they had found nothing. Her earrings and engagement ring had been found at a pawnshop, but, even under the most forceful persuasion, the clerk could not remember who had pawned them. Tenderly Matthew touched the ring and hot tears seared his cheeks.

"Cap'n." Peljo popped his head inside the door, his voice full of barely suppressed excitement. "I've got somebody out here who says he has seen Miss Katherine."

Matthew's head shot up and he turned. "Who? Where is he?"

"On deck, sir."

Matthew crossed the room in two strides and ran up the steps to the deck. A man stood there, nervously wringing his cap.

"Who are you?" Matthew's voice rapped out.

The man gulped, frightened by the tall, unkempt, wild-eyed man before him. "Alfred, sir."

"All right, Alfred, describe this young lady you saw."

"Pretty, sir, dark blond hair, brown eyes, very tall. Talked funny, like a Yank."

"How was she dressed?"

"Dressed? I don't know; it had little flowers on it, I think."

"When was this?"

"Three or four nights ago, sir."

"What happened?"

"Well, me and my friend Ned was talking to her when this flashy-looking dandy comes up and stabs Ned."

"Just because you were standing there talking?" Matthew's voice was cold and hard as sleet.

The man cleared his throat and said, "Madman, I guess, sir."

"Is it not more likely that you were accosting this young lady?"

"We was just having a little fun, sir," Alfred whined.

Hampton's hand shot out and he grabbed the man by his shirt, lifted him up, and shook him. "Did you hurt her, you sniveling little—"

"No, no, I never touched her; I swear," the man squealed. "It was Ned, sir—honest."

Matthew stared at him with flinty eyes and said finally, "All right. Tell me what happened."

"Well, this man stabbed Ned with his cane, and—"

"With his cane?"

"Yessir. He had a little knife in the end of it."

"I've seen 'em like that," Peljo volunteered.

"Well, that's all. He stabbed Ned and I ran for my life."

"Leaving her there, of course."

The man squirmed.

"Well, describe the man with the cane to me."

"Flashy dresser. He had on a plaid suit—yellow and gray. And a fancy hat. And this cane."

"Sounds like a pimp. Is that what he looked like?"

"Yessir. But I don't know him."

Matthew turned to Peljo. "All right, Peljo, let's start looking for that man. Now."

Almost before the words were out of his mouth, he was gone, flying back to the seamen's dives. For hours his search was fruitless. But finally, early in the morning, a barmaid touched him on the shoulder.

"I heard you asking about that man with the cane."

"Yes." He looked at her eagerly. "You know him?"

"Maybe. Why you want him?"

"I think he's kidnapped a woman that—that I love."

The girl looked at him shrewdly. Then she said, "Well, you better find her quick then. That sounds like Parker; he works over at Pearl's. He gets girls for her."

"And where is this Pearl's?"

"I'll show you. But you won't be able to do anything by yourself. Pearl's got Parker and two guards; not to mention the customers."

"I can get several men. You just show me where."

"All right."

He delved into his pocket and crushed some money into her hand. "Wait right here while I get my men. I'll give you more when we get there."

The girl shrugged and nodded. Matthew rushed out to gather Peljo and his men. When he returned an hour or two later with his crew, armed to the teeth, the barmaid gaped in astonishment.

"You got an army there," she said.

"Not quite." Hampton smiled, filled with that ice-cold calm that always came just before battle was engaged. "Now lead on, dear girl."

She grabbed a shawl and hurried out into the cold of predawn. The streets by this time were quiet and littered with drunks. They followed the girl, silent and purposeful; Hampton had had no trouble enlisting their aid in finding Katherine. She had fed them when they were prisoners and tended them when they were wounded; they had long ago adopted her as their own.

Suddenly the girl stopped. "That's it. The one in the middle."

"Are you sure?"

"Yes."

"Good girl." He shoved more money into her hand and she scampered off.

Hampton strode to the front door and tried it. Locked. Calmly he shot the lock and then kicked the door open. Once inside the now-empty parlor, he picked up an ashtray and hurled it against a mirror. The crash brought a sleepy guard stumbling out; he stopped dead at the weapons drawn on him.

"I want to see Pearl," Hampton said.

"Pearl!" The guard's voice came out a whisper and he had to call again.

"Damn it, I had just gone to bed; what's going on?" Pearl stopped short at the head of the stairs.

"Madam, I have come about a new addition to your staff. A tall girl with dark gold hair and amber eyes—" he paused inquiringly.

Pearl's eyes bulged. "You can't be—"

Hampton laughed. "Matthew Hampton, ma'am. Has she threatened you with my wrath? Well she might. Where is she?"

"I don't know what you're talking about."

Hampton aimed his pistol and fired; a crystal chandelier crashed to the floor. Pearl set her face stubbornly.

Another chandelier fell. Then, in a burst of anger, Matthew dashed up the steps, grabbed her arm, and twisted it behind her.

"Where is she?"

"I don't know what you're talking about."

Hampton raised his pistol to her head. "Where is she?"

"Oh, all right," Pearl snapped. "I'll take you to her. Good riddance to her anyway. She broke one of my windows and gave Harry a lump on his head the size of an egg and damn near stabbed Parker to death."

Matthew roared with relieved laughter. "Oh, that's Katherine, all right. Take me to her. Peljo, come with me. The rest of you men, go through this house floor by floor, flush out all the guards and girls and customers. And break everything you find. Mirrors, furniture, wine bottles. Everything. Come along, Pearl."

He gave the spluttering Pearl a shove and she stalked off to the upper stairs.

Loud voices and crashes slowly pulled Katherine from her sleep. Her foggy mind could make no connection between her perception of the sounds and any identification of them. How far away everything seemed, how brightly colored. Faint laughter reached her ears and she smiled a little—Matthew. But of course Matthew was not here. Where was he? She tried to pull her fuzzy thoughts together, but gave up on it and closed her eyes, feeling herself float away, like a cloud on the air.

Matthew's pistol urging her on, Pearl climbed to Katherine's attic cubbyhole at a faster pace than usual. She unlocked the door and stepped inside, followed by Mat-

thew and Peljo. Matthew stopped dead at the sight of
Katherine asleep in the shabby bed, her face pale and
fragile. At the sound of their entry, her eyelids fluttered
open and she stared at them vaguely, no hint of recognition on her face.

Hampton had to swallow hard before he could speak.
"Katherine? Katherine, it's Matthew. Can you understand me? It's Matthew. I have come to take you home."

Katherine looked at him, frowning slightly. Suddenly
tears welled in her eyes and she lifted her arms up to him
like a child. "Matthew," she whispered.

Blindly Matthew shoved his gun into Peljo's hand and
went to Katherine. Wrapping her in the dingy sheet
which covered her, he lifted her tenderly in his arms.
Trustingly she put her arms around his neck and rested
her head against his shoulder.

"Matthew. I knew. I knew you would. I told her."

Matthew turned to leave, his face so cold and full of
fury that Pearl gasped and stepped back a pace.

"Peljo, set fire to this place. Madam, consider yourself
lucky that I don't cut your heart out."

He strode past her and out of the house, his boots
thundering on the stairs. Katherine slipped limply back
into sleep against his chest. Grimly he carried her
through the dawn-deserted slum streets, cuddling her
against him, his arms steel hard in rage.

Damn them. Damn everyone who had ever harmed
her, including himself. What had they done to her? Was
she drugged? Or teetering on the brink of insanity? She
had been so vague, so slow, so unlike Katherine. Had it
finally happened—was that stubborn spirit of hers fi-

nally broken? His heart felt as if an iron hand were squeezing it, squeezing it as if to remove all joy from it, all feeling, all happiness, until he would be left with only cold emptiness in his chest.

He boarded the *Susan Harper* and went down to his cabin, where he gently laid her down on the bed. Softly he pulled away the sheet from her body, barely suppressing a gasp at the sight of little purpling bruises scattered here and there over her body, smudges left by grasping, overeager hands. Careful not to wake her, he turned down the covers and slipped her into bed. Wearily he sat down on the edge of the bed himself, his head in his hands. Dear God, she would never forgive him. He would never forgive himself.

Slowly, sadly, he pulled off his boots, then stood to slip out of his clothes. He crawled in beside her and pulled her to his chest. Cradling her to him, he at last gave in to sleep.

Fourteen

$\mathcal{I}$t was hours before Katherine awoke. For a moment she thought herself in one of her dreams—lying in Matthew's arms, her cheek against his bare chest, the slow, even rhythm of his breathing a counterpoint to the gentle rise and fall of the ship. But gradually her still-hazy mind assured her that she was not asleep and dreaming; this was real.

"Matthew," she whispered. "Matthew." How had she gotten here? Why was it so difficult to think clearly? Thank God, at least the colors and distortions were gone.

"Mm?" he rumbled, still asleep.

"Matthew, wake up. I'm frightened."

His eyes opened. "Katherine? Are you all right?"

"Oh, Matthew." She squeezed herself against him. "Where are we?"

"My ship, love."

"Truly? Are we safe?"

"Very. We are on my ship, in my cabin with the door locked, and all around us on the ship are my men. No one can get to you or hurt you." He spoke softly, as to a child, and his arms tightened around her.

"Oh, Matthew." Suddenly the tears began to flow, spilling quietly down her face. "She said you wouldn't come, that you couldn't find me."

"But you knew better, didn't you?"

"I thought so, but I—I was so afraid you might not."

"I shall always find you, Kathy, you know that. Sweet Kathy. I won't let anyone hurt you." Softly he kissed her hair and murmured into it, "I love you."

"Matthew, you never told me about—about things like—"

"Like what, my love?"

"Like what he did?"

"Who?"

"Paul. The guard. He did—awful things to me."

"What?" His voice turned icy-cold.

"I can't—I can't talk about them. It's so horrid, so— oh, Matthew!" Suddenly she collapsed into tears and sobs shook her body.

Her story poured forth, coming out in fits and starts between choking sobs, so confused and nearly inaudible that he found it difficult to understand. But gradually he put together the pieces of her broken words, forming a searing picture of the pain and humiliation she had suffered at the hands of Paul and the unknown baron and the crowd of customers. A cold rage shook him, even as he calmed her, smoothing down her hair, gently rocking her in his arms, until finally, her emotions spent, she drifted into sleep.

He lay awake, staring blankly at the ceiling, his mind

tortured by the images he conjured up from her words. His hatred flamed—a fire both hot and cold, both searing and freezing. He would make them pay for hurting her, though they could never pay enough to heal her wounds. He lay there, his cold, hard purpose growing, until at last he gently disengaged himself from Katherine's arms and eased out of the bed. He dressed quickly, grimly, and left the room.

Again he sought out their barmaid-guide of the evening before. At the sight of his pale, set face, she said sympathetically, "Did you not find your woman, then?"

"Yes, I found her. And I am grateful for your help. But now I need some more of your help. Tell me where I can find the guard named Paul."

A frown touched her face. "Now that I don't know— since Pearl's burned this morning." Her eyes twinkled for a moment. "He sometimes sleeps with Maggie, down at the White Hare. Maybe she could tell you. He might have gone there with the House gone."

"Thank you." Matthew slipped a bill down the front of her low-cut dress between her swelling breasts. "You are an angel."

The girl smiled. "Lor', you're a fine one. That girl of yours is a lucky one, all right."

"I doubt she shares that opinion," he said, "but thank you, anyway."

"Well," she said, "if you ever need a sympathetic ear—or shoulder—"

He laughed and winked at her. "I'll remember you."

How easily it came with other women—the casual charm that captivated them. Once one of his mistresses had told him that he could wheedle a Yankee from his dollar. Why had he not used it on Katherine, the one woman who meant anything to him? Was it because she meant so much, was so special that he could not use the same charm he used so indiscriminately on others? Or because he wanted her so and was so blindly selfish to her desires that he just took without asking? Dear God, if only he had taken a little time and trouble to woo her; if only he hadn't been so rash and stubborn and over-confident!

At the White Hare, the tavernkeeper said that Maggie had not arrived for work yet and directed him to her flat. Matthew paused outside her door in the grimy hall and pulled his pistol. Perhaps she had not come to work because Paul had unexpectedly come to see her. He tapped sharply at the door and waited, listening to the noises within—surely there must be more than one person inside. The door opened a fraction and a girl's suspicious face peered out.

"Hello," Matthew said briskly. "I was told I could find Paul here."

"Why should you be looking for Paul?"

"I want him to do a little job for me. Could I see him?"

"Maybe." She relaxed a little and Matthew, seizing the slight advantage, flung his weight against the door and burst into the room, shoving the girl in front of him.

At his entrance, a half-naked man leapt from the bed. It was the same guard whom he first encountered inside Pearl's.

"You!" the man exclaimed. "What do you want now?"

Hampton advanced menacingly into the room. "Paul, I presume?" His smile was thin and bloodless.

"Yeah. What of it?" he said with a show of bravado. "Think you can take me without your army?"

"I want a name from you."

"You won't get it."

"Indeed?" Hampton's lip curled into a sneer.

"Damn you, I'd like to meet you when you ain't hiding behind that pistol."

"Well, you shall have your chance. You see, I intend to use a knife on you." Slowly, deliberately, he pulled a long glittering sailor's knife from his belt and reholstered his gun.

Paul gulped and stepped back a little at the deadly light in the captain's sea-gray eyes. Slowly, gracefully, Hampton moved toward him, his arms extended, half-crouching in the eternal knife-fighting stance.

"I ain't got no blade," Paul whined, sweating and backing away.

"That's true. But at least you aren't tied down—as you found it necessary to tie a girl to overcome her."

"She run away—I had to tie her. It was Pearl; she told me to."

Suddenly, Matthew flashed in and then back out, cutting a long slash down the big man's arm. Fresh red blood welled out and the girl gasped.

"Tell him what he wants, Paul," she urged.

"Shut up, Mag!"

"Katherine told me what you did to her."

"Some girls like it," Paul excused himself.

"And if they don't, you force them to do it anyway."

Paul rushed him, but Matthew neatly sidestepped him and drew his blade swiftly across his back. For the next few minutes Paul crashed about the room, alternately rushing Matthew and dodging his knife, until finally he stopped, winded and covered with sweat and blood from a hundred tiny cuts. Matthew faced him, his knife ready, still cool as death.

"Good God, man, whose name do you want?" Paul gasped, his eyes glazed with pain and terror.

"Another man assaulted her, a baron. She did not know his name. That's the name I want."

"I don't know his name," Paul said, and Matthew slashed at him, cutting across his chest.

Blood gushed out and Maggie went into hysterics, yelling at the huge guard to tell him the name.

"I don't know. I swear to God I don't know. She wouldn't tell us their names, the high and mighty ones. Didn't want us ruining her business by blackmailing them. I swear it. She never called him anything but 'His Lordship.' But Pearl knows—she can tell you."

"And where is Pearl?"

"A hotel—the Crescent."

"If you're lying—"

"It's the truth. I swear it."

"Then, for your information, I shall give you more than you deserve—a quick death." Matthew's arm flashed out, his knife spinning from his hand.

The big man fell, Matthew's knife in his heart. Maggie stared, too numb with fear to even scream, as Matthew retrieved his knife and wiped the blood from it, then returned it to his belt. He turned toward her and she shrank away.

"I suggest you dump him in the street and forget you ever saw me. Do I make myself clear?"

"Yessir. I wouldn't go to the constable, sir—never. I'll do just like you say."

"Good." He left the room without glancing back.

He found Pearl very reluctant to talk, even staring down the muzzle of his pistol. His Lordship, she explained, was very powerful; he could ruin her. It wasn't until he recounted Paul's death and paused meaningfully that she broke down and told him that it was Arthur, Lord Kenwick, that he sought. Matthew thanked her with a smile that made her shiver and left.

The sun was sinking as he approached Lord Kenwick's gracious town house. The air turned chilly as the sun disappeared, but Matthew didn't notice it. He let the doorknocker fall with a crash.

"Yes?" A haughty butler opened the door.

"I want to see Lord Kenwick."

"I am sorry, sir, but His Lordship is indisposed right now—"

Hampton shoved him aside and entered. "Goddamn it, where is he? Must I shout for him?"

"Sir!" The butler looked shocked. "Really, I must insist that you leave at once."

"Morgan, what is going on here?" snapped a crisp British voice, and Matthew looked up at the stairs to see a pale, disdainful-looking man.

"Milord, this man just—" the butler began.

Hampton cut into his explanation. "Lord Kenwick?"

"Yes?" The man's eyebrows rose haughtily.

"I would like to talk to you."

"Is it your custom to barge into a gentleman's home like this?"

"No, not into a *gentleman's* home." Matthew accented the word insultingly, and the butler gasped at his effrontery.

"I think you'd best explain yourself," Kenwick snapped.

"I think you'd prefer that we talk in private."

Kenwick looked at him for a moment, then shrugged and led him into the drawing room. Hampton closed the door after them.

"Well?" Kenwick turned to him. "What is the meaning of this?"

"I have come to call you out."

The Englishman stared. "You mean a duel?"

"Precisely."

"You must be mad! I've never even seen you."

"No, but you have dishonored a lady—*my* lady."

"Now see here, sir, I never—"

"Her name is Katherine, though you may not have bothered to call her by name. Let me jog your memory. She was the frightened, helpless girl you disported yourself upon two nights ago—the one tied to the bed. Ah, I see you remember."

"The whore?"

"Yes. The whore." The Southerner's voice was as brittle and dangerous as thin ice.

Kenwick laughed. "You must be joking. You've come to defend the honor of one of Pearl's doxies? She was a delicious little piece, of course, quite enjoyable, but hardly something to fight over. After all, she is there for the price—"

The sudden flame in Hampton's eyes made him cut short his words. Good God, he thought, the man is insane.

"That girl was no street girl selling her favors. Surely even an animal like you must have seen her breeding; do you think skin as fair and soft as that comes from the slums? She is the daughter of a wealthy Bostonian, a pampered, sheltered girl who had never known harshness or pain until—" He stopped to regain control of his voice. "She has never felt any man's touch but mine, and that but a short time—and God knows I never touched her in your manner."

"Your wife?" Kenwick looked startled. "I had no idea she was of gentle breeding."

"You mean you had no idea she had anyone to protect her. You know, everyone knows, that many of those girls are there unwillingly. Didn't Pearl ask you to subdue a recalcitrant girl? Couldn't you tell she wanted none of you? Yet you forced yourself upon her, and in the vilest way. I demand satisfaction, sir."

"Indeed? A gentleman doesn't duel with just any boor who happens to—"

"Damn it, man, it is only because you are a so-called 'gentleman' that I give you this chance and don't kill you on the spot as I did her other tormentor. If you refuse my challenge, however, I shall be forced to do so."

"My seconds will call on yours," Kenwick said stiffly.

"Good. Ensign Fortner, of my ship, the C.S.S. *Susan*

Harper, shall act as my second." Hampton strode to the door, then turned and smiled humorlessly. "If it makes you feel any better, you won't be killed by anyone of low birth. My grandmother traces our family back to an exiled noble of the court of Charles I." He bowed shortly and left the room.

Katherine awoke, her head much clearer than before. Matthew! She sat up—he was not there. For a moment she was gripped by the cruel fear that it had been only a dream, and her heart raced, but she forced herself to be calm. Wasn't this the familiar cabin of the ship? His cabin? She closed her eyes. Her battered mind and body could not quite grasp that she was safe, that they couldn't get her.

All the memories of the past days—some sharp and some mercifully hazy—filled her mind, and she felt sick and ashamed. Her body felt sticky and dirty and crawling with unspeakable filth. Oh, Matthew. Had she told him all about what they had done to her, or had that been a dream? It was so mist-enshrouded, it was difficult to tell. She had the sick feeling she had told him—was he filled with disgust for her? Oh, please, no. Matthew would understand; he wouldn't think her vile; he knew about these things.

The door opened and she looked up, her heart pounding in fear and hope. It was Matthew, looking so lean and strong and handsome that tears sprang into her eyes. She looked away, unable to meet his eyes, hating herself, her own unclean, violated body. They had dirtied her everywhere; there was not one pure spot on her body, not a single place that belonged only to him. Oh, God, she could not even offer herself to him in gratitude. She had nothing to give; they had taken it all from her. She wanted to throw herself at him, to kneel in submission, and promise herself to him for as long as he wanted her, promise to no longer fight and resist, but to give her body to him totally, give him all the things he had wanted from her, promise to do anything to please him. But she couldn't; she could not offer her body, made vile and repulsive by their touch, to him. It was sickening to think of putting her soiled body against his.

"Katherine?" His voice was gentle. He felt shaken by the sight of her abjectly huddled on the bed. Oh, God, she wouldn't even look at him. "Are you all right?"

"Yes, Matthew." Did he still want to hear his name on her lips? She would scream it from the rooftops now, if he asked it.

"I have brought you a bowl of soup. Can you eat a little? It smells delicious." His tone was coaxing.

"Yes, please; I'm hungry."

He gave the bowl to her and watched her gulp it down. Still she wouldn't look at him.

"Not so fast," he said. "You'll make yourself sick, and burn your mouth besides."

She forced herself not to gobble it. He was standing so close she could feel his breath on her hair. She wondered what he was thinking.

The soup made her feel better, and when she handed back the bowl she forced herself to look at him. His face looked tired and sad.

"Oh, Matthew," she whispered.

His heart lurched at the caress in her voice, and he bent to touch her arm. Frantically she scrambled out of his reach.

"Oh, no," she pleaded, "oh, please don't touch me." Didn't he see how dirty she was? He mustn't put his hands on her, mustn't soil them on her filthy skin.

Matthew paled and retreated. "Oh, God," he whispered, "what have I done?"

He turned and quickly left the room. Katherine ran to lock the door after him, then ran to the wash basin and thoroughly scrubbed every inch of her body until her skin was red and raw. She picked up the sheet that he had wrapped around her at Pearl's and tore it and stuffed it piece by piece into the stove. Next she changed the sheets she had slept on; even they seemed contaminated. After that she felt somewhat better.

Matthew leaned against the railing for a long time, staring out to sea. At last he turned and called for Peljo.

"I want you to go into the city, check the hotels, and see if Dr. Rackingham is still here. If he is, bring him to me."

"But, Cap'n," the little man expostulated, "have you lost your wits? You just found Miss Katie and now you're going to give her up to that old fool?"

"Peljo, I will do what I think best, and I would appreciate it if you kept your opinions to yourself."

Peljo choked back his response and left quickly. Matthew turned back to the sea. He must let her go; he knew it now, had known it since the moment he had realized that he loved her. She despised him; his very touch filled her with fear and disgust. From the first she had wanted only to escape him, but he had held her, brutally insensitive to the anguish she suffered, berating and teasing her for her shame at what he had done to her, constantly inflicting himself upon her—call it what it was: raping her. Well, he had broken her, he and the men at Pearl's. Now she cringed from his touch, too scared to even fight him any longer. He had killed Paul for it, and tomorrow he would kill Kenwick. Nor would the other villain go unscathed; perhaps his punishment on himself would be even worse—for he was going to give her up, hand her over to Dr. Rackingham. Let her escape from him and pray that her slow Yankee lieutenant would be able to teach her the ecstasy that lay dormant in her body. He clenched his fists at the thought of another man exploring her body, tasting its sweetness, arousing her. He saw her lovely long legs twined around him, heard her moans of desire. With supreme effort, he wrenched his mind away from the picture he had created, only to find it replaced by a worse one—her writhing in pain and fear beneath Kenwick's hands.

His tortured thoughts were interrupted by the aging doctor who approached him, tagged by the glowering Peljo. The doctor's face was so suspicious that Matthew had to smile fleetingly.

"Dr. Rackingham, I've decided to release Miss Devereaux into your hands."

"I *knew* you still had her."

"Actually, I did not at the time, but that's of no matter. Miss Devereaux escaped and I am afraid suffered a rather sordid and—and harrowing experience." He turned and stared back at the sea, his voice carefully toneless. "Even I cannot bring myself to cause her any more grief. So I am letting her go. She needs someone to look after her, help her home. She's—" He paused, struggling to keep control of his voice. "She is feeling rather bad, you see."

Rackingham stared. "Good God, what happened to her?"

"She will tell you if she wishes to," Hampton said shortly.

"Of course, but—poor girl."

"I have a condition, Doctor."

"Oh?"

"I want everything about what has happened to her kept quiet. I want to keep as much scandal as possible from her. I trust in your discretion—I know very little about proprieties."

The man stiffened. "It is a little late to be thinking about her reputation, isn't it?"

"Yes, but I can hardly undo what is done, Doctor. The best I can hope is to cover it up. Could you manage to combat the rumors—say we slept in different cabins?"

"Yes, but you know how little effect that will have against rumor. And has it occurred to you that she might be—with child?"

Matthew looked at him, stunned. "Pregnant? My God—what's to be done? I would raise the child; perhaps she could remain here until it's born. People will talk, of course, but they wouldn't *know.*"

"Captain Hampton, if you are in fact concerned about Miss Devereaux's honor, if you do regret what you have done, why don't you marry her? Give her the protection of your name."

"Sweet Jesus, man!" Hampton swung toward him and in the dim light Rackingham saw the naked pain in his face. "Do you think I wouldn't gladly marry her? I love her," he rasped. "But she would never consent; she despises me. She cringes at my touch." His voice broke and he turned away.

"Have you asked her?"

Hampton shook his head.

"Captain, you did not see, as I did, the way she hung by your bed all through your illness, the way in which she took care of you. I think that inside she is fonder of you than she cares to admit."

"A lot has happened since then, Doctor, none of which would endear me to her. I am afraid that at the moment she must hate all men."

"Nevertheless, to guard against disgrace, especially if she is carrying your child—"

"You do not know Katherine very well if you think that. She sticks steadfastly to her principles and ignores the consequences. However, I shall ask her."

There was a moment of silence and then Rackingham asked, "When is she to leave?"

"I think she should rest another night. She's still a little shaky. Tomorrow morning, I guess." He could not bring himself to separate from her just yet. "I have a rather early appointment and I shan't be here. Perhaps it would be best if you left then."

"When is your appointment?"

"Six o'clock."

The older man raised his eyebrows, but said nothing. It sounded like a duel—what had gone on here since he left the ship? Poor Katherine; perhaps it was best not to inquire.

"I have a few things I bought for her; she probably will refuse to take them. Would you please take them along? Perhaps she might accept them later."

"Yes, of course." Rackingham felt a twinge of sympathy at the suffering underlying his quiet tone.

"Thank you." Hampton shook his hand, and the doctor took his leave. Matthew took a deep breath and headed for his cabin.

Katherine was in bed but not asleep. She looked a little better, not so pale or vacant-eyed, but she still acted shy and afraid. Hampton forced himself to smile at her.

"How are you, Katherine?"

"Better. Why did I feel so strange and dizzy? Why did everything look funny, all out of shape and brightly colored?"

"I think they must have drugged you. So you wouldn't resist. Fortunately, I think it's made your memories less sharp."

Katherine sat up and hooked her arms around her knees. Why was Matthew standing across the room like that? She wished he would come sit beside her, hold her hand; she would feel better that way.

"Katherine, are you pregnant?" he blurted out, then cursed himself for being a clumsy fool.

She looked at him in surprise and said, "What?"

"Are you carrying my child?"

"I—I don't think so." She blushed and ducked her head.

"Do you even know how to tell?"

"I'm not sure. You get sick at your stomach. But the old ladies never really tell you about it if you're unmarried."

He grimaced. "Lord, they love to keep you ignorant, don't they? Some have morning sickness, but others don't. The best sign is if your periods stop."

She blushed again and said in a tiny voice, "No, Matthew."

"Good." He paused and stared into space. Finally he plunged in. "Katherine, I apologize to you for what I have done; I am afraid I have been very cruel. I did not mean to be; I was simply too selfish to see what harm I was doing to you."

She said nothing, simply stared in amazement, and he hurried on. "Anyway, I have decided to let you go. You are no longer my prisoner. Dr. Rackingham will come here tomorrow morning to get you. You won't be afraid with him, will you?"

Numbly she shook her head. He was sending her away! She began to tremble. Why was he sending her away?

"I didn't tell him what happened to you. I thought you would not want me to. He will take you home and help you try to gloss over what happened. He—he thought you might consider marrying me." He picked up a paperweight from the desk and rolled it in his hand, fixing his gaze on it. He cleared his throat. "Would you, Katherine? I would take care of you and never intrude upon you. Nor would I hold you to your wifely duties; it would be a marriage in name only, of course. We could have separate bedrooms, and you would have a lock on your door."

"Oh, no!" Katherine gasped. That was it: he no longer desired her. He was filled with disgust at her unclean body, just as she was. Rackingham was trying to make him marry her, but he wanted to be rid of her, would not even touch her if they married. She was swept by a wave of shame; she was repulsive to him.

In a shaking voice she said, "I will go, Matthew."

His fist closed around the paperweight so hard that the muscles of his forearm bulged. "All right. I will just sleep here in the chair tonight, if you don't mind. So you won't be afraid. I bought you this box of things in London. Please take them with you."

"All right."

Without undressing, he turned off the light and settled down in the chair to sleep. Katherine pressed her hand against her mouth to hold back the tears. Oh, God, what was she to do now, all alone?

In the chill of early dawn, the sound of approaching horses was clear and crisp. Matthew watched silently as the carriage pulled to a halt and Kenwick and his second stepped out. The baron looked Britishly cool and calm. Matthew felt his stomach knot; in a moment the baron would be Britishly cool and dead. Britons were fools; the thing they did best was die. Witness the Crimea, where they had floundered about incompetently and claimed triumph because they had fallen so well.

Impatiently Matthew waited through the formalities: checking the pistols, choosing them, the request by the judge for reconsideration. They stood back to back, then at the signal paced away, turned . . . his body sideways to present a narrow target, Matthew fired, saw Kenwick recoil as the bullet struck him, and then felt a sudden spear of pain and a blow that knocked him flat as Kenwick's bullet slammed into him.

"Captain, Captain, please wake up." Fortner's anxious voice seeped into his brain.

Matthew made a determined effort to open his eyes, then closed them against the glare of the rising sun. He heard Fortner exclaim in relief. So the son of a bitch had hit him. Again he opened his eyes to see Fortner's boyish face floating above him.

"Are you all right, sir? Can you stand?"

"Of course I can stand," he said gruffly. "Is he dead?"

Fortner's eyes lit in admiration. "Indeed he is, sir. Cleanest shot I ever saw."

"Good. Then I suggest you and I visit a doctor."

The doctor cleaned his wound and pronounced him lucky the ball had gone clean through and not lodged in his arm. The oversize fee they left compensated his curiosity.

When they reached the ship, they were greeted by Peljo's sour face. "Well, she's gone, sir. Crying like a baby, too."

Matthew felt as if the wind had been knocked out of him. "Shut up, Peljo."

He shook off Fortner's supporting arm and walked to his cabin. It looked the same, except for the swelling emptiness of her absence. Matthew sat down at his desk and propped his head on his good hand. This afternoon he would return to London and spur Redfield to come up with that mission of his. He hoped grimly that it was suicidal.

He wondered how the War was going. The reports from the British correspondents were of course outdated and probably inaccurate as well. It sounded bad for Lee; they were steadily losing ground. No surprise to the Navy; they had been losing since the War began. He shrugged. What did it matter? Doomed country; the gallows waiting at the end for a Rebel pirate; Shel gone and half his friends, maybe David now, too; the family bankrupted. To hell with it. If he had had Katherine— well, that would be something to live for—a new life with her, children, dreams, hopes. But now, well, might as well be like the British and make a good end. He opened his desk to pull out a bottle of whiskey and a gleam of silver caught his eye. He reached in and pulled it out— Katherine's silly little popgun. Softly he ran a finger down the handle. Scalding tears slid down his face and splashed upon the metal.

NEW YORK

Fifteen

*A*fterward Katherine could hardly remember the first few days away from Hampton; it seemed as if she had done nothing but eat, sleep, and cry. While they waited for a ship leaving for the States, Dr. Rackingham kindly left her alone, realizing that sleep would heal her far better than any of his ministrations. So she lost herself in sleep, too shattered to face her broken world—the terror of her aloneness, the emptiness without Matthew, the intense self-disgust. She never left her room, taking her meals there, too. She locked the door and kept a chair under the knob, and checked the locked windows a hundred times a day.

Gradually, however, her fear began to recede, especially after they boarded the ship for New York. At sea, insulated by the encircling ocean, she could feel more secure. She took long walks around the deck, and the brisk sea air revived her. Her brain began to function again, and all the horrors that lurked at the back of her mind she was able to separate and bring to the forefront one by one where she could focus the light of reason on them and gradually wither them to nothingness. Day by day, she felt her strength of character returning, growing to fight the turmoil within her. And as it did, she realized that she must fight to regain herself. No one could restore her but herself; she had to destroy all the demons on her own.

First she had to recover her own self-respect, and that was the most difficult part. Each day she coached herself in all the reasons why she was not to blame for what had happened, why she was not the wrongdoer, why she must not hate and punish herself. Her humiliation lessened, she began to look straight at people again and not off to the side. Her first understanding, painful acceptance of Hampton's rejection passed, and was replaced by bitter resentment and anger. Oh, yes, it was fine for him to take her, willing or not, and be maddened when she protested. But if other men took her, then she was no longer fit for him. It did not matter that they had raped her; it did not matter that he had known far more women than she had men. Oh, no, all that mattered was that someone else had used her, and therefore he no longer wanted her. Damaged goods, that's all she was, and so he tossed her aside.

And how stupid it was of her to be hurt because he no longer wanted her. Naturally, she had focused on him during her trials and had viewed him as her savior because he had charged in with his huge, commanding presence and taken her from her tormentors. She had been consumed with gratitude and so ready, even eager, to repay him by throwing herself at his feet. That was why she had wanted so to cling to him, and been so destroyed when he sent her away. But now that she could put things in their proper perspective, realize her gratitude for what it was, and recall that it was his fault that she had been put in a position where he had to rescue her, she could see that it was silly to be hurt. After all, had he not done what she had been begging him to do all along?

The days at sea slipped by and Katherine's mental recuperation sped along, helped by pleasant conversations with the doctor and their friendly games of chess and large chunks of time spent alone to quiet her nerves in sewing or to soothe her raw emotions in reading. Her irrational fears died; her firm jaw and clear, straight gaze returned; her spirit revived. But nothing helped fill the aching emptiness inside her. Sadness darkened her eyes; she was slower, quieter, less likely to return a witticism. It seemed as if there were always a steel band around her chest—squeezing, squeezing. No wonder, she told herself, since her life was ruined. No man would have her now; she would be shunned by Society, doomed to while away her life in the musty company of Aunt Amelia. That was reason enough, surely, for her to sob her heart out nearly every night.

It was some time before she could bring herself to open the box he had given her. She wanted no more to do with it than he had, but finally curiosity won out: why, and what had he bought for her in London? On top lay a little white box; inside a delicate gold chain nestled against black velvet. She gasped at its simple, fragile beauty and hurried to clasp it around her throat and preen at her image in the mirror. A faint smile curved her lips. Damn the man, he had excellent taste. She returned to the box and pulled out a lace and ivory fan, beautifully carved, and lovely, lacy, enticing underthings. Her smile broadened. Shocking, really, and no protection from the cold, but how subtly provocative against one's bare skin, the sort of thing one wore only to have taken off. She blushed at her thoughts, a little ashamed of herself that she could feel a tingle of excitement at the thought of sex after the awful things she had been through. Sternly she put aside the underthings and dove into the box again, retrieving this time a nightgown that made her blushes seem inadequate. White, gossamerlike, pristine yet completely revealing. Quickly she undressed and slipped it on. It clung softly to her, concealing nothing, yet somehow was more enticing for the gauzy hint of covering it gave. Dreamily she looked in the mirror. She would have put it on and the fragile chain also, and then walked toward him, so that the slit sides revealed alluring glimpses of her bare flesh. And he would have smiled that little, almost mocking grin, his eyes burning, watching her, not moving. When she reached him, he would have reached out and slid his fingertips down her, grazing her breasts and stomach.

Good heavens, what was she doing? Standing about dreaming wanton daydreams! Hurriedly she jerked off the filmy gown and redressed, then opened the box to pull out bolts of cloth—deep rose, emerald, and— breathtakingly beautiful—pale gold satin. She touched them softly; he must have selected them carefully, for the colors were just right for her. He had thought of her in London, taken the time to select things to please her, things that were meant only for her and no one else.

How could he have done that and then rejected her so coldly? For that matter, why had he even bothered to save her, just to throw her out? Hadn't he whispered "I love you" as he comforted her? Or had that only been a delusion caused by that drug they had given her? Had he said it? Meant it? Was it possible that her defilement had so completely destroyed his feeling for her? No, he could not have said it; he could not have loved her and then rejected her so. She felt the salty taste of tears and realized that she was crying. Would she never stop all this weeping? Sternly she wiped away her tears, returned all the presents to the box, and shoved it out of sight.

The voyage was a long one, as the ship sailed first to Nassau and spent several days exchanging cargo before continuing its journey to New York. Katherine was glad, especially for the sunny, sleepy days in Nassau. The longer she delayed facing Boston, the better she would feel. But at last the vessel docked in New York City, and Katherine and the doctor continued their journey to Boston on the train.

Rackingham telegraphed her father from New York, and when they stepped off the train they found the Devereaux carriage waiting for them. A smile of genuine welcome split the coachman's professionally blank face for a moment, and Katherine smiled back, but felt a pang that her father had not come himself. She found it hard to reenter the restrained, formal world of Boston society after the tumultuous, emotional weeks spent with Matthew. The streets, the buildings, even her own house as they approached it were all so familiar, and yet somehow so strange. She was gripped by a sudden, icy realization that she no longer belonged here, and she wanted to cry. Was there anyplace she belonged now?

The butler opened the door and led her to the drawing room, where Mr. Devereaux and Aunt Amelia awaited her. Her father hugged her joyfully and her aunt burst into tears. Katherine kept hold of her father's hand, hoping that soon the barrier of her strangeness would fall. She was overjoyed to see them again, of course, but—why did she feel so sad, as if something was missing? Before long, pleading travel weariness, she retired to her room, leaving her relatives to talk to Dr. Rackingham.

"Oh, Miss Kate! I'm that glad to see you!" Pegeen ran to her and gave her a hearty hug.

Katherine returned her hug and then closed her bedroom door. Somehow she felt better here with her maid.

"Oh, miss, you have no idea how dreadful it's been without you."

"Well, I have missed you, too, Pegeen. In fact, I discovered that I hardly knew how to do a thing for myself!"

The Irish girl laughed, then suddenly sobered. "Oh, Miss Katherine, was it very dreadful? I—he didn't harm you, did he?"

"No." Katherine sat down on the bed, tired. "He didn't harm me."

"I knew he wouldn't. They all said he was a Rebel devil and no telling what he would do to you. But I thought he was a fine gentleman, even in chains like that. And the way I had seen him look at you, I knew he wouldn't hurt you. He just wanted to—you know."

"Yes, I know."

"It's dreadfully exciting to think how much he must have wanted you, kidnapping you like that, right in the teeth of the Navy."

"I am sure he loved the danger of it."

"But he must have known how much worse they would be to him for taking you as well as escaping."

Katherine sighed. "Matthew fears nothing, I found—and for good reason. Oh, Pegeen." She turned to her, her face suddenly alight. "If only you had seen him in the midst of battle. He's magnificent; so audacious." Katherine, for the first time having a receptive audience, found herself pouring out all her memories of his bravery and skill and determination: the battle, the storm, tricking the captain of the *Susan Harper*.

Pegeen was enthralled and elated at the change in her mistress. She seemed so much prettier, warmer. "But, mum, why ever did you leave him?" she burst out.

Katherine's face closed and she looked away. "He is a wonderful sailor and fighter, Pegeen, but not particularly good at being a human being. He's arrogant, selfish, and cruel. Besides, how can you think that I would live in sin willingly with any man?"

"I am sorry, miss; I know you are a good, moral woman. It's just that—well, you seem to love him."

"Don't be absurd, Peg. I am simply aware of his attributes as a captain. Also, I am grateful to him for saving me from something quite dreadful."

"What?" Pegeen asked, her eyes wide.

"Frankly, a life in a brothel."

"Saints preserve us, mum! You mean you was actually in one of them places?"

"Yes, unfortunately. But Captain Hampton rescued me. And then he let me go. He no longer wanted me, after—"

"Oh, Miss Kate." Pegeen hastened to put a comforting hand on her arm. "How terrible! He is a wicked man for turning you out like that. I can't see why men think it's so awful for a girl to have slept with other men, while they have any number of women they want. And especially when it wasn't even your fault. They are so unfair!" Her poor mistress—men were such beasts. Anyone could see she was eating her heart out for him, for all her saying she didn't love him. But *he* threw her over because some other man had raped her. Pegeen felt a sudden urge to find that handsome scoundrel and choke him to death. Poor Miss Katherine, whatever would she do now?

The doctor stayed on with them for several days, urged by Mr. Devereaux, who realized how much he owed to the old gentleman. Katherine was grateful for his company; he was the only person now who was secure and familiar. Though they never talked of Matthew, she knew the shared experiences of Matthew's ship would be gone from her forever when he left. Besides, he was the only relief from the company of her aunts—and they were almost more than Katherine could bear.

Aunt Amelia, true to form, was weepy and forever trying timidly to comfort her calm, strong niece. If it had not been so irritating, Katherine would have found it amusing. Aunt Amanda, however, amused her not at all. That worthy matron came to call the day after Katherine's return, her face a study of righteous pity and for-giveness.

"Poor child," she sighed tearfully, hugging Katherine to her massive bosom. "Thank God you have been re-turned to us."

Katherine forbore to comment that they had hardly been on the best of terms when she left. Amanda wiped away an imaginary tear and seated herself wearily.

"This time has been such anguish for me, for us all. Why, poor James—"

"Please, Aunt Amanda, spare me," Katherine said dryly.

"He was quite driven to distraction," his mother said firmly.

"I am sure that would not be too difficult."

"Katherine, you are the most ungrateful child! Why, that boy is willing to marry you, even now, just to save your good name!"

"I am sure that is very kind of him, Auntie, but I shan't require such a dreadful sacrifice from him."

"Well, I doubt your penniless lieutenant will have you now, although he may be even that anxious to trap your fortune."

"I intend to release him from his obligation," Kather-ine said evenly.

"Of course." That seemed to improve her aunt's humor and she smiled again. "Naturally the family must close ranks now. You can depend on Amelia and me to stand by you. If only you had listened to me and stayed home, like a decent young girl, instead of traipsing down to those docks every day, none of this would have happened. I trust that now you will depend on my advice and perhaps we will be able to lessen this blot on the Fritham name."

"Whatever are you talking about?" Katherine said coldly.

"I am talking about what we must do now. I think that after a while, if you stay quiet and don't cause any further fuss, *and* if you marry James, after a proper time, of course, to prove—" She paused meaningfully.

"That I'm not pregnant?" her niece snapped, and Aunt Amelia gasped and began to fan herself.

"Katherine, please, no doubt being around that Rebel monster has made you forget what few manners you once had, but if you ever expect to be allowed to enter a decent house again, you had better learn a little propriety!" Amanda said heatedly. "Until now, your peculiar notions have been tolerated because of your name, which you have managed to besmirch through your stubborn, headstrong ways, and from now on, you'll have to tread lightly, or you will never get even a toe into Society again."

"But I have done nothing wrong!" Katherine blazed. "Why should Society be closed to me?"

"Whether it was willing or forced, you are still a fallen woman; and remember, if you had not flaunted yourself down at the docks—"

Katherine leaped to her feet. "You're convicting me on no evidence. How does all Boston know what happened to me—how do you, for that matter? I tell you, and Dr. Rackingham will verify—"

"Really, Katherine, it hardly matters what happened.

Just the fact that you were in that beast's company for so long condemns you."

"This is outrageous! I will not stand for it."

"Dearest, please," Amelia interjected timidly, "Amanda is right. You are in disgrace, child. You cannot go out as you once did. Certainly not to the yards. Or even to the opera or the theater. And, of course, we shan't be invited to any parties."

"And you expect me to just fade out of sight like that? Hole up in here with you and never go anywhere? Just sit over my needlework all day or read uplifting novels?" The rage boiled up within her and spilled over. "Well, I'll be damned if I will! I am not to blame for what happened, and I will not be judged on supposition, either. I intend to readopt my way of life, just as it was! In fact, I think that I shall have a dinner party this very week!"

She stormed out, leaving the two stunned women staring after her.

Almost immediately, she regretted her words. She had absolutely no desire to see anyone, let alone face a whole room full of avid, curious faces. But she had rashly committed herself, and she had to brazen it out.

The thing was a disaster from start to finish. Half the people she invited coldly refused, and the others came out of morbid curiosity. Lillian Stephens was one of those who came, her face full of malicious triumph. Her father, once Katherine's suitor, assiduously avoided her. The rest conveyed disapproval even as they plied her with questions, all studiously skirting the matter of her downfall.

"How awful for you," Lillian said, demurely casting down her eyes. "Is that pirate really such a devil as they say?"

"Don't be silly," Katherine said calmly, though she felt a sudden stab of pain. Oh, if only Matthew were here, he would—he would what? Why, just put his hand against her arm to support her and look at them with that icy stare, and none of them would dare look at her in that shocked, superior, disapproving, eager way. "He was a perfect gentleman the entire time, even though I was his hostage. Did you not find him an exceptionally courteous man, Dr. Rackingham?"

"Why, yes, I did," the old man lied stoutly, though his eyes twinkled at her in shared mirth. "Gave Miss Devereaux and me the best cabins, while he and his ensign slept with the men."

"Indeed?" Mary Whitman said slyly. "I had understood that Southern men were really shocking and not at all genteel."

Katherine was seized with a sudden desire to describe her true adventures, just to see the shock on their faces, but she forced herself to remain calm. "Oh, my goodness, no, where social graces are concerned, I know of no one but the English who can match them." She suppressed a smile, thinking of the Englishmen she had met! "And I believe he was quite the bravest man I ever met."

"Why, Katherine," Lillian said innocently, "you have turned into a Rebel lover."

"Hardly. I just don't blind myself to their good points."

"Absolutely." Dr. Rackingham jumped in to draw

their fire and led into a rambling, boring, fictitious account of their days at sea.

Katherine's one charge at the bastions of Society finally ended, and she did not try it again. No one called on them or invited them to social gatherings. Her life settled down into a frustrating, boring regimen of idle handwork and socializing with Aunt Amelia. Her father adamantly refused to allow her to return to her work at the shipyards.

"My Lord, Katherine," he said when she broached the subject, "how can you think I would expose you to danger like that again? I have been consumed with guilt ever since he kidnapped you. If only I hadn't been so selfish, it would never have happened. But because I needed you there, I let you work, even though I knew I should not have. I certainly shan't make the same mistake."

"Good heavens, Father!" Katherine stared at him. "Surely you can't believe that there is anyone else capable of doing what Matt—Captain Hampton did. Or rash enough to even try it, for that matter. Besides, the prisoners are not allowed to work there now, so there is no possibility that it could happen again."

"Katherine, I simply cannot risk it. There are other things that could happen. It simply is not a safe place for a woman. Besides, it was scandalous before, when your name was spotless, but now, with your reputation already so—"

His daughter rose, her voice cold as ice. "Please, Father, you need say no more. I quite understand your desire that I not blacken your name any further. In fact, if you will give me a modest stipend, I shall be happy to change my name and move to another city. Someplace far away, of course—California, say? Or would you prefer I moved to another country? France might accept me, ruined as I am."

"Katherine, please, there is no need to act like this. I am only thinking of you. It's your safety and reputation I'm thinking of."

"Father!" she snapped. "I have been kidnapped, raped, and abused—by more men than Matthew Hampton; I have been in a battle, tended wounded men, and lived through a North Atlantic storm; I have stabbed one man and tried to shoot another. And now you expect me to spend the rest of my life knitting and sewing?" Violently she stormed out of the room, leaving her father staring after her.

Though she icily avoided her father, he did not give in and permit her to go back to work. Daily she and Pegeen took a brisk walk, but that took up very little of her time. She read a great deal and spent a large amount of time daydreaming. She grew quite tired of knitting mufflers and stockings and monograming handkerchiefs and doing needlepoint. Then she was seized with the idea of making Matthew's material into dresses. For the first time since she had returned, she enjoyed what she was doing. Eagerly she and Pegeen pored over pattern books and fashion magazines and cut and sewed. The rose pink she turned into a simple day dress with a scoop neck and puffed sleeves, remembering how Matthew had said the little muslin dress had shown off her beautiful chest. The emerald wool they made high-necked and long-sleeved, with a touch of lace at collar and cuffs to soften it. She tried them on and Pegeen declared the dusky pink one lovely and the green one simply elegant. And then they fashioned the gold satin into a lovely ball gown. Katherine knew there was no point; she would never have the chance to wear it, but she didn't care. She made it to wear for Matthew, not to wear for Boston. The neck was low-cut and square, exposing the elegant column of her neck, the creamy, soft expanse of her chest, the swelling tops of her breasts. The sleeves were narrow and tight and came to a point on her hands, accenting her slender hands and delicate wrists. The skirt belled forth in yards of material, making her waist appear tiny. It was very simple and understated, but suited to her; when she put it on, her hair and eyes and gown all seemed to blaze and shimmer and her skin looked invitingly warm and golden. He knew, she thought, he knew how I would look in this. He saw the beauty in me that no one else ever had. She grimaced; damn him—why did it have to be such a heartless, cold man who saw her beauty?

Carefully she folded her golden gown in tissue paper and stored it away. Her emerald dress was packed away in mothballs to save for winter. But the pink one she wore, much to the disapproval of Aunt Amanda, who pronounced it quite sinful. Katherine, however, was like a child after her first taste of sweets. After all, Boston couldn't keep her from shopping. She and Pegeen bombarded the stores, buying shoes and cunning hats and gloves and ribbons and hair combs and parasols. Most of all, they bought yards of material and the latest *Godey's*. Katherine was not about to entrust herself to the Boston dressmakers. If she was outside the pale, so be it; she would dress just as she pleased. So she and Pegeen made her dresses, their nimble fingers turning out a gold-and-white-striped traveling suit that looked good enough to eat, a frosted green morning dress that was scalloped around the bottom so that frothy white lace peeked out, a chocolate brown silk evening gown with a figured brown and tan bodice and a sweeping train, and countless others, all suited to her coloring and style and attributes, without a spinsterish one among them.

Aunt Amanda seemed on the verge of a seizure over Katherine's buying sprees and the sort of clothes she was making. It was shocking, she declared. She should, by all rights, be meekly hiding her shame, yet here she was out in public, buying positively gaudy clothes, acting not one whit ashamed. She was, in fact, dangerously close to acting like a loose woman. Katherine simply laughed at that and said, "But, Auntie, that's what I am."

One afternoon, as Katherine sat in her father's study, trying to puzzle out a book on naval strategy, the butler entered to tell her that she had a caller.

"A caller?" she repeated, startled.

"Lieutenant Perkins, Miss Katherine."

"William!" Katherine sprang to her feet, and the book in her lap went tumbling to the floor. "What is he doing here?"

The butler said impassively, "What shall I tell him, miss?"

Katherine recovered herself enough to say, "Show

him in, of course. I shall see him in here—and there is no need to inform my aunt that he is here."

Something close to a smile flickered briefly, but he said only, "Very good, miss."

Katherine picked up the book and replaced it on the shelf, all the while trying to bring her mind into some sort of order.

"Katherine!" Lieutenant Perkins paused in the doorway, struggling for control.

"William." She dropped him a nervous little curtsy.

He crossed the room in two strides and took her hand and kissed it tenderly. "Oh, Katherine, my dear, are you all right?"

"Yes, very." She blushed, confused. "Please sit down, William."

He sat down, pulling his chair close to hers, and once again took her hand in his.

Katherine smiled at him stiffly. "I thought you were on the blockade."

"No; we are stationed in New York now. I wrote your father as soon as we docked, inquiring about you, and he telegraphed me that you were home and safe. So as soon as I could finagle a pass, I caught a train up here."

Katherine looked at him and then back at her hands. "William, you must know that I have to call off our engagement."

"What? Katherine, don't be silly."

"I am afraid I am quite a scandal," she said lightly.

"You cannot think I care about that! Katherine, my only concern is that you are safe and well. Why, I could kill that scoundrel with my bare hands, if he weren't already dead, but—"

"Dead?" she echoed, stunned. "Hampton is dead?"

He shrugged. "He suddenly disappeared about a month or so ago in England. No one seems to know for sure, but the word is that he killed a nobleman in a duel and that he was wounded in the arm. Then the arm got infected, and the last anyone heard he was in London on the verge of death, and then he simply dropped out of sight. The Rebels say he has gone home, but they are just trying to conceal his death, because he hasn't attacked a single ship or put into port anywhere. And his ship, the *Susan Harper*, left England under a new skipper. When we put into port and heard that he had died and there was no mention of you, I wrote your father immediately to see if he had heard from you."

Her head whirled; she felt dazed, as if all the air had been knocked out of her. Dead? Matthew could not be dead. Blindly, she groped for something to catch hold of in what he had said.

"He killed a nobleman?"

"No one knows for sure. They say he dueled some baron in Liverpool."

"Liverpool?" Her heart began to thud heavily. "Why?"

"Something unsavory about a girl in a—" he blushed, "the kind of place a lady wouldn't know about."

That meant a brothel. He had killed a Liverpool nobleman over a girl in a brothel. Not her baron, surely. Dear God, if he had been killed because of that maniac's abusing her! Dear God, if he was dead! I will die, she thought numbly, I will die.

"Katherine, don't look like that. It was stupid of me to even mention his name. Just put him out of your mind completely. Forget about all that has happened. I shall make it up to you, I swear."

"No. William, please, I cannot discuss it now." She could feel the tears forming behind her eyes, the hysterical sobs welling up in her throat. "Come back tomorrow, if you must have an explanation, but right now I—" Suddenly she darted from the room and up the stairs to her bedroom.

William stared at the empty doorway in surprise. Poor Katherine. Why had he been such a fool as to even mention Hampton's name? He should have realized the horrifying memories it would dredge up for her. Poor, dear girl.

Matthew dead! The words pounded in her brain. All the unhappiness she had felt before seemed as nothing compared to this deep pain slashing through her. He could not be dead; she could not live if he was dead. She sat numbly on the side of her bed, staring at nothing. Her first, violent storm of tears was over, and now, spent, she had to face the fact of his death, bring her spinning world into some kind of order. Perhaps—there was always the hope that he wasn't dead. William had not known for a fact that he was dead; it was only surmise. For a moment she clung to that bright hope, then sternly put it away from her. No, it was better go to ahead and accept it now. He had been on the edge of death and then disappeared. What other explanation could there be? If Matthew were alive, he would have sailed on the *Susan Harper* or some new ship. If he were alive, he would be out there fighting. There was no escaping it: Matthew was dead.

She rose and went to the window to stare out into the black night. Oh, why had she not stayed with him, accepted his reluctant offer of a mock marriage? Perhaps she could have saved him somehow, nursed him day and night as she had during his fever. Or maybe even kept him from the duel. Oh, God, if that duel had been because of her; if that baron was her tormentor—she leaned her forehead against the window, the tears streaming down her face again.

"Miss Katherine?" Pegeen entered the room to help her undress. Her manner was excited. "They said Lieutenant Perkins had come to call on you. Isn't it grand his being here? Oh, miss, whatever is the matter? You have been crying."

Katherine attempted a smile. "It is nothing, Pegeen."

"He didn't say anything to upset you, did he?"

"Oh, no, Lieutenant Perkins is kindness itself. I am afraid it is I who must hurt him."

"What do you mean?"

"I cannot marry him."

"Why ever not, mum?"

"Oh, Pegeen, I would make him a wretched wife. I could not give him any love; I have nothing left in me to give."

"Sure, now, and that's a wild way to talk," Pegeen said, her brogue thickening in her excitement.

"No, it is true. Oh, Pegeen, can't you see? I love Matthew Hampton!"

The maid sighed. "I was afraid of that."

"And now—he's dead." Katherine's voice broke, and the tears began to flow again. "Matthew is dead!"

"Oh, Miss Katherine." Pegeen enfolded her in a warm hug. "Oh, whatever shall we do?"

"I haven't even—oh, damn, I'm not even carrying his child! I have nothing of him, absolutely nothing. Peggy, I can't go on; I cannot face life knowing he is nowhere in this world."

"Oh, Miss Katherine." Pegeen's ready tears mingled with her mistress's, and the two girls clung to each other, sobbing.

How horribly ironic it was that his death had made her realize she loved him. For she knew at last, too late, that she loved him, that all her hatred and fighting had been but pretense. She had simply been too scared and stubborn to acknowledge it.

She remembered his face, the slow, sardonic smile, the way his eyebrows lifted in amusement, his long-lashed gray eyes, sometimes the cold gray of steel, other times the stormy gray of the Atlantic, or now and then lit by the fires of desire or anger. She remembered his soft, velvety drawl, with the hint of iron beneath; his lean, hard body, the firm grip of his fingers under her arm as they strolled the deck, the comforting strength of his arms around her as he carried her away from Pearl's. And she cried for him and all the joy that might have been hers, had she not thrown it away.

Katherine managed to face her family the next morning, her eyes red-rimmed from tears and a sleepless night. It was more difficult to keep her composure that evening before William's loving concern. Katherine nervously twisted his ring and observed irrelevantly that she must have lost weight, for his ring was loose on her finger. Taking a deep breath, she plunged in, "William, you are a wonderful man, and very honorable, too, to still want me to marry you. But you must see that it's impossible."

"No, I do not see."

"William, please don't make this any more difficult," she whispered.

"Katherine, I love you."

"You are such a fine man, and you would be a kind and devoted husband, I'm sure, but I cannot marry you. It would be so unfair to you—no, let me finish. My reputation is ruined." She smiled mirthlessly. "I'm a fallen woman."

"Do you think I care about that? It was not your fault what that blackguard did to you. Katherine, I want to take care of you, make you forget what happened."

"But the world would—"

"The devil take the world! We need not live in Boston. We could live in New York, or anyplace where ships sail. We can start a brand-new life; no one would know."

"We would know. I would feel guilty all the rest of our lives. It is not just that I am—stained. I would make you an awful wife. I could never give you anything; I am drained of all emotion. I don't think that I shall ever be able to feel anything for anyone again. And it would be so unfair to shackle you with a wife like that. You will get over this hurt, and then you can find yourself another girl, one who will love you and be a proper wife for you."

"Katherine, I don't want any other girl."

"William, please." She looked away from him, agonized. She couldn't bear to tell him that she had never truly loved him, that she loved someone else, that she was tied to a memory. The pain and shock in his eyes would be too much for her.

"Are you saying that the physical side of marriage repels you, that you could not—"

"Yes, William, I couldn't sleep with you—or anyone else." Except one man, a man who's dead now. "That's part of it."

"Katherine, I could be patient. In time, you would change the way you feel; I'm sure." He stared at the carpet, unable to meet her eyes.

She felt a twinge of exasperation. Why must he be so embarrassed and roundabout? "No, William," she said firmly, "it simply would not work." She pulled his ring off her finger and held it out to him.

He stared at it for a moment, then finally took it. Stiffly, he rose and took his leave. Katherine stifled a little sob. Why, oh, why, did everything have to be so unfair?

Grimly, Katherine plodded through the days, wrapped in her grief, barely noticing the world around her. The summer wore to a close. Dimly she was aware that far to the south, the Confederacy was crumbling under the two-pronged attack of Grant and Sherman; Lee's army was on its last legs. Why did they hang on so stubbornly in the face of imminent defeat? Why not just give in and be done with it? She smiled wryly. For the same reason, she guessed, that she clung to life even though all hope and joy was gone—stubbornness, pride, desperation—God knew what it was.

At night, alone in her bed, she remembered Matthew's lovemaking, his hard hands gentle against her skin, his deep kisses and tingling caresses, and she ached with emptiness and unfulfilled desire. She had never guessed that she would miss him physically, that her loins would burn for him and her flesh tremble at the thought of his touch, that she would feel she could die from wanting him. Why, oh, why, had she so stubbornly refused to give in? Why had she held back when her body had wanted to let go, to return his love? Bitterly she regretted it now: her life stretched before her so full of waste and emptiness—if only she had snatched at that chance of happiness, however brief it might have been.

Now she realized, too late, that he had not been entirely the selfish monster she had thought. He had tried to bring her enjoyment, had concerned himself with her pleasure. She knew now, after her experience at Pearl's, that he need not have, that he could have gotten his own quick satisfaction from her without any effort to arouse her. Pearl's had taught her what true cruelty and debasement were; what he had done to her was not that. Many times he had offered her so much more than just being the passive object of his lust. He had wanted to converse with her, to take her to the heights of passion with him, to have her company, to give her things. And she had coldly, stubbornly refused. She had been the one who

kept them apart and separate, who insisted that they
remain in their respective roles of conqueror and victim.
If she had not been so pig-headed, she could have rev-
eled in the sensual joy he gave her—the sensual joy they
could have *shared*. She could have told him whatever she
wanted; he would not have been shocked by anything
she said. He had enjoyed her wit, laughed at her quips;
she could have entertained him with her quick mind,
instead of always having to curb her tongue. Had she
asked, no doubt he would have taught her how to navi-
gate a ship—or anything she wanted to know.

Now, bitterly and too late, she saw her own folly. She
had loved Matthew, but had thrown away happiness
with both hands. Now he was dead, and her life was an
aching void.

It was one evening when she was in this black mood
that her father called her into his study. There was a
peculiar twinkle in his eye and an air of suppressed
excitement about him.

"Katherine, how would you like to go to New York to
visit your cousin?"

"Who?" Katherine asked in astonishment.

"Angela Van der Vries. You remember, you went to
her wedding about seven or eight years ago."

"Oh, yes, I remember; a pretty blond girl, wasn't she?"

"That is the one. She has written inviting you to
spend a few months with her."

"But she is only a distant relative, Father; our grand-
parents were cousins or something." She regarded him
suspiciously. "Why on earth does she want me to come
stay with her?"

Josiah shrugged. "I don't know, really." He didn't add that he suspected it was because he had sent her a telegram angling for an invitation for Katherine. "Probably she's lonely, with her husband away at the War. Anyway, wouldn't you like to go? Get away from Boston for a while. Why, you could go shopping."

Katherine had the feeling that her father had had a great deal to do with the invitation. But what did that matter? Nothing mattered anymore. Her father wanted her to go to New York, and her life would be this same dead gray wherever she went. Nothing could ease the pain and bitter regret that were her constant guests. So if her father wanted her to go, she might as well. At least she would be away from her aunts.

"All right, I will go," she said indifferently.

Josiah felt like lifting his hands with glee. His scheme was working. He did not know what foolish notion had made his daughter reject Lieutenant Perkins, but he felt sure that the young man still loved her. Let her get down there in New York, with him around all the time, and surely Perkins would be able to woo her back and lift her from this dreadful gloom.

Katherine, with Pegeen beside her, stepped nervously off the train. "How shall I ever recognize her, Peg? I can't remember at all what she looks like."

"Miss Devereaux?" A tall man dressed in livery approached.

"Yes?"

"I'm Adam Clough, the Van der Vries's coachman.

Madame is waiting for you in the carriage. Is this your luggage?"

"Yes, please," Katherine replied, and he picked up one of her trunks and led them to the elegant carriage outside.

"Cousin!" a tinkling voice cried as Katherine stepped inside the carriage and was enveloped in taffeta and lace and crinoline.

"Cousin Angela, how nice," she managed to murmur and settled back into her seat, where she was able to get her first real look at her cousin.

Angela was a little doll of a woman, pretty, blond, and fragile. In her late twenties, there was still a girlish winsomeness to her, though her elegant coiffure and carefully applied makeup added a certain stiffness to her looks. She was dressed in the height of fashion, her skirts wide and her waist tiny, and a charming little bonnet adorned her curls, the flared straw brim framing her face. Her manner was effusive, and she leaned over to grasp Katherine's hand several times as she poured forth her "sheer delight" at her cousin's coming to see her, just in time for "the Season."

Angela really was quite happy to see her, though her nose for scandal had twitched a little when she received Josiah Devereaux's telegram. She remembered her cousin as a rather gawky, ill-at-ease, unattractive girl, and her first sight of Katherine in her plain brown traveling dress confirmed that. But she welcomed the idea of having a visitor. Besides, how well her cousin's height and strange looks would offset her own delicate beauty.

Angela Van der Vries kept up a constant chatter as

they drove through the streets of New York, pointing out places of interest and people she knew. Katherine found her conversation difficult to follow and soon gave up trying. New York was noisy and active and somehow even looked freer and looser than Boston. It would be better here, she told herself firmly, and smiled hesitantly at her cousin.

Angela's home was a gracious red brick house bordering the Battery, and the inside was rich, though rather ornate for Katherine's taste. Katherine was eager to go to her room for a little rest, as Angela suggested, simply to get away from her hostess's nonstop prattle. Her room was very pleasant and comfortable, with a large window that looked down upon the side yard. A large oak shaded her room, so that it was cool even in the summer. Very nice, Katherine told herself. I will like it here, I think— but then why do I feel like crying?

Angela gaily attended rounds of parties, dances, and teas, and went to the theater, the ballet, and the opera, always escorted by a gaggle of officers stationed in New York. Katherine thought, with a spurt of amusement, that her father had certainly missed the mark when he surmised that Angela was lonely for her husband off at the front. Katherine never accompanied her, even on her daily round of calls. Grimly she endured the afternoon visitors to Angela's house, but she could not bring herself to go out among people. She could not bear the laughter and light chatter, the gaiety, the entertainment. Everything seemed gray and flat to her; she could do nothing more than stare into space or busy her hands with mindless knitting and needlework. Her bright new clothes were never worn; now their very beauty offended her. Only her drab old grays and browns and blues seemed to fit her world.

Cousin Angela found Katherine even more of a mouse than she had remembered. She never said or did anything, just huddled over her sewing, prim and dreary. Angela did wish she would be more cooperative about going out; it would appear more respectable to have Katherine along as a chaperone. Some of those obnoxious old matrons were beginning to whisper that Angela was a little fast. Well, let them talk—she tossed her head. But it would be better if she could just persuade Katherine to come along with her.

It was with this view in mind that she sat in the drawing room with Katherine one afternoon, trying to tempt her into coming to the McFarland ball with her the next evening. "But, Katherine, you have no idea how much fun you would have. Truly. Since the War, this town is just chock full of the most fascinating people."

Katherine smiled vaguely; she hardly heard Angela anymore.

"Why, just last week, the most charming Navy commander arrived here. He is assigned to the naval base, and really is the handsomest man I have ever seen." Angela's eyes sparkled; she found the commander exceptionally attractive, and it seemed to her that he had quite favored her with his attentions.

"Really?" Katherine murmured, and Angela launched into a description of her favorite, of which Katherine heard not a single word.

" . . . and he's from Maryland," Angela was saying when Katherine stirred from her daydream. "The most charming manner and a Southern accent. I tease him by telling him he sounds just like a Rebel. Really, Katherine, you must meet him; I know you would just adore him."

Katherine felt a stab of pain. She hoped she would never meet him; she thought she would probably die if she heard a slow, lazy drawl like Matthew's.

"What is his name?" she asked without interest.

"I swear, Katherine, you haven't heard a word I've said! I just told you his name. It's Jason Forrest."

As if on cue, the butler entered the room, a calling card on the little silver tray. "Commander Forrest to see you, madame," he intoned.

"Oh, show him right in, Jenson." Angela turned to Katherine excitedly. "What luck! Here he is; you'll have a chance to meet him."

Yes, what luck, Katherine repeated dully to herself. She rose to her feet, thinking madly of escape, when suddenly the doorway was blocked by a tall blue figure. Katherine looked at him and her knitting dropped from her hands, one needle rolling across the carpet to rest at his feet.

Matthew!

Sixteen

*A*ngela stared at her cousin; why on earth was she acting so peculiarly? Two bright red dots stood out on her cheekbones and she was staring at their caller as if she had just seen a ghost. And Commander Forrest was acting most peculiarly, too. Astonishment and joy and excitement fleetingly mingled on his face and then disappeared into his usual charming, slightly sarcastic mask. He bent to retrieve Katherine's knitting needle and crossed the room to hand it to her.

Their hands touched briefly and Katherine shivered. "Ex-excuse me," she stammered. "It's just that you startled me."

"Of course," his voice was caressing. "But, please, you must not run off like a frightened doe."

"No, of course not," Katherine said and giggled nervously.

She wanted to throw her knitting up in the air and dance madly about the room, to throw her arms around him and smother him with kisses, to laugh hysterically. Matthew was alive! Dear God, he was alive. Who cared what he was doing here or why he was masquerading in a Union naval uniform and assuming the name of Jason Forrest? Just so long as he was here, alive and unharmed. It was insane, but she could have cried with pure happiness.

Angela felt a twinge of exasperation. What on earth had transformed Katherine? She seemed to glow and her eyes shone with a strange light. Really, she must tell her gawky cousin not to wear her heart on her sleeve like that; anyone could tell she was quite smitten with the commander. It was almost indecent, the way her eyes devoured him. And why did Jason Forrest keep his eyes riveted so on that plain spinster? Angela had suggested very prettily that he come to charm her dull cousin out of her shell, but there was no need for him to go this far!

The pretty Mrs. Van der Vries tried to pull the attention back to herself by introducing them.

"Katherine Devereaux," he repeated, his tongue lingering over the words. "What a delightful name. Are you French?"

"Heavens, no. Boston born and bred," she said, struggling for a light tone. She must gain control of herself or Angela would suspect something.

"Ah, Boston, a lovely city," he said gravely, his eyes twinkling.

"Then you have visited there?" Katherine responded to the devil in his eyes.

"Oh, yes. I only regret that I never had the pleasure of meeting you."

"No doubt you were too—" she paused, a smile

twitching at her lips, "too chained to the business at hand to do any socializing."

His wickedly handsome smile flashed across his face. "Indeed I was, Miss Devereaux. I was at that time, you see, requisitioning ships and supplies."

"Commander Forrest, you never told me you had been to Boston." Angela pouted prettily. She felt left out, as if the other two were speaking in a foreign language.

Matthew favored her with his melting gaze and said, "Somehow, it never came to my mind. When I am around you, your beauty chases all else from my mind."

"No doubt Captain—excuse me—Commander Forrest has visited so many places," Katherine murmured.

He inclined his head in assent.

"Have you been to England, Commander?" she prodded.

"Many times. I find it a truly charming place."

"Mm. Gracious people."

"Such interesting places to visit."

"Quaint lodgings."

Katherine felt exhilarated, as if she were floating at least ten feet in the air. Matthew was alive and grinning at her devilishly, playing verbal games with her, daring her to unmask him. She felt like tossing back her head and laughing as she had not laughed in ages. She smiled at him archly, provocatively, and was pleased to see his jaw muscles tighten. He desired her; she knew it. She was beautiful and in control and back into the contest with him, matched perfectly with her opponent, each win a win, and each loss somehow a win also.

"Mrs. Van der Vries," Matthew said, playfully accusatory, "you never told me how lovely your cousin was. Come now, confess, why have you been hiding her?"

"Oh, Commander!" Angela's laugh was a trifle brittle. "The fact is, Katherine just refuses to go anywhere. She is engaged, you know."

"Cousin Angela, that was ages ago!" Katherine protested mockingly.

"Unhappy man," Hampton murmured sympathetically. "But now that it has ended, surely you will stop refusing invitations."

Katherine smiled slowly and saw the almost imperceptible widening of his eyes in response. "Perhaps."

"Then allow me to urge you to attend the McFarland ball tomorrow evening."

Just as Angela opened her mouth to say that Katherine had flatly refused to come, Katherine said firmly, "Oh, yes, I quite plan to accept that invitation."

Angela gaped at her, and Katherine stifled an impulse to tell her to shut her mouth.

"Till tomorrow then," their visitor said, standing. "I am afraid I must take my leave now."

They protested politely and he was heartbroken, but firm. He bowed over Angela's hand and then Katherine's, his lips barely grazing her fair skin. That alone was enough to send a delicious shiver through her.

Matthew was alive! When he left them, Katherine dashed out of the room without a glance at her astounded cousin. Calling for Pegeen, she ran to her room, tearing out hairpins as she ran. Inside her room, she skinned out of her drab dress.

"Miss Katherine, what—" Pegeen halted in the doorway, struck speechless at the sight of her mistress, clad only in her chemise, her hair tumbled down about her shoulders, her face alight with joy.

"Oh, Pegeen!" Katherine took her by the shoulders and danced her around the room. "Pegeen, he isn't dead at all! He is alive and I am going to a ball tomorrow night."

"Who? What are you—do you mean Captain Hampton?"

"Of course I do. Who else? Pegeen, we've got to find a way to fix my hair. And get rid of that dress; burn it or something. I don't care. Get my new clothes ready. Oh, Pegeen, I'm so excited I can hardly breathe!"

"Oh, mum, but whatever is he doing here?"

"I haven't the slightest idea—and I don't care. He's parading around as a Union commander named Jason Forrest. And Peg, if you tell another soul, I shall kill you. I mean it; not one person, even one of the servants."

"Oh, no, mum, never." Pegeen glowed with empathetic happiness.

Katherine smiled idiotically at herself in the mirror as Pegeen experimented with her hair. Alive! He was alive and here. She had seen him, seen his smile, his dark gray eyes, his browned, strong hands. He had touched her hand, had sat across the room from her, so close she could have reached him in two steps. He was alive, and she felt as if she could soar as easily as a gull.

Her thoughts were scattered, disconnected; she could only feel. The world had turned suddenly bright and sunny; she wanted only to don one of her brilliant new dresses and dance in Matthew's arms. She wanted to be beautiful for him; she would be beautiful—she felt beautiful. He would want her again; she would make him want her. They would begin anew, everything forgotten, and she would entrance him, entice him, until he would take her away and once again make love to her.

Who cared what the world would think, or what was right or wrong, or which one of them won in their battles of will? She had learned her lesson: the only important thing was to love him and share pleasure with him and grab her one chance at happiness. And everything else be damned!

Matthew stepped out onto the street, feeling his spirits soaring precariously. He had agreed to undertake this suicidal mission out of sheer despair. After Katherine left him, he had felt lower than he ever thought possible. Plagued by a low but unremitting fever from his wound, haggard from lack of sleep and ceaseless self-recriminations, he had felt as if he would die from loving her, wanting her and not having her. Neither whiskey nor women could ease the pain. He cursed himself for letting her go and hated himself for wanting to keep her against her will. He was tortured both night and day by hot, lustful dreams in which she moaned in ecstasy beneath him, and nightmares in which he saw her brutalized again and again at the brothel.

So when Redfield had laid out this scheme, the most appealing thing about it was the near-certainty of death in it for him. But to find Katherine here like this! When he saw her standing in that room, thin and pale, her gold eyes dark with sadness, it had taken every ounce of willpower in him not to sweep her into his arms. And then she had lightly bandied words with him, smiling and looking up at him provocatively, her eyes amber beneath the thick fringe of her lashes. He thought of the way she had looked at him when he first entered, her face glowing, her eyes alight. Surely that had been love, not hate, shining out of those eyes at him. He would see her again, hold her in his arms in a waltz tomorrow night, steal a few moments alone with her on the terrace. He began to whistle, then stopped abruptly when he realized that the tune he was whistling was "Dixie."

Katherine turned slowly before the mirror, checking to make sure every fold of the soft gold satin gown was in place. Behind her, Angela watched enviously her slow rotation in the powder room mirror. It just wasn't fair, she told herself, that her ugly duckling cousin had turned into such a swan. Her gown was beautiful and shimmering and revealed her bosom to a point just short of indecency. Her hair was pulled back from her face and arranged in artless curls falling from the crown. Her perfect, shell-shaped ears were adorned with simple gold studs, and around the base of her slender, regal neck lay a fragile gold chain. The effect was stunning. Somehow she looked majestic and exotic all at once, and Angela felt like a colorless child beside her. She could not imagine how Katherine had managed such a complete transformation, but she had no doubt that that golden glow of her skin and eyes was due to the imminently eligible Commander Forrest. And she had the uneasy feeling that her dowdy cousin was about to pull off the catch of the Season.

"Well, Cousin, I am ready to go down now. Coming?" Katherine asked her.

Angela smiled. She was not fool enough to make her entrance in Katherine's shadow. "No, dear, you run along. I simply must speak to Rosemary Clifton first."

"All right." Katherine smiled, headily suspecting Angela's true reason. She swept out of the powder room door and paused at the top of the stairway, her eyes searching for Matthew. She began to descend the broad stairs, her wide skirts trailing the marble. Her right hand clutched the ivory fan fiercely, as she willed him to look up and see her. Already men had noticed her and were clustering about the bottom of the stairs. Then casually he glanced around and saw her and stopped in midsentence. Lazily he smiled at her entrance, but she had seen the way his entire body had stiffened when he saw her and the fierce blaze that had sparked in his eyes before he regained control of himself. She favored the room with a dazzling smile, and a barely audible sigh ran around the ballroom.

Katherine was the hit of the evening. She had not really considered that possibility. Her dress had been for Matthew; she had wanted to stir his senses, tease him, enflame him. Her own senses had been in a whirl ever since she saw him again. She had not been able to sleep or eat from the excitement that raged in her. A thousand questions spun in her hand, and she could not untangle her own turbulent emotions. Only two things seemed clear to her: he was alive, and somehow she must rekindle his desire for her. It had not occurred to her that she might produce similar effects on other men as well.

She found herself besieged by officers in blue, all begging for a space on her dance card. It was a heady feeling for a former wallflower. Laughing, smiling, flirting, she danced the night away. The only thing spoiling the evening was the fact that Matthew had not approached her at all. Then suddenly, she saw him striding purposefully across the floor toward her, and she waited for him breathlessly, almost faint with fear and hope and excitement.

"I believe this dance is mine," he said, cutting off an approaching swain, and she moved into his arms without a murmur of protest.

His hand was firm against her waist as he guided her about the floor, their bodies a very correct distance apart. But the grip his other hand maintained on hers was anything but seemly. She followed him easily; he danced well, lightly, and she felt as if they were floating around the floor. It was all perfect: it felt so right, so good, to be in his arms, to be staring, entranced, into his gray eyes, devilishly alight. She felt as if she could whirl around the floor like this forever.

At last she managed to find her voice enough to say lightly, "You have neglected me, Commander Forrest. Quite shamefully, too; I haven't seen you all evening."

"Oh, but I have seen you. The crowd around you has been too thick for me to get close. Besides," his teeth flashed in his tanned face, "I couldn't let you have it all your own way, could I?"

"Well, I can see you're as conceited as always," she snapped, and he burst into laughter.

"Oh, Katherine, you look so beautiful I could devour you."

"Right here on the dance floor?" she teased.

"Right here." His voice was husky. "Kathy, when this dance is through, walk with me on the terrace."

Her heart began to pound violently, and her voice was barely more than a whisper: "All right."

"I see you wore my chain." He didn't add that he had been quite shaken when he saw her coming down the staircase in that alluring gown cut from his cloth and his chain hung enticingly about her silken neck. Surely that was a clear statement that she had forgiven him.

She smiled. "Your fan also. And your dress. And some other things you gave me." She smiled meaningfully.

His breath caught in his throat at the idea of the flimsy undergarments he had given her lying soft against her skin. The music wound to a close, and she took his arm for him to lead her to the terrace. Fanning her flushed face, she noticed with pleasure that his arm trembled under her hand. Once outside, they walked to the far end of the colonnade, beyond the lighted windows, where the darkness covered them. He faced her, suddenly realizing he had no idea what to do. Should he try to explain to her, enlist her silence? Beg her to forgive him? He longed to kiss her, but was afraid he might frighten her off.

Gently he touched the chain about her neck; the metal was warm with the heat of her body. Softly his fingers traveled downward, lightly brushing the tops of her breasts, slipping down between her breasts and back up, tracing intricate designs about her chest. Both of them stood still, their eyes locked, almost afraid to move for fear of breaking the pleasure of his touch, painful in its intensity and lack of fulfillment.

Finally, Katherine broke the spell by taking his hand between hers and lifting it to her lips. Softly she kissed the palm, then each fingertip; for an instant she held his hand to her cheek, then again kissed his palm.

"Katherine." The word came out almost a groan.

"Matthew." She took his other hand and began to kiss it the same way. "Matt. Matthew. 'See how I say your name?' " she quoted shakily. He felt wetness on her cheek. Tears? "He said you were dead." There was a catch in her voice. "I thought you were dead."

"As you can see, I am very much alive." He slid his fingers along the soft angles of her face. "Oh, Katherine, I haven't felt so alive since the last time I saw you."

She stretched up on tiptoe and kissed him, a brief whisper of a kiss, but his arms tightened around her and he kissed her deeply, hungrily, his tongue caressing hers, and she responded, pressing her lips to his, her tongue playing with his. His hands roamed her body, delving into her bodice to fondle her perfect breasts. Hungrily he bent to kiss them. To his amazement, he felt her hands traveling over his chest, sliding down his legs.

"Oh, God!" He pulled away from her.

"Matthew!"

"We have to go back in now."

"Matthew, why?" She pressed her body into his, felt

the shudder that shook his body. He wanted her; she could feel it.

"We have been out here too long already. Soon people will notice we are not there and, if we stay out here long, your reputation will be ruined."

"I don't care; it already is."

"Perhaps in Boston; not here."

Her hand slipped between the buttons of his uniform, caressing his chest.

"Katherine, please, you are torturing me."

"Then take me. Can't we slip into the garden, back behind the hedges?"

"My love, I can think of nothing I would rather do than abscond with you to the garden and make love to you. But we can't! Don't you see? Your reputation would be in shreds. I cannot blacken your name here, too. It would be different if I could take you with me when I leave, but I can't. It's far too dangerous. I would have to leave you here, fair game for all the scandalmongers, without me here to protect you. Otherwise I would say 'reputation be damned,' because I have never wanted anyone so badly as I want you now."

"Later, then, we will meet somewhere. I can slip out of my room anytime. I shall come to your room. It won't be like it used to—I will do anything you say, I swear."

"Good God, can't I make you understand? I have to think of your future—and mine. If you were to be caught and I was embroiled in a scandal, soon my entire masquerade would be discovered, and I would be hanged as a spy. And you would be treated as a spy, too, knowing who I was and not revealing it. But even if we were not caught, as soon as I am done here, I have to leave, and frankly, I doubt if I shall manage to reach Virginia. I expect to die. And I cannot just take my pleasure of you and then leave you here, perhaps carrying my child, to face the world alone."

"If that is the case, I should think you would want to have your one last moment of pleasure, and I do, too. And these past few weeks, thinking you were dead, the thing I have regretted most bitterly is that I am not pregnant with your child!"

"Katherine, you are not thinking clearly."

She gave a short, bitter laugh and straightened her disarranged dress. "Oh, yes, I am thinking clearly—clear through to the obvious reason you refuse to take me— simply that you don't want me."

"Katherine—"

She brushed past him and marched into the ballroom without a backward glance. He leaned against the railing and sighed. God, what an unholy mess.

Katherine lay awake all night. She felt as if she had been hit by an emotional hurricane: first the agony of thinking him dead, then the exhilarating joy upon finding him alive, the spiraling passion that had engulfed her this evening, and finally, his second rejection of her. Now, bruised and buffeted, she tried to gather herself together and return to some stability, sort everything out and put it into perspective.

He did not want her anymore—how could she have forgotten that? He had rid himself of her forever back in Liverpool. Her happiness at seeing him had simply obscured that unpleasant fact. She had thought she had rekindled a passion in him, but obviously she had been mistaken. Katherine didn't believe his excuses for a second: he was the most irresponsible man alive, not one to be guided by fear for her reputation, or even for their lives. No, he was lying, for some reason pretending to be enflamed by her, but glibly fibbing his way out of bedding her. And the reason was obvious: he must keep her on his side because she could identify him to the authorities. One word from her and he would be on the path to the gallows. So he must keep her happy by paying court to her, but could not bring himself to make love to her.

Sternly, she shook herself. What did it matter? She had known Matthew did not love her, or even desire her any longer. All that was important was that he was alive. She could see him and hear his voice and feel the warmth of his lazy grin. At least she could revel in that. He would continue to come to see her, and they could continue their verbal games. She could drink in the pleasure of seeing him, and she would not press him again to make love to her. No, she would be her old self, sharp, light, amusing; she would not plague him with her love. And perhaps, if she could manage to look pretty enough, some of his old desire for her might reignite.

But what was she to make of his reason for being here? He must be here as a spy or saboteur; she was betraying her own country by not revealing his identity. Katherine felt stricken with guilt. She knew she would never identify him: that would mean certain hanging for him as a spy. Yet how could she, ardent Unionist and abolitionist that she was, allow him to bring harm to her country? Her love for Matthew had not changed her opinion of the South or of the rectitude of the Northern cause. The South was almost defeated now, but whatever Matthew was trying to do—and she had no doubt but that he would accomplish it—could prolong the War, cause more lives to be lost. And she could not just toss away hundreds of men's lives for her love of a Rebel spy.

I must stop him myself, she thought. That is the only way. I must find out what he is here for and somehow dissuade him or foil his plans.

And upon setting that task for herself, she finally drifted off to sleep, just as dawn broke.

She awoke late the next morning and spent a long time getting dressed; she wanted just the right dress and just the right hair style. Then she sat down to wait, trying to cover her nervousness with needlework. But looking at her uneven stitches, she knew that she would have to tear them all out and start over again. Angela stuck with her, plying her with curious questions and gossiping about the party, until Katherine felt that she would scream. At last, unable to endure the boredom or her cousin's chatter, she went for a stroll, taking her maid with her for propriety.

A block away from the house, she saw Hampton coming toward her. "Miss Devereaux," he said, sweeping off his hat and bowing. "What luck! I was just coming to call on you."

His eyes swept over her. She looked like a delicious confection in a frosted silk of broad purple and white chevron stripes. A dainty straw hat perched on her curls, a lavender feather curving fetchingly downward to brush against her cheek. Matthew felt a distinct desire to gather her up in his arms and kiss her right there on the street.

"Commander Forrest, what a pleasant surprise," Katherine murmured, her eyes twinkling.

"And Pegeen," he smiled at the pert redhead, "are you still breaking hearts? You made my crew quite worthless, you know."

Pegeen giggled. "None of your blarney now, Captain Hampton. You don't need it to get me to leave you alone."

"Thank heaven you are Irish." He winked at her and offered his arm to Katherine.

She flashed him a dazzling smile, and they walked off together, Pegeen trailing discreetly several paces behind.

"You have changed, Katherine."

"Have I? In what way?"

"You are more beautiful than ever. You seem to have accepted your beauty."

She looked up at him through her lashes and smiled. "You thought me beautiful; no one else ever had. It made me look at myself in a different way. And I decided to be daring; I was quite an outcast anyway—I had nothing to lose."

"Katherine, I am sorry," he began, but she tossed her head and said, "Old cats!" so furiously that instead laughter bubbled up out of his throat.

"Don't laugh. It is true; they are. Wouldn't even speak to me! God knows they were all dull enough, but compared to being shut up all day with only Aunt Amelia! *Her* only topic of conversation is the Fritham family tree. Oh, except for funerals; she is quite enamored of them, too. Of course, Aunt Amanda did come over to scold me, and her son Jamie, too, to slobber over my hand and tell me how he was willing to marry me, despite my wicked past."

"Ah, another suitor," he said lightly.

"Mm. One of your Boston cash registers."

"Katherine, couldn't we find some place more private than the street to talk?"

"There is a little park a couple of blocks from here."

"Good. To the park, then."

A few minutes later they were ensconced on a stone bench, hidden by spreading trees, with Pegeen on guard at the gate. Matthew took her left hand in his and lightly stroked the ring finger.

"Has your stupid lieutenant beat a retreat, then?" he said sarcastically.

She snatched her hand back and said heatedly, "Oh, you are a fine one to talk about deserting me! For your information, Lieutenant Perkins did not break off our engagement. He loved me and was very sweet and told me that it didn't matter about you and that he would be patient and—" She choked in fury.

"What a magnanimous man he is," Hampton said dryly. "He seems such a paragon, I only wonder why you broke your engagement. I assume one of you must have cried off, since you no longer wear his ring."

Katherine clenched her fist. How could she have forgotten what an infuriating man he was! She wanted to hit him for his lazily mocking tone, to wipe that derisive grin from his face.

"Yes, I called it off, not that it is any of your business. I was not going to saddle him with a tainted wife; I have more respect for him than that. He deserves better than your leavings! Yours and quite a few other men's—"

"Shut up," he said grimly.

"Oh, so that hit home, did it?" she said, perversely pleased and wounded. "You don't like to be reminded of that, do you? That I have been handled and used by others; that you were not the only one to take me!"

"Katherine, for God's sake, please—"

"Oh, I know, your delicate masculine ego," she said bitingly. "You cannot stand to think that your property has been touched by someone else, can you? That made me quite unworthy of you, didn't it? So low and common!"

"Don't be stupid, Katherine; you know very well—"

"Yes, I know very well! There is no need for you to pretend that it isn't so, that you still want me. Do you take me for an imbecile? Don't you think I know that you are hanging about, professing mad passion for me, so that I will not reveal who you are? Well, you don't need to bother, because I won't tell them. I have no desire to spread my shame all over New York, too."

He stared at her, amazed. "Katherine, you half-wit, do you think I am *pretending* to desire you?"

She leaped to her feet in rage. "Of course I think that. I don't believe your protestations about 'my reputation'—what a joke! When you wanted me, you weren't halted by any such concern!"

"Good God, girl, are you taking me to task because I am *not* carrying you off and raping you this time? You're insane!"

"Oh, am I? Well, thank you very much. I would rather be insane than be a low, blackhearted scoundrel like you! You are a snake, and spying is the perfect profession for you. And I shall tell you something else: you are not half the man Lieutenant Perkins is. He doesn't care about my past. He didn't throw me over because another man had raped me, as you did."

"As *I* did! Katherine, I asked you to marry me. Is that what you call throwing you over?"

"Oh, yes, you asked me—because Dr. Rackingham forced you to! But you didn't want me. You would not even touch me. Because I was spoiled; because other men had raped me. I was not fit for you any longer, was I? Of course not. I was stupid enough to tell you what happened, and immediately you rushed to get Dr. Rackingham to shuttle me off. And you think I am fool enough to believe you are suddenly burning with passion for me now? Well, I am not; so don't waste your time on me. Go ahead and do whatever treacherous thing it is you came here to do. I will not betray you. Just don't come near me again. I despise you, and I hope I never have to see your face again!"

She whirled and ran down the path out of the park. Matthew simply stared at her, stunned. His mind could not quite comprehend what she had said. He sat down heavily on the park bench. Back in Liverpool she had not wanted to go. For once he had decided to do the honorable thing: he had released her because he loved her. And she thought he had cast her away because he did not want her—and she despised him for it. Suddenly he began to laugh. What idiots they both were!

Two days later, Matthew sat at his desk in naval headquarters, thoughtfully staring out the window. This was his last day here; soon he would be either dead or back home. Yesterday he had finally located the hiding place of the Navy's new ironclad that he had been sent to destroy. Tonight he would blow it up and escape to the South—provided, of course, that he was not killed in the process. At any rate, it would be over, and Katherine out of his reach.

And he had been unable to see her to explain the ridiculous mix-up, to apologize and declare his love for her. In one sense, it did not matter; no doubt she had lost whatever feeling she had held for him. It seemed as though everything he did in connection with her was wrong and gave her more reason to hate him. But in another way, it mattered very much: he could not stand to die letting her believe for the rest of her life that he had not loved her. At least he could give her the satisfaction of knowing she had been the only woman to capture his heart.

However, the lovely Miss Devereaux refused to see him. Each time he called, the butler announced that she was not at home. He wrote her a letter, but she returned it unopened. Wildly, he thought of forcing his way into the Van der Vries house and tracking her down, but stopped himself; breaking into the house of a prominent citizen was hardly the way to avoid detection. And he could not scuttle his country's welfare for his own affairs of the heart.

"Ah, Commander Forrest," a voice boomed.

Hampton winced. He recognized the voice of Major Lindale, a deadly bore from Nantucket. Resignedly he turned to greet the man—and suddenly turned ice-cold. Lieutenant William Perkins stood beside Lindale.

"Major Lindale." Matthew forced his voice to remain calm. Surely Katherine had not given him away to her former fiancé.

"Forrest, I'd like for you to meet somebody here. Lieutenant Perkins, Commander Forrest. Perkins is from my hometown; just happened to run into him as I was coming over here to see you. Thought I would just bring him along to meet you."

"Lieutenant Perkins." Matthew greeted him with the stiff condescension of a senior officer.

"Commander." Perkins saluted. There was no flicker of recognition in his eyes, only the blank boredom of someone who had just spent several minutes with Major Lindale.

"Perkins here is on a blockader; sailing tomorrow for Wilmington."

Hampton felt an insane desire to laugh and say that was his plan, too. Perkins continued to look at him and saw a small frown line crease his forehead.

"Excuse me, sir," he said, "but I feel that I have met you before."

Once, at the Devereaux yards. "Perhaps you were stationed in Philadelphia?" Hampton said coolly.

"No, sir."

"Well, perhaps we have met each other in passing." He shrugged, dismissing it. "Glad to have met you, Lieutenant. Good luck."

"Thank you, sir." Perkins saluted upon recognizing the dismissal in his voice and escaped gratefully. He had been afraid he was stuck with Lindale for hours.

Perkins went to a restaurant for his last meal ashore. Forrest's face nagged at his memory; there was something faintly familiar about him. What a stupid thing to spend his time on—stubbornly he shoved it out of his thoughts.

After dinner he strolled past the Van der Vries house. Mr. Devereaux had written to tell him of Katherine's visit to New York and to urge him to call on her. William had not done it. He was haunted constantly by the thought of her, but he knew that Katherine had meant it when she broke off their engagement, and he would not force his presence on her against her wishes. Often, however, he walked past the house where she was staying, hoping for a glimpse of her. Tonight he leaned against the fence, staring hungrily at the lighted windows before him. In one room, he could see several blue-coated men and the blond woman he sometimes saw leaving the house. He did not see Katherine.

He leaned his head against the iron bars of the fence, still slightly warm from the day's sun. He remembered the taste of her lips in that last deep kiss as he left her the night of their engagement party. He remembered her smile, her wide, generous mouth, her low voice. That day when she had shown him around the ship the prisoners were working on and she had told him he could call on her. He clenched his teeth against the hot tears threatening to flow. Perhaps he could at least see her once before he sailed; not pressure her, just offer her his help and friendship, if she should ever need it.

Suddenly he stiffened and raised his head. That day on the ship . . . he had climbed down the ladder. There was tension in the air; a guard had stood behind Katherine and across from her a ragged prisoner with a bold face and cold eyes. Commander Forrest. Captain Hampton. Good God! Captain Hampton was in New York masquerading as a Union commander! He had stood not three feet away from the man he hated most in the world!

Perkins began to run. When he reached headquarters he found everyone long since gone, and he paused for a moment, thinking. Surely he would be in his quarters. He headed for the bachelors' quarters, but when he reached them, he found that Commander Forrest was not quartered there. The quarters were wartime-crowded and the newly arrived commander had been unable to get a room there. He was living in a room in town. William got the address and soon found Hampton's room. He knocked several times on the door but to no avail.

"Here now! Can't you see he isn't home?" said an irritable voice, and William turned to find a heavy, middle-aged woman clutching her wrapper to her.

"Is this where Commander Forrest lives?" he asked politely.

"Of course it is, but he's gone out. Why don't you come back later?"

"Are you by any chance his landlady?"

"Yeah. Why?"

"I am an old friend of the commander. We went to school together."

She regarded him suspiciously. "You don't talk funny like him."

"Oh, no, I don't mean when we were children. At the Naval Academy. I just got in today and learned he was here. I would very much like to surprise him. Do you think that you could let me into his room?"

She stared at him, apparently judging him; at last, the solid, honest look about him decided her in his favor.

"All right," she said and went back to her room to fetch her keys.

In a moment she returned and let him in. William lit the kerosene lamp on the table and surveyed the room. It was a spare, barren room. No wonder. A spy did not carry memorabilia around with him. William pulled a chair directly across from the door and sat down. Perfect. Hampton would open the door and be directly in his line of fire. He pulled his gun, turned out the lamp, and settled down to wait.

Stealthily Matthew climbed over the high wire fence, the bag of explosives slapping ominously against his back. Crouching, he ran through the shadows on the dock toward the squat outline of the ironclad. He slowed as he neared the gangplank and pulled his knife. The guard at the end of the gangplank leaned drowsily on his rifle. Hampton hurled his knife; it whistled through the air and the guard went down without a sound.

Matthew crept on board and down into the bowels of the ship, scarcely daring to breathe, but he did not encounter another guard. When he judged himself to be below the waterline, he planted his charge against the metal wall of the ship's hull. Taking a deep breath to calm himself, he lit the fuse. Then he turned and sped up to the deck and back down the docks toward the fence. He sprang at the fence and scrambled up it.

"Hey! You! What are you doing? Stop right there!" an angry voice called, and Matthew heard running steps behind him. Cursing, he swung over the top of the fence. The man behind him fired and Matthew plummeted to the ground. With a great roar, the ironclad went up in a flash of light. A flying piece of metal caught Matthew's pursuer in the head and he fell.

Hampton lay on the ground, the wind knocked out of him by his fall. He struggled to catch his breath; there was a searing pain in his head. He felt his head; it was sticky with blood. The bullet must have grazed him, knocking him out and sending him crashing to the ground. Painfully, he stood up and staggered away, driven by desperation. He must not be found here.

At last he reached the streets. Several times he almost lost consciousness. Someone hurrying toward the noise bumped into him and he almost cried out. His side was throbbing in pain, and he thought he must have broken a rib. Thank God it was so dark the stranger had not seen the blood streaming down his face. He had to keep wiping it out of his eyes. He forced himself forward; he would not be caught and hanged. At least he would make it to New Jersey and the little sailboat that awaited him there. Better to die at sea.

At last he reached his boardinghouse and stumbled up the stairs to his room. Fumbling, he managed to unlock the door and open it; he leaned briefly against the doorjamb.

"Come in, Captain Hampton." Suddenly the room sprang to light. Dully Hampton stared at Perkins sitting across the room, holding a gun on him.

"Damn."

Seventeen

*K*atherine was torn from her sleep by the muffled boom. She sat straight up in bed, her heart pounding. She looked at the clock. Almost midnight. What had awakened her? She left her bed and went to her window, but she could see nothing but the oak tree. On tiptoe she went down the hall to a front window. In the distance, probably down by the Navy yards, a glow lit the sky. A fire?

Suddenly she was shaken by a wave of fear—it had something to do with Matthew; she knew it. She scurried back to her room and began to scramble into a dress. She shoved her feet into some slippers and snatched up a shawl against the cool night air. She started for the door, then stopped. If she left through the house, she might awaken Angela and the servants. Darting to her window, she pulled it open and reached out. She could just touch a limb of the tree. When she was a child, she had often escaped the house via the tree by the back hall window; she hoped she could still do it. Taking a deep breath, she grabbed the branch and swung out. Hand over hand she slid down the limb until she found footing. Holding her skirts up about her waist, she clambered down the tree and dropped to the ground. Then she took off at a run, driven by fear for Matthew.

Racing through the streets, she cursed herself for not seeing him the past two days. She had fled home in a rage and fallen on her bed in sobs. When she had finally pulled herself together, she realized that she could not trust herself around him; she could not hide the turbulent emotions he roused in her. It would be easier for both of them if they did not see each other. So she had refused his calls. But now she hated herself for her folly; if only she had more control over herself and had talked to him, maybe she could somehow have kept him from this.

Blindly she scurried along, finding herself part of a curious crowd rushing down to the docks to see what was going on. She pulled the shawl up over her head to hide her bright hair and shadow her face. She was not sure she was going the right way. Pegeen had wormed Matthew's address from some poor naval clerk and they had ridden past it in a cab: she could not keep from seeing where he lived, like a tongue returning to a sore tooth. But on foot and in the dark, she was unsure of direction. Still she plunged on, not stopping to think what a silly, harebrained thing she was doing. The only thing in her mind was the terrible conviction that Matthew needed help.

Matthew stepped inside the door and closed it. He leaned back against it for support; his head was spinning and he felt weak; every breath hurt.

"So you recognized me," he said.

"Not at first," William said, "but later I remembered."

"Are you going to kill me?"

"Not unless you force me to. I plan to take you to the authorities. You are an escaped prisoner and a spy."

"Saboteur," Matthew corrected, calmly wiping the blood from his forehead with one arm.

"Then that explosion I heard was your doing?"

Matthew smiled faintly. "Your new ironclad."

"Captain Hampton, please unbuckle your gunbelt and drop it. And your knife, too; I have heard you carry a knife."

"I am afraid I left my knife behind; I was rather in a hurry." Matthew dropped his gunbelt as he studied the lieutenant's grim face. No chance of mercy from that one. His only hope was to shake him up and make him drop his guard. He curled his lip in contempt. "You are a fool not to kill me. I would if the situation were reversed."

"I am sure you would." Perkins rose. "However, I plan to take you to headquarters."

Matthew shrugged. "Have you seen Katherine today?"

For an instant fear flickered in Perkins's eyes and Matthew smiled. "No, of course you haven't. She is not at home, you see." Casually he crossed the room and sat down at the table.

"What are you saying?" Perkins said grimly.

"Just that she is someplace else, waiting for me. I imagine she will get rather impatient when I don't return, especially since she is tied to the bed."

Matthew saw the hand holding the gun tremble a

little. Good; he was hitting home. If he could just manage not to pass out before his chance came.

"Damn you, Hampton, if you have touched her, I will kill you."

"But then how would you know where to find her?" Matthew grinned mockingly. "I suggest a more reasonable approach to the problem: an exchange. I give you the girl, and you give me my freedom."

William was silent, studying him.

"Of course, I shall be sorry not to have her on my trip home," Matthew prodded. "She was an amusing little chit. Always gave you a nice little romp in bed."

"Shut up."

"Ah, but I forgot; you wouldn't know about that, would you? You were always too much the gentleman, weren't you? Shall I tell you what it is like?"

"Shut your filthy mouth, you son of a bitch!"

Matthew shrugged. He was afraid he could not even stand up, let alone overcome a man with a gun. His vision kept blurring and he felt on the verge of losing consciousness.

"All right," Perkins said, more quietly. "Take me to her and I will let you go."

Suddenly the door burst open and Katherine pelted into the room, crying, "Matthew, are you—"

She stopped dead at the sight of Perkins holding a gun on Matthew. "Oh, my God!"

"Katherine!" William looked at her. Normally Matthew would have seized the opportunity and gone for Perkins's gun, but he had barely staggered to his feet before Perkins's gaze was back on him.

"Matthew, what happened to your head? Are you all right?"

Hampton slumped back into his chair. "You chose a damned inopportune moment to show up, Katherine. I had just told your friend here that I had you tied up somewhere."

"Katherine, you are all right?" William asked anxiously.

"Of course I am. Why shouldn't I be?"

"He said—"

"Oh, he was lying to you; he is very good at that. William, what are you doing?"

"I am about to take him back to headquarters. Hampton, get up and turn around. Katherine, can you tie him up?"

"Well, of course I can, but I am not going to. William, you cannot do this. They will hang him."

"It is better than what he deserves."

"Your friend has a refined sense of honor, my dear. He plans to let the government wreak his revenge for him," Matthew sneered, and Perkins glared at him, stiff with rage.

Katherine could feel the animal hatred stretching between the two men, the tension palpable in the air.

"Matthew!" she snapped. He seemed to be goading Perkins, as if he wanted to drive him to violence. "You are in a pretty poor position to be hurling insults. William, please listen to me. Please, don't send him to his death. Please. He saved me once—more than once. He brought our ship through a terrible storm and then another time he rescued me from a brothel."

"Katherine!"

"I couldn't tell you, William; I am embarrassed. But it is true. If it weren't for him, I would be dead by now, probably."

"If it weren't for him, you would not have been in danger in the first place," Perkins retorted. "Katherine, you are too softhearted. Why should you care what happens to him? He kidnapped and raped you. Why do you want to save him?"

"Because I love him!" she flared. She swallowed hard at the stricken look in his eyes. Softly, she continued, "I am sorry, William, but it's true. That is why I could not marry you; I had fallen in love with him."

William stared at her in shocked disbelief, and her voice dropped to a whisper: "Please, I know how awful you must think me, but if you ever had any love for me, please don't kill him. I would die if they hanged him."

"Goddam it, Kathy, don't beg him for me," Matthew said harshly.

"Then you went with him willingly?" William forced out the words, his voice tortured.

"Never! She never came to my bed willingly. I forced her every time." Matthew pulled himself out of the chair.

"Matthew, for God's sake, would you be quiet!"

"No, I will not. I won't have you debase yourself to this—"

"Matthew, you are out of your head. Please sit down and keep your mouth shut before you get yourself killed. William, please, please, for my sake."

"All right," William said tiredly. Katherine felt tears start at seeing the pain and contempt in his eyes. "I will leave you to him. I won't tell anyone who he is. My ship leaves tomorrow, so you need not worry that I will change my mind. I wish you luck, Katherine."

He left the room and Katherine turned to Matthew, tears streaming down her face.

"He is a fool," Matthew rasped. "I would have killed me in his place."

"Oh, shut up!" Katherine snapped. "Not everyone is as primitive as you. He is a fine gentleman."

"Then why didn't you go with him if you admire him so much?"

"Because I love *you*, damn it," she shouted.

He smiled weakly. "Kathy, my love, come here. I am afraid I cannot—" He sat down heavily.

"Matthew!" She flew to his side.

He had fainted, and his face was ashen. She grabbed a cloth and poured water on it and cleaned his wound, a narrow furrow along the left side of his head. Now what? She could not let him remain here. Soon they would be bound to suspect Commander Forrest, especially when he did not show up at work the next day, and then they would come here looking for him. But even when he came to, he would be in no condition to travel. She had to find someplace where he could recuperate. Certainly she could not take him to a hotel looking like this. The only thing she could see to do was to take him back to her room.

"Matthew, wake up." She shook him and dabbed at his face with the cold, wet cloth. "Matthew, please."

His eyelids fluttered open. "Kathy," he said thickly. "So damned noble, I could kill him."

"Matthew, please, I know it is hard, but you must get up and come with me. We have to leave; you must not black out again or we are both ruined. Do you understand?"

He nodded and his eyes grew clearer. "I understand. I am sorry, Kathy. Help me up."

She pulled him to his feet and put her arm around him to support him. He winced at her touch.

"Side hurts," he explained. "I think I broke something. I fell several feet. Maybe I have a concussion, too. God, my legs feel like rubber."

"Lean on me; I'll try not to hurt your side. And please don't pass out."

It seemed to take hours to get home. Matthew was sometimes alert and able to walk, at other times he slumped against her so that she had to lean against a wall to keep them upright. But the people they passed seemed to assume that he was drunk and left them alone. When they reached the Van der Vries house, she stopped, nonplussed. How on earth was she to get him up to her room? If they went in through the house, they would surely awaken the entire household—but neither was he fit to climb the tree.

"Matthew," she whispered.

He mumbled incoherently against her neck. "Shot him. No, not really. If you asked for him, I'd have given him to you."

"Matthew, please listen. Please wake up."

He smiled at her glassily. "Only I'd-a kept you—bargain, you see. 'Cause I'm not noble."

"I know that. Listen to me, Matthew. Can you climb

that tree? We either have go to in the front and not make a sound—or climb that tree. Do you understand?"

"Yes." He struggled to clear the fog in his brain. "I can climb it."

"Are you sure? Perhaps we should hide you in the gardener's shed."

"I can climb it." He looked at her, his gaze clear and sharp.

"All right. Then quick, before you pass out again."

He pulled himself up, smothering a cry at the sharp stab in his side. She hiked up her skirts and followed him. He climbed quickly and surely and crawled out the limb to her window. For a moment the world began to swim before his eyes and he clung to the branch, but then it passed and he swung onto her windowsill. Katherine scrambled in after him. Matthew looked at her bared legs and smiled.

"How very improper, Miss Devereaux."

"Well, I can see you are all right," she snapped.

"But of course," he said, smiling, and then quietly fainted.

Katherine caught him before he fell and eased him onto the bed. She tore a petticoat into strips and bandaged his head, then cautiously felt his ribs. It seemed to her that some were broken, but she did not quite know what to do about it. So she just took off his shoes and pulled the covers over him. Then her knees gave way and she sat down quickly in a chair.

She was awakened by Pegeen's horrified whisper, "Oh, Miss Katherine, whatever is going on?"

Katherine blinked at her, trying to collect her scattered wits. Pegeen locked the door behind her and hurried over to the chair where Katherine had fallen asleep.

"Oh, God, I forgot to lock the door," Katherine groaned and repressed the hysterical laughter trying to bubble out.

"Mum, why are you sleeping in the chair? And what is he doing here?" Pegeen blushed. "I—I mean, all bandaged and all; he looks—"

"Well, he isn't," Katherine snapped. "He just passed out, that's all." She rose and went to feel his pulse—still strong. "Oh, Pegeen, we are in the most terrible mess." Hurriedly she described the events of the night before. "And now what are we to do? I don't even know what to do about a broken rib." She felt on the edge of tears.

"Well, my brother Tommy once got three ribs broke in a brawl at a pub, and all they did to him was wrap a bunch of bandages aroud him real tight. I can do that; I watched."

Katherine attacked her petticoat again, and they pulled Matthew up and Pegeen tightly bound his ribs. By the time they finished, Katherine had regained control of herself.

"All right, now, Pegeen, I am going to stay in here all day. You go out and say I have the vapors from fear, because of the explosion last night. Make sure no one comes in here except yourself; I will keep the door locked. Bring me my meals on a tray, as big as you can make them without arousing suspicion, because Matthew will need to eat, too. Don't let Angela call a doctor; convey the idea that I am just having an attack of ladylike fear. And find out all you can about that ironclad's being blown up."

"How did you know already that—" Pegeen began and then stopped, her eyes wide. She swung her gaze toward Matthew. "You mean he had something to do with that?"

"Pegeen, the less you know about this the better for you. He is a dead man if they find him, and I probably will be, too."

Pegeen gulped. "Yes, miss. I understand. I will keep my mouth shut and my ears open."

After the girl left, Katherine settled down in the chair to wait, her gaze fixed on Matthew's pale face. Terror welled up in her, but she stubbornly fought it down. Somehow she would find a way to do it.

He did not regain consciousness until midafternoon. She jumped, her heart pounding, when at last his eyelids fluttered open. He looked bemused; then his eyes fell on her and he smiled weakly.

"Katherine."

"Shh." She rushed to his side and leaned down close to his face to whisper. "You must not talk or make any noise. You are in my room at my cousin's house, and they must not discover you."

He nodded to show his assent and took her hand and brought it to his lips. In a moment, he drifted back to sleep. He slipped in and out of sleep all afternoon, but she managed to keep him awake long enough to get some food into him. Again she spent the night in the chair, afraid to sleep beside him where she might bump against his sore ribs. Toward morning she was awakened by the sound of his voice. He was mumbling in some dream. She covered his mouth with her hand to muffle it, and that awakened him. He caught her wrist and tried to rise; the pain in his side brought recollection and he relaxed.

"Can we talk now?" he whispered.

Katherine sat on the bed beside him and leaned down so that their faces were inches apart. "I guess so, if we whisper. Everyone's asleep, and the walls are thick."

"Kathy, you were a fool to bring me back here; you are risking your neck."

"Well, I could hardly leave you there to be caught, could I?"

"Now, don't get all ruffled," he grinned. "I am very grateful to you. But I am also very concerned about what might happen to you."

"Well, nothing is going to happen to either one of us so long as we keep quiet; no one here will suspect. I played sick today. Tomorrow, I shall lock the door whenever I leave. Pegeen is the only servant who ever comes in here. And Angela won't come in if I am not here. Peg and I will sneak food up to you, so you won't starve. You can just lie here and be lazy while they are searching for you all over the place. They will never think to look here. No doubt they think you have fled New York."

"I cannot stay here forever."

"No, but you can stay here a few days until the search has cooled a little and you have grown a beard to make you less recognizable. You are in no condition to travel anyway."

He frowned, but acquiesced and went back to sleep. Katherine could not sleep, however, and waited impatiently for Pegeen to bring their breakfast. At last Pegeen came in with a huge tray filled with food. "What on earth will the kitchen staff think?" Katherine giggled.

"I told them you always ate like a horse after one of your attacks."

"Attacks? Good heavens, Pegeen, what did you tell them was the matter with me?"

The maid laughed merrily and did the imitation of a grand lady having the vapors which she had performed for the servants. Katherine protested lightly as she ate one of the rolls and sipped at a cup of coffee.

"Matthew," she whispered, "wake up. Here is a huge, hot breakfast."

She helped him sit up and solicitously fluffed up the pillows and put them behind his back. He attacked the food hungrily, while Pegeen dressed Katherine's hair. Pegeen chattered about the general shock over the explosion, which the newspapers were attributing to local copperheads.

"I haven't heard a word about Commander Forrest," she said, setting down the brush to admire her work.

"Whatever that may mean," Katherine said, getting up and beginning to dress.

As Pegeen helped her into her clothes, she felt Matthew's gaze on her and glanced over at him. He was looking at her, a slight smile on his face. She blushed; she had been used to dressing and undressing before him, but somehow Pegeen's presence made it embarrassing. His smile broadened, and she looked away.

She spent the day pretending to be terrified at the bombing. "Madmen!" she declared to Angela. "Absolute madmen, and they are still on the loose! We might all be murdered in our beds. I know I shan't sleep a wink until they are caught. In fact, I think I ought to leave New York altogether and return to Boston, where it is safe."

Katherine played her part so well that she soon had her susceptible cousin wondering if perhaps she ought to remove her household to their summer estate on the Hudson, even though the Season was in full swing. Katherine did nothing to dissuade her; if Angela was not in New York, there would be no danger of discovery if her father sent a letter to her in New York after she was supposed to be at home in Boston. For Katherine's intent was to pretend to return to Boston; in reality, she would take Matthew south. The only problem was how she was to accomplish that.

As the days passed, she found she had another problem: keeping Matthew down. He soon regained full control of his faculties and was climbing the walls with impatience and boredom. Katherine gave him books to read, but that helped little. He wanted to be up and gone, and forced rest and silence and the pain in his side which kept him there all combined to put him in a black mood.

"Katherine," he whispered one night after she had undressed and slipped into a nightgown.

"Shh," she admonished and went to him.

"I am leaving tomorrow."

"Don't be silly. How far do you think you will get? You know your side won't allow you to ride a horse, and they are watching the train station."

"Well, it is better than lying here starving to death."

"How unfair! Pegeen and I bring you plenty of food."

"Yes, and you are going to get caught. Katherine, can't you understand that the longer I remain here, the more likely you are to be discovered?"

Katherine sighed. "I know." She looked at him thoughtfully. "I guess your beard has grown enough. Shall we leave the day after tomorrow?"

"*We?*" he repeated ominously.

"But of course. Surely you don't think I would just throw you to the wolves."

"You are not going."

"I am."

They glowered at each other. Finally Katherine said, "Oh, be reasonable, Matthew. You are going to need help and you know it. Besides, I have thought of a ruse, and you need me to carry it off."

"What?" he said warily.

"I thought of it while looking at your bandaged head. I shall bandage your entire head and eyes, and you will be a poor blind soldier and I your devoted wife taking you home. Who would suspect us?"

"No."

"Why not?"

"It's too dangerous for you. What if someone asks me for identification or my discharge papers?"

"Who would badger a blinded soldier? And if they did, I would simply burst into tears and embarrass them so they would take any lame excuse of ours, just to get rid of us."

"They will be looking for a commander."

"Yes, but not a private in the Army."

"And where do you intend to come up with a private's uniform?"

She smiled. "Pegeen has cousins here in New York, one of whom is a private in the Army—or was, rather. He got shot in the leg and is home again and quite willing to sell his old uniform."

He swore softly. "All right, then, damn it. Would you like to tell me where we are going?"

"Well, I wasn't sure about that," she faltered. "I was going to ask you."

"I find that surprising."

"Oh, Matthew, please don't be cross." Tears started in her eyes.

He touched her face tenderly. "I am sorry, Kathy. Sweet girl; here you are being so brave and resourceful and saving my neck, and I growl like a bear at you. It's just that I feel so helpless lying up here all day, and I hate myself for putting you in danger." He kissed her hand. "We shall go to Philadelphia. There is a shipper there who has traded with us from time to time; I can sail on one of his ships." He paused and then said, "And you can, too, if you wish."

"Thank you, I don't want your gratitude."

"Well, you have it, whether you want it or not. You also have my heart."

She jerked her hand back and said shakily, "Hush. Go to sleep now."

"Katherine, if you sleep in that chair again, I will scream the house down."

"I am afraid I might hurt your ribs."

"Then lie on the other side, goose. I want to tell you something, and you are going to listen."

She lay beside him, nestling naturally against his shoulder. "Kathy, did you mean what you said to Perkins the other night? That you loved me?"

"What if I did?"

"Don't be so damn prickly, or I will have to take my whip to you yet. Do you love me?"

"Yes!" she hissed.

Softly he kissed her ear. "And I love you. Now, don't protest. If you will think for a minute, you would realize that I am not the sort to pretend to love someone out of gratitude."

She lay stiff and unyielding against him. "Then why did you send me away?"

"Because I loved you. I didn't *want* you to go. But you recoiled from my touch—"

"Oh, Matthew, I couldn't let you touch me. I felt so soiled and unclean; I could not let you dirty your hands on what they had touched."

"Katherine, my love, why didn't you tell me?"

"I was so ashamed."

"Girl, I wanted to keep you and hold you and make you forget those bastards, but I was sure you despised me. You had told me so all the way across the ocean, and I was to blame for your escaping and getting thrown into that brothel. I was being so damned noble—and it's the last time I will ever try that, believe me."

"Oh, Matthew." A laugh gurgled from her lips.

"Anyway, I want you to know; in case I die."

"Don't say that."

"I love you. I have never loved any other woman in my life." He nuzzled her neck. "You are the most beautiful, intelligent, brave, desirable creature I have ever met."

"Matthew," she breathed and raised her lips to his.

His mouth consumed hers hungrily. "Katherine, please, let me love you. Give me my last night—the one you offered me the other night." His lips roamed her neck. "Did you mean it?"

"Oh, yes, Matthew; but you shouldn't—your ribs!"

He grinned wickedly. "You shall just have to be gentle with me, my love." His hands tugged at her nightgown and eagerly she helped him pull it off. "Kathy," he breathed. "You are so lovely. It's worth the pain; I shall welcome it, enjoy it."

His hand traveled her body; she quivered beneath his touch, shy and uncertain as a virgin. "Matthew, I don't know what to do—to please you, I mean. I'm not resisting. I want to please you. It's just that I don't know how."

"Just relax; that will please me. Relax." He kissed her deeply as his hands caressed her. His mouth strayed down her body, his lips searing her skin, while his hand found and aroused her soft, secret places. Katherine, for the first time letting her defenses down, trembled with passion at his touch. She returned his caresses and smiled to hear him moan with desire at her inexperienced touch.

She groaned at the almost painful delight he brought to her. "Matthew, I love you; I want you. Love me, please. Please," she whispered.

His voice was incoherent, muffled against her skin. Greedily he took her mouth in a fierce kiss as he entered her, their bodies blending in a shattering explosion of pleasure, one blinding moment of death and rebirth and perfect unity.

Eighteen

Softly Matthew kissed Katherine awake; she smiled at him shyly and glanced away. He chuckled deep in his throat.

"My demure little girl," he teased. "You were less inhibited last night."

She buried her face in his shoulder. "Was I—were you—disappointed?"

He stared down into her eyes. "No, my love; it was the most beautiful thing that ever happened to me." Then it was he who felt embarrassed and looked away.

"I love you," she whispered and kissed his shoulder. "I would do anything for you. I am sorry for all those times I was so stubborn and refused you."

"No, I was a brute to force you." He smiled briefly. "Shouldn't rush your fences, as Shelby would say. I was just so impatient to have you; you drove me mad with desire. You still do, you know. That clean, rose-petal smell of you; your hair; those wild golden eyes. Did you know how wide and inviting your mouth is? Cries out to be kissed." He suited his action to his words, covering her mouth with his.

When at last he pulled his lips away, she said shakily, "No, Matthew, the house is awake; they will hear us. And Pegeen will be here with breakfast."

"Are you refusing me?" he mocked.

"No, oh, Matthew, no." She covered his face and neck with kisses until it was he that pulled away.

"Oh, girl," he said unevenly. "When we sail, I am going to lock us into our cabin and do nothing but make love to you. And we won't have to be quiet anymore; I intend to make you moan and whimper and scream with desire. But for now, you are right; this is no time to give ourselves away. So you hop out of bed and get dressed before I forget our safety and take you here and now."

"Yessir," she saluted and scrambled out of bed.

He watched her dress, a faint smile on his lips. She blushed a little at his warm gaze, but did not turn away. It was still a little embarrassing, but also pleasing. She felt proud of her ability to stir him.

Matthew felt bombarded with new sensations. It was scary, this new, fragile little thing nestling in them both; he could so easily break it with a careless word or action. He hardly knew how to tenderly nurture their seedling love. It made him feel immensely strong and powerful and at the same time weak and bound. It fogged his thinking, made him take her with him when it was safer for her to stay, and made him revile himself for thus exposing her to danger even though her plan made sense. What a tremendous responsibility lay on him now—to protect her, think of her, control his selfishness, his temper.

"Katherine," he whispered fiercely, and she hurried to

him. "I love you; trust me; believe me. Even though I act stupidly or unkindly, please don't turn away."

"Matthew." Her throat felt too full to speak, and tears glistened in her eyes. She took his hands and squeezed them tightly.

Pegeen's entrance with their breakfast interrupted their communication of silence, and both of them suddenly discovered that they were starving. When they finished, Katherine went downstairs to tell Angela that she had decided to leave the next day, as she was absolutely unable to sleep a wink for fear they would all be murdered in their beds. Angela grew quite agitated at the idea that she would be left alone, and the house soon hummed with the activity of two hurried departures.

Katherine wrote a letter to her father, and gave it and a bundle of money to her maid. "Now promise you will go home and not give this to Papa until two weeks have passed."

"Oh, yes, mum, never fear," Pegeen answered stoutly.

The maid packed up Katherine's clothes and hers in the trunks, then stuffed a dress and a few other necessities into her own worn carpetbag for Katherine to take to Philadelphia. Katherine quietly added the flimsy nightgown Matthew had given her. When we get out to sea, she said to herself determinedly, then I will wear it; and we *will* get there.

The household retired early after their hard day. Katherine, forcing herself to remain still as Pegeen brushed her thick hair, knew she was far too nervous to sleep. Tomorrow they might be heading straight for their deaths. And the responsibility lay on her shoulders, for

Matthew would be sightless and vulnerable with the bandages over his eyes. She had not realized before just how much she depended on him to master all the crises. She bit her lower lip and looked over at him.

He smiled at her, that warm, lazy smile that seemed to melt all her bones, apparently concerned only with watching her hair being brushed out.

After Pegeen helped her into her nightgown and left the room, she turned and crossed the carpet toward him.

"Take off that silly nightgown," he ordered, and she obeyed him, teasingly lingering over the buttons.

"You vixen," he laughed as she crawled into bed beside him.

"Any complaints?" She pretended to be aloof.

"Not one." He pulled her to him and murmured against her hair, "Tomorrow night I shall have to play lady's maid and brush your hair, with Pegeen not around."

She smiled at the thought, her gold eyes darkening seductively, and he drew in his breath sharply. Slowly, tenderly, he began to make love to her, patiently building the fires of her passion, until she had to clench her teeth to keep from sobbing out her desire. Expertly his fingers enflamed her, brought her to a shuddering ecstasy, his mouth on hers muffling her involuntary moan. She clung to him, limp with satisfaction.

Katherine blushed at her own wild passion, and his eyes glinted with amusement. "Wanton," he whispered, his voice making it a caress.

* * *

Before dawn, Matthew rose and dressed in his private's uniform, then eased himself out the window. Clenching his teeth against the stab it caused in his ribs, he swung down the limbs and dropped to the ground. Katherine tossed down the carpetbag, blew him a kiss, and closed the window. He picked up the bag and began his walk to Saint Patrick's, their agreed meeting place.

Upstairs in the house, Katherine anxiously waited for the time to pass. She paced the room, started dressing a hundred times and stopped, and checked and rechecked her reticule to make sure the wad of notes and pouch of gold coins were still there. When at last Pegeen came in with the breakfast tray, she was too nervous to eat a bite. After crumbling a roll and sipping at a cup of coffee, she shoved the tray aside and began to dress. For the sake of anonymity, she wore one of her old gray dresses and a plain bonnet; catching sight of herself in the mirror, she grimaced. How had Matthew ever seen through all that to the wilder creature locked inside her?

And then at last, there was Adam to carry down her trunks, and she and Pegeen were scurrying down to the carriage, stopping only to hug Angela goodbye and tip the staff. The ride to the train station seemed interminable, and then Adam insisted on seeing them onto the train and into their seats before leaving.

"I thought he was going to stay until the train began to move!" Katherine exclaimed, jumping to her feet.

Pegeen, now that the actual moment of parting had arrived, began to cry. Katherine gave her a quick, fierce hug.

"Don't cry, Peg; I shall be all right, truly. Matthew

always wins. And think how happy I will be. Remember to wait two weeks. Oh, Pegeen, I shall miss you; you have been my dearest friend."

"You better go now, Miss Katherine," the girl said tearfully. "And may Saint Christopher watch over you and keep you safe."

Katherine fled, almost in tears. Hurriedly she returned her ticket to Boston and purchased two to Philadelphia. There was a two-hour wait for that train, and she forced herself to make her way slowly and calmly to the cathedral. Mass was over and the huge church nearly empty; it was easy to spot Matthew kneeling on one of the back rows, to all appearances deep in prayer. Quietly she slipped in beside him.

"Thank God," he hissed. "My knees were about to give way."

"Don't be flip," she said severely and squeezed his hand.

They found a hiding spot behind the confessionals, and Katherine pulled a swath of gauze from their bag and quickly began to wrap it around his eyes. Soon all of his head above his nose was encased in white.

"I can't see a damn thing," he complained.

"Matthew, please, we are in a church."

He chuckled. "Boston-proper to the end."

"Oh, hush, and take my arm. Carry the bag with your other arm. Ready?"

"Lead on, MacDuff."

They had to wait an hour in the station for the train to arrive. Though Katherine carefully schooled her face to look only sorrowful, without fear, she squeezed Matthew's hand until he winced. He, however, now that he was in the midst of danger, was possessed of his battle calm. Katherine marveled at him. Had it been she who was sitting helplessly blindfolded, surrounded by enemies, she would have been reduced to abject terror by now.

The journey turned out to hold no fear except that which their minds imposed. Katherine trembled at the sight of a blue uniform, and her stomach churned with trepidation at every stop. Each new passenger made her tense, and any look cast their way made her sure they had been discovered. She felt every single minute of the long day; it seemed as though it lasted for years.

When they reached Philadelphia, they found a hansom cab and Katherine directed it to the address Matthew had given her. It was the office of a shipping merchant, Mercer & Sons, seemingly a very prosperous one. Katherine told the secretary of their desire to see Mr. Mercer, and the secretary haughtily told them to wait.

"May I inquire your names?" he asked.

"I represent a shipper from Havana; Hampton is the name," Matthew said. "I believe Mr. Mercer has dealt with my firm a few times before."

The secretary returned moments later and ushered them into Mr. Mercer's office. The man behind the desk was a portly gentleman, at the present a trifle pale.

"See here," he began to bluster as soon as his secretary left, "what the devil are you doing here? Next week is my last load; I absolutely refuse to run any more risks."

Matthew calmly unbandaged his head. "Indeed?"

"Yes. It's a losing proposition now, and you know it. You fellows can't last much longer, and I think the authorities are on my trail."

"Well, don't worry. I have not come to ask you to sell us any more goods. What I need is passage for two on your next ship."

Mercer peered at him. "Oh, is that all?" he said sarcastically. "My God, man, what are you doing here? I thought you escaped from Fort Warren months ago."

"And so I did. But I returned, you see, and now I need passage out. Anywhere will do. Bermuda. Cuba. A Confederate ship."

"Are you insane? Do you realize what would happen to me if they found out I helped you escape?"

"I know what will happen to you if you do not help me," Hampton returned easily.

The man glowered at him. "Don't threaten me, Hampton. Turn me in and your goose is cooked."

"No, I shan't run to the Navy with the information," Matthew said judiciously. "But if I am unable to get out of the country and am captured, believe me, your name will be the first word on my lips. I will have nothing to lose, after all. Unlike you."

"The first ship I have doesn't leave until next Tuesday. It sails for Nassau; the *Sea Nymph*, under Daniel Josephs."

"Ah, then it is a load for us?" Matthew said, and, at Katherine's puzzled look, explained, "Only one of his captains knows of Mr. Mercer's connection with us. Greatly reduces the risks. Besides, some of his men show a bothersome tendency toward patriotism."

"I should hope so," Katherine said, glaring at Mercer as if he were some loathsome, crawling creature.

"Please, dear, be a little more forgiving," Matthew said, amused. "He is helping to save our necks, you know."

Mercer returned her glare. "And who might you be, Miss High and Mighty?"

"That's none of your business," Matthew snapped. "She is with me, and that is all you need to know."

"All right." Mercer raised his hands pacifically. "I shall tell Josephs. He will leave at dawn on Tuesday."

"We shall be there," Matthew promised and rose. "Very nice to have finally met you face to face."

"I wish I could say the same," Mercer said dryly.

Katherine gave vent to her feelings as soon as they reached the street. "That man—he is a spider, a gruesome thing that preys on both sides! Traitor to his own country, and gouges your side with ridiculous prices, no doubt. A snake—that's what he is."

"Calm yourself, please. You ought to be grateful to him. Without him, we would be in a much worse plight."

Katherine grimaced. "I am not so sure. It is days until Tuesday, and here you and I will be all that time, just like sitting ducks."

"Well, frankly, Katherine, we do not have much choice."

"I know," she said grumpily and fell into a brief silence. Then she began again, more cheerfully this time, "Well, what are we to do now?"

"Get a hotel room, I suppose, and hide for a few

days." He looked down at her devilishly. "I think we shall be able to find something to occupy our time."

Katherine laughed and blushed and turned to look in a shop window to hide her awkwardness. "Matthew," she said, stopping dead-still. "Look at this."

"What? That hat? Not your style at all."

"No, silly. See that man in the gray suit? Looking so intently into that haberdashery? See his reflection in this window?"

"What about it?"

"Well, when I stopped and looked in this window, I saw him. He was looking at us, and when he saw us stop, he whirled and started looking into that window."

Hampton frowned. "You think he is following us?"

"I don't know. It's just that he acted so peculiarly."

"Well, it won't hurt to lose him. Come along."

They quickened their pace; behind them, the man in the gray suit quickened his. They made several turns and still he followed. Matthew's frown grew.

"There's something wrong here," he said. "We better get back to Mercer and tell him. I think perhaps his office was being watched. It is almost dark now, so we should be able to lose him. See that alley ahead? When we reach it, turn into it and run. But don't make a move until we are in it?"

"All right." She tightened for flight and dropped her hands to her sides to lift her skirts to run when the chance came. As the alley loomed beside them, Matthew took her hand and hissed, "Now!"

They tore down the alley, the carpetbag Matthew carried banging awkwardly against his leg. He dragged her along, twisting and turning down dark streets and alleys. Katherine concentrated on just running and trusted Matthew to elude their pursuer. At last he came to a stop and pulled her into a dark doorway. They waited, trying to catch their breath. There was no sign of the man in the gray suit.

"Now, to tell Mercer," Matthew said and started off again.

Mercer had left the office, but a night watchman was able to give them his address—for the proper monetary inducement, of course. They quickly caught a cab and gave the driver the address. Soon they found themselves in a pleasant area of tree-lined avenues and spacious houses.

The cab pulled up before a fence-enclosed house, and the two disembarked. Matthew paid the driver, and as the cab clattered off, they stepped up to the gate, but Matthew stopped Katherine with a hand on her arm. She looked up, puzzled, then followed his gaze. The front door of the house had just opened, and a blue-coated officer stepped out. He was followed by Mercer, who was flanked by two armed guards. Katherine gasped and turned to Hampton. He nodded grimly.

"He must be under arrest. Take my arm and let us take a casual stroll down the street."

Her heart pounding, Katherine obeyed him. They walked briskly and soon out of sight of the house. "Oh, Matthew, what are we to do? If they have arrested him, they'll stop his ship from sailing. And he will doubtless tell them about us."

"First thing is to head for the docks and find the *Sea*

Nymph. Perhaps it has not yet been impounded and, if it hasn't, we can persuade Josephs to sail immediately. I have dealt with him; I think he will recognize me and believe our story."

"And what if it has been impounded?"

"Then you and I shall flee for the border and try to enter Virginia by land."

"And get shot by one army or the other, no doubt."

"No doubt."

It took them some time to find a cab in this residential district; Katherine felt they must have walked halfway to the docks before they came upon one. After they finally got the cab, it did not take them long to reach the docks. Matthew quickly jumped out, but when Katherine started to follow suit, he stopped her.

"There may be guards around; there could be trouble. And I don't want you involved in it. So you stay right here until I come back. And if I don't come back in a reasonable time, you leave and head straight back for Boston. Understand?"

"But, Matthew—" she began to protest.

"Katherine, I mean it," he said firmly. "I shall never forgive myself for the danger I have put you in already, and I refuse to expose you to any more than is absolutely necessary."

Her lips twitched angrily, but she managed to refrain from arguing.

Hampton gave a low chuckle. "Ah, Katherine, you have learned restraint."

He vanished into the darkness of the docks. Katherine waited anxiously, her ears straining to hear any sound.

It seemed ages before she finally heard Matthew's returning footsteps. He was smiling, and she quickly jumped out of the carriage and paid the driver. Matthew picked up the bag and cheerfully guided her across the docks.

"I found it," he said. "There was one Yankee watching it and I crowned him. Then I went aboard and talked to Josephs. Thank God he believed me and is even now preparing to sail. Katherine, I think we—"

The words stopped in his throat as suddenly a soldier loomed up in front of them, pistol in hand.

"Stop right there."

"What the devil!" Matthew snapped, managing to sound like an outraged citizen.

"I saw you leaving the *Sea Nymph,*" the stranger said accusingly. "And I just found the guard I was to replace out cold and trussed up in an alley."

"Guard?" Matthew asked innocently. "I fail to see what that has to do with us. Nor do I see why you have been spying on me."

"I think you see perfectly well. And there's certainly no harm in my taking the two of you back to headquarters to explain why you are carrying baggage to a ship that is carrying contraband."

"Contraband! What nonsense!" Matthew growled.

"Oh, no, whatever are we to do!" Katherine wailed. "Now Papa will discover us and send me off to my sister's in the country, and we shall never see each other again! Oh, Corporal, you don't understand! I have the most terrible, sternest father, and he won't let me marry Henry. And so we were eloping. Only you are spoiling it all!" She burst into tears, and the guard looked a trifle uneasy.

"Now, miss—" His voice was placating.

"Oh, I can tell that you are a kind man underneath. Oh, please, please, help us!" She flung herself upon him in supplication, and with both hands shoved hard against his gun hand.

Hampton immediately threw himself upon the luckless soldier and sent him sprawling; the gun went flying off through the air. Katherine scrambled after it, but when at last she found it and turned to aim it at the soldier she found that Matthew had just effectively dispatched him with his fists.

"Oh, God," she said, and the gun slid from her trembling fingers.

"Quick, help me tie him," Matthew hissed as he dragged the body into a dark doorway.

She followed and knelt beside him, her shaking knees giving way. Hurriedly they pulled off the man's belt and tied his hands. Matthew tied his feet with his own belt as Katherine gagged him with her scarf.

"Come on now, let's go." Matthew pulled her to her feet, grabbed their bag, and hurried her across the docks to the waiting ship.

Once on board, Katherine refused to go below. She could not bear to sit in fear in a cabin, with no idea of what was going on. Instead, she leaned against the railing, gripping it tightly, scarcely daring to breathe as the ship slowly edged away from the docks. Quietly, stealthily, they unfurled the sails a little at a time as the ship drifted out to sea, until at last they were in full sail. The lights of the city began to dwindle, and now a good breeze caught their sails and sent the ship skidding across the waves.

"We are off." Matthew's voice sounded behind her and she jumped. He had been helping the sailors to slip away from shore.

"Are we safe?"

"I think so. Even when they find the guards, I don't think they will give chase. A half-loaded merchant ship is not that important."

"Matthew." She leaned against him in relief, and he folded his arms around her.

"My brave, good girl," he said and kissed the top of her head. He was filled with tenderness for her as he thought of the way she had risked everything to help him. Tossing aside pride, country, reputation, she had helped him to escape, put her very life in danger, while asking nothing in return. When she had saved him from Perkins, she had not even thought he loved her; in fact, she had thought he had scorned her. And even now, she had not asked him for any commitment.

"Katherine, I love you," he breathed against her ear.

They made their way down toward their cabin. When they reached it, Katherine began to dig in their bag, pulling out something she would not let him see.

"I have been thinking," he began, and she looked at him inquiringly. "Tomorrow, I think that I shall have Captain Josephs exercise his power and marry us at sea. Or would you prefer to wait for a proper minister?"

She stared at him, her eyes shining. "Matthew, do you

mean it? You don't have to, you know; I mean just because I—"

He laughed. "Do you still not know me enough to know that I would not marry out of a sense of duty?"

She laughed, tears sounding in her throat. "Oh, Matthew. Yes, I will marry at sea, or anywhere else you want. I love you."

"Keep looking at me like that, girl, and I may find myself ripping the clothes off you—again."

"Oh, no, you don't. I have a surprise. Turn your back."

He raised his hands in mock resignation and obeyed. "I thought that you had lost your girlish modesty."

She giggled. "Just wait."

He heard the swish of her petticoats hitting the floor and smiled to himself.

"All right; you can look now," she said, and he turned. He gasped at the sight of her, unable to speak.

She stood clothed in the filmy white nightgown he had bought for her; the soft material clung to her, revealing every lush line of her body, and the slit sides teasingly parted over her smooth flesh. He felt a trembling begin within him.

"Girl, you are a marvel," he said huskily.

He crossed the space between them and swung her into his arms. Laughing, she clung to him as he carried her to the bed.

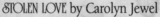